P9-DEE-737

# Criminal Intent

ALSO BY SHELDON SIEGEL

*Special Circumstances*
*Incriminating Evidence*

Sheldon Siegel

G. P. PUTNAM'S SONS
*New York*

This is a work of fiction. Names, characters, places, and incidents either are the product of the author's imagination or are used fictitiously, and any resemblance to actual persons, living or dead, business establishments, events, or locales is entirely coincidental.


Published simultaneously in Canada

G. P. Putnam's Sons
*Publishers Since 1838*
a member of
Penguin Putnam Inc.
375 Hudson Street
New York, NY 10014

Library of Congress Cataloging-in-Publication Data

Siegel, Sheldon (Sheldon M.)
Criminal intent / Sheldon Siegel.
p. cm.
ISBN 0-399-14917-1
1. San Francisco (Calif.)—Fiction. 2. Ex-police officers—Fiction.
3. Divorced people—Fiction. 4. Ex-clergy—Fiction. I. Title.
PS3569.I3823C75 2002 2002019054
813'.54—dc21

Printed in the United States of America
1 3 5 7 9 10 8 6 4 2

This book is printed on acid-free paper. ♾

BOOK DESIGN BY KATY RIEGEL

For Margret McBride, Katherine V. Forrest
and Elaine and Bill Petrocelli

# Criminal Intent

# Chapter 1

## "He's Definitely Dead"

> Richard "Big Dick" MacArthur was once a promising young director. Now he churns out B movies on his best days and soft-core flicks on his worst. For those of us who remember his early work, it's a sad waste of an extraordinary talent.
>
> —Film Critic Rex Lucas
> *San Francisco Chronicle*, Friday, June 4

"He's dead, Mike," the familiar voice says without the slightest hint of emotion. Even in the middle of the night, Rosita Carmela Fernandez, my ex-wife and current law partner, exudes calm professionalism. If we had demonstrated such reserve in our personal dealings a few years ago, we might still be married.

My eyes strain to adjust to the darkness in the unfamiliar bedroom as I fumble with my cell phone. A moment later, I'm able to focus on the green numerals on the clock radio. Four-fifteen A.M. It's June fifth and I'm freezing. Another glorious San Francisco summer. I ask, "Who's dead, Rosie?" I'm not much for guessing games before dawn.

"Richard MacArthur."

Three decades ago, Richard "Big Dick" MacArthur was heralded as the second coming of Stanley Kubrick. He made his first movie, *The Master*, when he was only twenty-five. It was nominated for best picture and he won the Oscar for the screenplay. Then he formed his own production company to make what he liked to call "high-quality art films." Some of his movies were more artistic than others, but all were over budget. He hit the skids a couple of years later when he depleted his bank accounts to cover the monumental cost overruns on his films. His lavish spending habits eventually pushed him to the brink of bankruptcy. In recent years, he's kept his creditors at bay by churning out formula action movies and soft-core flicks. If you believe the papers, the debts of MacArthur Films rival those of some third-world countries.

Notwithstanding his spotty track record, Big Dick still had a knack for convincing the major studios to pony up big bucks for a mainstream film every few years. The results have been mixed. His baseball film, *The Lead-off Man*, grossed over a hundred million dollars. The ill-fated sequel, *Extra Innings*, seemed longer than the seventeen-inning game it portrayed. Most of his spare cash has gone to pay alimony to his two ex-wives and to maintain his winery in Napa, where his Cabernets are on a par with his B-movies. His new film, *The Return of the Master*, is scheduled for release next week. It's being touted as yet another attempt to return to mainstream respectability. We'll see. The early buzz has been lukewarm.

My brain shifts into second gear. I sit up in bed and reach for the lamp. For most people, a call before the sun comes up means serious trouble. When you make your living as a criminal defense attorney, it comes with the territory. Most of my clients don't have the common courtesy to get themselves arrested during normal business hours. I turn on the light and glance at the elegant four-poster bed and the sleek oak dresser. I look out the picture window that frames Alcatraz Island, but all I can see is a layer of thick fog. I remind myself that this fashionable condo on Telegraph Hill isn't exactly the working-class neighborhood in the outer Sunset where I grew up. Then again, this isn't exactly my condo.

I ask Rosie, "Where did they find him?"

"Baker Beach. Sounds like he may have fallen off the deck of his house."

Whether it was movies, divorces or houses, Big Dick did everything on a scale that was larger than life. His mansion is perched at the top of a rocky precipice in the exclusive Sea Cliff neighborhood just west of the Presidio and has a panoramic view of the Marin Headlands and the Golden Gate Bridge. It's an exclusive corner of town. The *Chronicle* magazine reported that he took out a three-million-dollar mortgage when he bought the house.

I fight to clear the cobwebs and ask, "Are they sure it's Big Dick?"

A pregnant pause. "Oh, it's Big Dick," she says. "He's definitely dead."

Rosie. She's one of the best criminal defense attorneys in Northern California. We met when we were working at the San Francisco Public Defender's office and got married after a whirlwind romance. She liked the idea of being married to an ex-priest. I liked the idea of being married. We called it off three years later on account of irreconcilable living habits. That was nine years ago. Unfortunately, we have an uncanny ability to push each other's buttons. Shortly after we split up, Rosie left the P.D.'s office and opened her own shop and I went to work for the white-shoe Simpson and Gates law firm at the top of the Bank of America building. We were reunited three years ago when the firm showed me the door because I didn't bring in enough high-paying clients. Rosie took me in, and we've been law partners ever since. It isn't an ideal arrangement, but we've always been better at working together than living with each other.

"Angel left the message," she says. "The police picked her up in the parking lot at the south tower of the Golden Gate Bridge."

Uh-oh. This is going to hit close to home. Angelina Chavez is MacArthur's third wife. He's old enough to be her father, and she's starring in his new film. She's also Rosie's niece, but there's a lot more to that story. Rosie isn't just Angel's aunt. She's her surrogate mother. Rosie's younger sister, Theresa, got married when she was eighteen and had two children. Angel's younger brother died of lymphoma when he was five, and her father left home a short time later. Theresa became addicted to antidepressants and alcohol while Angel was still in high school. She's been in AA for a couple of years. Angel spent a lot of time at our apartment when Rosie and I were married. Notwithstanding her family issues, she was a good student and got a scholarship to study drama at UCLA. She did some part-time modeling work and summer theater in college. This led to a recurring role on *All My Children*.

Angel met Big Dick at a party. He took an immediate liking to her and gave her a couple of small parts in his movies. They got married about a year ago, much to the dismay of the Fernandez clan, Rosie and Theresa included. Angel's starring role in *The Return of the Master* is her big break. She used her first advance check to buy her mother a small condo in the

Mission District, not far from the house where Rosie grew up. Theresa has filled her modest apartment with photos and other memorabilia of her daughter.

I ask, "What was she doing at the bridge at this hour?"

"She didn't say."

This is uncharacteristic. Angel has a level head for a young woman who now travels in limos. Notwithstanding the temptations, she's managed to keep her feet on the ground and stay out of trouble. I ask, "Where is she?"

"The Hall of Justice."

"Why didn't they take her home?"

"I don't know." She has few details. We talk for a couple of minutes. I can hear the tension in her voice when she says, "I can't leave Grace by herself. And you know how she feels about Angel. She's going to be very upset."

Grace is our ten-year-old daughter. She lives with Rosie, but she stays with me every other weekend. Her bedroom walls are covered with her cousin's photos from *InStyle*, *Elle* and *Vanity Fair*.

Rosie adds, "I sure as hell don't want to take her to the Hall at this hour."

A highly commendable parental decision.

"Can you go down? I'll take Grace to my mother's, then come find you."

"I'm on my way, Rosie." I pause and ask, "Are you going to be okay?"

There's a hesitation before she says, "Yeah." She stops for an instant and adds, "Mike?"

"Yeah?"

"Thanks."

A VOICE FROM BEHIND me asks, "Rosie?"

I turn around. "Who else?"

"Naturally." Although Leslie Shapiro's delicate features and dark brown hair suggest she's in her mid-thirties, the crow's feet at the corners of her intense eyes reveal a woman who celebrated her forty-eighth birthday last September. She's a year younger than I am. She asks, "Why does your ex-wife always call when we're together?"

The room still smells of the aromatic candles that were burning a couple of hours earlier. Leslie has a taste for the exotic. "It just seems that way," I say.

We've been seeing each other for about six months. She asked me out for a drink after a bar association dinner, and one thing led to another. In a perfect world, judges and defense attorneys wouldn't sleep together—it creates certain inherent conflicts of interest—but it isn't a perfect world. It's still hard for me to refer to a sitting California Superior Court judge as my girlfriend. It's even tougher for the daughter of a California Supreme Court justice and a member of a prominent Jewish family to admit she's sleeping with an Irish Catholic criminal defense attorney who used to be a public defender and a priest.

For the time being, we're keeping our relationship to ourselves. At least we think it's a secret. Rosie knows about it, of course, but the rest of the San Francisco legal community is in the dark. For the moment, so is Judge Shapiro's family. We're reaching the point where we must consider a more permanent arrangement. This will get complicated. She's on the short list for the next opening on the Federal District Court, and mercifully, I haven't appeared in her courtroom since we started dating, but that could change at any moment. I guess you could say the practice of law makes for some strange bed partners.

"Just business," I say.

"It had better be." She's wearing only a UC Berkeley T-shirt, and she stands and pulls my face close to hers. Her eyes never leave mine as she kisses me and then lets go. "I sleep with only one man at a time," she says. "I expect the same from you."

We've covered this territory. "Not a problem," I say. "My relationship with Rosie is purely professional these days." This hasn't always been the case. We used to spend a fair amount of time rolling around together even after we got divorced. Old habits. The recreational aspects of our relationship came to a halt about a year ago when Rosie started going out with an attorney from the D.A.'s office. They broke up earlier this year. Rosie was seeing him when Leslie asked me out.

Leslie gives me a softer look. "How is Rosie feeling?"

"Not bad, all things considered." Rosie was diagnosed with breast cancer last fall. She had no apparent symptoms, she was very good about doing self-exams, and she had a mammogram every year. You never know. Her doctor called it Stage II infiltrating ductal carcinoma, or IDC, the most common type. It starts in a milk passage, or duct, then breaks through the wall and invades the fatty tissue. If untreated, it can spread to other parts of the body. I learned quickly that the severity of the disease is classified into four stages. The higher the stage, the more serious the cancer. Thankfully, they caught it early. She had a lumpectomy in January and six weeks of radiation, and the early tests suggested the treatment was successful. I'm hopeful. True to form, she's fighting with stoic intensity. She went in for her regular tests last week.

"What's the story with Richard MacArthur?" she asks.

"He's dead. His wife was picked up at the Golden Gate Bridge a little while ago."

"What was she doing there?"

"Beats me."

She gives me a skeptical look. "I've read about her."

"She's only twenty-five." I tell her about her modeling career and soap opera roles. Then I give her an abbreviated version of her relationship with her husband.

"Do you think she had anything to do with his death?"

"It's too soon to tell. She's talented and ambitious. He's an egomaniac." If you believe the tabloids, they've been sniping at each other on the set for six months.

She asks where they found the body.

"Baker Beach. They think he fell off the deck of his house. It's about a ten-story drop."

She cringes. "Accidentally?"

I shrug. "It could have been an accident. Or a suicide." I leave any other possibility unspoken.

She reflects for a moment and adds, "Forgive me for asking, but doesn't it seem a little odd to you that Angelina Chavez called you and Rosie for legal advice?"

It's a fair question. For the most part, Rosie and I practice criminal defense law by the seat of our pants from the second floor of a tired three-story brick building at 84 First Street, a block from the Transbay bus terminal. We run a low-margin operation just above the El Faro Mexican restaurant in a suite that once housed Madame Lena, a tarot card reader who assured us that we would have good luck if we took over her lease. Our new space is actually a slight improvement over our old offices in a defunct martial arts studio around the corner on Mission Street, next door to the Lucky Corner Chinese Restaurant. We moved last month when our old building was torn down to make way for a new high-rise. The Lucky Corner was also a casualty of urban renewal. The San Francisco culinary landscape will never be quite the same. We pay our bills by cutting deals on drunk-driving cases and representing small-time hoodlums and an occasional drug dealer. At least the drug dealers usually have some money to pay us. On a really good day, some poor corporate executive who has been charged with securities fraud will call us. Lately, there haven't been many good days. Rosie's illness has required her to cut back her practice. We get calls from people in Sea Cliff about once a decade.

Despite our modest surroundings, Rosie and I have had our share of high-profile cases. Three years ago, we represented an attorney from my old firm who was accused of gunning down two of our former colleagues. It was a media circus. A year later, Rosie and I defended the San Francisco District Attorney when he was charged with murdering a young male prostitute in a room at the Fairmont Hotel. We got a lot of attention for that one, too. Although it's fun to see yourself on the news every night, those cases are the exception to our day-to-day existence.

"There's a perfectly logical explanation," I say.

"And that would be?"

"She's Rosie's niece."

Leslie considers this news for a moment and says, "You never mentioned it. You've been withholding evidence from me, Counselor."

I give her a quick grin and a glib answer. "You didn't ask."

This elicits a grin. "Have you withheld any other material information from me?"

"No, Your Honor."

Her grin disappears. The Honorable Leslie Shapiro gives me a judicial nod and says, "The conventional wisdom says you shouldn't represent family members. It gets too personal."

"You can't always follow the conventional wisdom."

"This is going to get messy, isn't it?"

"Absolutely."

# Chapter 2

## "I Don't Remember"

> My husband's later work has not received the critical acclaim that it deserved. He will be recognized as one of the great directors of his generation. I am very grateful to have had the opportunity to work with him on *The Return of the Master*.
>
> —Angelina Chavez, KGO Radio

IT TAKES ME fifteen minutes to drive through the empty streets from Leslie's condo to the Hall of Justice, a monolithic, six-story structure at Seventh and Bryant that takes up two city blocks and houses the county jail, the criminal courts, the D.A.'s office, the chief medical examiner and the Southern Police Station. A blanket of thick fog envelops the mausoleum-like gray building as I push my way through the assembling media horde on the front steps. The guard at San Francisco's temple of criminal justice isn't happy to see me as I walk through the metal detector. The darkened building has an eerie calm at this hour. My dad was a cop who worked nights out of Southern Station. He used to say you could see ghosts in the hallways.

I present my State Bar card and driver's license to the desk sergeant who is sitting in front of a panel of television monitors at the intake center in the new jail wing, known to the cops as the "Glamour Slammer." The antiseptic, modern-looking facility was opened in the early nineties and is squeezed between the old Hall and the elevated 101 freeway. The warehouselike structure is covered in frosted Plexiglas and is the first thing tourists see as they approach downtown. It's our way of saying "Welcome to San Francisco!"

The sergeant buzzes me into a holding area that smells of industrial-strength disinfectant. A wiry man with a military bearing, a shaved head and utilitarian street clothes is waiting for me. Inspector Jack O'Brien is a former undercover cop. Now in his early fifties, he was rewarded with a promotion to homicide twenty years ago after he single-handedly brought down a drug ring in the Tenderloin. He gives me a perfunctory handshake and says, "Ms. Chavez is in the interrogation room."

It strikes me as curious that he's here instead of at the MacArthur house. I try for a nonconfrontational tone. "Jack," I say, "what's going on?"

His hawk nose sits above a neatly trimmed mustache on his leathery face. The deep scar that runs the length of his right cheek is a reminder of his undercover days. "MacArthur's body was found on Baker Beach at three-thirty. That's all we know."

He knows more. Most homicide inspectors work in teams. Not Jack. The cantankerous, tight-lipped workaholic refused to be paired when his last partner retired over a decade ago. I ask, "Do you know how he died?"

"Too soon to tell."

"Care to venture a guess?"

"No."

It's the answer I expect. I suggest to him that it may have been an accident.

"Maybe." He says he doesn't know the time of death. "A neighbor found the body."

Seems like an early hour to be out on a cold, foggy beach. "He was out for a stroll in the middle of the night?"

"He was walking his dog." He tells me the neighbor's name is Robert Neils. He runs a small investment firm downtown. He could put together a billion dollar venture capital fund if he and his neighbors pooled their resources.

I ask him if Neils is a suspect.

"I haven't talked to him yet."

"Why is Ms. Chavez here?"

"We had to take her somewhere."

Not good enough. "Why didn't you take her home?"

"We wanted to talk to her."

"You could have talked to her at home."

He hesitates for a beat and says, "We decided to do it here."

He's holding something back. "Why?"

"We're checking out her story," he says. "I can't tell you anything more."

You mean you *won't* tell me anything more. "Is she a suspect?"

He repeats, "We're checking out her story."

Not a very enlightening answer. "Why is she in the jail wing?"

"It's the best we could do. There was nobody available over in homicide."

Bullshit. Even in the middle of the night, there are always uniforms around. I try again. "Are you thinking of charging her?"

This time he responds with a shrug.

Stalemate. I want to keep him talking. "I understand she was picked up at the bridge."

"We got a call from the security patrol at three forty-five. They found her passed out in the driver's seat of a Jaguar registered to her husband."

"What was she doing in his car?"

"We have no idea. It was parked near the concession stand in the view lot at the south tower. The lights were on and the engine was running. We sent a black-and-white right away." He says he doesn't know how long she'd been there.

Seems decidedly odd. "Did she know about her husband?"

O'Brien gives me a circumspect look and replies, "She said she didn't. The uniform told her. She was very upset."

I'll bet. "I still don't understand why he didn't drive her home."

"Her husband's body was there. The officer thought it would have been traumatic."

"And bringing her down here seemed less so?"

He scowls and says, "The officer discovered she was driving on an expired license."

"It doesn't mean anything. She spends a lot of time away from home. Under the circumstances, couldn't you have just given her a ticket?"

"We had to bring her in."

I don't like the sound of his voice. There's something else going on. "Come on, Jack," I say. "You have my word that I'll bring her back here later today to sort this out. Let me take her home so she can begin making arrangements for her husband's funeral."

He runs his finger across his scar. "Look, Mike," he says, "under any other circumstances, I'd have given her a pass."

There's a "but" coming.

"But there's another problem." He chooses his words carefully. "The officer did a routine visual search of the area in plain view of the interior of her car."

Uh-oh. Cops use code words such as "routine visual search" and "in plain view" when they're concerned about the admissibility of evidence. "What did he find?"

"A Baggie filled with cocaine. Probably about three ounces."

Christ. "Where?"

"Front seat." He repeats, "In plain view." Then he adds, "We could have let the expired license and maybe even the DUI slide, but we couldn't let the coke go. We had to bring her in."

I try not to show any reaction. "Where's the car?" I ask.

"We've impounded it."

"Did you find anything else?"

"Not yet."

Now I choose my words carefully. "Are you going to file possession charges?"

"We haven't decided."

It's the correct response. "Has she told you anything?"

"She said she wanted to talk to you." He pauses and corrects himself. "Actually, she wanted to talk to your partner."

"I'd like to see her."

ANGEL LOOKS NOTHING like the actress in the airbrushed magazine photos that are tacked to the walls in Grace's room. She's sitting on a heavy wooden chair in an airless interrogation room. Calvin Klein has given way to an orange jumpsuit. O'Brien provided the change of clothes. Your fashion options are limited in the Hall. Her waif-thin five-foot-five-inch frame looks frail. Her long, dark hair has given way to an unkempt tangle. Her saucer-shaped eyes stare straight down at the linoleum floor, and her cheeks are covered with dried tears. Her full lips form a tight line across her face. Although she's sometimes difficult to read, the demeanor of the poised, outgoing actress has given way to a look of desperation. She hasn't said a word for ten minutes.

"I can't help you if you won't talk to me, Angel," I say.

She glances up at me for an instant, then her eyes return to the floor.

I wait. Five minutes pass. Then five more. I was a public defender for seven years and a priest for three. In both occupations, you learn patience.

Finally, she breaks the silence. "When is Aunt Rosie going to get here?"

"Soon. She had to take Grace to her mom's house."

"My husband is dead," Angel says, "and you're here to baby-sit me until Rosie can find somebody to stay with Grace?"

Essentially, that's true. "I'm here to help you." In reality, I'm here to make sure she doesn't say anything to the cops until Rosie arrives. For the time being, I leave out any mention of the expired driver's license or the coke. We'll get to that soon enough. "Why don't you tell me what happened."

Her grimace transforms into a frown. "I have to get out of here, Uncle Mike."

I try again. "We'll get you out a lot quicker if you talk to me."

Silence. I hear a knock. Inspector O'Brien opens the door and lets Rosie in. Angel's red eyes brighten. "I'll be outside," O'Brien tells us. The door slams shut.

Rosie glances toward me and then walks across the room to hug Angel. She whispers to her, "We'll take care of everything, honey." She gets Angel to say that except for a splitting headache, she's feeling okay. Even in a windowless room in the Hall of Justice at five in the morning, Rosie is somehow capable of lending an air of normality. She begins to ease her niece into a discussion of last night's events. "Angel," she says, "you know I have to ask you what happened. And you understand it's very important to tell me the truth."

Puppy eyes. "Uh-huh."

"What have you told the police?" First things first.

"Nothing. They said they were looking for me." She swallows hard and adds, "They told me Dick was . . ." She can't finish the sentence.

Rosie keeps her tone measured as she says, "You didn't know?"

She shakes her head.

Rosie's tone is soothing. "That's okay," she says. "Let's start from the beginning."

Angel swallows back tears. "This is hard."

"Take your time, honey." Rosie's eyes dart in my direction. You can often tell more about your client from body language than words. We'll compare our impressions later.

Angel is looking at the floor as she says, "We had dinner and a screening of the movie at the house." Big Dick's B movies paid for certain amenities like a private theater.

"Who was there?" Rosie asks.

"Dick, of course. And Daniel and his wife."

Daniel Crown is Angel's costar in *The Return of the Master*. The gorgeous hunk began his career in a series of commercials for a once-trendy men's sportswear manufacturer. He parlayed the publicity into a brief stint on a syndicated game show, followed by a couple of guest appearances on a steamy evening soap opera. This led to a small part in one of Big Dick's movies. His career is on the cusp. The window of opportunity for muscle-bound studs is often pretty short. *The Return of the Master* could propel him into the next generation of leading men or send him reeling back to game show oblivion. Roger Ebert said he has a chance to be a big star if he can stay away from the recreational pharmaceutical products that led to several drug arrests early in his career. Ebert said it was an even bet that Crown's career would go either up like a rocket or up his nose.

Crown's wife, agent, manager and spokeswoman, Cheryl Springer, is a former advertising executive who started her own talent agency. Crown is her first major client and her meal ticket. Supposedly, he doesn't go to the bathroom without her permission, and he's managed to stay clean under her watchful eye. In an effort to avoid the temptations of the Hollywood crowd, they gave up their West Hollywood condo last year and moved to Marin County.

Angel says, "Dick's son was there."

Rosie had the privilege of meeting Richard MacArthur, Jr., at Angel's wedding. She described MacArthur the younger, whom she dubbed "Little Richard," as an antagonistic rodent who supervises his father's B-movie assembly line and aspires to direct his own films. Young MacArthur has a reputation for doing whatever it takes to get his father's movies made on time and under budget. He's willing to run into a brick wall a hundred times if that's what it takes to get a movie in the can. Although he lacks finesse, his skills are a perfect complement to those of his father, whose budgetary shortcomings are legendary.

Unfortunately, Little Richard's directorial debut was costly proof that certain skills cannot be transmitted genetically. His limitations were brought to light a few years ago when he wrote and directed his only feature, an amateurish rip-off of *The Blair Witch Project*. The *Chronicle* called it the *Ishtar* of the new millennium. The few audience members who stayed beyond the first ten minutes of the debacle complained of motion sickness from the hackneyed use of handheld cameras. His father did little to enhance family harmony when he expressed his embarrassment over his son's failure to a national audience on the *Today* show. Holiday gatherings at the MacArthur household must be a riot.

Angel adds, "Marty was there, too."

Martin Kent is a Hollywood insider. An attorney, agent, talent scout and entrepreneur, he's represented some of the biggest names in the motion picture industry for three decades. He's been Big Dick's business manager and personal consigliere for almost thirty years. The silver-haired, smooth-as-fine-Scotch Kent was a young lawyer at a Century City firm when MacArthur hired him to negotiate his production contract with Universal for *The Master*. He took a liking to the fastidious ex-Marine and became his first client when Kent started his own agency, which he relocated to Northern California a few years ago. *Business Week* described Kent as a man whose unlimited resourcefulness has been tested with alarming regularity. When MacArthur was on the verge of bankruptcy, Marty was able to cut deals with his creditors. When Big Dick was arrested for buying cocaine from an undercover cop, Marty got the charges dropped. He's on a first-name basis with every major studio boss and the head of every large drug- and alcohol-rehabilitation center in Southern California.

More recently, Kent has been on the news because he's the point man on a controversial joint venture to build a new headquarters for MacArthur Films in China Basin, just across the Lefty O'Doul Bridge from PacBell Park. The rusted-out rail yards have been barren for decades. When a new UCSF medical center campus began to rise south of the site, the long-neglected parcel became more valuable. It's turned into an economic and political hot potato. The city tried to put together a low-income housing project, but the funding fell through. That's when the redevelopment agency gave tentative approval to turn China Basin into Hollywood North. The locals have been raising hell ever since.

She adds, "Dom was there."

Dominic Petrillo is the bombastic chairman of Millennium Studios, which is providing the funding for *The Return of the Master* and is the majority investor in the China Basin project, where it plans to house its headquarters along with five hundred computer graphic artists. If you believe a *Wall Street Journal* story last year, the term *egomaniac* doesn't adequately capture his essence. An arrogant, hyperactive former development boss at Disney, he is trying to transform Millennium from a sleepy art-film house into a major Hollywood player. The early results have been mixed. *The Return of the Master* is the first big-budget production that Petrillo "greenlighted," and he has a lot riding on it. His ruthless methods are publicly scorned and privately admired by his competitors. One major studio executive said negotiating with Petrillo is like dealing with Charles Manson, except Manson has more charm. There are rumors that Millennium's investors will be out for Petrillo's head if *The Return of the Master* doesn't put up big numbers. I've never had the pleasure.

"Anybody else?" Rosie asks.

Angel rolls her eyes and says, "The guy from Vegas—Carl Ellis."

Rosie gives me a knowing look. Ellis is another reason the residents of China Basin are furious. He's been a lightning rod for controversy since his company was selected as the general contractor. He underbid the local construction firms by almost ten million dollars. One San Francisco contractor said Ellis will never be able to deliver the finished project at that price. We'll see. Some have suggested that Ellis had access to his competitors' bids, and there have been accusations of graft and payoffs. The *Chron-*

*icle* described Ellis as a greedy bastard who would sell out his mother to turn a fast buck. The *Examiner* went so far as to say he has ties to organized crime, a charge Ellis and his attorneys have vehemently denied. Then again, my friends in Vegas tell me nobody will respect you down there if you don't have some real or imagined contacts with the mob.

"What was he doing at the screening?" I ask.

Angel says, "He wanted to see the movie."

Ellis doesn't strike me as a film buff. On the other hand, he has a reputation as a shrewd businessman. Millennium is borrowing millions to provide the bulk of the financing for the China Basin project. MacArthur Films is supposed to get a ten-million-dollar loan from Wells Fargo Bank to finance its minority interest in the project. If *The Return of the Master* bombs, Millennium and MacArthur Films may not be able to fulfill their commitments. Perhaps Ellis was trying to gauge the creditworthiness of his new business partners. The project is undoubtedly in jeopardy now.

"How was the party?" I ask.

Angel is starting to settle down. "It was fine," she says. "I don't know if the movie was any good or not—I hate watching myself—but we had champagne, and they started discussing the China Basin project. They were smoking cigars when I excused myself and went upstairs—I was tired and I hate smoke."

Rosie asks, "What time was that?"

"A few minutes after one." Her face takes on a pained expression. She turns toward the wall and says, "That's the last time I saw Dick."

Rosie puts her arm around her niece's shoulder and says, "It's going to be all right, honey."

"Sure," she replies in a barely audible tone.

Rosie lowers her voice and asks, "Was everybody still there when you went upstairs?"

"Yes. I had a glass of champagne and I took a shower, and went to bed around one-thirty. The next thing I remember is somebody knocking on the window of my car at the bridge."

There is something in the sound of her tone that troubles me. Angel developed a pretty good poker face when her mother was drinking. I ask, "What time did you drive there?"

"I don't remember."

What? I glance at Rosie, who picks up the cue. She struggles to keep her tone nonjudgmental. "What do you mean, honey?" she asks.

Angel holds up her hands and says, "I don't remember going to the bridge."

Come again? This elicits a puzzled look from Rosie, who asks, "Do you recall anything from the time you went to bed until the time the patrol officer knocked on your window?"

"No. I must have blacked out."

Rosie's lips twitch. "Angel," she says, "has this ever happened before?"

Her response is a barely audible "Yes."

"How many times?"

"A few."

"More than twice?"

"Three times. All in the last couple of months."

Rosie takes this in without any visible reaction. Then she leans toward her niece and asks, "Do you know what caused them?"

Angel shakes her head rapidly and says, "I'm not sure."

I get a quick glance from Rosie. She turns to Angel and asks, "How much champagne did you drink last night?"

"A couple of glasses."

"Enough that you probably shouldn't have gotten behind the wheel of a car?"

"I don't know."

"Inspector O'Brien told me you took a breath test."

"I didn't think I had a choice."

You can refuse, but your license will be suspended. "You did the right thing," Rosie tells her, "but you didn't pass."

"I know."

"And I understand your license had expired."

"I was supposed to send in the renewal. I got busy and I never got around to it."

"That's okay, honey," Rosie says. An expired license is the least of our problems. She takes a deep breath and asks, "Did you take anything else last night?"

Angel closes her eyes and whispers, "I did some coke."

Rosie's voice remains perfectly level when she asks, "A lot?"

"Enough."

Christ. I remind myself that Rosie's niece isn't a baby anymore.

Rosie asks, "Where did you get it?"

"It isn't hard to find."

Rosie searches for the right words. "Are you doing coke . . . regularly?"

Angel closes her eyes and whispers, "No."

"Did coke cause your blackouts?"

"Maybe."

Rosie shoots me a knowing glance and says, "Inspector O'Brien told me they found a bag of coke on the front seat of your car."

Angel says in a barely audible tone, "They told me."

"I have to ask."

She stops Rosie with a raised hand. "I didn't put it there."

"Any idea who did?"

"I don't know."

Rosie isn't letting go. "It looks suspicious."

"I know how it looks."

Rosie tries again. "It will be difficult to explain if they find your fingerprints."

Angel holds her hands up and says, "I understand."

Rosie is giving her every opportunity to come clean. "They may charge you with possession," she says.

Angel doesn't respond.

Rosie tries once more. She takes her niece's hands and says, "Angel, this is me—Aunt Rosie. Just between us. What you say in this room is completely confidential. Okay?"

Angel's eyes are staring straight down when she says, "Okay."

"Is there something you want to tell me?"

Angel clenches her jaw. She looks like the poised actress again when she says, "Do you think I'd drive around with a bag of cocaine sitting on my front seat?"

Rosie looks at me. Then she turns back to her and says, "No, Angel." She pauses and then asks, "How were things with you and Dick?"

She answers too quickly, "Fine."

"I have to ask," Rosie says. "There were reports on TV about arguments."

"Everything was fine, Aunt Rosie."

"And you were getting along last night?"

"Yes." Angel's eyes turn a gleaming cobalt. She gestures with her index finger. "Look," she says a little too emphatically, "Dick wasn't a perfect husband to his other wives, but he was good to me. Always."

"Angel," Rosie says, "was he seeing anybody else?"

"No."

"Are you sure?"

"Absolutely."

I'm not. Big Dick's track record isn't stellar. He was still quite married when he ran off with Angel.

Rosie looks at Angel and waits. I can hear the buzzing of the fluorescent lights.

Angel exhales. "Look," she says, "I'm not naive. I've heard the rumors. At one point I got so concerned I hired a private investigator to watch him."

Well, that's not a good sign. "Who?" I ask.

She rearranges her face into an ironic grin. "Your brother."

This elicits a discernible sigh from Rosie. My younger brother, Pete, is a former cop who works as a P.I. He lost his badge about ten years ago when he and some of his buddies at Mission Station got a little too enthusiastic breaking up what they thought was a gang fight, only it turned out to be two hormone-charged teenage boys who got into a fight over a girl. One of the boys suffered a concussion when Pete hit him, his father was a lawyer. . . . The result was predictable. He's still bitter about it. "Why did you call Pete?" I ask.

"How many P.I.'s do you think I know? I couldn't very well have asked my husband for a recommendation."

True enough. "Did he find anything?"

"Just more rumors."

My eyes dart toward Rosie, but I don't say anything. I'll get the real story from Pete.

The door opens and Inspector O'Brien enters. "I need to talk to your client," he says.

"I'm afraid I can't let you do that," Rosie replies.

"This will take just a minute."

"I haven't decided whether I'm going to let you question her," Rosie says.

"I didn't come to question her."

"What's this about, Jack?"

O'Brien turns to Angel and says, "Angelina Chavez, you are under arrest."

Hell. Angel had been leaning against the wall. She sinks to the floor. Rosie goes over and puts her arms around her.

"Come on, Jack," I say. "You're going to charge her with possession? Don't you think she's been through enough tonight?"

O'Brien turns to me and says, "If it were just possession of a few ounces of cocaine, we would have gone home by now." He turns back to Angel and says, "Angelina Chavez, you are under arrest for the murder of Richard MacArthur. You have the right to remain silent."

Angel starts to fold her body into a ball.

"You have to be kidding," Rosie says.

"I'm not," O'Brien responds. Then he completes the recitation of the Miranda warnings.

Angel dissolves into tears.

"She had nothing to do with this," I insist.

O'Brien is unimpressed. "That's what she's telling you."

"What's the evidence?" I ask.

"You'll find out everything in due course." He looks at Angel and says, "Ms. Chavez, I'm not allowed to question you unless your attorney gives me permission to do so."

"Damn right," Rosie says. She points her index finger at Angel and adds, "I don't want you to say a word."

O'Brien takes this in and says, "It doesn't prevent me from offering you some free advice. I would suggest that you tell us everything you know. At least tell your attorney the truth. It will make things easier on everybody."

He's trying a standard ploy. If you can convince a suspect to say something to her attorney, she is much more likely to repeat it to somebody else—even the cops.

I look at Angel and repeat Rosie's admonition to stay silent. She looks as if she's in a trance.

Rosie helps her to her feet. "I don't want you to talk to anyone," she says. "Not the police. Not the guards. Not anybody. Understand?"

Angel begins to sob uncontrollably. Her voice takes on a childlike tone. Her breath is coming in gasps when she wails, "They're saying I killed my husband, Aunt Rosie."

Rosie takes both of her hands and looks into her eyes. "I don't want you to talk to anybody," she repeats. "Do you understand?"

Angel is shaking. She nods and manages to say "Yes." She's still sobbing as O'Brien leads her toward the booking area.

# Chapter 3

# "It Was Covered with Blood"

> Just when you think you've seen everything, some bastard comes up with a new and horrific way to kill somebody. I've been doing this for a long time and you'd think I'd be jaded by now, but it still makes me sick when I have to secure a crime scene.
>
> —Inspector Jack O'Brien. KGO Radio
> Saturday, June 5. 6:30 a.m.

"I don't have time to talk," Inspector Jack O'Brien tells us a few minutes later. He's standing by the elevator just outside the intake area.

Angel is in booking. She's being photographed, fingerprinted, strip-searched and showered with disinfectant. Her last vestiges of self-respect will disappear when she receives a freshly washed jumpsuit.

Rosie tries to strike a conciliatory tone. "I was hoping we might be able to talk."

O'Brien punches the elevator button and says, "The arraignment is Monday." The elevator door opens. We get inside with him, and the door closes.

Rosie says, "Just a couple of minutes, Jack."

He knows we're fishing. "I have to get out to the scene," he tells us. "I assume your client doesn't want to talk to me."

Rosie nods. That would be correct.

"Then I have nothing to say to you. We'll talk after the arraignment."

Rosie keeps her tone measured. "Come on, Jack. This makes no sense. Her first starring movie is coming out next week. It's her big break. Why would she have killed her husband?"

"You'll have to ask her. You won't let her talk to me."

Rosie tries again. "Her husband may have been drunk. He probably fell off the balcony. She's already lost her driver's license—charge her with a DUI or even possession of cocaine, but don't push a murder charge."

O'Brien takes in Rosie's appeal with the stoic cynicism of one who has heard multiple permutations of every conceivable story at least a dozen times. "Are you finished?" he asks.

"Yes."

He doesn't take his eyes off the elevator door. "It was no accident," he says. "Somebody hit him and pushed him off the balcony."

"How do you know?" Rosie asks.

"We know."

"Are you saying he was already dead by the time he hit the ground?"

"I'm not the medical examiner. There was a significant trauma to the back of his head. The paramedics said his skull was cracked."

I interject, "He could have fallen and hit his head on a rock."

"Somebody definitely whacked him on the deck," O'Brien says.

"How do you know?"

"We know."

Dammit. "How do you connect this to our client?"

"She was there. She admitted she'd had a lot to drink. She was probably high on something, maybe coke. There was the coke in her car."

"You don't know how it got there."

This elicits an eye roll. "She tried to flee."

Rosie insists, "You don't know that for sure."

"Sure we do. How else did she get to the bridge?"

"Somebody could have driven her."

"She was sitting in the driver's seat."

"She wouldn't have stopped in a public place if she was trying to flee."

"She was drunk and high. She got as far as she could and pulled off the road." O'Brien's voice drips with disdain when he adds, "She's lucky she didn't kill somebody else."

It's difficult to surmise how much of this conversation is pure bluster. I say, "You aren't considering other possibilities. There were a lot of people at the house, and he wasn't exactly the most beloved character in town."

He looks at us knowingly. "Your client can't provide any explanation."

Rosie fires back, "That's your job. You won't get past the arraignment."

"Yes we will."

"Just because you found cocaine in her car doesn't mean she killed her husband."

"We found something else in the trunk."

Uh-oh. Rosie darts a glance in my direction. "What?" she asks.

O'Brien gives us a triumphant look. "Her husband's Oscar statue."

"So what?" I say. "It was his car. He probably put it there himself."

"I doubt it." We get to the ground floor and the elevator door opens. "It was covered with blood," he tells us. "We're going to test it, but I'll bet you it matches her husband's."

# Chapter 4

# "That's Where He Landed"

> This is a quiet neighborhood. I can't believe something like this happened in Sea Cliff.
>
> —Robert Neils, KGO Radio
> Saturday, June 5, 7:00 a.m.

"There's the deck," Officer Pat Quinn says to me. He's pointing up toward a balcony that extends the length of the second floor of the back of the MacArthur residence, a white stucco palace that hangs perilously at the top of the ridge overlooking Baker Beach. We're standing at the edge of the water about fifty yards behind the house, just outside a ribbon of yellow crime-scene tape. A zigzagging stairway has been carved into the rocky embankment to provide access to the public beach. A short retaining wall at the base of the stairs is covered with barbed wire and NO TRESPASSING signs, as well as a locked iron-mesh gate. The residents of Sea Cliff value their privacy.

It's seven-fifteen. Rosie stayed at the Hall to have a heart-to-heart talk with Angel about the Oscar. Then she was going to try to find a judge who might be willing to discuss bail. I followed Jack O'Brien out here to get a closer look at the scene of Dick MacArthur's demise. He's inside the house. I got as far as the foot of the driveway, where I found Pat Quinn.

The MacArthur/Chavez mansion is at the end of a short cul-de-sac known as North Twenty-fifth Avenue. There is an access gate next to the driveway that leads to a path through the adjoining open space down to the beach. Pat Quinn and his colleagues have cordoned off the house, North Twenty-fifth and a stretch of the beach. They have the thankless job of supervising the scene until the photographers, video cameramen and field evidence technicians, or FETs, complete their respective tasks. My dad used to say you get only one chance to investigate a crime scene. You have to get it right the first time.

Pat is doing me a favor. He took me on a roundabout trek just outside the restricted area so I could see where they found the body. Most defense attorneys wouldn't receive similar cooperation. Most defense attorneys weren't in the starting backfield with Pat at St. Ignatius.

The moist air smells of salt water. From where we're standing, it would take about twenty minutes to walk along the beach and through the Presidio to the Golden Gate Bridge. At the moment, the orange towers are shrouded in fog. I can barely make out the lamp at the Point Bonita Lighthouse in the Marin Headlands across the bay. If we're lucky, the fog may lift by noon. Then again, maybe not. Summer in San Francisco.

The house is on the toniest street in one of San Francisco's most affluent neighborhoods. Sea Cliff is a far cry from the bungalow in the flatlands where I grew up. It's an enclave of elegant white mansions tucked on the bluffs in the northwest corner of the city that was considered suburban when it was built at the turn of the century. To the west lies the Lincoln Park golf course and the Pacific coast, known as Land's End. Big Dick's neighbors serve on the boards of the opera and the symphony and play dominoes at the Olympic Club, where I tended bar when I was in college. They include two movie stars, the CEO of a large database developer, the former chairman of Wells Fargo Bank, the orthopedic surgeon for the Niners and the managing partner of the city's largest law firm. A fixer-upper in this part of town will run you more than two million bucks. A place like MacArthur's would set you back at least triple that.

Not to be outdone, Big Dick's son lives in his own ostentatious, turreted castle two blocks inland at El Camino Del Mar and McLaren. His piece of the American Dream was hopelessly out of place among the stucco mansions when he bought it two years ago. He hasn't endeared himself to his neighbors by adding a third story to his eyesore and covering every inch of his lot with an unsightly pool that looks as if it was transported straight from one of those big resorts on Maui. Little Richard's concept of style is a little different from that of his neighbors.

Officer Quinn points toward a spot near the gate. "That's where he landed," he says. "Just outside the retaining wall." A team from the coroner's office is huddled around the body, which is covered by a black tarp.

We don't say anything for a moment. I hear the foghorn from Alcatraz. Then I look into the round face of my old high-school buddy. "Could you tell what happened?" I ask.

He shrugs. "I just secured the scene, Mike."

I try again. "Come on, Pat," I say. "Just between us."

"Off the record?"

"Off the record."

"He fell off the balcony like a load of bricks. It's a straight shot from the deck to the spot where he landed facedown. Very messy. There's no way he could have survived the fall."

The crime-scene photos are going to be gruesome. "Any chance he jumped?"

"No. Somebody hit him."

"How could you tell?"

"There was blood on the balcony. You don't have to be Rod Beckert to figure out that somebody cracked open his head."

Beckert is the chief medical examiner. He's standing next to the body and talking into a miniature tape recorder.

"Got it," I say. "Was there blood inside the house?"

"I didn't see any."

"What about footprints?"

"I couldn't tell."

I won't get much from Pat, which doesn't stop me from trying. I ask him about weapons.

"None." He reflects and says, "I hear they arrested the wife. She's pretty."

I nod.

He doesn't look at me when he asks, "So, did she do it?"

He's a good cop. Just because he's showing me the scene doesn't mean he won't troll for information. What's good for the goose is good for the gander.

"No," I say.

"Are you sure?"

"Yeah."

"Jack O'Brien is sure she did."

"He's wrong."

"He's good."

"I know."

Quinn casts another glance at the body. Then he turns back to me and says, "Sounds like the old story, Mike. Pretty young woman. Mean old man. Betcha there's a big insurance policy. It wouldn't be the first time a woman did her husband."

This isn't a made-for-TV movie. Angel is Rosie's niece. She stayed at our house when her mother was working late. "She's a kid," I say.

"Sometimes kids do stupid things."

Angel doesn't. "Her movie is coming out next week."

"Doesn't mean anything."

"Maybe not."

He continues to probe. "What was she doing at the bridge?"

"I don't know, Pat."

"Sounds to me like she was trying to run."

I respond with a shrug and try to change the subject. "Any witnesses?" I ask.

"Just the guy who found the body. His name is Neils." He points to the house next door to the MacArthur's and says, "He lives there."

"Did you talk to him?"

"No." He gestures toward the cove at the far end of the beach where a man is standing next to one of those sleek hunting greyhounds with long legs and a painfully narrow head that are all the rage. "That's him," he says.

"Have you talked to anybody else?"

"We're still trying to figure out who was here last night."

I give him a list of the names Angel mentioned. It can't hurt to give them some options. "What about MacArthur's son?" I ask.

"What about him?"

"Has anybody talked to him?"

"We can't find him," he says. "Nobody was home when we knocked on his door."

Where the hell is he? "What time was that?"

"Around four. We tried the phone. We tried his cell. No answer. We have somebody waiting for him at his house."

Very curious. "Anybody else?"

He responds with a shrug. "We're interviewing the neighbors. Except for the guy who found the body, no witnesses so far." He tells me he has to go back up to the house. "Stay outside the tape, okay?"

"Sure thing," I say. "Pat?"

"Yeah?"

"Thanks."

"I'VE GIVEN MY STATEMENT to the police, Mr. Daley," Robert Neils tells me. "I don't want to talk about it again." He emphasizes the word *don't*.

We're standing at the edge of the cove at the west end of Baker Beach, about the length of a football field from the MacArthur house. He looks like an investment banker: tall, tan and fit. His athletic dog tugs at a long leash. The wind beats against his nylon jacket, but his silver hair doesn't move.

"We're trying to help your neighbor," I say.

He heaves an impatient sigh. "I was walking my dog. He was off the leash. He found the body by the wall and started barking. I had my cell with me. I called the police."

"Do you always walk along the beach at that hour?"

"Every day. The markets open at six-thirty. I try to get to the office by five." He looks at the greyhound and gives me a half smile. "He's bred to run," he says. "He needs exercise. I like to turn him loose when nobody's around."

A sensitive gesture. "Do you get up at that hour on weekends, too?"

"I've been doing it for thirty years."

"Was anybody else around?"

"No."

I ask him how well he knew his neighbors.

"Not very well. Dick kept to himself. Angelina moved in after they got married."

"What were they like?"

He scowls. "Noisy. There were always people around." He adds with palpable contempt, "We've lived here for twenty-five years. This *used* to be a quiet area."

I ignore the dig. "Did you see anything last night?"

"We live next door," he says. "Everybody in the neighborhood knew when they threw a party." His dog tugs at the leash. "My wife and I have quiet habits. They don't."

I seem to have touched a nerve. I try again. "Anything out of the ordinary last night?"

"Just the dead body by their gate."

"Other than that?"

"No. Cars were coming and going. People were talking loudly on the deck."

"Did you hear anything unusual?"

He looks at the house and says, "I heard shouting around a quarter to three this morning. I told the police."

"Did you recognize the voices?"

"No."

"Could you tell if they were male or female?"

"I don't know."

I ask him if he heard anything else.

"A car pulled out of their driveway."

"Did you get up to check it out?"

"Mr. Daley, I don't get up every time I hear loud noises next door." He throws a rock into the bay and then turns back to me. "They were difficult neighbors," he says. "Most of us on this street won't be heartbroken if Ms. Chavez decides to sell the house to somebody with quieter habits."

---

"DID YOU HAVE any luck finding a judge?" I ask Rosie. My cell phone is plastered against my right ear. I'm still at Baker Beach, and she's in her car.

"The duty judge said no. I called the clerks for Judge Mandel and Judge Vanden Heuvel. They said they'd get back to us." She thinks for a moment and adds, "I'm not optimistic."

Neither am I. "You could talk to Leslie," I suggest.

"I thought about it. That would have put her in a tough spot."

Indeed. Me, too.

"And I didn't think she'd grant bail," she adds.

"Probably not."

She leaves the bottom line unsaid. Angel is going to be staying at the Hall until Monday.

I ask, "What did she have to say about the Oscar?"

There's a pause. "She has no idea how it got into the trunk of the car."

"Just as she had no idea how she got to the Golden Gate Bridge."

"Right."

"Just as she had no idea how the cocaine got into her car."

"You aren't helping, Mike."

Duly noted. I shift gears and tell her about my conversations with Quinn and Neils.

She asks if there's a chance Big Dick committed suicide.

"Doubtful. Pat said there was blood on the deck. He was sure somebody hit him."

"How reliable is he?"

"Very."

"And the neighbor?"

"Seemed like a straight arrow." I tell her about Neils's description of shouting on the deck and the car pulling out of the driveway.

I hear her sigh. "Well," she says, "we've gone from a serious problem to a multidimensional disaster. Angel is falling apart. My sister is going to be a basket case."

"We'll get through it."

"We have no choice."

I look out toward the bridge. I can make out the roadway, but the towers are still blanketed in fog. "How are you holding up?" I ask.

"I'll be all right."

"You sound tired."

"I'll be okay."

She never stops pushing ahead. I hear a blast from the Alcatraz foghorn. Then I say, "So, what do you think? Do you believe Angel?"

The phone goes silent for a moment. Then she says, "She's my niece." She hesitates for an instant and throws it back at me. "Do you?"

I answer honestly. "I'm not sure. You know her better than I do."

Her tone turns adamant. "She isn't a killer."

I take a deep breath of the cool air. "Look," I say, "I'm trying to give her the benefit of the doubt, too. But we're going to have to try to remain objective. She isn't just your baby niece anymore. She's twenty-five. She's been out on her own for a long time. She's a college grad and an actress." I pause and add, "And her story has a lot of holes."

"I'll keep that in mind."

"You can't let your personal feelings cloud your judgment. There's too much at stake."

"This case is already personal."

"Then let's consider bringing in somebody else—someone who will be more objective."

"Absolutely not."

"Then let me take the lead. You're too close to her."

She doesn't hesitate. "She's *my* niece."

I know this tone. I'm going to lose this argument. "Does that mean you believe her?"

Now it's her turn to parry. "We don't know her story, Mike. We've barely scratched the surface. What's the first thing I taught you when you came to work at the P.D.'s office?"

"Not to sleep with your colleagues."

"Very funny. What's the second thing?"

"The facts are your friends. Get as many of them as you can before you make any judgments about your client's case."

"Right. Think about it. What do we really know?"

I reflect for a moment and reply, "There was a party and a screening at the house." I rattle off the names of everybody who was there. "The neighbor says he heard shouting and a car pull out. MacArthur's body was found at three-thirty. It looks like somebody nailed him on the head. Angel drove to the bridge."

"She was *found* at the bridge. We don't know how she got there."

Come on. "Do you really think somebody put her into the car and drove her there?"

"I don't know."

"Fine," I say. "For now, we'll just say she got to the bridge somehow. She was drunk. She had an expired driver's license. She did coke. They found a Baggie of it in her car."

"Which she says she knew nothing about. We don't know who put it there."

"Do you really think it was planted?"

"I don't know that, either. Let's see if they find any fingerprints."

I'm not sure if she's trying to convince me or herself. "Come on, Rosie," I say. "There was a bloody Oscar in the trunk. What do you make of that?"

She hesitates for a moment and says, "It could be a setup."

"It's a damn good one. Do you really believe that?"

"I don't know. We shouldn't rule out the possibility. The pieces fit together perfectly—maybe too perfectly. They found her at the bridge—a public place where she was easy to find. If she was trying to flee, she wouldn't have stopped there."

"Maybe she stopped because she was drunk and high. Maybe she couldn't drive."

"Maybe. The coke in the front seat ensured she'd be taken in and the car searched. Lo and behold, they found the Oscar—the supposed murder weapon—in her trunk. It's too perfect."

Not so fast. "Come on," I say. "If somebody was trying to frame her, they could have left her at the house with the bloody statue in her hand.

Why risk taking her all the way to the bridge? Somebody could have seen them."

"It looks more plausible if she was trying to flee."

She's grasping. "I don't buy it. If you're going to go to the trouble of framing somebody, why would you have planted them in a public place that's crawling with security guards?"

The phone goes silent.

I add, "It would have been impossible to plan. You couldn't have counted on the fact that she would have passed out. And we have no evidence she was drugged by somebody else."

Rosie is silent for a moment. Then she suggests, "Maybe it was a crime of opportunity."

"Maybe." I look down the beach. "What about her clothing?" I ask. "What was she wearing when she was arrested?"

"A sweatsuit."

"Is that what she was wearing when she went to bed?"

"No. She said she was wearing a nightgown."

Odd. "How did she end up in the sweatsuit?"

"She doesn't remember."

"Long-sleeved?" I ask.

"Yes."

"Then there would have been blood on it if she hit him. Was there?"

"No."

"She could have changed into the sweatsuit after she hit him," I suggest.

"Or somebody could have changed her clothes while she was passed out," Rosie says.

Seems unlikely. "Why wouldn't they have left her in the nightgown?"

Rosie has no good answer for me.

I observe the coroner's van driving down the beach. Presumably, they're getting ready to move the body. "It begs another question," I say. "What happened to the nightgown?"

"She says she doesn't know."

This seems to be her answer for everything. I try to shift to another subject. "There's still no motive," I say. "Why would she have killed Big Dick? He gave her a break."

There's a long pause. "I was wondering the same thing," she says. "I asked her about their relationship again. She insisted she and Dick were getting along fine."

Now I really want to talk to Pete. "Do you believe her?"

I hear a loud exhale at the end of the line. She finally gives a little. "I'm not sure. She was a little too animated when she said it."

"What about life insurance?" I ask.

"There was a million dollar policy. Angel was the beneficiary."

Christ, Pat Quinn's instincts are pretty good. "That's a million-dollar motive," I say.

"It doesn't prove anything," she says.

"It doesn't help. Have you been able to find MacArthur's son? The cops haven't been able to locate him."

Her answer surprises me. "I just got off the phone with him."

Really? "Where did you track him down?"

"Napa. He was at the winery."

What? "When did he go up there?"

"Last night, after the party. He said he left the house a few minutes after two."

He drove straight across the bridge. "Was he by himself?"

"As far as I know."

"Was he rational when you talked to him?"

"As rational as a person could be under the circumstances. I told him we'll need his help with the funeral arrangements. He's on his way home."

"When can we talk to him?"

"Later this afternoon. He said he'd meet with us for a few minutes at his house."

Good. "Were you able to reach Marty Kent?" Presumably Big Dick's business manager and fix-it man should be able to assist us.

There's a long silence. Then Rosie tells me Kent's adult son answered the phone at Kent's house when she called. "His son had no idea where his father was," she tells me. "It seems he never made it home last night."

# Chapter 5

## "Family Matters"

The proposed China Basin studio project is an example of graft and influence peddling at its most blatant.

—Investigative reporter Jerry Edwards
*San Francisco Chronicle*. Saturday, June 5

"My daughter didn't kill her husband," Theresa Chavez says. Rosie's sister is sitting on the tired beige sofa in her mother's white bungalow at Twenty-fourth and Bryant in the Hispanic enclave in the Mission District, just south of downtown. It's a few minutes after ten. Although the tension is palpable, the Fernandez clan has long mirrored the quiet dignity of Rosie's mother, Sylvia. If somebody in the Daley family had been arrested earlier today, the finger-pointing and recriminations would just be starting.

The aroma of fruit, vegetables, rice and beans wafts through the two bedroom house that has served as Fernandez family headquarters since Rosie's parents scraped together a down payment four decades ago. The place probably cost them about twenty thousand dollars. With a new coat of paint and a little work, Sylvia could get almost a half million for it today. Not that she'd ever sell. She's been living by herself since Rosie's father died about ten years ago. She makes ends meet. She won't even treat herself to a dishwasher, although she did accept a microwave from us when she turned seventy a couple of years ago. The handmade lace curtains that I first saw when I met Rosie still hang above the windows that look out on the steeple of St. Peter's Catholic Church. Black-and-white high school graduation photos of Rosie, Theresa and their older brother, Tony, sit in tidy silver frames on the mantel. A larger color photo of Grace hangs on the wall near the postage stamp–sized kitchen. A wedding picture of Rosie's mom and dad sits on the end table. The resemblance between Rosie and Sylvia is striking.

"I have to see Angel," Theresa says. There is panic in her red eyes.

"I'll take you down there in a little while," Rosie assures her.

"She never should have married Richard MacArthur," Theresa adds. She fires off a round of questions. Has she been arrested? On what charge? Will they set bail? What happens next?

Rosie patiently answers her sister's questions in a measured tone.

Theresa is fighting back tears. She's forty-four, a year younger than Rosie. A large woman with bloated features and tired eyes, her alcohol problems have led to an irregular heartbeat and high blood pressure. I glance at her high-school graduation photo. It's hard to believe the woman sitting before me was once the pretty girl in the white dress who was the prom queen at Mission High. Now she lives by herself in a small condo three blocks from here. A life once full of hope and seemingly endless potential is littered with disappointments. A failed marriage. The death of a young child. Bouts with depression, diabetes and alcohol.

Theresa's life revolves around her baby, Angel. Their relationship has gone through many stress points over the years. They barely spoke when Angel was in high school and Theresa was on the bottle. They came to a brief reconciliation when Angel went to UCLA and started working as an actress. Things hit another speed bump when Angel announced she was going to marry Dick MacArthur. Theresa came to the wedding, but the tension was unbearable. Angel extended an olive branch when she invited her mother and Rosie to her house last Christmas, but Rosie described it as an "uncomfortable" event. Angel visits her mother at least twice a week at her condo, but Theresa won't go to Angel's house anymore. It's an uneasy truce.

Sylvia talks quietly to Theresa in Spanish. I have seen Sylvia lose her composure only once, when Rosie and I were engaging in an ill-conceived custody battle. She pooled her resources with my mother and they told us we had to put our differences aside for Grace. I came to my senses a short time later, and the world became much brighter. She says to Theresa now in a tone that leaves no doubt, "Rosita and Michael will take care of everything." She gives us an authoritative nod and adds, "Family matters."

Grace has a serious look as she walks in from the tiny bedroom that Rosie used to share with Theresa. Tony slept on a cot in the dining room. "I saw you on the news, Daddy," she says as she gives me a hug. The top of her head comes up to my chin. She's the spitting image of Rosie and, by extension, Sylvia. "You said Angel was innocent."

"She is."

"Then why did they arrest her?"

Rosie answers for me. "It's a big mistake, honey."

Angel spent a lot of time at Rosie's house when she was growing up. She used to baby-sit Grace and became something of an older sister to her, and the bond between the first cousins is undeniable. Grace worships her, in fact. Angel had promised to take Grace to the premiere of *The Return of the Master*, but it looks as though those plans may have to be put on hold. Grace says in an even tone, "Angel didn't kill her husband, Mommy."

Rosie gives her a comforting nod. "I know, sweetie," she says. "Daddy and I are going to take care of things."

"Can I help?"

She's only about fifteen years from getting her law degree. "We need to do some lawyer stuff. Maybe you can help Grandma around the house."

"How about if I check the Internet to see if I can find anything about Angel's case?"

"That's a good idea," I say. Sometimes, your parental decisions are somewhat less than stellar when you find yourself in the middle of a murder investigation.

Rosie's brother lets himself in. Tony owns a produce market on Twenty-fourth. It's a grind, but his customers are loyal and he scratches out a living. "There are reporters outside," he says as he closes the door. "I told them we have no comment."

His instincts are good. He hugs his mother, Theresa, and then Rosie. "Helluva time for a family reunion," he says. He's a couple of years younger than I am. His chiseled body has the weight-lifter look. His wife died of leukemia right after he bought the market, and since then, he's spent most of his time running his business and going to the gym. His daughter,

Rolanda, graduated near the top of her class at Hastings last year and had her pick of big downtown firms, but following in the footsteps of her misguided aunt and ex-uncle, she decided to become a criminal defense attorney. Now she works with Rosie and me. I admire her values and question her sanity. Tony loves to talk about his daughter the lawyer.

"I got here as soon as I could," he says. "They said on the news they've charged Angel with murder. They're crazy, right?"

"Of course," Rosie says. She fills him in. His focused expression never changes. Tony never went to college, but he should have. He's a smart guy with good judgment who never panics. Rosie says to him, "Can you stay here for a little while with Mama?"

"Sure."

Rosie turns to Theresa and says, "Get your stuff. I'll take you down to see Angel."

"I'm ready," Theresa replies.

I offer moral support. "Want some company?" I ask.

Rosie's eyes dart in Theresa's direction and then back toward me. "No," she says. "I'll meet you at the office."

"MIKE," TONY SAYS to me, "can I talk to you for a minute?" We're sitting at his mother's kitchen table. Sylvia is in the bedroom talking on the phone. Rosie and Theresa just left.

"Sure."

He lowers his voice and says, "I haven't mentioned this to Rosie or to Mama." He pauses and adds, "Or to Rolanda."

Uh-oh. "I won't say anything unless you tell me it's okay."

He takes a sip of coffee and leans forward. He says in a low whisper, "There's something going on in the neighborhood."

There's always something going on in the Mission. The blue-collar community that was home to Irish immigrants fifty years ago is now inhabited by a mix of working-class Hispanics and high-tech yuppies. Rents have shot up. Independent businesses like Tony's are struggling to stay afloat. The longtime residents don't want to give up their neighborhood without a fight. I don't blame them.

"In this part of town," he continues, "you have to scratch a few backs to stay in business." He gives me a sideways glance. "Do you understand what I mean?"

I nod. This is Tony's polite way of saying that in the Mission, it isn't uncommon—and some would say it's essential—for businesses to pay protection money to the local gangs. In all the years he's owned the market, he's been robbed only twice. In both instances, they caught the bad guys within hours. It isn't a news flash that there are also payoffs in the produce business. "You do what you have to do," I say. I try to cut to the chase. "Is this a gang issue?"

He drums his finger on the table. "It's more complicated." He glances toward his mother's bedroom and then adds, "Armando Rios stopped by the store."

Rios is a high-school buddy of Tony's who became a lawyer and is now a local political operative. His official title is Chairman of the Mission Chapter of the San Francisco Democratic Steering Committee, but his influence extends much farther. He used to be a law partner of the mayor, and he knows his way around city hall. He has the goods on everybody. In the vernacular of San Francisco, he's what we call an "expediter," which means he's a one-stop shopping center for political connections. If you need a building permit, Armando can get it for you. If you need somebody to make a few inquiries of the mayor, he's your guy. If you want to build a new movie studio, he'll make sure your permit application finds its way through San Francisco's byzantine planning process. He claims he is simply providing a legitimate service to his clients. Perhaps. Most of us believe he's nothing more than a shameless—albeit well-compensated and highly effective—influence peddler. I ask, "To what did you owe the honor?"

"You know about the redevelopment project in China Basin?"

"Hollywood North," I say. "What about it?"

"The neighborhood groups are howling."

This is an accepted part of the urban-planning process in San Francisco. You can't build a single-car garage for your house, let alone a movie studio, without some turbulence. The same groups try to derail every major development plan. Certain antigrowth lawyers appear on TV every few weeks to complain about another new building, which they always describe as a blight upon our community. Then the attorneys for the developers get their turn to proclaim that the project will enhance the quality of our lives for centuries. The truth usually lies somewhere in between. If the project is particularly big, the mayor will get into the act. It's free publicity and great theater. The script never changes. Some of the plans get approved and some don't. It's just how we do things.

"I thought it was a done deal," I say. The *Chronicle* said the permits are going to be issued after a perfunctory final hearing in a few weeks.

"I thought so, too," he says, "but Armando said there may be a competing proposal."

"I thought the low-income housing deal was dead."

"It is. They're talking about something else."

"What is it?"

"A bigger office park."

Just what we need. "The redevelopment agency will never go for it."

"They might. Apparently, it will include some condos."

"How many?"

"About five hundred."

Not bad. "Any below-market units?"

"A few. It's just window dressing. The rest will be very expensive. The smallest will run at least half a million dollars."

So much for trying to increase the stock of affordable housing. "It's better than nothing," I suggest.

"I suppose."

"What does this have to do with you?"

"Armando said the partners in the China Basin project have invested millions in start-up costs and plans. A lot of people like the idea of building a movie studio."

Unlike the working-class city of my youth or the mythical "Baghdad by the Bay" described by legendary *Chronicle* columnist Herb Caen, modern San Francisco is becoming a town of million-dollar condos, designer restaurants and movie moguls. Grumpy natives like me mourn the loss of our home. Rosie says we're going to wake up one day and find San Francisco has turned into an enlarged Carmel.

I'm becoming impatient. "Tony," I say, "this is all very interesting and I can see where Big Dick's death may have some ramifications for the studio development, but I still don't see why Armando came to see you."

"The studio guys are getting nervous. The head of the redevelopment agency is unhappy because the studio project doesn't include housing. Some of the business owners in the Mission and on Potrero Hill spoke out against it at the earlier hearings. They wanted a guarantee that locals would get first crack at jobs."

I try again. "So?"

"They aren't taking any chances this time. They're trying to get the neighborhood businesses to sign a letter to the redevelopment agency in support of the project."

"What's their pitch?"

"They'll give first priority for jobs to people from the neighborhood."

Sure they will. The kids from Mission High won't be getting too many of those high-tech computer graphics jobs unless they happen to have graduate degrees from Cal, Stanford or MIT. "You realize they'll give priority to the locals only for the low-paying jobs," I say.

"It's better than nothing. This isn't an affluent neighborhood. Most of the kids don't go to college."

"What about low-income housing?"

"I'd love to see it as much as you would, but the city doesn't have the money to finance it. I didn't take Armando's word for it—I asked around."

"And the competing proposal?"

"It may be nothing more than rumors."

I don't see a problem. "If you like the project, sign their petition. If you don't like it, don't sign. What's the big deal?"

He leans back in his chair and says, "They have a lot riding on the China Basin project. Some heads will roll if it gets shot down."

"So?"

"Armando said they're willing to make it worth my while to ensure my support."

Now I get it. Suffice it to say, this would not be the first time in recorded history that money has changed hands in order to facilitate a particular result with local governmental authorities. "How much?" I ask.

"Twenty thousand."

Not bad. It's reassuring to know the universal language of graft, corruption and bribery hasn't changed since I was a kid. "And all you have to do is sign the petition?"

"That's about it."

It isn't illegal to sign a petition. The wisdom of accepting the gratuity is a more interesting question. "So," I say, "are you going to take the money?"

He hesitates for an instant and says, "What if I do?"

"It isn't a great idea."

"I'm aware of that. Is it illegal?"

"It depends. If you don't report it, and the IRS finds out about it, they may come looking for you. They may never find you, and I'm not inclined to make a citizen's arrest. If you use it for an illegal purpose, you can get into serious trouble."

"What's an illegal purpose?"

"You should avoid paying bribes to local governmental officials."

"That's good advice."

"I'm a good lawyer." I catch his eye and say, "Let me give you some practical advice. I'm going to forget that we ever had this conversation. If you haven't taken the money, I'd suggest that you don't. If you've already taken it, I'd encourage you to give it back and stay out of this mess."

"I get your message loud and clear." He folds his arms and adds, "There's a catch."

There always is. "What's that?"

"If I don't cooperate, I have it on good authority the city health inspectors will find some serious violations at my market."

"How serious?"

"Enough to put me out of business."

Christ. "Anything else?"

"Yes. I must graciously agree to make a donation to the Mission chapter of the San Francisco Democratic Steering Committee."

I should have seen it coming. Cash is still the mother's milk of politics. To the untrained eye, it will appear that a group of businesses in the Mission and Potrero neighborhoods will sign a letter supporting the studio. They will also make a series of relatively modest contributions to the steering committee. For political purposes, this will look far more palatable than a single large contribution from a Hollywood studio or a sleazy Vegas developer. If my guess is right, the money from Tony and his neighbors will be funneled into the war chest for the mayor's reelection campaign. Rios knows what he's doing. "How much?" I ask.

"Ten thousand."

At least they're willing to let Tony keep half. "Who's putting up the money?"

"I'm not sure. Armando wouldn't say."

In circumstances such as this, there are some questions that are better left unasked. There are also only three logical contenders: Ellis Construction, Millennium Studios and MacArthur Films, or any combination of the three. I ask, "And if you don't make the contribution, you're in trouble with the city. They got you."

"Yeah," he says.

"It stinks," I say.

"That it does."

Time to turn the cards faceup. I lower my voice and ask, "Did you take the money?"

He hesitates, but his expression doesn't change. "Not yet," he says.

"Are you going to?"

"If I have to."

"How is it going to work?"

"Armando will give me ten grand in cold, hard cash. The other ten will go straight into the coffers of the steering committee on my behalf before I can get my hands on it. I guess they didn't trust me to make an illegal campaign contribution all on my own."

We sit in silence for a moment. I ask, "How many other businesses are involved?"

"I'm not sure. Maybe a dozen."

"Has anybody said anything to you about it?"

"No."

"It might blow over," I say. "Maybe nobody will find out."

"Maybe." He scowls. "There are a lot of people involved. The studio project is a high-profile deal. The *Chronicle* came out against it. The press may start asking questions."

It's possible. The *Chronicle* has given the project daily coverage for the last few weeks. One of their pieces was an exposé on Ellis Construction that was distinctly not flattering. "What do you want me to do?"

"For the moment, nothing," he says. "I may need you if something happens."

"I'll take care of it," I say. Sylvia walks into the room and I add, "Family matters."

# Chapter 6

# "I Need Your Help with Something"

> Fernandez and Daley is a boutique law firm specializing in criminal defense matters in federal and state courts. Flexible fee arrangements are available.
>
> —San Francisco Yellow Pages

"How did things go with Angel and Theresa?" I ask Rosie.

"Fair." She's sitting behind stacks of paper piled on her gunmetal-gray desk. A framed photo of Grace in her baseball uniform is in a prominent spot next to her computer. It's only one o'clock, but it's been a long day. She takes a drink of Diet Coke and says, "A lot of crying. Some yelling. Half the time I had no idea what they were talking about. One minute they were discussing the release of the movie. Next they were fighting about something that happened when Angel was in high school. It ranged from the mundane to the dysfunctional. It probably wasn't much different than every other conversation they've had for the last ten years."

Rosie. The unyielding voice of perspective.

I glance out the open window. Our building is the last remnant of an area that used to be skid row. Now we're surrounded by high-rise office buildings that sprouted during the go-go days of the late nineties. I glance out the open window. The unique aroma of bus fumes and burritos wafts through the room. You get used to it.

A consultant recently told me we shouldn't describe our firm as "small." We're supposed to market ourselves as a specialty "boutique." He's never seen our office. We lose any chance of portraying an upscale image as soon as our clients walk in the door. When we decided to take over the space from Madame Lena, we hired an architect to draw up plans for a significant remodeling job, but cooler heads prevailed after we moved in and the upgrade went on hold. Maybe it's just as well. I've started to become attached to the astrology posters in the small room where Madame Lena used to look in to her crystal ball. It now doubles as Rosie's office and our conference room.

"I should have brought you with me for moral support," she says. "You can be very soothing. Especially when you talk in your priest-voice."

I give her a wry smile. "They try to teach you how to do it at the seminary, but the best of us are born with the gift." Complete strangers tell me their life stories in elevators. It's a mixed blessing.

She isn't finished. "Did you ever worry about giving somebody some bad advice?"

"That's one of the reasons I got out of the business." It wasn't the only one. I was terrible at church politics and had no knack for fund-raising. At times I was more screwed up than the people I was supposed to be helping. A priest on Prozac isn't very effective. One of my seminary classmates convinced me it was okay to leave before my depression consumed me.

She asks, "Did you ever screw up? I mean royally?"

I'm not sure I appreciate this line of questioning. "Sure. One time a guy confessed that he was cheating on his wife. I made him do his Hail Marys and I told him he should talk to his wife and maybe get some counseling."

"Sounds about right so far."

"Then he went home and beat the living daylights out of her. She almost died. They split up. I felt terrible about it."

She's sorry she asked. "What do you do if you're a priest and you screw up?"

I give her a grin and say, "Same thing every other good Catholic does—go to confession. We got to absolve each other."

"Sounds like a good deal to me."

"I always thought so. It's like being in a club. We were pretty honest about it most of the time. The guys who did the really horrible stuff never told anybody."

She says, "Next time, you're coming with me. Angel and Theresa don't scream quite as much when somebody from outside the immediate family is around."

Families. The venom exchanged by parents and children can be frightening. I used to fight with my dad. We never came to blows, but the shouting often went on for hours and the recriminations lasted for years. I used to joke about the fact that I crammed eighty years of guilt into the first twenty years of my life. It doesn't seem so funny to me anymore. It was worse for Pete. My dad was never the same after our older brother died in Vietnam. Tommy was a star quarterback at St. Ignatius and Cal before he volunteered for the Marines. When he didn't come back, my dad took out his frustrations on Pete, who was still living at home. I think he became a cop to show him he was just as tough as his old man. Angel and Theresa are a lot like Pete and my father. If you put them together in the same room, there will be an explosion within fifteen minutes. You can set your watch.

"Where's Theresa?" I ask.

"Back at my mom's house. She's a wreck. Thank goodness Tony is there."

"Did Angel tell you anything else?"

"She's sticking to her story. She doesn't remember a thing from the time she went to bed until they found her at the view lot at the south end of the bridge."

At least her story hasn't changed. Then again, I hope we won't have to hang our hat on her explanation in front of a jury. I take a drink of weak coffee from a mug with Grace's picture on it. "Any word about Martin Kent?"

"It's been reported to the police. He's officially a missing person."

"His wife must be a basket case."

Rosie grimaces. "She died about a year ago, Mike. He has a grown son who said this is very unusual behavior for his father."

I ask her if she'd heard anything more from the police.

"I saw Jack O'Brien at the Hall. He told me they found Kent's car at the MacArthur house. They're checking to see if anybody saw him leave. Maybe somebody gave him a ride. He might have called a cab. I suppose it's possible he left on foot."

It seems unlikely that he would have walked home. His house is in the

Marina District behind the Palace of Fine Arts. It would have been about a five-mile hike through the wooded Presidio.

I ask, "Is there any chance O'Brien will consider Kent as a suspect?"

"He's certain Angel did it."

"But is he open to suggestion?"

"Are you asking whether he's considered the possibility that Kent hit Big Dick, loaded Angel and the Oscar into the car and drove to the bridge, and then disappeared off the face of the earth?"

"Essentially."

The corners of her mouth turn up slightly. "I might have suggested it to him."

"Was he buying it?"

"Not yet." She winks and adds, "Give him time. He'll come around."

We'll see.

I hear a familiar female voice say, "You two look like hell. Have you been up all night?"

Carolyn O'Malley marches into Rosie's office. Our new partner was a take-no-prisoners prosecutor for two decades. She joined us two years ago after she was unceremoniously purged from the D.A.'s office after she got into a fight with her former boss. Her transformation to the defense side didn't take long. She's a petite woman, barely five one, and you might be inclined to underestimate her. If you did, you'd be making the mistake of your life. We couldn't manage our practice without her.

I smile and say, "Pretty close."

Carolyn and I grew up in the same neighborhood. We attended the same church and we went out for a few years when we were in high school and college. I asked her to marry me, but she said no, and she ended up going to law school in L.A. and I went to the seminary. It was a long time ago and we were kids. With a quarter of a century of hindsight, I've come to realize that it was probably little more than a youthful infatuation, but young love can bite very hard. I tore myself up for a couple of years after we split. She later admitted to me that she had done the same to herself. It isn't a relationship I would ever try to reheat. She's too independent and I'm too stubborn. On the other hand, after a few glasses of wine, I do sometimes wonder how things might have worked out if we had stayed together.

Rosie opts for understatement. "We have a new case," she says. "We've been asked to represent Angelina Chavez."

Carolyn's eyes light up. She lives for moments like this. It isn't unusual to find her in the office on weekends or late at night, because her personal life is a mess: two divorces and an intelligent, but rebellious, son from her first marriage who lives with his girlfriend and goes to State. Ben makes extra cash by working as a bike messenger. The girlfriend is trying to set some sort of record for number of body piercings. Carolyn takes it very hard. "We haven't had a big case in a while," she says.

It's true. It's been almost two years since we were asked to defend the former San Francisco D.A. on the male prostitute murder.

Rosie's niece, Rolanda, joins us a moment later. She looks a lot like Rosie, and she's going to be a terrific attorney. She says, "I've been monitoring the news and the police band. Jack O'Brien is telling anybody within earshot that he has compelling evidence against Angel." She glances down at a manila folder and adds, "Carolyn and I have already started putting together subpoenas."

Rolanda already has excellent instincts for someone who has been practicing law for only a year. She's thinking two steps ahead. It's the sign of a good lawyer.

I tell Carolyn and Rolanda about my visit to Baker Beach and my conversations with Officer Quinn and Robert Neils. "The arraignment is Monday," I say. "Between now and then, we need to find out everything we can about Dick MacArthur."

"And Angel," Rosie adds. She rattles off the names of the other people who were at the screening.

"We're on it," Carolyn replies.

"I want you to dig up whatever you can about the China Basin project," I say. "And see if you can find out anything about Martin Kent."

Rosie looks around at the team. "Let's get to work," she says.

"YOU GOT A MINUTE?" Carolyn asks. She's standing in the doorway to my office.

"Sure."

She gives me a concerned look and asks, "Are you okay?"

"I'm fine." I'm just terrific. My ex-niece-in-law has been arrested for the murder of her husband. My ex-wife, law partner and best friend has cancer. My ex-brother-in-law could be hauled in at any moment because he may have accepted a bribe. My girlfriend has commitment issues. I'm doing just great.

She chews on her lower lip and says, "I need your help with something."

My antenna goes up, because Carolyn never asks for help. "A legal question?"

"Yes." She swallows hard and says, "And a personal one, too."

Something in her tone troubles me. "What is it, Caro?" She permits only a few people from the old neighborhood to call her by her childhood nickname.

"The same thing as always."

"Ben?"

"Of course."

I hold my palms up and ask, "What is it?"

"There was a rave out near Candlestick last Sunday."

"I heard about it. Sounded like it got a little out of hand."

"It did. The cops arrested a bunch of kids . . . and Ben was one of them."

"What's the charge?"

"Possession of a controlled substance."

"Which one?"

"Ecstasy."

Hell. "First offense?"

"Let's just say it's the first time he's been arrested."

Got it. "Has he been arraigned?"

"Yes. I put up the bail." She sighs. "I thought about leaving him in for a night. It might have taught him something."

"The holding tank at the Hall is a tough place to learn a lesson. Besides, he's fundamentally a good kid. He's going to find himself one of these days."

"I hope so." She frowns. "I worked at the Hall for twenty years. I put a lot of people in jail. I prosecuted a lot of kids." She struggles to keep her composure. "Do you know how hard it is to go down there and bail out your own kid?"

"I can't imagine."

"It was humiliating for both of us. I felt like such a failure. The cops were decent about it, but you could tell they were getting a chuckle about a defense attorney's son being in jail."

"You should have called me. I would have gone with you."

"I couldn't."

"It will all get worked out," I say.

"It has to."

"Did he do it?"

"He claims he was in the wrong place at the wrong time. He was holding a backpack when the cops came in. He didn't know there were drugs inside." Her face takes on a pained expression as she says, "I don't know if I believe him or not."

"How can I help?"

She heaves a long sigh and asks, "Will you represent him? I'm too emotional about it. And I'm too close to him. He's tuned me out."

As if I don't have enough on my plate already. This isn't exactly a great time to take on yet another case. "Of course," I say. "Who's the prosecutor?"

"Lisa Yee."

This isn't good news. She's been prosecuting cases for about five years, and she's the smartest lawyer in the D.A.'s office. She's also the most meticulous. Unlike many of her contemporaries, she has no political aspirations of her own. She *likes* to go to court.

"I've tried a couple of cases against her," I say. "She's very bright and seems fairly reasonable." I look her in the eye and ask, "Do you have any history with her?"

"Nothing out of the ordinary. We were colleagues. I respected her. I think she respected me."

I ask her when the preliminary hearing will be held. It's a perfunctory legal proceeding to decide whether there is sufficient evidence to hold Ben over for trial.

"Thursday."

"And the judge?"

"Leslie Shapiro."

*She doesn't know. What do I do? What do I say?*

She pauses and adds, "I worked with Leslie on a few cases when she was a D.A. It was a long time ago, but she's a good judge—firm, but very fair. I like her."

So do I. I'm busted. I have no choice. "Caro," I say, "there's something I have to tell you about Judge Shapiro. This has to stay in this room."

She gives me a perplexed look and says, "What is it?"

"We're seeing each other."

Her head snaps back. "Socially?"

"Yes."

"Does Rosie know?"

"Yes."

Silence. She takes a bite out of her fingernail and says, "For how long?"

"About six months."

She leans back in her chair and opts for understatement. "It's not the smartest thing you've ever done."

"I realize that." She has no standing to make moral judgments, but I refrain from saying so. Her career at the D.A.'s office ended badly after she had a fling with her former boss. She freely acknowledges it wasn't the smartest thing she's ever done, either.

I hear the sigh that I heard so many times years ago when we were dating. "I can't let you do it," she says. "It's a conflict of interest. I'll have to find somebody else."

"That would be the right thing to do."

"Yeah." She pauses and says, "I don't want to impose this on Rosie. It may be a conflict for her, too."

"She'll do it if you ask."

"I know. She has a lot on her mind." The frustration in her eyes is palpable.

"Look," I say, "Let me talk to Lisa. Maybe I'll be able to get the charges dropped."

"And if you can't?"

"I'll refer it to Randy Short. He's expensive, but he's very good."

"Mike," she says, "this may be a little more complicated than you think."

It usually is. "How's that?"

"I'm getting bad vibes from the D.A.'s office. Lisa said they want to use Ben's case to set an example. Her boss is running for reelection. She wants to show she's tough on drugs."

"Politics shouldn't have any impact on this case," I say.

"Politics has an impact on *every* case."

It's true. "I'll talk to Lisa," I say. "I think I can fix this before it gets out of hand." I tell her I want to meet with Ben right away.

She says she'll arrange a meeting. "You can bill us at the standard hourly rate," she says.

"You get family rates. It's on the house."

"I can't let you do that."

"Yes, you can. I won't accept money from you, Caro."

"I want Ben to understand it costs something to make these problems go away."

"Fine," I say. "I'll do it by the book. I'll have him sign a client engagement letter and I'll ask him for a two-hundred-and-fifty-dollar retainer. I'll tell him we're going to bill him at our standard hourly rates. But I won't take his money—or yours."

"What will it take to make you change your mind?"

"You can't."

I catch the hint of a smile. "Did I ever tell you you're a good man, Michael Daley?"

"You used to mention it from time to time. Right before you started focusing more on my shortcomings."

I catch a glow of appreciation in her eyes. There is a side to her that makes me sad. I wish she could experience the joy with Ben that I feel when I'm with Grace. "I know it's ancient history," she says, "but sometimes I think I would have been better off if I had said yes to you all those years ago."

So she wonders about it, too. I give my head a mental shake. My plate's a little crowded to revisit my history with Carolyn. I can't think of anything better, so I cop out with a cliché. "We were very young," I say. "It probably wouldn't have worked out."

She won't let it go. "Unlike my husbands, *you* were always there for me," she says. She swallows hard and adds, "It's taken me a long time to realize how important that is."

She's exceeded my capacity for rehashing another failed relationship. "You'll get through this, Carolyn," I say.

"I don't want to lose my son."

"You won't. I promise."

There are tears in her eyes. She hugs me. Then she turns and heads for the door.

I stop her just before she walks out of the room. "Caro?" I say.

She turns around and her eyes get bigger. "Yes?"

"We're going to need a lot of help with Angel's case."

"I know." She pauses and says, "Is Rosie okay? She looks tired."

"She's waiting for more test results."

"She's going to be all right," she says.

"I hope so. I'm not sure she's going to have the stamina to take this case to trial."

"I'll be there."

It's my turn to swallow. I flash back almost a quarter of a century and I can't remember what we spent so much time fighting about. "Thanks, Caro."

"THERE'S SOMETHING ELSE we need to discuss," Rosie tells me as she takes a seat on the corner of my desk.

"What is it, Rosita?"

"Angel can't afford to pay us."

Come again? "She lives in a big house in Sea Cliff. She was married to Dick MacArthur. She drives a Mercedes SUV."

"Prenup. She had nothing going into the marriage. Dick bought her cars and jewelry and other toys. He gave her an allowance, but he controlled the money. It's all in a trust. She can't get to it."

"What about the money for the new movie?"

"She used most of her advance to buy the condo for Theresa."

I'm not inclined to suggest that we ask Theresa to take out a mortgage on her condo to pay for Angel's legal fees. "What about the studio? Won't they fund her defense?"

"They've advanced everything they owe her. They've even given her some extra money. She spent every penny on Theresa's condo. They may try to distance themselves from her."

It wouldn't surprise me. Millennium may not want to be associated with an accused murderer. "Who administers the trust money?"

"Her husband."

He's dead. "Anybody else?"

"Marty Kent."

Swell. He's a missing person. "Does anybody else have authority to access the cash?"

"At the moment, no."

"So, we're going to have to do this for free?"

"At least until Angel collects on the life insurance policy."

If she ever does. The insurance company won't pay as long as Angel's case is pending. Rosie and I have done our share of pro bono work for the poor and needy, but this case could extend our resources. We have no line of credit. We have to pay the rent. We have to pay Rolanda. Grace has to eat. "Is there any way she might get her hands on some cash?" I ask.

"She said she'd try. She can't afford to pay another defense attorney. A P.D. won't have time to put together a case."

That's true. "Have you talked to Carolyn?"

"She's agreed."

I knew she would.

"Besides," Rosie continues, "Angel's family."

I don't hesitate. "I'm in."

"Thanks. There's something else." She takes off her reading glasses and brushes back her short, graying hair. I can tell what she's about to say is hard for her. "I'm not sure I have the energy to take the lead if this goes to trial."

This has been a recurring theme since Rosie became ill. I have no good answer. Her fire is still there, but the glow isn't as strong. She's been fighting her entire life for respect. Now, she's fighting for her life. I think back to when we first met: how we promised we'd always be there. I think of the day Grace was born. I skip past the unhappy times, the acrimonious divorce and the custody hearings. I reach across and take her hand. "Carolyn and I will take the load, Rosie," I tell her. "Rolanda will help."

Her eyes flash an unspoken thanks. We talk for a few minutes. As she's heading for the door, she asks, "How are things with Leslie?"

My relationship with Judge Shapiro has been a bone of substantial contention. All things being equal, I wouldn't be dating a judge. We all get lonely. Among other issues, Rosie is troubled by the fact that Leslie has been unwilling to make our relationship a matter of public record. Rosie says it's unhealthy. I know she's right. You draw your lines where you choose. It didn't help that I found a new girlfriend around the same time Rosie got sick.

"Things are fine," I tell her. It's just a bit of a lie. Leslie and I enjoy each other's company and we have a great deal in common. And God knows, the sex is good. On the other hand, the secretive nature of our relationship troubles me. I'm not sure there is a long-term future. Leslie doesn't like to talk about commitments.

"Is she getting used to the idea of telling a few more people about your situation?"

"I think so."

"Why is she so reluctant?" Rosie asks.

"It's complicated."

"No, it isn't." She shakes her head and asks, "What do you see in her?"

"She's funny, smart and independent."

Rosie's expression doesn't change. "So?"

I give her a coy look and say, "She reminds me of you."

This gets a smile. "Why can't you act like every other guy your age and go out with some beautiful, nubile young law student with large breasts and a tight ass? Why do you always insist on getting infatuated with intelligent older women?"

I smile and say, "I have more depth than you think."

---

"YOU MUST HAVE SOMETHING better to do than to stare out the window and feel sorry for yourself." My brother Pete is standing in my doorway. He's a shorter, stockier version of me, with darker hair and a mustache. He's wearing a chocolate bomber jacket and faded jeans, and he hasn't shaved. He doesn't sleep much. It's in the job description if you're a P.I.

"Have you been working?" I ask.

"Of course."

"Anything interesting?"

"The usual. Unfaithful husband." He looks around my tiny office and gives me a wry grin. My furnishings might be described as "modern thrift store." Law books cover my tired wooden desk. Manila files have taken up residence on my two dark brown, vinyl-upholstered chairs. A large poster with the signs of the zodiac adorns my wall. It was a housewarming present from Madame Lena. I have all the accoutrements of a first-class criminal defense attorney.

I ask, "Did you get anything good?"

His tone is flat as he says, "I always get something."

I glance out the cracked window toward the alley that separates our building from the high-rise just behind us. I look at the grim young man who sits in a cubicle and stares at a computer screen all day. The view was far better when I was working for Simpson and Gates on the top of the Bank of America Building. It was only three years ago. It seems longer.

I study my reflection in the window. My hair is now more gray than light brown. The crow's feet are now permanent fixtures in the corners of my eyes. I'm looking every minute of my forty-nine years. "Do you have time to work on another case?" I ask. "It could be a high-profile matter and it's for an existing client of yours."

He's five years younger than I am. He lived at home with our mom for many years. He was married briefly. Then he moved back home when he got divorced. Pete kept the house when our mom died two years ago. It must be odd for him to be living in the house where we grew up. His face rearranges itself into a half grin. "Angel?" he asks.

"Yep."

The half grin turns into a full smile. "Pretty young actress. Big film producer. Hollywood. Lights. Camera. Action."

"I take it that means you're available?"

"Absolutely. What have you found out?"

He knows at least as much as I do. "She was picked up at the bridge. They arrested her."

He gives me a look that suggests he's thinking *duh*. "Uh, thanks," he says. "I knew that. What was she doing at the bridge?"

"She doesn't remember."

"Let me guess. She denies everything."

"Yep." I fill him in. His eyebrows go up when I tell him about the Oscar in the trunk.

He scratches his chin, a mannerism he inherited from our dad. He tugs at his mustache. He has a large repertoire of nervous ticks. "I hear another guy is missing."

"Martin Kent. He was MacArthur's business manager."

Pete cuts right to the chase."You want me to find him?"

"It would help."

"Done." He pauses and asks, "What did Angel tell you about her husband?"

It's a test. He's comparing the story she told him with the story she told us. "She said she had suspicions that he was cheating. She said you were looking into it, but hadn't found any definitive evidence."

"And you believed her?"

Our eyes lock. "Pete," I say, "were you able to confirm that Big Dick was cheating?"

"Let me put it this way," he says. "I don't have any pictures. I didn't catch him in bed with anybody." He tugs on his ear. "Having said that, the answer is yes. I am sure he was cheating on her. But that's just the tip of the iceberg."

# Chapter 7

# PETE

> Being a P.I. is a lot more glamorous on TV than it is in real life. You just keep working until you find what you're looking for.
>
> —PETE DALEY

MY BROTHER has taken off his jacket and is sitting on my windowsill. He's nursing a cup of coffee. "Their marriage was a disaster from day one," he tells me. "I have friends in L.A. who work security for the studios. They gave me the skinny. Big Dick was a control freak. He orchestrated every move she made. He told her how to dress and what to say. The quid pro quo was that she got a starring role in *The Return of the Master*."

"When did she hire you?" I ask.

"About three months ago."

"What made her suspicious?"

"There's a reason MacArthur was married three times. If they cheat with you, they'll cheat on you. Angel may be young, but she's no dummy. She has more street smarts than your average twenty-five-year-old. She knew what she was getting into. He was spending a lot of time in L.A. on postproduction. She called me when he stopped coming home on weekends. He was having an affair with a model named Maureen Sheridan. Very sexy. She appeared in a couple of Madonna's videos. She's had everything done. She probably had her boobs done twice. Legs that go from here to L.A. I don't think she and MacArthur were just reading scripts when they got together."

"Why weren't you able to nail him?"

"They were careful. They arrived separately at the Beverly Hills Hotel. I couldn't get any pictures."

"Do you have any idea how long he was seeing her?"

"About three years. She's a single mom with a two-year-old son. I don't know if MacArthur was the father. He was cheating on Angel the entire time they were married."

He was a pig. Then again, Angel knew from the beginning that he had demonstrated an utter contempt for the institution of marriage. "Does Angel know about this?" I ask.

"I told her about it a couple of weeks ago."

"How did she take the news?"

"Badly." He reconsiders and says, "Very badly. She's in a state of denial. She told me she wouldn't believe it until I showed her some pictures."

We look at each other in silence for a moment.

"There's more," Pete says. "Those rumors about problems on the set were true. Her husband was unhappy with the film."

"And their marriage?"

"She was going to take a big hit there, too. He made her sign a very one-sided prenup. He kept control of all the money. If he divorced her for any reason, she got nothing."

"Even if he cheated on her?"

"*Especially* if he cheated on her. That was the whole point. He had an easy out, no matter what."

"And if he died before the divorce was final?"

"His will trumps the prenup. She's entitled to the house, her car, half of his cash and securities and half of the stock of MacArthur Films."

"Who gets the rest?"

"His son."

Really. "Angel and young Richard will each own half the company?"

"Yeah." He arches his eyebrows and adds, "They hate each other. They'll never be able to work together. One of them is going to end up buying the other one out."

Unless one of them is a murderer or Angel's husband amended his will without telling anybody. "What do you know about the son?"

"He's an obnoxious twit who's going through a nasty divorce. It isn't his first. I wish his soon-to-be ex-wife had hired me to watch him. I would have dug up some pretty juicy stuff. He's also a solid producer of crappy movies. He'll do whatever it takes to get the job done. In some respects, he was the only reason MacArthur Films was still in business. When he was at his best, his father was a good writer and a great director, but he had no idea how to deal with the business side of production. Little Richard is a lousy writer and a terrible director, but he's very good at the nuts and bolts of producing movies." He shrugs and adds, "His father never appreciated his skills. They barely spoke."

"Why did Big Dick leave him half of everything?"

"Other than Angel, he's the only family he had left."

I ask the million-dollar question. "Was he planning to file for divorce?"

"I think so."

"How could you tell?"

"The guy to watch was Martin Kent. He kept MacArthur out of trouble."

"Now he's a missing person."

Pete says, "Kent had a couple of meetings with Frank Grossman."

Grossman is a barracuda in the guise of a divorce lawyer, who takes great pride in his "scorched earth" approach to family law. His business cards contain the motto "We take no prisoners." He handled Big Dick's first two divorces and he probably prepared Angel's prenup. It's unlikely he'll talk to us because of client confidentiality. All the more reason for us to find Martin Kent. I ask, "Anything else I should know?"

"Nothing that's admissible."

"Anything that's inadmissible?"

"Maybe."

"Did you do anything illegal to obtain it?"

"Depends on your definition of illegal. I have some sophisticated recording equipment. It allowed me to listen in on some of Big Dick's conversations with Dominic Petrillo."

"Where were you?"

"The room next door to MacArthur's at the Beverly Hills Hotel."

"I take it you weren't a registered guest?"

"That would be correct."

"You realize breaking and entering is frowned upon."

"For the record, I didn't break anything. I just entered. Coincidentally, I had my recording equipment with me. I never go anywhere without it."

"Technically, taping other people's conversations without their permission is a crime."

"I won't do it again any time soon. Do you want to know what I heard or do you want to lecture me on the federal and state wiretapping statutes?"

We won't be able to use any of this in court. I ask him what he heard.

"It seems Petrillo and his friends at Millennium Studios weren't real happy with the early buzz on *The Return of the Master*. Petrillo was talking about delaying the release."

If Petrillo didn't like the movie, he could have pulled the plug. It's hard to imagine Big Dick could have double-crossed him to such an extent that Petrillo would have killed him. We have no evidence to suggest he did. "What does that have to do with MacArthur's death?"

"Maybe nothing. I thought you might like to know."

"Is there a chance you were keeping the MacArthur house under surveillance last night?"

"No. Angel told me to keep my distance."

We sit in silence. A cheating husband. A lousy movie. A nervous studio. A tenuous development project. A lot of questions. I look out the window toward the guy in the cubicle.

Pete asks, "Where do you want me to start?"

"I want you to find Martin Kent."

"Got it. What are you going to do?"

"Rosie and I promised MacArthur's son that we'd pay him a condolence call this afternoon."

# Chapter 8

# Little Richard

> My father was a kind and gentle soul whose body of work will be his lasting legacy. The industry has lost one of its shining lights, and he will be missed. Construction of the MacArthur studio complex will begin as planned.
>
> —Richard MacArthur, Jr. KGO Radio
> Saturday, June 5. 3:00 p.m.

"That's disturbing," Rosie understates when I tell her about my conversation with Pete. "Angel hasn't been particularly forthcoming about her relationship with her husband."

We're heading west on Geary toward Little Richard's house. The afternoon rush-hour traffic is heavy. My Corolla cooperates as we pass Japantown, but sputters when I hit the gas to climb the hill near Kaiser Hospital.

"If Pete says Big Dick was fooling around," I observe, "I'm inclined to take his word for it. And if he said Petrillo was unhappy about the movie, I think it's true."

"I'll talk to Angel about it. It won't be a pleasant conversation."

No, it won't. "We need to get copies of the prenup and the will," I say.

She agrees. Then she adds, "Even if Pete's right, none of this proves anything."

"It gives her motive."

Rosie nods. We drive in silence for a minute.

I ask, "Did you have a chance to talk to Nicole?"

"Briefly."

Nicole Ward is the San Francisco D.A. and is running for reelection in November. She comes from a prominent family and is considered one of the great young hopes for the California Democratic party. She has insatiable political ambition and plays exceptionally well on the evening news, and it also doesn't hurt that she's drop-dead gorgeous and perhaps the most eligible single woman in the Bay Area. She gained a certain amount of notoriety early in her career when it was revealed she had worked her way through law school by modeling lingerie for Victoria's Secret. She's more than just a pretty face. She's an effective prosecutor and one of the most unpleasant people on the face of the earth.

"What's her temperature?" I ask.

"White hot. She's already talking about the death penalty."

She always does. A law-and-order zealot, Ward would send shoplifters to the gas chamber. "Do you have any idea which A.D.A. will be assigned to this case?"

"I think she may keep it herself," Rosie says. Most cases are assigned to the assistant D.A.'s. It is unusual, but not unheard of, for a D.A. to handle a case personally. Ward might see this as an opportunity for some free media time. She is well aware of the fact that she is, in the vernacular, "media-genic." She had the hormone-charged anchorman from Channel Seven eating out of her hand when he tried to do a "serious " interview last week. Rosie gives me a sly grin and adds, "You can ask her about it. She's agreed to meet with us tomorrow morning."

"On a Sunday?" I say.

"This is a big case," Rosie says. "She's going to play it for all it's worth."

"MR. MACARTHUR will see you now," says an exotic-looking woman with a seductive low voice, jade eyes, olive skin and purple lips. Her straight black hair cascades down the back of a white satin blouse and tight black leather pants hug long, slender legs. Hoop-style earrings balance on either side of her round face. A dozen bracelets adorn each of her wrists. There is a ring on each of her fingers.

"Thank you," I say.

It's five-thirty. Rosie and I have been waiting for fifteen minutes in the two-story foyer of Little Richard's six-bedroom monstrosity. When we walked in the door, we were greeted by a life-sized wooden sculpture of our host dressed in formal attire. It seemed a bit ostentatious to me. An original Picasso hangs above the circular stairway. The artwork cost considerably more than my college and law school educations. I can picture young MacArthur standing in the hallway next to his statue and greeting his Hollywood pals.

The woman leads us under the stairway. I see a dozen people standing in small groups in the living room. There doesn't appear to be any substantial mourning taking place. I recognize Daniel Crown, Angel's costar, as he talks on his cell phone. He looks like a young Paul Newman. Everybody in the living room is talking on a cell phone. One guy seems to be carrying on two conversations at once by placing a cell phone against each ear. I guess that's what they call multitasking.

We pass through a remodeled, restaurant-quality kitchen, where the aroma of freshly cooked pasta and pesto sauce greets us. Then we follow the woman up a back stairway. The carpet and the walls upstairs are snow-white. The sleek furniture is chrome and black leather. The artwork is modern. The ambiance is sterile, almost icy.

"Terrible tragedy about Mr. MacArthur's father," I say to the woman.

She gets a faraway look in her eyes. "Yes," she replies. "You could say that."

I suppose I could. I glance at Rosie as we pass an art piece composed of a miniature video screen showing a beautiful, naked woman who keeps repeating the words "I am perfect."

"Richard turns her off at night," explains the woman with the rings and the bracelets.

I smile back at the image. I would find it unnerving to have talking artwork in my home.

The dark-skinned woman gives me a playful grin. "She isn't real," she explains. "She's a cyber model. The artist is developing quite a following."

A very talented artist indeed. If things don't work out for him in cyber art, I suspect he'll have a promising career in cyber porn.

I'm still not sure if this woman is Little Richard's servant, friend or mistress. She may be all three. There are no signs that MacArthur's soon-to-be-ex-wife still lives in the house. "Are you a friend of the family?" I ask.

"Oh, no, sir." She licks her lips. "I'm Mr. MacArthur's personal assistant."

I'll bet. You aren't anybody in the movie business unless you have a personal assistant. I try for an innocent tone when I ask, "What's your name?"

"Eve."

How biblical. "Do you have a last name?"

She shakes her long hair. "No, Mr. Daley. It's just Eve."

First there was Cher. Then there was Madonna. Now there's Eve. "Fair enough, Eve," I say. "Why don't you call me Mike?"

"Fair enough," she repeats. "Mike."

"Do you live nearby, Eve?"

"In the Marina."

"Were you here last night?"

"Yes."

I ask her what time she went home.

"After Richard went to his father's house."

"That would have been around eight?"

"Yes."

"And you were at home the rest of the night?"

"Yes."

A woman of few words. "Did you hear from Mr. MacArthur last night?"

"Not until this morning. That's when he told me the terrible news."

I ask her if she spends a lot of time up here.

"Yes. Mr. MacArthur works from his home. My job is a full-time position, although he gives me extra time when I have a film role."

"You're an actress?"

"Yes."

I don't recognize her. "Where can I see your work?" I ask.

She smiles. "I have a small part in *The Return of the Master.*" I don't recognize the names of any of the other movies she mentions. I wonder if any of them can be found in the adult section of our local video store.

I ask, "Do you know Angelina Chavez well?"

"We're friends. We worked together on a couple of projects." She hesitates for an instant and adds, "I tried to facilitate communications between Angelina and Richard."

I decide to be coy. "They don't get along?"

Her eyes turn down. "No." She parries my questions when I try to probe.

"We may want to ask you a few more questions," I say.

She hands me a business card that says simply Eve. There's a post-office box, a phone number and an e-mail address. She motions us toward a door at the end of the hallway. I can hear loud voices inside. The shouting is followed by guffaws. Eve opens the door, and a bearded man with an expanding gut walks out of the room. Dominic Petrillo looks older and more disheveled in person than in his photos. He's early sixties, about my height, with a full head of dyed black hair, a scraggy beard and a deeply lined leathery face. His small eyes are hidden behind tiny wire-rimmed spectacles. He kisses Eve on the cheek and says good-bye. He looks at Rosie and me and frowns. He doesn't say a word as he brushes past us.

"Mr. Petrillo," I say. "I'm Michael Daley. We're representing Angelina Chavez."

He gives me an icy glare and says, "I know who you are. I have to get back to my hotel."

"Can we speak to you for just for a moment?"

"I'm late. Call me at the office." He barrels toward the stairway. Rosie follows him.

I turn around and look at Eve, who puts a finger to her lips and motions me into the room. "Please, Mr. Daley—I mean Mike." She escorts me into the office. Then she excuses herself and closes the door behind her.

Little Richard's office has an unobstructed view of the Golden Gate Bridge. The fog is starting to roll in, but I can see the Marin Headlands and the top of Mount Tam. At the moment, I would rather be up there with Grace.

"Come in, Michael," he says in a raspy, high-pitched voice. His tone is businesslike, almost cheerful. He's a young man, probably mid-thirties, with slicked-back hair and expanding jowls. He looks like his father. He's sitting in a tall, ergonomically correct leather chair behind a desk made of a Plexiglas slab resting on a stainless-steel base. A speakerphone, a laptop and a black coffee cup with a logo of Richard MacArthur Films are sitting on his otherwise spotless desk.

He accepts my condolences with perfunctory thanks. "I'm pressed for time," he says. "I'm trying to finalize the arrangements for my father's memorial. Of course we still have to deal with the release of the movie."

Of course. The door opens and Eve comes in. He points toward his coffee cup. She nods. She leaves the room and returns less than a minute later with a carafe. She fills his cup. He doesn't thank her. For that matter, he doesn't even acknowledge that she was there. Without a word, she turns and walks out the door.

Young MacArthur tugs at his black silk shirt. "She's very conscientious," he says.

I'm sure. "She's your assistant?" I ask.

"Yes. She's also an actress. We think she has great potential. Her mother is Caucasian and her father is Filipino. That's why she looks so, uh, interesting."

"Where did you find her?" I ask.

"The Mission District. We gave her a role in the new film. She has many qualities."

I presume this means that she's very good at taking shorthand. A copy of Friday's *Daily Variety* and an old photo of MacArthur and his father sit on one corner of the credenza. Next to it is a picture of Little Richard in the driver's seat of a vintage Ferrari. I remember reading that he likes to refurbish cars. Conspicuously absent are signs of a spouse or children. The walls are filled with posters from his father's movies and pictures of classic autos.

I start slowly. "Kind of sparse furnishings," I observe.

"I don't like to let anything detract from the view," he says, without looking at me. "I try to keep all of my stuff out of sight."

His stuff would also include Eve, I presume. I say, "I didn't realize you were meeting with Dominic Petrillo."

He turns his gaze from the windows and eyes me suspiciously. "We have a movie coming out on Friday."

"Are you still planning to release it on time?"

"Yes. And we're trying to get final approval of the studio project."

"I've read a lot about it."

He slumps back into his chair. "It is a monumental pain to get approvals to build anything in this town." He tries for a conciliatory tone. "Now I have this mess on my hands.

I decide to try the high road. "I'm terribly sorry about what happened, Richard."

He regains his composure. "You and me both," he replies. "Biggest fucked-up mess I've ever seen."

When I was a priest, I heard many people try to describe their feelings after the death of a parent. This is the first time I've ever heard the term *fucked-up mess* used in this context.

There's a knock on the door. Eve lets Rosie in. I ask her if she talked to Petrillo.

"He said he'd meet with us tomorrow." She faces MacArthur and says, "Angelina asked us to find out about the arrangements for the funeral."

"You could have called," he says.

"We wanted to talk to you in person."

"You know Angelina and I haven't always gotten along."

As far as I can tell, they haven't *ever* gotten along. Rosie asks again about the funeral.

MacArthur pulls a cell phone out of his pocket and flips it open. I didn't hear it ring. It must have been on vibrate mode. He turns away from me. "Yeah," I hear him say. Then he adds, "Right." Then his neck starts to turn red and he says, "No way. Tell them to go fuck themselves. Tell them we have a deal." His voice gets louder with each passing insult. He spends another five minutes berating the poor soul who had the audacity to question him. Then he snaps the phone closed and says to me, "I work with a bunch of fucking idiots."

Nice guy. Then again, it wouldn't surprise me if he does, in fact, work with a bunch of fucking idiots.

"What were we talking about?" he asks.

"The funeral."

"Yeah." He pauses. "There isn't going to be one."

No funeral? Big Dick MacArthur is going to his final reward without a final extravaganza? A tribute? "I take it this was your father's wish?" Rosie asks.

"Yes." He gives me a sheepish grin. "He had something a bit more elaborate in mind."

This is beginning to sound more like it. I ask him what that might be.

"He's going to be blown up."

"Excuse me?"

"You heard me."

I realize my mouth is wide open.

"You see," he continues, "the Northern California Neptune Society offers a unique service. First, they cremate the body."

Sounds pretty conventional.

"Then they take your ashes out on a boat called the *Naiad*. Then they shoot your ashes up in fireworks. That's how they're scattered."

I look right into his tiny eyes to see if there's any chance that he might be kidding.

"I'm not making this up," he insists.

I glance at Rosie. How are we going to explain this to Angel?

"It's in his will," he adds. "He read about it and loved the idea. I just talked to his lawyer. All the arrangements were made a long time ago." He gives me the name of a reputable probate attorney whom I've met. I can vouch for the fact that he has no sense of humor. If he says Big Dick is going to be blown up, then by God, he's going to be blown up.

"Who are the beneficiaries of the will?" I ask.

"That's confidential."

"Richard," Rosie says, "it will become a matter of public record when the will is submitted to probate. We're going to find out."

He gives her a cold stare. Then he confirms what Pete told us. Angel gets the house and the car. She and Little Richard split the rest of it, including the stock in MacArthur Films, except he gets to keep the keys to MacArthur Cellars. It looks like he's about to become a gentleman vintner. "Of course," he says, "we plan to contest the will. We think it is entirely inappropriate that Angelina would receive anything under the circumstances."

"How's that?" I ask.

"She killed him."

"You don't know that."

"I'd put money on it."

We volley back and forth on the subject of Big Dick's death for a few moments. Then Rosie says, "When is the memorial ceremony going to take place?"

"We're hoping they'll release the body tomorrow. We're shooting for Tuesday," he says, not intending to make a pun.

"Angelina would like to be there," I say.

He stops cold. "You're kidding, right?"

"No, I'm not."

His face starts to turn bright red. "The marriage was a sham. She just married him to get into his movies. No way I'm gonna let her come."

"If she wanted to get into his movies, why would she have killed him?"

He drums his fingers on his Plexiglas slab. "Because her performance was a disaster. My father pointed it out to her last night. He wasn't subtle about it."

"It makes no sense," Rosie says.

"It's free publicity," he argues. "The tabloids will be all over this."

"You're suggesting she killed her husband as a publicity stunt?" Rosie says.

"You got it."

"That's preposterous."

Little Richard folds his arms like an angry eight-year-old and says, "She's not welcome at my father's memorial."

"She was his wife," Rosie says. "She has every right to be there."

I notice little beads of sweat forming on his forehead. "It's disrespectful." He wags a chubby finger in my face. "She was never part of the family."

Now he's starting to sound like Al Pacino in *Godfather II*. "Richard," I say, "where were you last night?"

"Are you accusing me of something?"

Rosie interjects, "No. We're just trying to figure out what happened."

"I've already talked to the cops."

"Maybe you can tell us what you told them."

"I was at the same place Angelina was—the screening."

"Who else was there?"

He rattles off the names of Daniel Crown and Cheryl Springer, Dominic Petrillo, Carl Ellis and Martin Kent. "It was a VIP event," he says.

"What time did you leave?"

"Around two."

I ask him if anybody was still there.

"Ellis and Petrillo left at one forty-five. They went back to the Ritz in Petrillo's limo."

"And the rest?"

"Crown and Springer left a few minutes before I did. Marty was still around."

"You didn't hear anything or see anything unusual?"

"Your client was high as a kite. In her case, that wasn't unusual."

I ignore the dig. "Where did you go?"

"I walked home to get my car. Then I drove up to the winery."

"It was two o'clock in the morning."

"I was supposed to be at a charity auction this morning."

"Can anybody corroborate your whereabouts?"

"Danny Crown and Cheryl Springer can. So can Petrillo and Ellis. You can talk to Marty Kent."

"He's missing."

He becomes silent for a moment. "So I understand."

"Do you know where he is?"

"No idea."

"Did anybody go with you to the winery?"

There is a slight hesitation before he says, "No."

"And you drove back by yourself?"

"Yes."

"When was the last time you saw Angelina?"

"Around one. I thought she went to bed." He pauses for effect and adds, "I guess not."

At least this corresponds with Angel's timeline. "You didn't see her after that?"

"No."

"Was Marty Kent upset?"

This elicits a rapid nod. "Yeah. He was worried about the movie. And he thought the China Basin project was a bad deal for us."

I ASK ROSIE what she thought of MacArthur's son as we're driving downtown a little later.

"It's about what I expected," she says. "I have a very finely tuned asshole sensor. It was blaring the entire time." She gets a faraway look in her eyes. "There's something else that seems curious to me. He said he drove up to Napa by himself."

"So?"

"When I called the winery, a woman answered the phone. I may be mistaken, but it sounded a lot like Eve."

ANGEL IS INCREDULOUS. "They're going to shoot Dick's ashes up in a Roman candle?"

Rosie and I are with Angel in her cell at seven o'clock Saturday evening. Rosie just finished explaining the arrangements for the memorial. "I checked with the probate attorney," I say. "He said that the fireworks were written into Dick's will."

"Richard never told you about his final wishes?" Rosie asks.

Angel looks at the ceiling. There is desperation in her eyes. "He's making this up, right?" she says. "He's playing some sort of sick joke. There must be something we can do."

"Realistically, honey," Rosie says, "there isn't much." We can spend the next few days trying to stop the memorial or we can use our time more productively trying to gather evidence.

"Fine," Angel says. "Let them cremate Dick. Let them shoot him up in fireworks. But I want to be there. I'm his wife. I have every right."

"We'll see what we can do," Rosie says.

"What about bail?"

Rosie explains that there will be an arraignment at two o'clock Monday. Angel will plead not guilty, and we'll ask the judge for bail. "The district attorney will oppose it," Rosie says.

"So when do I get out of here?"

"I'm not sure, honey. The judge is a former prosecutor. The D.A. is going to argue that you tried to run." She tells her that there's little chance she'll set bail if the D.A. proceeds with a charge of first-degree murder.

Angel struggles with her composure. The tears flow freely as she slumps into the heavy wooden chair. "No one believes me, Aunt Rosie."

"You have to trust us, Angel," Rosie says.

"I didn't do anything."

Rosie changes the subject. "What can you tell me about a woman named Eve?"

Angel tenses. "What would you like to know?"

"For starters, what's her real name?"

"Evelyn LaCuesta. We went to the same high school, and we did a couple of modeling jobs together. She wants to be an actress."

"What is she doing now?"

"She's Richard's assistant. Which means she does whatever he says."

"Does that include sleeping with him?"

"Probably, but nobody is supposed to know about it. He's getting divorced again, and it's gotten acrimonious. He's trying to show that his wife was cheating on him. He doesn't want anybody to know he was cheating on her."

It's an old story. I ask, "Do you trust her?"

She answers immediately. "No, she's very ambitious. She'll do anything to land a part in a major film."

"Even lie about a murder?"

She doesn't hesitate before she responds, "Absolutely."

Rosie and I glance at each other. "Angel," Rosie says in a soft tone, "we understand you may stand to inherit a large sum of money from your husband."

She shrugs, but her eyes never leave Rosie's. "I wouldn't know."

"You never read his will?"

She becomes indignant. "I didn't marry Dick for his money. I signed a prenuptial agreement to prove it. I loved him."

Rosie takes her hand and says, "Honey, it turns out that you may be entitled to a lot of money under the will that you wouldn't have been entitled to under the prenup."

"So?"

"The prosecutors are going to emphasize the fact that Dick's death at this time will result in your receiving a large windfall—much more than you would have received under the prenup if you had gotten divorced."

"Who said anything about a divorce?"

"We understand Dick consulted a divorce attorney. You can put two and two together."

She sits in stunned silence for a moment. Then she says, "You're saying they think I killed Dick for money?"

"We need to be prepared to address that possibility."

She remains defiant. "I have no idea what's in my husband's will, Aunt Rosie. Dick asked me to sign the prenup. It may not have been the smartest thing I ever did. If the prosecutors want to make something of it, there's nothing I can do."

"We have another problem," Rosie says. "We talked to Pete."

Angel's eyes dart in my direction, but she doesn't say anything.

"Honey," Rosie continues, "we understand he gave you information that suggested Dick was seeing another woman."

Angel freezes.

Rosie says, "Can we talk about it?"

Angel exhales heavily and whispers, "He didn't have any proof. He didn't have any pictures. It was all just rumors."

"Pete is very thorough," Rosie says.

"I trust my husband." She wipes the tears out of her eyes and says, "I won't believe he was cheating on me until somebody brings me pictures."

"There may not be any pictures," Rosie says. "You hired Pete, so you must have suspected something. It doesn't look good."

"I know how it looks," Angel says. "Do you think I would have killed my husband because I suspected he was seeing another woman? Do you think I would have done it a week before my first film was coming out?"

Rosie looks her straight in the eye and says, "No." She runs her fingers through her hair and says, "There's a more fundamental problem."

"What's that?" Angel asks.

"This is going to sound harsh."

Angel steels herself.

Rosie lays it on the line. "You lied to us. You led us to believe Pete had told you Dick wasn't seeing anyone else."

"He still hasn't proven to me that he did."

"Be that as it may, you misled us."

Angel appears genuinely contrite. "I'm sorry, Aunt Rosie."

"Honey," Rosie says, "I need to know if you've lied to us about anything else."

"No."

"Have you stretched the truth?"

"No."

"Have you left anything out that we should know about?"

Angel bursts into tears. "What do you want from me, Aunt Rosie? Do you want to take me down to Father Aguirre at St. Peter's to confess that I lied?"

Rosie holds up her hands and says, "That's not the point. If you want us to represent you, we need to know you're telling us the truth—good, bad or ugly. We can't represent you effectively if you lie to us. Understood?"

Angel's voice is barely a whisper when she says, "Understood." Then her eyes go gray and her shoulders start to shake violently as she starts to sob. Rosie takes her niece into her arms.

# Chapter 9

## "I Made a Deal with God"

> I try not to judge my clients. I ask them to tell me the truth and I listen to their stories. In many cases, it's in your client's best interests to arrange for a plea bargain. Making deals is an important part of an overworked system.
>
> —Rosita Fernandez
> *San Francisco Daily Legal Journal*

"Daddy," Grace says to me, "is Angel going to go home soon?"

I study the troubled look in her eyes and think of the life-sized poster of her movie-star cousin hanging on the back of her bedroom door. I recall the countless times Angel has taken her to the movies or shopping. "Yes, honey," I say. "It's all a misunderstanding."

"Mommy says she gets a little mixed up."

"Just because you're mixed up doesn't mean you would hurt somebody."

We're sitting in Sylvia's kitchen at eight o'clock the same night. Rosie is at the grocery store. The practice of law doesn't always allow for a lot of free time to handle some fairly basic needs, such as shopping for food.

Grace swallows a bite of pizza and takes a sip of Diet Coke. Rosie drinks the same stuff from the time she gets up in the morning until she goes to bed. The culinary apple doesn't fall too far from the tree. Sylvia is watching CNN in the living room. Theresa finally fell asleep in the spare bedroom. Grace takes her plate to the sink and returns with an Oreo for each of us. I hand mine back to her and nod toward my ex-mother-in-law. "See if Grandma wants a cookie."

She does as she's told. Sylvia gladly accepts the cookie and kisses Grace on the cheek. There's something special about grandmothers.

I look at my daughter. She has Rosie's dark brown eyes and olive skin. She looks a lot like Sylvia, too. Her short, curly hair is a little lighter, suggesting she has a few Daley genes. Her round face and full lips are pure Rosie. She's already pretty. She's going to be beautiful. When Sylvia, Rosie and Grace are together, it's as if you're looking at time-lapse photos of the same person. Grace is the spring, Rosie is the summer and Sylvia is the autumn. "Daddy," she whispers, "can I ask you something?"

"Anything, sweetie."

She lowers her voice and asks, "Is Mommy going to die?"

*Oh, boy.* The question elicits a discernible glance from her grandmother. Sylvia doesn't miss a thing. I'm caught off guard, and I do what every good lawyer would do under the circumstances—stall. "Why do you ask?"

"I heard Mommy crying again last night."

There are things they don't teach you in law school. Or in priest school, for that matter. "Mommy had a bad night. We've talked about this. She's getting better."

She pouts. "I know. But Mommy says the cancer isn't all gone."

"No, it isn't."

"So she isn't all better."

"Not quite." I take her hand. "Look, honey, Mommy is doing everything the doctor tells her to do. She's taking her medicine and she's going to get better."

"Do you promise?"

*What do I say?* "I promise."

"I'm worried, Daddy."

"So am I."

"I don't want Mommy to die. It made me sad when Grandma Margaret died." Grace took it very hard when my mother died about two years ago. She was too young to remember when my dad died, and she never knew Rosie's father.

"I don't want Mommy to die, either," I tell her. "That would make me sad, too."

"Even though you're divorced?"

"Even though we're divorced."

She reflects for a moment and asks, "Are you going to get married to Judge Shapiro?"

She shares her mother's directness. "I don't know, honey. Maybe someday. We're just getting to know each other. Would that be okay with you?"

Her lips form a thoughtful frown. "I don't know. We're just getting to know each other, too."

Touché. "Nothing is going to happen anytime soon. And I won't do anything without talking to you about it first. Okay?"

"Okay." She glances at Sylvia for an instant and then turns back to me. "Daddy, would you and Mommy ever think about getting back together?"

We've talked about this on many occasions. She knows my standard answer. "Probably not, sweetie. We tried, but we weren't very good at being married."

"Maybe you could try a little harder next time."

I suspect there are few ten-year-olds who share Grace's wisdom. We sit in silence for a moment. Sylvia picks up the remote and turns off the TV.

Grace's dark eyes look directly into mine when she whispers, "I'm scared, Daddy."

So am I. "It's okay," I tell her. "Maybe we can be scared together."

"You won't get sick, too, will you?"

There's a lump in the back of my throat. "No, sweetie. I'll take good care of myself."

"Promise?"

"I promise."

Grace gives me a hug and heads off to the living room. Sylvia walks in. I give her a helpless look. Priests are supposed to know answers to questions like that. I ask, "Did I say the right thing?"

"Some questions don't have easy answers." She senses my unease and adds, "You did fine, Michael."

MY CELL PHONE CRACKLES. "You didn't tell me MacArthur got whacked by his own Oscar," Leslie says to me. "You have to admit, there's a certain poetic justice to it."

I'm driving north on Doyle Drive toward the Golden Gate Bridge. Leslie is at her place. I pass the parking lot on the east side of the toll plaza where Angel was found this morning. I'm on my way to Rosie's house.

I ask, "How did you find out about the Oscar? The police haven't released any details."

"I work at the Hall of Justice."

"Do you usually discuss the evidence in a pending murder investigation?"

"We have no secrets at the Hall. We're all doing our best to find the truth." She pauses and adds, "There's also an exception if the case involves a movie star. Then all bets are off."

"And what do you do if the movie star is represented by the world's sexiest criminal defense attorney?"

She chuckles and says, "We need to be sure counsel is competent. In the interests of justice, we designate a Superior Court judge to review the attorney's qualifications. In this case, I have graciously agreed to take on the responsibility for becoming familiar with your credentials."

I can't resist feeding her the straight line. "How familiar?"

"Intimately."

"I was hoping you were going to say that."

"Does that mean we're still on tonight? I'd like to begin my due diligence right away."

"I need to ask for a continuance."

"On what grounds? You know I don't like to grant continuances in my courtroom."

She doesn't grant them in her bedroom, either.

"There are extenuating circumstances," I plead. "I need to get together with Rosie to talk about Angelina's case."

"The court is not amused."

"Neither is the defense attorney."

"I may need to hold you in contempt. The penalties are quite severe."

"I'll make it up to you "

"I'll make it worth your while."

"What did you have in mind?"

"I'll do that thing where I wear my robes."

It's my favorite. "I need a rain check."

"That doesn't sound tempting to you?"

"If you get any more tempting, I'll drive off the bridge."

Another chuckle. She asks, "Is this what people call phone sex?"

"I'm not an expert."

"Is there anything I can do to change your mind?"

"Not likely."

"Let me try. I'm sipping a glass of Pride Mountain Merlot and watching the fog come in over Coit Tower. I'm not wearing anything."

"I'm pulling over."

"I'll stop."

"Don't."

This elicits a laugh. I decide to switch to a more serious subject while she's in good spirits. "So," I say, "have you had a chance to think about our discussion from the other night?"

"Which one?"

"Where I asked you whether you want to make our situation a little more permanent. You know—maybe tell a few other people we're an item."

The phone goes silent for a moment. "I haven't had much time to think about it." She hesitates and adds, "It's complicated."

"Take your time. No pressure."

She ponders for a moment and says, "I love being with you, Mike. You know that, don't you?"

"Yes. And I love being with you, too."

"It's just that our relationship will have a ripple effect. You appreciate that, don't you?"

She still asks questions like a prosecutor. She frames them in a manner to elicit the response she wants.

"Of course."

Her tone is more tenuous when she asks, "Do I have to give you an answer right now?"

"No. Will you give me an answer soon?"

"Yes." She changes the subject. "Everybody at the Hall is talking about your case. Nicole is going to handle it herself."

"She wouldn't be looking for some free TV time, would she?"

"Just because she's behind in the polls? Of course not. That would be wrong."

I ask her what else she's heard.

"O'Brien is saying he's got your client nailed. The blood on the Oscar matched MacArthur's."

"I thought you guys weren't supposed to talk about this stuff."

"We aren't. So, did she do it?"

"You aren't supposed to ask that question."

"And you aren't supposed to be sleeping with a judge. Did she?"

"No."

"What will it take for you to reconsider your position and enter a guilty plea?"

"Are you trying to fix this case?"

"*Fix* is such a harsh word, Mike. I'm an officer of the court. Let's just say I'm trying to resolve it in the interests of justice."

"You aren't supposed to do that, either."

She plants her tongue in her cheek and says, "I'm doing this as a public service. If the case moves forward, the Hall will be swarming with media. Do you know how bad the traffic is around here?"

"I'm familiar with the problem."

"So, what's it going to take to get a guilty plea and avoid gridlock?"

"You know that red teddy you were wearing the other night? I'd like to see you and your teddy at your place tomorrow night at nine o'clock. We can discuss your proposal for relieving congestion." I pause and add, "The teddy is optional."

"On behalf of the citizens of our fair city, you're on."

"DID PETE FIND ANYTHING?" Rosie asks me.

"Not yet. He's camped out down the street from Little Richard's house."

We're sitting in her living room watching the late news. Rosie and Grace live in a rented bungalow on Alexander Avenue, across the street from the

Little League field in Larkspur, three suburbs north of the Golden Gate Bridge. I live in a cookie-cutter one-bedroom apartment about two blocks from here. We'll never resemble Ozzie and Harriet in any meaningful way.

Rosie stares at the TV. The media frenzy is fully engaged. Angel is the top story. A distraught Little Richard says his father's loss is a great tragedy. Then he faces the camera and says *The Return of the Master* will be released on time. The show must go on. Next they talk to a subdued Carl Ellis. He says the China Basin project will proceed as scheduled. I guess that show must go on, too.

"In a related story," the blow-dried anchor continues, "police are still trying to locate attorney and businessman Martin Kent, whose car was parked down the street from the MacArthur residence."

The camera cuts to the gate of a Marin County mansion. A harried-looking Daniel Crown expresses his sympathy. "It's a great loss to our business," the movie star says. Then a woman with a horrific bleach-blond friz and a salon-enhanced tan steps in front of him and says he'll have no further comment.

"That would be Crown's wife?" I say.

Rosie nods. "I wouldn't want to meet Cheryl Springer on a dark street out in the Bayview." Rosie turns off the TV and says, "I'll bet you the movie will be released on time. Big Dick's death is great publicity."

"You're so cynical," I say.

"You're so right."

We discuss our meeting with Nicole Ward tomorrow morning. Grace is sleeping on the sofa. She fell asleep in Rosie's car and again when she got home, and Rosie wouldn't let me carry her into her bedroom. Sometimes Rosie just wants to be with her. At times, she can't take her eyes off her. It's as if she's trying to paint a picture in her mind—to keep a snapshot of Grace with her at every instant. She hasn't slept well since she was diagnosed with cancer. It's almost as if she wants to hold on to every waking moment as long as she possibly can.

"Were you able to reach Carl Ellis?" she asks.

"Briefly," I say. "I caught him by phone at the Ritz. I was surprised he talked to me."

"And?"

"He said he left Big Dick's house with Petrillo at a quarter to two. And that the studio project will proceed as planned."

"Anything about a competing proposal?"

"He said it was too late to consider alternate plans. They're moving forward."

"And Angel's behavior?"

"He said she'd had too much to drink." I tell her he had no idea where Kent is.

She nods. "His story squares with Little Richard's."

"Yes it does." I tell her Ellis was on his way back to Vegas.

Rosie shakes her head and says, "It doesn't help."

"Did you expect him to confess?"

"No." Then she adds, "I need you to take a trip to Vegas—sooner rather than later."

"I'll go down there in the next couple of days."

She shifts gears. "Sorry your date with Leslie got screwed up."

"We'll get together another time." I decide to leave out any mention of our little high-tech rendezvous on the Golden Gate Bridge.

"I hope things work out for you." She reflects and adds, "If it's what you want."

I look at my ex-wife and say, "I think it is."

"Do you love her?"

Now it's my turn to pause. "I'm pretty sure."

"Does she love you?"

"It's complicated."

"Yes or no?"

"She's working at it."

"Are you ready?"

"I think so."

"Do you want to get married?"

"Not anytime soon. We both know the risks."

"That we do." She looks at Grace and says, "She asked me about you and Leslie."

"Me, too."

"What did you tell her?"

"Nothing major will happen anytime soon."

"How did she react?"

"She's taking a wait-and-see attitude."

"She's wise beyond her years."

"She's been through this before."

"It's different this time," she says. "She has good instincts. She knows you're serious. She wouldn't have asked me about it otherwise." She reflects and adds, "She has a lot on her plate right now."

"I know."

"She'll need a period of adjustment for this. I need you to be gentle with her, Mike."

"I will."

She swallows and says, "It's nice to have somebody to hold you at night. I miss that."

Beautiful Rosie. I'm falling in love with Judge Leslie Shapiro, but Rosita Carmela Fernandez will always be my soul mate. "You'll never be alone, Rosie."

She gets a faraway look in her eyes. "If things don't work out with Leslie—" she says. Then she stops herself.

"What is it, Rosie?"

"Never mind."

"Come on."

"I can't." She mulls things over for a moment and changes the subject again. "How much longer do you want to keep doing this?"

"Hanging out with you?"

"Practicing law."

I go with the standard answer. "As long as I can. It's what I do."

"Don't be glib. Don't you ever get tired of dealing with other people's problems?"

"Sometimes. It's still easier than being a priest."

"How's that?"

"If a defense attorney screws up, the client ends up in jail. If a priest screws up, the client ends up in hell."

"Some people think it's about the same."

"Not the way I learned it."

"Do you think it might be time to take a break?"

"Maybe. I'm not sure what I would do with myself."

"You could hang out with Grace and Leslie. You could even spend some time with me. You know. Go out for coffee or something appropriately platonic for two old friends."

"I'd like that."

"Or you could even do something useful. Did you hear anything more from the dean?"

My alma mater, Boalt Law School, received a large donation to start a program to give law students hands-on experience working on death-penalty cases. They've been looking for somebody to supervise the clinic. Dean Dwyer thinks I have the right stuff. I'm not so sure.

"He called again," I say.

"You'd be perfect," she says.

"He doesn't realize how godawful I am at administration. The program would go broke in a year."

She gives me a knowing smile. Rosie is very familiar with my shortcomings with business and money. She will always be the managing partner of our firm. "I think Professor Michael Daley has a nice ring to it," she says.

So do I. "I'd miss the courtroom."

"You could train a dozen young attorneys every year to do what you do. You could hang out in Berkeley. You could chase pretty young coeds."

"Now, that would be fun."

"Why are you trying to talk yourself out of it?" she asks.

"I'm just not sure I want to do it."

"You're going to be fifty next year, Mike."

"Which means I can do this for at least another twenty years."

"Don't you want to retire someday?"

"We can't afford it. Grace won't get out of law school for another fifteen years."

"What about all the money you put away in the Fernandez and Daley Keogh Plan?"

"Twenty-seven thousand dollars doesn't go as far as it used to."

She feigns exasperation. "You're going to do this until you drop, aren't you?"

She knows me too well. "Probably. I can't seem to let go."

"We're not as young as we used to be."

"We're not as old as we're going to be."

"What did you tell him?"

"I'd think about it."

She sighs. "It wouldn't kill you to take a job where you might get a regular paycheck."

"I wouldn't know what to do with it. Besides, I wouldn't want to be responsible for breaking up Fernandez and Daley."

"I'll understand."

"Maybe it's something *you* should think about," I say. "I could mention it to the dean."

"I'm a trial lawyer, Mike. I'm not a teacher."

"Sure you are. You taught me everything I know about sex."

She smiles. "That was like teaching a preschooler. The job at Boalt would require me to teach law students."

"Do you want me to say something to the dean?"

"I'll think about it."

She'll never do it. There's an excitement in her eyes when she's in court. It would be very difficult for her to give it up. "How are you feeling?" I ask.

"Fair." She turns serious. "I spend my life waiting for test results."

"You're going to be fine."

"I hope so, Mike."

I walk over to her and give her a hug. As I turn to leave, I see her looking at Grace, who is curled up with a Winnie the Pooh that she got at Disneyland. "She's beautiful," Rosie says.

"She has your eyes."

Rosie gives me a knowing grin. "She's going to break a few hearts."

"Just like her mom." We look into each other's eyes. There are tears in hers. "She's scared, Rosie," I say.

Her lips turn down. "I know." A year ago, we would have been sitting on the sofa drinking wine. Now, Rosie drinks a lot of water. It's almost as if she thinks she can wash the cancer out of her system. "So am I."

"It's okay to be scared."

"I know that, too." She extends her hand to me. I take hers in mine. "I've got everything worked out," she says. "I made a deal with God."

"You did?"

"Yeah. Didn't you do that when you were growing up?"

"All the time. I still do." I smile. "So what's your deal?"

"I promised God I would stop swearing if I can live long enough to see Grace's graduation from high school."

"I see. And have you negotiated a deal to see Grace's graduation from Cal?"

"Not yet. I'm having my people get in touch with God's. I was talking to Father Aguirre over at St. Peter's. He said God is going to launch a website. You'll be able to do everything by e-mail."

"Even confessions?"

"Yes. You'll go straight to the top. It will cut out the need for a middleman."

"What about the clergy?"

She gives me a wry grin. "They'll be necessary to perform ceremonies like weddings and funerals, but there will be cutbacks and downsizings."

"Sort of like what happened to live bank tellers after they put automated teller machines on every corner?"

"Exactly."

"Sounds like I got out of the business just in time." I lean over and kiss her on the cheek. "You're a marvel, Rosita."

She kisses me back, lightly on the lips. "What do you think about my deal?" she asks.

"It's a pretty good one."

She turns serious. "But do you think God will go for it? You were the priest. You had the pipeline. You must know something about deals with God."

"I've made a few of them over the years, too, Rosie."

"Did they work?"

"Most of the time." But not all the time.

"Do you still believe that God listens?"

"I think so."

"Do you think God's listening to me right now?"

"I'm sure of it."

She looks back at Grace. Tears stream down her face. "I just want to see how she turns out when she grows up," Rosie says.

"You will," I whisper.

"Promise?"

"I promise."

IT'S A FEW MINUTES before midnight when I open the door to my apartment just behind the Larkspur fire station. I toss my jacket onto the beat-up oatmeal-colored sofa and I pull the last Diet Dr Pepper from the refrigerator that's been sitting in the kitchen since the fifties. I salute the dishes that are stacked in the sink. I set the soda down on my butcher-block table and I hit the "play" button on my answering machine. There are messages from all the local TV stations and newspapers. An unlisted number isn't much good in our high-tech world.

I listen to a message from Nicole Ward. "Just confirming our meeting tomorrow morning," she says. It's only ten hours away. "We should have a great deal to talk about."

The final message is from another familiar source. "Michael," the husky voice says, "it's Leslie. Please call me on my cell. I'll be waiting up for your call. I have a surprise for you."

I punch in Leslie's number. A sexy voice answers on the first ring. "Hello, Michael," she whispers.

"How did you know it was me?"

"I give this number to a very select group of people."

"I'm honored."

"You should be."

"You said you had a surprise for me."

"I do. I heard you had a tough day."

"I did."

"There's a beautiful, naked, sexy woman. She wants to see you."

Damn. "I thought we rescheduled for tomorrow night, Leslie. It's a little late for me to come into the city."

"You don't have to do that."

"How's that?"

"Come into your bedroom, Michael. I've been waiting for you."

It's so hard to find judges who make house calls. I can feel my heart starting to pound. I walk across my living room and open the door to my bedroom. I find Leslie lying in bed with a sheet pulled over her. She's still holding her cell phone. I ask, "Why didn't I hear your cell phone ring?"

"I put it on vibrate mode. I wanted to surprise you."

"You did. It's very sweet of you to come over, Leslie."

She smiles and says, "I told you I don't like to grant continuances."

# Chapter 10

## "They Found Him"

Fort Point was built in the 1850s. It has witnessed the Civil War, two world wars, countless earthquakes and the construction of the Golden Gate Bridge.

—Golden Gate National Recreation Area information pamphlet

"Are you awake, Mick?"

"I am now, Pete." I fumble the phone and struggle to get my bearings. I can feel Leslie's breath on my cheek. Her eyes are closed. I whisper, "What time is it, Pete?"

"A few minutes after six."

"Don't you ever sleep?"

"You don't have to get snippy."

A job with regular hours is sounding better all the time. I turn on the light. Leslie opens her eyes. She leans back and gives me an inquisitive look. Then she pulls the sheet over her body. She mouths the word, "Rosie?"

I shake my head.

She tries again. "Who?"

I cover the mouthpiece of the phone and say, "Pete."

She sighs. Then she leans back onto the pillow.

Pete tries again. "Mick? Are you listening?"

"Yeah."

He hesitates and asks, "Are you by yourself?"

"Yeah."

"Right." I can hear the chuckle in his voice when he says, "Rosie?"

"Never mind."

"Good for you."

"Shut up, Pete."

"Anybody I know?"

"No."

"When do I get to meet her?"

"We'll talk about it another time."

"Same old story. I'm working and you're fooling around."

I sit up and say, "You have my undivided attention. Why did you call?"

"They found him."

"Who?"

"Martin Kent."

Yes! "Where?"

"Fort Point."

Huh? It's a restored Civil War–era installation at the base of the south anchorage of the Golden Gate Bridge. "What the hell was he doing there?"

"He washed up next to the retaining wall. He's dead, Mick."

Hell. "Did he jump?"

"I don't know. I heard about it on the police band. They've already dispatched a couple of black-and-whites."

"Where are you?"

"On my way to the fort."

"I'll meet you there as soon as I can."

I'm pulling on a pair of slacks when I hear Leslie's voice from behind me. "This is becoming a familiar story," she says.

Busted again. I turn to her and say, "I'm sorry." I tell her about Kent. "I have to get to Fort Point."

She runs a finger across her lip. "Do you think the relationship gods are trying to tell us something here?"

"I wouldn't read too much into it."

Her eyes turn softer. "You really have to go, don't you?"

"Yes."

"You're the most conscientious man I've ever met, Michael Daley. You aren't helping me fall in love with you."

"I'm trying, Leslie."

"I don't know if this is going to work."

"Why not?"

"A lot of reasons."

"The federal bench?"

"That's an issue," she acknowledges. "But not the real one."

"What *is* the real issue?"

"I've been single for a long time. I've never mentioned it, but I was married once."

This is news. "When?"

"I was in college. It lasted less than a year."

"It was a long time ago."

"I know. And the one bad experience shouldn't color my judgment—but it has. I like my independence. I'm used to having things my way. I promised myself I wouldn't get seriously involved with another man unless he was almost perfect."

That's a pretty tall order. "How do I stack up?"

"You're pretty damn close—maybe as close as I'm going to find."

Not bad. "What's the problem?"

"I need your attention."

"I'm all yours."

Her eyes flash. "No, you're not. You have other responsibilities—big ones. You have your practice, which seems to involve a lot of late-night phone calls."

Fair enough. "The last couple of days have been unusual."

The hint of a grin. "I understand. But you also have Grace and Rosie to worry about."

"I can't change it. They're part of the package."

"I know. This may sound selfish, but I don't want to share you—especially with your ex-wife."

This is a new angle. I tread cautiously. "You seem to get along okay."

"On a professional level, yes. I'm not so sure we'll do so well on a personal level."

"Why?"

"You still have feelings for her."

There's no point denying it. "I always will."

"I don't want to be looking over my shoulder."

"You won't have to."

She shows a hint of irritation. "Come on, Mike. It's clear to everybody who sees you together. You have stronger feelings for each other than most of my married friends have for their spouses. You have a daughter. You work together. And you can't seem to untie the knot. How do you think I feel when I see the two of you together?"

"You shouldn't be jealous of Rosie." I realize I sound defensive as I say it.

"I am."

"It isn't that sort of a relationship anymore."

"Before I can make any real commitment to you, I need to know you won't be leaping back into each other's arms."

"We won't."

"I'm not so sure." For the first time since we've been seeing each other, I think I see tears welling up in her eyes. This is unusual. She once told me judges aren't allowed to cry.

"I want this to work out," I tell her. "I want *us* to work out."

She regains her judicial composure. She kisses me and says, "We'll talk about it later. Your brother is waiting for you at Fort Point."

"YOU DON'T SOUND GOOD," Rosie tells me.

"I'm tired," I say. I'm talking on my cell as I'm driving to her house.

"Is something wrong?" she asks.

"They found Martin Kent."

"I know. My mom heard it on the radio."

It shouldn't surprise me. Sylvia wakes up at four-thirty. "Can you find somebody to stay with Grace?"

"I've already talked to Melanie and Jack." Her neighbors have a son who is Grace's age. We impose upon them more frequently than we should.

"I'll be there in five minutes," I tell her.

"Are you okay, Mike?"

"Why do you ask?"

"Something in your voice." She hesitates and says, "Something with Leslie?"

She knows me better than anybody. "I'm fine."

FORT POINT is a masonry building located twenty-five stories directly below the deck of the Golden Gate Bridge. It was called the Pride of the Pacific when construction was completed during the Gold Rush. At the time, its four tiers of cannon were considered a state-of-the-art deterrence to a naval attack on California. It turns out they were never tested in battle.

Rosie, Pete and I are standing in the fog next to a cyclone fence between the outside wall of the fort and the bay. The spot is a popular turnaround for runners and cyclists who come here from the Marina district. The park service put up a sign with a picture of two hands. It's customary for the runners to touch the hands before they turn back. A more imposing warning next to it says, NO ADMITTANCE—THIS AREA SUBJECT TO FALLING OBJECTS DURING BRIDGE REPAIRS. Although traffic is light at seven-fifteen on Sunday morning, we can hear the cars and trucks barreling across the deck.

The police have cordoned off an area about the length of a football field on the narrow access road that hugs the bay. Officers are huddling around the body of Martin Kent, which is covered with a black tarp. The papers will note that he washed up at almost the exact spot where Jimmy Stewart plucked Kim Novak out of the water in *Vertigo*. Inspector Jack O'Brien is supervising another crime scene. The coroner's van, a paramedic unit and four police cars are parked just outside the yellow police tape.

I gesture toward O'Brien, who looks visibly troubled. "We seem to have found another body," he says. "Do you think you can persuade your client to talk to us about it?"

"No," Rosie answers.

I ask him if he knows what happened.

"Too soon to tell. The watchman found him at five-thirty. He called us."

"Did he jump?" Pete asks.

He shrugs. "I don't know. He was pretty banged up."

"What about gunshots or stab wounds?" I ask.

"None."

I ask him about other evidence of foul play.

"I'm not the medical examiner."

"Do you have any idea how he got to the bridge?"

"No. You shouldn't assume he went off the bridge."

I won't. "Any telltale signs on his clothing?"

"He's been in the water for a while. We'll have to wait for the coroner's report."

I survey the scene and ask, "Have you been able to connect Kent to MacArthur's death?"

"Not yet."

"Is it safe to assume they're related?"

"We aren't assuming anything."

Pete looks toward the body and points to a distraught middle-aged man who is talking to the police. "Is that Kent's son?" he asks.

"Yes. He identified the body."

"Mind if we ask him a few questions?"

O'Brien starts walking away. "This might not be an ideal time."

He's right. "We'll talk to him later," I say. "He needs a little time to himself."

"THAT'S WHERE they found Angel," Pete tells me. We've driven up to the area known as the east view lot at the south end of the bridge. He's gesturing toward a parking space about fifty feet from the concession stand. The yellow police tape has been removed. A cool breeze is gusting as we're standing among the tourists next to the statue of Joseph Baermann Strauss. Every San Francisco schoolkid learns he was the chief engineer for the bridge. Construction of his masterpiece began in 1933 and was completed four years and twenty-three million dollars later. Next to Strauss is a display of the cross-section of the main cable, which is more than three feet in diameter.

"Did anybody see her park the car?" I ask. I glance at the tacky snack bar emblazoned with the words BRIDGE CAFÉ. Just past the Strauss statue is the Roundhouse Gift Shop, a circular building that used to be a restaurant. It's been a souvenir shop since the late eighties. Like most natives, I haven't stopped in this touristy area since I was a kid.

"The security guard didn't see her drive in," Pete says. "They haven't found any other witnesses so far. The snack bar and the gift shop were closed."

We walk past the gift shop and through a garden area. The fog is starting to lift, and I can see patches of blue sky above the towers. The cool air smells of salt water. We pause at the open cyclone-fence gate at the entrance to the walkway on the east side of the bridge deck. A sign says pedestrians may walk across the bridge from 5 A.M. until 9 P.M. The gate is topped with barbed wire.

"He couldn't have gotten out on the deck if he was here before five," I observe.

Pete studies the gate and says, "He could have climbed over it."

I look at the barbed wire at the top and say, "That would have hurt."

"He probably wasn't worried about cuts if he was planning to jump. If there wasn't any traffic, he could have hopped over the barrier onto the roadway and walked around the gate."

"He might have been hit by a car."

"There isn't much traffic at four in the morning."

I look at the tollbooths adjacent to the snack bar. You have to pay only when you're heading southbound. "Somebody at the toll booth might have seen him," I say.

"Maybe not. Only four lanes were open at three-thirty yesterday morning."

I ask him about patrols.

"The bridge has its own security force. A couple of officers watch for potential suicides. We should talk to the guys who were on duty last night."

We walk onto the deck and head north. I stop for a moment and look over the side. Fort Point is directly below us. I can see the yellow police tape forming a semicirclular arc around Kent's body. "He couldn't have jumped from here," I say. "He would have landed in the middle of the parade ground."

Pete nods. We continue walking for another hundred yards or so. A tall chain-link fence was added above the original iron guardrail several years ago to deter suicides. It extends only partway to the south tower. If Marty Kent didn't want to climb the higher fence, he needed to walk only a few hundred feet north.

When we reach the south tower, the skies are starting to turn dark blue and we can see Alcatraz to the east. I glance over the side and look down over the murky waters of the bay. "I wonder what Marty Kent was thinking." I say to Rosie.

"This may have been the last thing he saw," she says.

I can feel the blood rushing to my feet, and I take a step back from the rail. He may have flown over two hundred feet straight down into dark, ice-cold water at full speed in the middle of the night. Rosie and I look at each other for a moment without speaking.

Pete glances out at Alcatraz and says, "Just because his body washed up at Fort Point doesn't necessarily mean he jumped. It may be a coincidence that Angel and Kent were both at the bridge. Maybe they came in the same car. Maybe they were in on something. Maybe they were mad at each other. Somebody could have driven both of them." He turns back to me and says, "The one thing I do know is that we shouldn't jump to any hasty conclusions."

# Chapter 11

# The Princess of Bryant Street

During my tenure as district attorney, we will earn the respect and admiration of law-enforcement officials across the country.

—San Francisco District Attorney Nicole Ward
*San Francisco Chronicle*. Sunday, June 6

The chief law-enforcement officer of the City and County of San Francisco is glaring at me through oval-shaped brown eyes that sit just above her high, sculpted cheekbones. Nicole Ward's stylish cotton blouse and light slacks suggest she was lifted directly from the pages of a Nordstrom's ad. Her creamy complexion complements her shoulder-length auburn locks. She wrinkles her prim nose as she says to me, "You don't seriously think any judge in his right mind will grant bail to your client, do you?"

Beneath the sleek veneer, she's a street fighter who plays for keeps and wins more often than she loses. The battle is on.

"We're going to ask for bail," I say.

"We'll oppose it."

It's a beautiful Sunday morning. Most San Franciscans are drinking coffee, looking over the Sunday *Chronicle* and perhaps thinking about a hike on Mount Tam. Rosie and I have an audience with the woman Rosie calls the Princess of Bryant Street. We're sitting in the overstuffed chairs in the ceremonial D.A.'s office on the third floor of the Hall. A few years ago, the citizens of our fair city elected an egomaniac named Prentice Marshall Gates III as our D.A. His first official act was to have this office remodeled with oak paneling, elegant leather chairs and plush carpeting. He was better at picking furniture than trying cases. Although Gates left the scene two years ago, his furniture is still with us. It would cost at least fifty grand to rip out the paneling and the carpets and replace them with something a bit less ostentatious. Thus, Nicole Ward gets to sit in nice digs. The daughter of the CEO of a biotech firm wears the accoutrements of power well. While style will get you a long way in San Francisco, it would be a huge mistake to underestimate her skills as a prosecutor.

Rosie says, "She isn't a flight risk. She can't go anywhere without being recognized."

Ward leans across her immaculate desk and says, "You shouldn't expect special treatment from this office just because your client is a celebrity."

Believe me, we don't.

Ward glances at the miniature bronze scales of justice sitting on her credenza and adds with melodramatic self-righteousness, "Equal justice under the law. We respect every defendant's rights. We treat everybody the same."

I don't doubt her.

She points an index finger at us and says, "She tried to flee. She drove to the bridge. If she hadn't been intoxicated, she'd be in Oregon by now."

Rosie takes in the calculated diatribe with stoic silence. You're bound to lose if you get into a pissing contest with Nicole Ward.

"The arraignment is tomorrow at two," Ward says. "We're before Judge McDaniel."

Not a great draw for us. Elizabeth McDaniel is a veteran Superior Court judge who moved down the hall from the D.A.'s office a few years ago. Although she is thoughtful and exceptionally bright, she's never met a prosecutor she didn't like.

Ward adds, "I assume your client is going to plead not guilty."

"That would be correct," Rosie replies.

"Then we'll see you tomorrow."

"Nicole," Rosie says, "I was hoping we could take a few minutes to discuss the case."

"There's nothing to discuss."

Rosie scowls. "If you didn't want to talk, why did you agree to see us?"

Ward doesn't hesitate. "Professional courtesy. Nothing more."

How magnanimous. "What about Martin Kent?" Rosie asks.

"He's dead. You know as much as we do. We're investigating."

Thanks. I ask, "Do you know how he died?"

"We aren't sure."

"Did he jump off the bridge?"

"We aren't ruling anything out."

Rosie isn't giving up on a suicide yet. "Why would he have killed himself?"

"We don't know."

"You mean you won't tell us."

Her eyes narrow. "I mean we don't know. We just opened an investigation. We talked to his son, who said he saw nothing unusual in his father's behavior. We're talking to the toll takers and the bridge security force. We're trying to find anybody who might have seen him." She cocks her head and adds, "Who knows? Maybe your client was involved in his death, too."

Rosie ignores the cheap shot and observes, "Surely you've considered the possibility that Kent might have been involved in MacArthur's death."

"The thought had crossed my mind."

"You could even put together a plausible scenario where he might have killed MacArthur and then jumped off the bridge."

Ward gives us a sarcastic grin and says, "You left out the part where he decided to frame your client for murder along the way."

Rosie isn't giving in. "It's not beyond the realm," she insists. "His car was still at MacArthur's house. He could have driven my client to the bridge."

"Yeah, right," Ward says. "Then he carefully moved her into the driver's seat, put a bag of coke in the car and stashed the blood-splattered Oscar in the trunk."

"You're the one who keeps saying you shouldn't rule anything out," Rosie says.

Ward isn't buying it. "If he had just committed the perfect crime and framed your client, why would he have killed himself?"

Why, indeed? Rosie and I look at each other, but we remain silent.

Ward's tone becomes less strident. "Look," she says, "putting aside the posturing, we have enough evidence to get your client's case to trial."

I ask, "Would you mind telling us about it?"

"We'll have plenty of time after the arraignment."

"How about a preview?"

"She was at the scene. We found the murder weapon in the trunk of her car. She tried to flee. You can connect the dots."

It's enough for the arraignment. We'll know more before the preliminary hearing in a couple of weeks. We debate for a few more minutes, then an intense young Asian woman with delicate features and short, jet-black hair walks into the room without knocking. At barely five feet tall and dressed in khaki pants and a beige sweater, Lisa Yee isn't an imposing physical presence. However, she carries herself with supreme self-confidence. I've never heard her raise her voice. She wins with brains, not histrionics. She extends a delicate hand to me and seems genuinely apologetic when she says, "Sorry to interrupt."

Ward acknowledges her colleague and turns to us. "I'm sure you've met Lisa Yee," she says. "I've assigned her to help me with this case."

More bad news. Yee has taken a half dozen murder cases to trial during her tenure as a prosecutor. She's won every one of them. "Nice to see you again," she lies.

"Same here," I say.

She starts right in. "We got the fingerprint analysis on the Oscar."

That's quick. The crime lab is putting in some overtime. More important, Yee's appearance at this precise moment was undoubtedly carefully orchestrated.

"What did you find?" Ward asks.

Now I'm sure this has been rehearsed. Ward wouldn't have asked the question if she didn't already know the answer.

"The victim's fingerprints."

No surprise there.

"And Angelina Chavez's fingerprints."

"It doesn't mean a damn thing," Rosie says. "They lived in the same house. She could have handled that statue any time."

"She handled the murder weapon," Ward replies. "How do you figure the statue found its way to her car?"

"That's your job," Rosie says.

Ward doesn't respond.

I ask Yee, "Did you find any other prints on the Oscar?"

Yee glances at Ward before she says, "Yes."

"Whose?"

"We don't know yet. We haven't been able to match them."

At least it may give us some other potential suspects. "How many others?" I ask.

"At least four," Yee replies. "Maybe more."

Rosie darts a judgmental glance at Ward and says, "That shows somebody could have planted the statue in the car. That's four other suspects you're choosing to ignore."

Ward gives us an incredulous look and says, "The murder weapon was found in the trunk of your client's car."

"You don't know how it got there." Rosie replies.

"You don't have to be a rocket scientist to figure it out."

I ask Yee, "Did you find any fingerprints on the trunk?"

She squirms. "Just the victim's," she replies.

At least they didn't find Angel's. "How do you figure my client put the Oscar in the trunk?"

"She could have opened the trunk without leaving prints. Or she could have used the trunk release inside the car."

I ask if she found fingerprints on the trunk release.

Her light complexion turns bright red. "No."

"Did you find any prints on the steering wheel?"

"Yes," Yee says. "We found prints from the victim and Angelina Chavez."

"Anybody else?"

She glances at Ward and says in a subdued tone, "Martin Kent."

"Really?"

"And we're still trying to identify some smudged prints."

Rosie looks at Ward and says, "How do you suppose Kent's prints got onto the steering wheel, Nicole?"

She glares at Rosie without responding.

Rosie adds, "There are many possibilities. You shouldn't rule anything out."

Ward's delicate cheeks turn crimson. "It's staring you right in the face," she insists.

"You're jumping to conclusions," Rosie says.

Ward turns back to Yee and asks her about the blood on the Oscar.

"Type O," she says. "It matches the victim's blood type."

Ward is pleased. She turns to Rosie and asks, "How do you explain that?"

"We'll wait for the DNA tests. Millions of people have type-O blood. I'm one of them."

I interject, "So am I." Then I ask, "Did you find any blood on my client's hands or clothes?"

Ward hesitates for just an instant before she says, "No."

"How do you figure she was able to hit her husband with an Oscar without getting blood on her hands and her clothes?"

"She washed her hands. She changed clothes."

"When?"

"After she hit her husband, but before she got to the bridge."

Her tone isn't convincing. "Have you found the bloody clothes?"

Ward casts a helpless glance at Yee before she says in a quiet voice, "No."

It doesn't exonerate Angel, but it's a hole in their case. It inches us closer to reasonable doubt. We snipe at each other for a few more minutes, but Ward doesn't give in.

Rosie isn't finished. "Why would she have killed her husband? He gave her a shot to be a movie star. Her first big film is coming out on Friday. What's her motive?"

Ward gives us a sardonic smile. "The oldest one in the world: money. There's a million-dollar life-insurance policy. There was an ironclad prenup. She would have gotten nothing if he divorced her. By killing him before he was able to divorce her, she'll get half of his assets under the will, which overrides the prenup. He *was* going to divorce her."

Hell. I'd hoped they wouldn't find out about all that yet. Fat chance. "Where did you get the information about the insurance and the prenup?" I ask.

"MacArthur's son."

At least we know where his loyalties lie. We ask her for copies.

"Let me give you some friendly advice," she says. "Person to person. Friend to friend."

Asshole to asshole.

"Your client is in serious trouble. She has no plausible explanation. If she can't come up with a better story, you'd better start talking to her about pleading."

The games begin.

"It's premature to talk about a plea bargain," Rosie says. "You're going to end up dropping the charges."

"No, we won't," Ward replies. "I'm a reasonable person. I'm only asking you to talk to her. Convince her to come clean."

She isn't offering anything.

"Off the record," she continues, "I might be willing to go down to second degree if she cooperates. It would take the death penalty off the table."

It would also mean a minimum sentence of fifteen years. Rosie gives her an indignant look and asks, "You're really thinking about the death penalty?"

"Absolutely."

They stare at each other. They're both posturing. Rosie says, "Is that an offer?"

"No." Ward hesitates for a moment and adds, "It's a suggestion. Try it out on your client. Maybe it will encourage her to tell the truth. It would be good for her conscience."

It would also be good politics for Ward. She can take full credit for resolving the case if she can get a quick confession. If Angel doesn't plead, it's unlikely the case will be concluded before the election.

"I'll mention it to her," Rosie says.

"See you at the arraignment."

Angel's voice has a sound of desperation. "A plea bargain?" she says. We're meeting with her in a consultation room in the Glamour Slammer. It isn't going well.

"I'm reporting on our discussion with the D.A.," Rosie says. "I'm not recommending it."

"Good." Angel glares at Rosie. "It's out of the question."

"I was pretty sure you would say that." Rosie asks Angel about her night.

She tilts her head back and sighs. "Horrible." Her lips form a tight ball. "My roommate is a drug dealer."

"Did something happen?" Rosie asks.

Silence.

"Angel?"

Her eyes fill with tears. "I couldn't sleep. I was just lying on my bunk."

"And?"

"When the guard was away, she attacked me."

Rosie takes her hand. "She hit you?"

"Not exactly." She closes her eyes. "She covered my face with her pillow. I tried to push her off, but she was too strong." She glances around the gray room. "I thought I was going to die."

Rosie swallows hard. "Did you tell anyone about this?"

"She said she'd kill me if I did." Her voice is filled with palpable fear when she says, "You have to get me out of here."

Rosie puts her arm around her.

Angel is shaking. "Everything's falling apart," she says.

Rosie holds her for a moment and whispers, "They found Martin Kent." She hesitates for an instant and adds, "He's dead."

Angel covers her mouth with her hand. She starts to breathe heavily. In between gasps, she says, "They killed Marty, too?"

Rosie is now holding Angel like a baby. "They found his body in the bay by Fort Point," she tells her. "They think he may have jumped off the bridge."

Angel is silent for a moment. Tears well up in her eyes. Her head drops. "He was very decent," she says. "He took care of his wife when she got sick. He was terribly upset when she died."

Rosie and I glance at each other. I ask, "Was he upset on Friday night?"

Angel gives us a stern nod. "He was furious at Dick."

"Why?"

"He thought Dick had cut corners on the movie. And he didn't like the China Basin project from the start. He had put up a lot of his own money—probably millions. He thought Dick gave up too much to Ellis and Petrillo."

Rosie looks at me for an instant and then gives Angel a drink of water. "Honey," she says, "we'd better take it from the top one more time."

# Chapter 12

# "People Don't Get to Hold Oscars Every Day"

> This statue may not be sold, conveyed or otherwise transferred (other than pursuant to bequests) without first being offered to the academy. Manufactured under world rights granted by Academy of Motion Picture Arts and Sciences to R.S. Owens & Co., Inc., Chicago, Illinois 60630.
>
> —Inscription on the base of the Academy Award statue

Angel's tone is flat as she adds little embellishment to the sketchy story she told us yesterday. There was a dinner and a screening at the house. She was there along with her husband and his son, Daniel Crown and his wife, Marty Kent, Dominic Petrillo and Carl Ellis. They drank champagne at twelve-thirty. Everybody was still there when Angel went upstairs at one.

Rosie tries to slow her down as she begins probing for details. "Let's rewind the tape a little," she says. "What time did people start arriving?"

"Around eight."

"How did everybody get there?"

Angel says MacArthur's son walked from his house. Kent came by car. Daniel Crown and Cheryl Springer drove in from Marin. Petrillo and Ellis were staying at the Ritz. Petrillo came in a limo and Ellis took a cab. The living room, dining room and kitchen are on the second, or middle, level of the house. The theater is on the lower level and the bedrooms are on the third floor. Dinner was served at eight-thirty. She gives us the name of the caterers, who arrived at six.

Rosie asks, "What time did the caterers leave?"

"During the movie. They left after they set up the champagne." She confirms that they watched the movie in the theater and went back up to the living room for champagne.

"And the deck is just off the living room?"

"That's right."

I ask whether anybody went outside.

"Everybody did. Dick and Marty and Carl were smoking cigars."

I've started drawing a diagram of the house. We'll want to inspect the interior as soon as the cops will let us.

Rosie asks, "Was anybody else around? Your housekeeper? Security?"

"No. We gave our housekeeper the night off. We have an alarm, but we didn't hire a security guard. We live at the end of a cul-de-sac. It's a quiet neighborhood."

"Did you hire a valet parking service?"

"No. It was a small gathering. There was room on the street."

They live on the only street in San Francisco where parking isn't a problem. "Angel," I say, "when I was at the house, I noticed an outside stairway from the deck to the beach." I ask if somebody could have gotten to the deck without having gone through the house.

She considers for a moment. She explains there is a locked gate down by the beach. Then she says, "Somebody could have climbed over the gate, but it's covered with barbed wire. The stairs go all the way up to the gangway between our house and the Neilses'. The gangway leads to our driveway. Our property is enclosed by a fence. We have a locking gate on the driveway and at the entrance to the footpath at the front of the house."

My drawing is becoming more detailed. I show it to Angel and say, "But there's just a short picket fence at the front of the house, right? And there's no barbed wire there."

"That's true."

"So if somebody climbed over the fence, he could have walked down to the deck."

"I suppose."

Rosie's eyes open wide and she asks, "Did you leave the driveway gate open on Friday night to make it easier for the caterers and your guests?"

Angel thinks about it for a moment and says, "Yes."

"So," Rosie says, "somebody could have come in from the street and gone to the deck."

"It's possible."

The flip side is also true. Somebody could have killed Big Dick and left the premises without ever going through the house. It may give us a little wiggle room to suggest various alternative scenarios to the police and the prosecutors.

"Where was your car?" Rosie asks.

"In the garage." She says it was in the usual spot on the left side.

"And Dick's?"

Angel tilts her head back and tries to remember. "In the driveway," she says. "Behind my car."

Rosie asks her why his car wasn't in the garage.

"The caterers were using his side of the garage as a setup area. They parked their truck on his side of the driveway."

"Did anybody else park in the driveway?"

"No."

This means Angel couldn't have pulled her car out of the garage without having moved Dick's car first.

I ask her about Petrillo's limo. "Was it parked in front of the house the entire time?"

"No," she says. "The driver went to get a bite to eat. Dominic would have paged him when he was ready to leave."

"Do you know the name of the limo company?" I ask.

"Allure. We use them all the time." She says she doesn't know the name of the driver.

Rosie tries to refocus Angel's attention back to the timeline. Angel confirms the champagne started flowing at twelve-thirty and she went upstairs around one.

"Honey," Rosie says, "where did you keep the Oscar?"

"On the mantel in the living room."

"Was it there Friday night?"

"Yes. Then I put it on the table with the champagne glasses. I thought it would make a nice centerpiece."

That would also explain how Angel's fingerprints found their way onto the statue, if they weren't there already. "Did anybody else touch it?" Rosie asks.

"Everybody did," she says. "We passed it around for good luck. People don't get to hold Oscars every day. Dick was holding it when we toasted *The Return of the Master.*"

It may also explain some of the unidentified fingerprints on the statue. Rosie tries to keep her engaged. "Where was it the last time you saw it?"

"On the table." Her tone is steady when she tells us again she has no idea how it got into the trunk of her husband's car.

Rosie shifts gears and asks, "Was anybody else upset that night?"

"Just Marty. As I said, he was unhappy about the China Basin project. He said they were having problems with the redevelopment agency. I heard him say he thought it was a lousy investment."

"Did you get along with him?" Rosie asks.

Angel tenses and says, "I didn't know him very well."

"Did Dick and Marty get along?"

The corners of Angel's mouth turn up slightly. "They were like an old married couple. They argued constantly, though Dick used to say he couldn't live without him. Everybody was under a lot of pressure. Dick had a temper, and so did Marty."

"Did either of them lose his temper the other night?" Rosie says.

"No."

"What happened after you went upstairs?"

Her story doesn't change. She took a shower, put on her nightgown and went to bed.

"When did you change into the sweatsuit?" Rosie asks.

"I don't remember." She says she doesn't know what happened to the nightgown.

I catch a hint of skepticism in Rosie's eyes. "You have no idea how you got to the bridge?"

"That's right."

I tell her about my conversation with her neighbor. This gets a discernable grimace. I ask, "Did you know them pretty well?"

"No. They kept to themselves."

"He said he heard shouts from your deck around three," I say. "Did you hear anything?"

"No."

We talk for a few more minutes. Rosie reminds her that the arraignment is tomorrow. "Just follow my lead," Rosie tells her. "When the judge asks for your plea, you should stand up and say 'not guilty' in a clear voice. Got it?"

"Got it."

"WE DIDN'T GET MUCH out of Ward," I say to Rosie as we're driving toward the Ritz for our promised audience with Dominic Petrillo.

She's in a contemplative mood. "I didn't expect much," she replies. Then she adds, "She's very pretty."

"She's also a good prosecutor. The judges love her."

"So does the press. She's savvy. She knows Angel is attractive. It couldn't hurt to give the judge a smart, beautiful prosecutor."

Trial work is theater. When you're in court, you use whatever you have at your disposal. Nicole Ward doesn't need to rely on good looks. That doesn't stop her. If I looked like her, I'd use it to my advantage, too. I ask, "Do you think Angel was telling the truth?"

She reflects for a moment and says, "Her story hasn't changed. That's good. On the other hand, there are still some gaping holes."

I'm a little surprised by her equivocation. "What's bugging you?"

"The three-hour gap from the time she went upstairs until she was found at the bridge."

"You don't buy the blackout?"

"Maybe, but I find it hard to believe she didn't hear anything at all. I have a lot of trouble where she says she woke up a mile away in different clothing in her dead husband's car."

So do I.

She adds, "I'd like to find out what happened to the nightgown."

"Me, too. I'll have Pete search the area between the house and the bridge."

"That would be a good idea."

Time for a reality check. I say, "You don't seriously think she's a murderer, do you?"

This time she doesn't hesitate. "I can't see it."

I trust her instincts. "But?"

"I don't think she's told us everything. And I'm certain she's shading it in a manner that's favorable to her."

"Every client does."

"I know. Still, I have a feeling she's holding something back."

"Like what?"

"I'm not sure."

"We might be able to get something from Little Richard," I say, "or some of the others who were there. We should try to get to the caterers, too. And I'm still trying to figure out how the China Basin project fits into all of this."

"Me, too."

I pull into the driveway of the Ritz. I look at Rosie and say, "Let's see what Dominic Petrillo can tell us."

"COULD YOU PLEASE call Mr. Petrillo's room," I tell the concierge at the Ritz. Rosie and I are standing in the understated lobby of what many consider San Francisco's finest hotel. The classical nine-story structure at the top of Stockton Street near Union Square was built as the headquarters for an insurance company. It has evolved several times and was converted into the Ritz in the early nineties. The dark wood walls and deep carpets create an elegant ambiance. Sunday brunch is being served in the five-star restaurant, known simply as the Ritz Carlton Dining Room. The inviting aroma of eggs, bacon, waffles and coffee envelops us.

The officious man in the dark suit eyes me suspiciously. He says in a clipped tone, "And you would be?"

"Mr. Daley and Ms. Fernandez. Mr. Petrillo is expecting us."

He glances at his computer screen and frowns. Then he folds his arms and juts out his chin. "I'm afraid Mr. Petrillo has checked out."

I try not to show my irritation. Angry outbursts don't play well at the Ritz. "When?"

"About an hour ago."

"Has he left the building?"

"I'm not sure," he says. He motions to a uniformed bellhop, who practically sprints across the carpet. He whispers into his ear, and the young man starts walking toward the restaurant. "He'll try to find Mr. Petrillo," he tells us.

"Is Carl Ellis still here?" I ask.

He recognizes the name immediately. The concierge at the Ritz has to be good at remembering names. "He checked out late last night."

Dammit. "I need to reach him," I tell him. "One of his business associates died suddenly yesterday. Do you know if he went to Las Vegas? I have some information for him about the funeral arrangements."

"He seemed upset," the concierge acknowledges. "He left in a hurry." That's all he'll tell me. He adds, "Please sit down while our bellman tries to find Mr. Petrillo."

I glance at Rosie and ask the concierge, "Where is your restroom?"

He motions down the hall.

"I'll be back in a moment."

Rosie catches my eye and says, "Me, too."

We head toward the fancy dining room. When we're out of the concierge's earshot, Rosie says to me, "Are you going into the restaurant?"

"Of course."

Her eyes gleam. We walk by a security guard who is on his way to the lobby. Rosie whispers, "Looks like they're calling out the troops to follow us."

"We really look like criminals. The first thing most big-time crooks do is introduce themselves to the concierge at a big hotel right before they steal the silver."

She smiles. I open the door to the restaurant. The wood-paneled room with heavy tables and velvet chairs has a clubby atmosphere. The smell of French toast is making me hungry. I'm operating on a couple of hours of sleep and almost no food.

The maître d' is standing behind a tall kiosk. He looks a little like Sir Alec

Guinness. He addresses me with a polished British accent. "Do you have a reservation, sir?" He pronounces it as if it were spelled "suh."

Rosie is standing to my left. She's scanning the dining room while I filibuster. "I'm afraid not," I say. I glance around the room. The tables are full. "We were supposed to meet Mr. Petrillo." I pause and say, "Is he dining with you today?"

"One moment, sir." His face rearranges itself into a scowl. He puts on his half glasses and studies his reservation chart.

Rosie nudges me. "There he is," she whispers. She points toward the corner of the room, where an unhappy looking Petrillo is sitting by himself.

"I think I see him," I tell Sir Alec. "We'll join him for a few minutes."

"Will you be dining with us, sir?"

"I don't think so. It looks like he's almost finished."

He escorts us to Petrillo's table, where he is talking on his cell phone. There is a sign by the door that requests patrons to turn off their cell phones, but guys like Petrillo play by their own rules. He scowls at us when we arrive. He cups his hand over the mouthpiece and says, "I'm almost done. Why don't you wait outside?"

"We can wait here for a few minutes," I tell him.

He gives the maître d' a helpless look and says, "It would be better if you wait outside."

I glance at Rosie, who gives me a quick nod. We don't want to make a scene with Sir Alec still standing here. "We'll meet you outside," she whispers.

"Right this way," the maître d' says. He leads us to the entrance. We wait just inside the door. I don't want Petrillo to give us the slip by going out through the kitchen.

Petrillo makes us wait for another fifteen minutes. I can see him gesticulate as he talks on his cell. His pained expression suggests his business matters aren't going well. Finally, he snaps his phone shut, finishes his coffee and heads in our direction. He opens the door and leads us into the corridor. "Business," he mutters. He offers no explanation.

Rosie jumps right in. "We'd like to ask you a few questions about what happened Friday night," she says.

He keeps walking toward the lobby. "Your niece has put us in a very difficult position," he says. "I've given my statement to the police and I'm already late for my plane."

Rosie keeps firing questions as we follow him. "Can you tell us what you saw?"

Petrillo responds grudgingly, "I didn't see anything. I got there around eight. We had dinner and watched the movie. We had a drink, and my driver took me back to the hotel."

"What time did you leave?"

"A quarter to two. Carl Ellis rode with me. He can confirm the time."

And provide an alibi. "Who else was still there when you left?" I ask.

He rattles off the names of Angel, Little Richard, Crown, Springer and Kent.

"Was anybody upset?" I ask.

"Everybody was in a great mood." He says he didn't see or hear anything unusual.

He isn't an especially convincing liar. We're approaching the concierge's desk when Rosie asks, "How was Dick MacArthur acting?"

"He was very pleased with the way the movie turned out."

"And Ms. Chavez?"

"She'd had too much to drink. In all honesty, her behavior was erratic." He asks the concierge to have the bellhop bring his bag to the curb. Then we follow him out the door.

Rosie asks about Kent.

Petrillo responds, "He seemed fine to me."

"He's dead," I say.

"That's what I understand."

"Do you have any idea if something was bothering him? Was anybody mad at him?"

"He was under a lot of pressure."

Rosie asks, "Is the movie still going to be released on time?"

"I hope so. Some of my colleagues believe it would be in bad taste to release the movie this week. It might appear as if we're trying to exploit Dick's death. From a business standpoint, I'd like to do it. We've already spent a lot on advertising and promotion. The theaters are booked. It would be expensive to pull back now."

His bottom-line view doesn't surprise me. He takes a business card out of his pocket and says, "Give me a call at the office if you want to talk some more."

A burst of cool wind hits me in the face. "Just a few more minutes of your time," I say.

The bellhop comes by with Petrillo's overnight case. "I'm late," he says.

Rosie and I watch him get into a waiting Lincoln. I memorize the license number. It says, "ALLURE1."

# Chapter 13

# "Since When Did You Start Hanging Out with Movie Stars?"

> We are continuing our investigations of the deaths of Richard MacArthur and Martin Kent. We are unable to provide any additional details at this time.
>
> —Inspector Jack O'Brien. KGO Radio
> Sunday, June 6. 1:00 p.m.

I find a parking space down the block from the office. Our humble corner of downtown is quiet on Sunday afternoon. A few reporters are milling around in front of our doorway. Rosie and I wave them away, and we head inside without comment.

The aroma of stale coffee greets us as we walk up the rickety stairs toward Rosie's office, where Carolyn greets us with a sarcastic smile. "How'd things go with Ms. Victoria's Secret?" she asks. There is no love lost between Carolyn and Nicole Ward.

I catch the hint of a grin from Rosie. "Great," she says. "She's going to drop the charges and issue a heartfelt apology. Then she's going to take us for dinner at Boulevard."

"You guys are good."

"Not that good," I say.

Carolyn turns serious. "Be careful with her. I've seen some good defense attorneys turn into Jell-O after she looked at them with those big eyes and gave them the million-dollar smile."

"I'm not so easily impressed," I tell her.

Rosie says, "Yeah, right."

I tell Carolyn that Lisa Yee is the A.D.A. assigned to the case.

This elicits a frown. "She's a good prosecutor."

"I know." I describe our meeting with Ward and Yee and our conversation with Angel. Then I tell her about our less-than-enlightening visit with Petrillo. She takes copious notes and asks a few pointed questions.

Rosie asks, "Anything from the police?"

"They aren't talking," Carolyn says. "Their reports aren't finalized. I'm sure they're going over them to make sure they're right."

This is undoubtedly true. The cops don't want to screw up a high-profile case.

Carolyn adds, "I've prepared the standard requests for documents. The D.A.'s office and the police are playing this by the book. They're saying they have solid evidence tying Angel to the murder, and they aren't releasing any additional information."

That's smart.

Carolyn smiles and says, "You have messages from all the TV and radio stations. CNN wants to talk to you. So does *Daily Variety*."

I say, "I trust you told them our client is innocent and we have no comment."

"Correct."

Carolyn is always thinking at least three steps ahead.

Rosie asks, "Did anybody else call?"

"Your mother. She said Theresa isn't doing too well. Pete checked in, too. He's watching young Richard's house."

"Did he find out anything useful?" I ask.

"Not yet. He said he'd talk to you later."

I ask her about Marty Kent.

"He checked out. For a guy who has spent his life in the movie business, there aren't any skeletons in his closet. As far as I can tell, he's a very solid guy. Born to an affluent family in L.A. Top of his class at UCLA and Harvard Law School. Served in the Marines. Moved here about five years ago. Married thirty years. His wife died about a year ago from cancer. Two grown children. No arrests. No funny stuff."

"Emotional problems?" I ask. "Financial problems? Depression? Substance abuse?"

"Nothing as far as I can tell. My friend at the redevelopment agency said he took his wife's death very hard."

I ask her what she's found out about the studio project.

"It's up for final approval by the redevelopment agency a week from Friday."

"Any word about a competing proposal?"

"Just rumors."

"We should try to find out everything we can before the arraignment," I say. I volunteer to go down to the Hall to see Inspector O'Brien. Maybe I can persuade him to let me see the inside of Angel's house. Carolyn agrees to track down the limo company and the caterers.

Rosie says, "I'm going to see Theresa and my mother."

"What about Kent's son?" Carolyn asks.

"Let's give him until tomorrow," Rosie says. "They just found the body this morning."

I ask, "And Ellis?"

Rosie smiles and says, "You could use a trip to Vegas."

"I'll make the arrangements." Then I say, "I think I'll have a talk with Daniel Crown and his wife."

Rosie gives me a sardonic grin. "You know Daniel Crown?"

"Not exactly."

"How do you figure a movie star will talk to you?"

"I know where he hangs out."

This elicits a bemused look. "Since when did you start hanging out with movie stars?"

"Do you want me to talk to him or not?"

"Of course. How do you know where to find him? This isn't Beverly Hills. They don't sell maps that show where the stars eat up here."

"I've seen him."

"Where?"

"I can't tell you."

"What do you mean?"

I raise an eyebrow and say, "It's a secret. If I tell you, you'll tell somebody else, then they'll leak it to the papers. Then the *National Enquirer* will show up and start taking pictures. He'll stop going there. The owner of the place will be very unhappy."

She's still trying to figure out if I'm pulling her leg. "I promise I won't tell anyone."

I glance at Carolyn. "Me either," she says. She pantomimes turning a key in front of her mouth. "My lips are sealed."

"Willie's Café in Kentfield," I say. "He goes there for coffee every morning after he drops his son off at school. He stands in line like everybody else."

"How did you find out about this?"

"Becky told me."

"And who is Becky?"

"I'm told she makes the finest lattes in the state of California."

"Since when did you start drinking lattes?"

"I don't. I stop there every Saturday and order black coffee."

"I didn't know you were becoming a connoisseur of fine coffee."

"A man can't live on Maxwell House alone."

Rosie gives me a broad smile. "You're serious."

"Indeed I am."

"What are you going to do? Stop by Willie's on the way to work in the morning and try to chat him up?"

"Essentially. He seems nice on TV. We could call his agent, but we won't get anything. We can send him a subpoena, but we'll only get a chance to talk to his lawyer. You got any better ideas?"

Rosie chuckles. "Knowing you," she says, "it's just screwy enough it may work."

"You can come with me. Would you like to meet him?"

"I'd love to. He's gorgeous."

"I don't think he'll try to make a pass at you at Willie's. They frown on that kind of behavior."

Rosie's face lights up. "I'll meet you there after I drop Grace off at school."

"Deal."

"What if he doesn't show up?"

"The French toast is superb."

I'M WALKING back to my office a few minutes later when Carolyn stops me in the hall. "Do you have a couple of minutes?" she asks. "Ben's here."

A moment later, I'm sitting on the windowsill in Carolyn's cramped office next door to mine. Her son, Ben Taylor, towers above her. His chiseled features are strikingly similar to his father's, an egomaniacal tax attorney with a big downtown firm with whom he no longer speaks. He's wearing baggy jeans and a Giants T-shirt, and his red hair is dyed an unnatural blond. A single gold earring hangs from his pierced left ear. His handshake is firm. He gives me a disarming smile and says, "I guess I really did it this time."

"We'll get this straightened out," I tell him. I've known him since he was a baby. He's a good kid who carries the all-too-familiar baggage. His parents divorced when he was three, and he never got along with Carolyn's second husband. He got good grades until high school, and that's when his rebellious nature succumbed to the many temptations presented to kids nowadays. He was an honors student his freshman year, but he barely made it to graduation and skated into State by his fingernails. He got a dose of reality when he moved into his own apartment. Then he started to apply himself toward school. He made the dean's list last semester and started talking about graduate school.

He looks down for an instant. Then he glances at his mother. I look at Carolyn and say, "Maybe you could give us a moment?"

She says, hesitating, "Sure." She heads down the hall.

Ben turns to me and says,"There was a party near Candlestick. I was the only person who wasn't drunk or stoned. I offered a ride to a guy from school. I was carrying his backpack when the cops showed up."

"What was in it?"

"Ecstasy."

This isn't the first time I've been asked to talk to somebody who has gotten in trouble over the popular drug. Ecstasy, or methylenedioxymethamphetamine, is a psychoactive chemical that was first synthesized a hundred years ago for use as an appetite suppressant. It comes in tablet form and became popular in the late eighties at late-night rave parties. Users experience great relaxation and profound positive feelings. However, it suppresses the desires to eat, drink and sleep, often resulting in dehydration or exhaustion. It can cause nausea, hallucinations, chills, sweats and blurred vision, and the aftereffects include anxiety, paranoia and depression.

"That stuff can kill you," I say.

"I know."

I ask him, "Did you take any?"

"No."

"Were you selling?"

"Absolutely not, but I was holding a backpack with a thousand dollars' worth of pills in it. I told the cops it wasn't mine, but they didn't believe me. They hauled in my classmate and found a couple of pills in his pocket. They charged him with misdemeanor possession, and then dropped the charges against him when he agreed to testify against me."

This is serious. "They've charged you with a felony. You could go to prison."

He swallows hard. "I understand."

I look him right in the eye and ask, "Are you telling me the truth, Ben?"

His eyes lock onto mine. His tone is emphatic when he says, "Yes."

If you're lying to me, I'll rip that earring off with my bare hands. "What have you told the cops?"

"Nothing." He darts a glance out the window and says, "It's one of the things you learn when your mother is a prosecutor."

"So, you've observed a few things along the way."

He gives me a serious look and says, "I know how it looks. I made a mistake. It shouldn't screw up my entire life."

I'm inclined to believe him. "Let me talk to the prosecutor and review the file." I pause and say, "You understand that legal representation costs money."

He nods.

"My billing rate is two hundred dollars an hour."

"I know." He says in a tenuous tone, "I swear I'm good for it, Mike." He hesitates and adds, "Do you think you can fix this?"

"I can't make any promises, but I think I can persuade them to reduce the charges to something more reasonable."

He tugs at his earring and says, "Thanks, Mike."

"DID YOU BELIEVE HIM?" Carolyn asks. We're sitting in my office a few minutes later. Ben just left.

"I think so. It's one thing to lie to your parents. That's a time-honored tradition. It's another thing to lie to your mother's law partner and former high-school sweetheart. That would be really embarrassing."

She gives me an uncomfortable grin. "Thanks, Mike."

Rolanda appears at my doorway. Her expression is serious. "Can I talk to you for a minute?" she says to me. "Something's come up."

Carolyn excuses herself. I turn back to Rolanda and say, "Is it about Angel?"

"No. It's about my father."

# Chapter 14

# "They Want to Ask Him Some Questions"

> We have been asked to conduct a full investigation of the China Basin project. We have received credible information suggesting that certain parties have attempted to influence the redevelopment process through questionable means. We will provide additional details at the appropriate time.
>
> —San Francisco chief of police
> Sunday, June 6

The door to my office is closed.

"I understand you spoke with my dad," Rolanda says. She could be Rosie's younger sister. Their voices are similar, and their inflections are identical. "Why didn't you tell me?"

"He asked me not to say anything to you."

Her dark eyes flash. "I just talked to him."

Uh-oh. "Where is he?"

"Mission Police Station. They want to ask him some questions about the China Basin project." She gives me a sharp look and adds, "He said *you'd* be able to fill me in on the details."

"I'm sorry, Rolanda."

"He's my father. I had a right to know."

"He was embarrassed. Maybe you'll have your chance to help him out." I pause and then ask, "Did they arrest him?"

"No. I told him we'd get down there right away."

I stand up and say, "Let's go."

"Don't you have to go see Inspector O'Brien?"

"Not until after we've talked to your dad."

The corners of her mouth turn up slightly.

I grab my briefcase. "Come on," I say. "I'll tell you about it on the way."

"WHAT'S GOING ON?" I say to Sergeant Dennis Alvarez, who is standing in an airless interrogation room at Mission Station, a modern, low-rise building on Valencia, between Seventeenth and Eighteenth, about a mile from Sylvia's house. Tony is sitting in a heavy wooden chair. His hands are folded on the table in front of him. He hasn't said a word since we arrived. Rolanda is sitting next to him.

Alvarez chooses his words carefully. "We have reason to believe Mr. Fernandez may have information about the China Basin project," he says. His guarded tone is cause for concern, because he's family. He grew up down the block from Rosie and Tony, and he was in Tony's class at St. Peter's. He's a tough cop and a straight shooter.

Tony says, "What's this 'Mr. Fernandez' bullshit? We've known each other for forty years."

Alvarez shifts on the balls of his feet, but doesn't respond.

Tony starts to say something and I stop him. Rolanda puts her hand on his and says, "Let's hear what Dennis has to say."

I turn to Alvarez and say, "Maybe we should discuss this outside."

Tony interjects again. "We'll discuss it right here."

Rolanda gives me a concerned glance. I see the determined look in Tony's eyes and say, "You don't need to talk to him, Tony."

"I understand."

Alvarez says, "We're looking for information."

Tony gives his friend the eye and says, "If all you wanted was information, why did you send a squad car over to the market? You could have called. I would have come right over."

Alvarez swallows. "Orders."

"From whom?" I ask.

"My captain. He got a call from the chief." He looks at Tony through tired eyes and says, "I apologize. I didn't mean to embarrass you."

Tony is seething. "I had a storeful of customers."

"I'm sorry about that."

"What's this all about?" Tony asks.

"We think money is changing hands in connection with the China Basin project."

Tony's expression doesn't change. He remains silent.

I say, "Tony runs a produce market."

"We think he may know something." Alvarez lowers his voice and says, "The chief got a call from Jerry Edwards at the *Chronicle*."

Edwards is an overbearing investigative reporter who spends his life digging up dirt on the mayor. He's also the self-appointed watchdog for graft. He's on a mission to stop the China Basin project. When he isn't brandishing his word processor at the *Chronicle*, he takes his gratuitous swipes on the morning news show on Channel Two. He took particular glee in hammering Carl Ellis when it was revealed he had been indicted a few years ago on charges of bribing local officials in Las Vegas. Although Edwards didn't mention it, the charges were dropped. His attacks have become more strident as approval of the project has gotten closer.

"He's been whining for two years," I say.

"He's working on another story. He thinks somebody is lining up support from the neighborhood businesses."

"It isn't illegal to exercise your first amendment right of free speech."

Alvarez shows his first sign of irritation. "Edwards claims somebody is trying to funnel cash to the local businesses to buy their support."

I feign indignation. "Let's assume he's right. As long as they report it, there isn't anything illegal about it."

"It stinks," he says.

That it does.

"There's more," Alvarez continues. "Edwards says money is being kicked back into the mayor's campaign chest. It's a charade to circumvent the limits on campaign contributions and buy influence." He points a finger at me and says, "That's when it becomes illegal."

Although he's a shameless publicity hound, Edwards is a good reporter. Sounds like he's got the whole scheme figured out.

"Look," Alvarez says to Tony, "I don't like to hassle my friends."

I believe him.

"We read the papers," he continues. "We watch TV. We have to look into it." He pauses and adds, "The last thing I need is to see my name in Edwards's column. And I really don't want to hear my name when Edwards does his shtick on *Mornings on Two*."

I ask, "What do you want from Tony?"

"I want to know if it's true."

Tony's eyes narrow. "Are you asking me if somebody offered me money?"

"Yes."

"People offer me money every day."

Alvarez strokes his mustache. "Come on, Tony. Did anybody involved in the China Basin project approach you?"

I interject, "You don't have to answer that, Tony."

He waves me off. He turns to Alvarez and says, "I'm not talking. Are you going to arrest me?"

Alvarez's tone becomes emphatic. "We aren't interested in you. We're trying to find out where the money is coming from."

Tony looks Alvarez in the eye and says, "I don't know."

"Is Carl Ellis involved?"

"Why don't you ask him?"

"We did. He's denied everything."

Tony gives Alvarez a sarcastic grin and says, "Big surprise."

"What about Dick MacArthur?" Alvarez asks.

"He's dead," Tony says.

"Was he involved?"

"I don't know."

I ask Alvarez, "What makes you think Tony would know anything about this?"

"His name was on a list of local businesses who were supposed to be approached."

"Who gave you the list?" I ask.

"Edwards."

"Where did he get it?"

"I don't know. He claims it came from a source in the neighborhood. This may be a big circle jerk for Edwards, but we can't ignore it."

Tony stares at the wall without saying a word.

Alvarez exhales heavily. He takes a seat at the table and talks directly to Tony. "Just between us," he says, "Edwards thinks this goes all the way to the mayor's office. You know the players. You can help us."

"Edwards sees more conspiracies than Oliver Stone," Tony says.

"We think you know something."

Tony is exasperated. "This isn't some chickenshit payoff to one of the gangs," he says. "This is real money. These guys play for keeps. I'm going to get my ass kicked."

"We'll protect you," Alvarez says.

"You can't," Tony replies.

"We will," Alvarez says. "I promise."

"If you're wrong, I'm dead."

"It won't happen."

"Damn right. There's no way I'm putting the finger on anybody involved in the studio project."

Alvarez becomes agitated. "Dammit, Tony," he says, "I need your help."

"There's too much at risk."

Alvarez's tone becomes less strident. "I was hoping to persuade you to help us voluntarily," he says.

"I'm sorry, Dennis."

Alvarez lowers his voice to a whisper. "We know you took the money."

Tony looks at Rolanda and then at me. "Don't say a word, Tony," I tell him.

Alvarez continues. "We've been watching Armando Rios. We know he went to see you. We know he sent somebody to deliver a payment. The money runner disappeared. We don't know where the money came from. We know some of it is being kicked back. We don't know where and we don't know how much."

Tony gives me a helpless look. I turn to Alvarez and say, "I'm instructing my client not to say anything more to you."

"Understood." Alvarez holds up his index finger and says to Tony, "Hear me out. We aren't after you. We want you to talk to Rios. We want the name of the bankroll. And we want the names of the businesses that are participating in the program."

Jesus. I try for a measured, but firm, tone when I say, "You're asking him to finger a powerful local political operative and some high rollers."

Rolanda adds, "Not to mention his friends and neighbors."

"I realize it's a lot to ask," Alvarez says.

"It's insane," I say.

"No, it isn't," Alvarez insists. "Nobody will touch him."

"If you're wrong," Tony says, "I'm out of business and maybe dead."

"We'll provide twenty-four-hour protection at the market. We'll put a squad car in front of your apartment. I'll sit in the damned police car if I have to."

Rolanda interjects, "There will, of course, be full immunity for my father, right?"

"The precise terms will have to be negotiated."

Rolanda's eyes flare. "There won't be any negotiation," she says. "Full immunity. We'll prepare the document."

"We'll work it out," Alvarez says.

"Hold on," Tony says. "This isn't a done deal. I want to think about it."

"That's fine," Alvarez replies.

"What if I say no?" Tony asks.

"My orders are clear. If you don't cooperate, I'm going to have to arrest you."

"On what charge?" I ask.

"Violation of the campaign finance laws and bribery of an elected official."

"You'll never be able to win that case," I say.

"Maybe not," he replies. "It isn't my call." Alvarez speaks directly to Tony. "I came to you first because we're friends. If you cut a deal now, we'll give you immunity and round-the-clock protection. I can't keep this offer open for long. I'm going to be talking to some of the other businesses. If somebody makes a deal before you do, they may get a better shake. More important, they may finger you. Things will get really sticky if you don't have an immunity agreement. It isn't fair, but it's the way things work."

"When do you need to know?" Rolanda asks.

"The day after tomorrow," Alvarez says. "I can give you until Tuesday at noon."

"DID YOU take the money?" I ask Tony. Rolanda, Tony and I are still sitting in the interrogation room. Alvarez has returned to his desk.

"Yeah."

Rolanda gives him a concerned look. "Why did you do it, Dad?"

"I didn't think I had any choice."

He probably didn't. "What do you want to do?" I ask.

"I don't know. Armando said the city inspectors would close my business if I didn't take the payment. Now the cops are telling me they'll arrest me unless I finger everybody who is involved. I don't even *know* everybody who is involved. I can't ask Armando." He thinks for a moment and says, "I don't want to go to jail or lose my business." He looks at Rolanda and adds, "I don't want to die, either."

"They're good at protecting people," I say.

"I run a retail business. I can't keep my doors locked. Anybody can walk into my store and pull a gun. If they make one mistake, I'll end up in a box."

We sit in silence for a moment. "You could take your chances in court," I say.

"My reputation will be ruined if I get arrested."

"Your customers are loyal."

"Not if they think I'm a crook."

Probably true. "You need to decide soon," I say. "Somebody else might cut a deal."

"You're saying it's better to be the first guy to cut a deal than the last."

"The first person usually gets the best deal. It's a fact of life."

"What are the penalties if I'm convicted?" he asks.

"A fine. Probably probation." I pause and say, "Maybe some jail time, Tony."

"I might be able to afford a fine," he says. "I can't do jail time. My business will collapse. I've worked too hard for too many years."

Rolanda takes his hand and says, "You won't go to jail."

He smiles at her and says, "I knew it would come in handy to have a daughter who's a lawyer."

Rolanda smiles. "What do you want to do, Dad?"

"I want to nail everybody involved in this smelly matter."

"If you give the money back," I say, "you might look like a hero." I turn to Rolanda and add, "The immunity agreement should say that Tony does not acknowledge any wrongdoing. In addition, if asked, the police will be required to say that Tony turned down the payoff. That should help keep his reputation intact."

"That isn't entirely true," Tony points out.

"It isn't an entirely perfect world," I tell him. "It shades the story in the right direction."

"That's a wonderful semantic victory for you lawyers," he says. "It's more important to me to stay alive long enough to enjoy my great moral victory." He turns to Rolanda and adds, "In the meantime, why don't you start preparing that immunity agreement?"

# Chapter 15

## "I Can't Tell You Much"

I just gather the evidence as carefully as I can. The prosecutors try the cases.

—Inspector Jack O'Brien, KGO Radio
Sunday, June 6. 4:00 p.m.

I'm sitting in my car in front of the MacArthur house, which is still encircled by yellow police tape. Rolanda took Tony back to the market. I'm parked behind a black-and-white. Two uniforms are standing in the driveway. Another officer is drinking coffee at the end of the cul-de-sac by the entrance to the path leading down to the beach. Except for the police presence, it's just another foggy afternoon in Sea Cliff.

Jack O'Brien agreed to meet me here at four-thirty. That was a half hour ago. I tried to reach him, but had to leave a message. Five minutes pass. Then five more. I wonder if I'm wasting my time. A familiar face comes up to my window. Officer Pat Quinn gives me a broad smile and says, "I didn't think a priest would be working on Sunday."

"Former priest," I correct him. "Have you wrapped up yet?"

"Almost. The FETs are almost done. We stand around and watch. Another two days of my life I'll never get back." He shrugs and says, "Jack called. He's on his way."

At least he's coming. "Did you find anything else that might be interesting?"

"Nothing that you haven't already heard about. MacArthur must have taken a nasty shot to the back of the head."

"Did you find any blood inside the house?"

"None."

I look at Angel's car, which is still parked in the garage. "Any fingerprints?"

"Just hers."

"Anything in the trunk?"

"The spare tire and a gym bag."

Uh-oh. I ask him what was in the bag.

"Sweaty clothes and a towel. It looks like your client went to the gym before the party."

She didn't mention it. "Any more on Martin Kent?"

"Not that I know of. Jack was going to talk to his son. He's late because he was sitting in on Kent's autopsy."

"Do you know the results?"

"You'll have to ask him."

I will if he ever gets here.

"So," he says, "now you're representing movie stars. Well, la—di—da, Here I am, just another guy from the old neighborhood trying to pay the bills." With Pat, what you see is what you get. He's a likable guy. If you meet him on the street and you look suspicious, he'll shove you up against a wall and stick his billy club into the small of your back.

I go with the standard reply. "It's my job. She's Rosie's niece."

"I heard." His smile disappears and he says, "Jack says they've got her. No doubt. No alibi. Are you thinking about a plea?"

"Too soon to tell. We're still trying to figure out what happened."

"You'd better figure it out soon."

My old friend Pat Quinn wanders back to his post in front of the house. I think of all the people from the neighborhood who became cops and firemen. A few are doctors and lawyers. I was the only priest. I think about Grace and wonder what she'll be doing in another thirty years.

I inhale the cool breeze. The saltwater aroma reminds me of the afternoons I spent in our backyard with my older brother, Tommy. The sun came out so infrequently that most of my childhood memories are of playing in the fog. I try to call Leslie, but get no answer. I call the office. Carolyn tells me Rosie is still at her mother's house. I call Pete's cell. He tells me all is quiet around the corner at Little Richard's house. I give him the license number of Petrillo's limo. Finally, after another interminable fifteen minutes, I see O'Brien park his unmarked gray Ford in front of the MacArthur driveway, and I get out of my car and walk toward him.

He gives me a perfunctory apology. "I can take you inside for a few minutes," he says. "You have to stay with me at all times. I will kill you instantly if you touch anything."

Got it.

The tour takes ten minutes. We walk carefully around the FETs, who are still inventorying evidence. He points out the bloodstains on the deck. He takes me inside to see the living room. The carpet is snow-white. Next he takes me up to the bedroom. He shows me the closet and armoire. Then he takes me downstairs to the ornate theater. It has velvet chairs and maroon curtains. If there's a smoking gun in this house, I'm not going to find it today.

We stop in the foyer by the front door. I ask him if they've found any new evidence.

"I can't tell you much." There is no malice or irritation in his tone.

"Come on, Jack," I say. "You must know the results of the autopsies."

"The results on MacArthur aren't official yet. They're still working on Kent."

"You must have a preliminary conclusion on MacArthur."

He shrugs as if to say, "You're going to find out anyway." He says, "They've ruled out suicide and natural causes."

"That leaves homicide," I say.

"Correct. The cause of death was a blow to the back of the head from a heavy object that fractured his skull. He also had broken bones from the fall."

"How do you know he was struck on the deck?"

"The blood splatter pattern."

I glance toward the living room and ask, "Did you find any blood inside the house?" I already know the answer, but I want to hear it from him.

"None."

"Doesn't that strike you as odd? How did she get to the car without dripping blood on the carpet or tracking it across the floor?"

O'Brien says, "She didn't necessarily walk through the blood on the deck. Just because there was blood on the Oscar doesn't mean it dripped on the floor. She didn't have to go through the house. She could have gone up the outside stairs and through the gangway. She could have gotten into her husband's car and driven off."

We'll have an interesting time making our respective arguments about the possibilities to a jury. I ask him to show me the gangway between the MacArthur house and the Neilses'.

He leads me out to the damp, cement-paved passage that smells of star jasmine. It extends from the front of the house to the rear, where it connects to a short stairway that leads up to the deck and a longer one that leads down to the beach. Stray garden tools are leaning against the fence, and a limp green hose hangs on the wall next to the controls for the sprinkler system. The FETs have already completed their work.

I ask if they found any blood out here.

"No."

"What about footprints?"

"None."

"How do you suppose she got to the car without leaving footprints or tracking blood?"

"She wasn't walking in dirt or mud where footprints would have been easy to find."

Not so fast. "There still should have been traces of blood," I say.

"Not necessarily. Although we found blood on the railing, there was very little on the floor of the deck. We think MacArthur was leaning out over the railing when he was hit. That's why he flopped over so easily and fell."

"That's certainly convenient for your theory," I say.

"It squares with what happened," O'Brien snaps.

I won't win this argument today, so I shift gears. "What was Angelina wearing when you picked her up at the bridge?" I know the answer.

"A sweatshirt and sweatpants."

"Did you find any blood?"

He hesitates for an instant. "No."

"Really? How do you account for that?"

He tries to be coy. "What do you mean?"

"If she hit him hard enough to crack his skull and project blood all the way back to the deck, surely there should have been some blood on her sweatshirt."

"Not necessarily."

He's bluffing. "How do you figure? The Oscar is about a foot tall. If she gripped it by the narrow part and hit her husband with the heavy base, her hands and arms would have been within inches of his head. If the blood flew back onto the deck, surely some of it would have hit her arms and maybe even her face."

"The blood missed her. Or she changed clothes."

Bullshit. "When?"

"Before she drove to the bridge."

I don't think so. I search for a tone of measured incredulity. "Where?" I say. "You just said there's no evidence she went back into the house."

"Outside. Maybe she changed in the car."

"You're saying she planted clean clothes in the car?"

"I said it's a possibility."

"It was her husband's car."

"So what? Maybe she planted some clothes in *her* car. Her gym bag was in the trunk."

I take the offensive. "What happened to the bloody nightgown? You haven't found it, have you?"

"We will," O'Brien says.

"I bet you won't. It doesn't exist."

"She got rid of it," he insists.

I dig in. "You're saying she got rid of the nightgown, yet she left a bloody Oscar in her trunk and a bag of cocaine on her front seat. Why would she have gotten rid of the clothes, but kept the coke and the murder weapon?"

He doesn't respond.

"Did you find any blood on her hands?"

There's a pause before he says, "No."

"How do you account for that?"

O'Brien gives me a serious glare. Then he points to the hose and says, "We think she used the hose to clean her hands and face."

"Did you find any fingerprints on it?"

"No."

"Why didn't she clean the Oscar at the same time?"

"I don't know. Ask her."

I'm not finished. I ask, "What about the Baggie with the coke? Did you find any fingerprints?"

"Your client's."

"I was assuming you would. Anybody else's?"

O'Brien clears his throat and says, "Daniel Crown."

Well, what have we here? This is the first mention of Angel's costar. "What did he have to say about it?"

"He admitted he did some coke Friday night." He scowls and adds, "He's agreed to cooperate fully with the investigation."

I'll bet. "How did his fingerprints get onto the Baggie?"

"He said he handled it."

"No kidding. But did he provide the coke?"

"He said he didn't."

Sure. He's probably still on probation from his last bust. "Are you planning to charge him with possession?"

"Not at this time."

"And did he know how the coke got into Angelina's car?"

O'Brien doesn't hesitate. "He said she put it there. He said she was high as a kite."

I've got to get to Crown right away. "Did he say anything about Kent?"

"He said Kent was nervous and distracted. Something was definitely wrong."

"Did he have any idea why?"

"The movie. The China Basin project."

"What time did Crown leave?"

"Two o'clock." He says Crown's wife left with him.

How convenient. They can alibi each other. "Was anybody still there?"

"Kent and MacArthur's son." He gives me a sideways look and adds, "And your client."

"And I take it Angelina's husband was still alive when Crown left?"

"Very much so."

"Is it possible somebody might have come back to the house?"

He's heard enough. "When are you going to face the facts? Your client is the only one with no plausible explanation. The sooner she starts telling us what really happened, the better off she'll be."

I don't engage. "What's the word on the Kent autopsy?" I ask.

"It was still going on when I came here to see you."

"Any hints?"

"Beckert said he drowned. He also had multiple traumatic injuries, probably from a fall. In other words, it looks like he jumped."

"Is it possible he was pushed?"

"You'll have to ask Rod. We aren't ruling out homicide."

"Did you talk to Kent's son?"

"He said there was no indication Kent was upset, depressed or otherwise suicidal."

"We understand his wife died last year and that he was under a lot of pressure in connection with the movie and the China Basin project."

"True. But he was used to dealing with stress. He said his father was not suicidal."

I'm not so sure. Crown said he was upset. So did Angel. So did Petrillo. "Do you believe his son or do you believe Daniel Crown?"

"We're still investigating."

It's the standard response. I ask if he left a note.

"No."

"Did anybody at the bridge see anything? Maybe a toll taker or a security guard?"

"We're still checking."

He's holding something back. "Nicole told me they found Kent's fingerprints on the steering wheel of Big Dick's car."

O'Brien purses his lips, but doesn't respond.

I'm not going to let it go. I ask, "How did his fingerprints find their way onto the steering wheel?"

He responds with a shrug. "We're checking into it."

"Surely you must have more than that?" I say.

He meets the question with an icy glare.

"Did you talk to Dominic Petrillo?" I ask.

"Yes. He left the MacArthur house with Carl Ellis at one forty-five. They went back to the Ritz together in Petrillo's limo."

It's the same story Petrillo told us. "Have you talked to the driver?"

"Yes. She confirmed the timing."

I ask him for her name. "Did you talk to Ellis, too?"

"Yes." His story matches Petrillo's almost perfectly. Either they've compared notes or they're telling the truth.

"Did Petrillo or Ellis see anything?"

"No."

"Was either of them mad at MacArthur?"

"Not as far as we could tell."

"And they knew nothing about what happened?"

"That's correct."

So they say. "Do you know where I can reach them?" I don't want him to know I've already spoken with Petrillo.

"Petrillo flew to L.A. Ellis went back to Vegas."

"Do you believe them?" I ask.

He responds in a measured tone. "We have no reason not to." He reflects for another moment and says, "That's all I can tell you for now."

I want to keep him talking. "Come on, Jack," I say. "You're going to have to share your information with me."

"That's all I can tell you for now," he repeats.

He knows California law requires him to show me everything he has sooner or later. The courts don't allow surprises in criminal matters. It doesn't make for great theater, but it puts everybody on an even footing. If I were in his shoes, I'd stonewall, too. They're still gathering evidence. The Kent autopsy is ongoing. That doesn't stop me from letting him know we're paying attention.

I try for a tone of reason. "Look," I say, "we can do this the easy way or the hard way. It will be a lot easier if we cooperate."

O'Brien measures his words. "I can assure you," he says, "that you'll get everything to which you're entitled at the appropriate time."

"And when might the time be appropriate?" I ask.

"We'll be in touch with you after the arraignment."

Carolyn has started preparing subpoenas for the police records and the autopsy reports. For that I'm grateful. I ask for the phone records for the MacArthur house and the cell-phone records for everybody who was at the screening on Friday night. We aren't going to get a tremendous amount of cooperation from the police.

# Chapter 16

# "It Can't Hurt to Ask Around"

Police are searching the Presidio and Baker Beach for clues relating to the murder of Richard MacArthur.

—*San Francisco Chronicle*
Sunday, June 6

PETE MEETS ME in front of the MacArthur house a short time later. It takes us twenty-five minutes to walk along Baker Beach past the Lobos Creek water treatment plant and the old military installation at Battery Chamberlin and then up through the Presidio to the bridge. We see police officers and a couple of the free-lance P.I.'s who work with Pete searching the area along the way. They haven't found anything relevant so far.

As we reach the administration building at the bridge, I observe, "It would have taken only five minutes to have driven here from the house."

Pete nods and says, "If the cops are right, Angel would have had plenty of time to have hit her husband and driven over here after everybody had left." He squints into the fog and adds, "There were places along the way where she could have stashed her nightgown."

"*If* there was a nightgown," I say.

"The cops will say there was."

I know. It worries me. I keep thinking they're going to call and say they've found it in a tree stump in the Presidio. I glance at Pete and say, "Your guys had better keep looking."

"They will." He looks around and observes, "Somebody could have walked from the house to the bridge. Or he could have walked back."

"We shouldn't rule out any possible scenarios."

We don't say much as we walk back along the wooded bluffs on Lincoln Avenue. I pull up my collar as the wind picks up. The cold doesn't seem to bother Pete. We stop at the intersection of Lincoln and Bowley, a narrow access road to the Baker Beach parking lot. There is a garbage can, a pay phone and a fountain. I take a drink of water. Pete pokes through the trash. I look up across the street at the old apartments known as Wherry Housing, where a few retired service people still live. The cheaply constructed buildings are now in a national park.

Pete is constantly looking around. He says, "She must have driven right by here."

I correct him. "Or somebody drove her."

"Yeah." He looks at the apartments and says, "Maybe somebody saw something."

"It was three in the morning."

"It can't hurt to ask around." He says he'll come back in the morning.

We head down Bowley and walk through the parking lot back to the beach. We stop at Battery Chamberlin, where four cannon fortifications were built in 1902. One of the 95,000-pound cannons has been restored, and Pete and I sit on the cement wall at the edge of the bay and stare out in silence as the saltwater breeze hits our faces. To our right is the Golden Gate Bridge. In front of us are the Marin Headlands. A quarter of a mile to our left is Dick MacArthur's house. A little farther to the west are Land's End and the Pacific Ocean.

Pete gives me a knowing look and says, "They're going to check every inch of this area, Mick. If they find a bloody nightgown, Angel is going down."

"They won't find it. It isn't here."

"How do you know?"

I don't. "Instinct." I give him a quick grin. "Just in case I'm wrong," I say, "tell your guys to be careful. If it's out here somewhere, it would be better if we find it first."

"DID YOU get anything useful out of O'Brien?" Rosie asks.

"Not much," I say. It's seven-thirty the same evening. I've returned to the office. Pete's back at Little Richard's house. I tell Rosie and Carolyn about my tour of the MacArthur mansion and my conversation with O'Brien. Then I describe my stroll with Pete to the Golden Gate Bridge. Rolanda is in her office putting together an immunity agreement for her father. I say, "There are things we can use to our advantage—things that don't fit."

"Like what?" Carolyn asks.

"Angel's nightgown," I say. "I can't figure out how and when she changed clothes."

Rosie says, "Maybe somebody changed them for her."

"Maybe. If she was framed, it means somebody was in the house, found her unconscious or drugged her, changed her clothes, took her downstairs and put her in the car. He also cracked Big Dick on the deck and found a way to put the Oscar in the trunk without leaving any tracks or getting any blood inside the house. He had the presence of mind to put the coke in the car. That's a lot of movement in a short period. It couldn't have been planned in advance." As I say all of it out loud, I begin to realize how contorted the frame-up scenario will appear to a jury.

"Maybe somebody spiked her drink," Rosie suggests. "Maybe more than one person was involved. Maybe they thought it would seem more realistic if they made it look like she was trying to flee."

"Other than the booze and the coke," I say, "we have no evidence that Angel was drugged. And it still leaves the nightgown. Why didn't they just leave her at the house with the Oscar and the nightgown?"

"Because there wouldn't have been any blood on the gown," Carolyn says.

"They could have wiped some of MacArthur's blood on it," I say.

Carolyn shakes her head. "The FETs are good at analyzing splatter patterns. If the killer tried to pick up some blood by rubbing the gown on the deck, the FETs would have known it was a setup. I tried cases where the defendant walked because the pattern didn't fit. They may be better off with no nightgown than one on which the pattern doesn't match."

"Are you suggesting the cops may not try too hard to find it?"

"I'm simply pointing out that the wrong pattern could undermine their case."

I'd rather know what happened. The last thing we need is for the gown to magically reappear on the eve of the trial. "You know all about splatters because you used to be a prosecutor," I say. "Your garden-variety murderer isn't so sophisticated. The chances that the people who were there on Friday night are so knowledgeable are very low."

"True. I'm just trying to give you some plausible options."

Frankly, a more plausible explanation is that Angel realized she was wearing a blood-splattered gown and somehow got rid of it on her way to the bridge.

Rosie asks, "How is O'Brien explaining it?"

"He's saying Angel hit her husband, went up the gangway, put the Oscar in the trunk, changed clothes and drove off."

"Where did she find the extra set of clothes?"

"They found her gym clothes in a bag in her trunk. They think her sweatsuit was in her car and she changed in the garage."

"And where did she get rid of the nightgown?"

"Somewhere between the house and the bridge. You can bet they're checking every garbage can along the way."

Rosie is skeptical. "Why didn't she get rid of the Oscar and the coke at the same time?"

"He didn't have any explanation for that."

"Do you find his version the least bit plausible?"

"I'm trying not to rule anything out." And I'd like to think I'm maintaining an appropriate level of professional skepticism about our client's story.

Rosie asks, "What else doesn't fit?"

"They found Daniel Crown's fingerprints on the Baggie," I say. "He told them he had no idea how it got into Angel's car."

"Sounds like Crown may be having a heart-to-heart talk with his parole officer."

He'll also be having a somewhat less pleasant conversation with his wife and manager. "It may give us an opening," I say. "We can start deflecting blame away from Angel."

"It's a start, but it only shows he may have shared some coke with her."

"It puts his fingerprints in the car," I say.

"But it doesn't tie him directly to Big Dick."

Carolyn adds, "And you can bet his wife will provide an alibi for him."

"I know. All of which leads us to another possible alternative."

Rosie says, "And that would be?"

"Marty Kent. Angel told us he was upset on Friday night. Crown and Petrillo told the police he was stressed about the movie and the China Basin project. He had a temper. He and Big Dick used to fight."

"It doesn't get you to murder," Rosie says.

"Not yet. On the other hand, his fingerprints were on the steering wheel of MacArthur's car. They have no explanation for how they got there."

"They were friends," Rosie points out. "It was a new Jaguar. Maybe Dick let him take it out for a test drive."

"Maybe. We should use it to our advantage until they come up with a better explanation. Kent is the one guy who would have had the presence of mind to have framed Angel." I point out that he was a lawyer and an ex-Marine who wasn't prone to panic and was trained to keep a level head at the sight of blood. He knew Angel had financial motives. "The same can't be said for anybody else who was there that night, with the possible exception of Little Richard."

Rosie hasn't quite bought in. She says, "So you want to blame it on the dead guy?"

"Essentially. He can't defend himself."

"If he had just killed MacArthur and orchestrated the perfect frame-up of Angel, why did he jump off the bridge?"

I don't have an answer. "I don't know for sure that he did. We shouldn't rule out Little Richard, either. He was there after everybody else had left.

He must have known about the will. He had a huge financial incentive. Maybe he hasn't told us everything he knows."

"You think he killed his own father?"

"He and his father weren't the reincarnation of Beaver and Ward Cleaver. Besides, I'm just saying he had the opportunity."

"You think he took Angel to the bridge and then drove to Napa?"

"Why not?"

Rosie gives me another skeptical look. "He drove *his* car to Napa. If he drove Angel to the bridge in his father's car, how did he get back to his house to pick up his car?"

"It would have taken only about twenty-five minutes to have walked. Maybe he took a cab or somebody picked him up."

"Who?"

"I don't know."

Suddenly, Rosie's eyes shine. "I have a WAG."

Carolyn gives her a quizzical look. "WAG?"

"Yes. W—A—G. Wild-assed guess."

"I'm listening."

"Eve."

I reflect for a moment and say, "It's plausible, I suppose." I think it over and add, "We don't have any proof that she did it."

"We don't have any proof that she didn't. We should ask her about it."

"She'll deny it."

"Why should we believe her?"

"We shouldn't."

"Do you have any other suggestions?"

Not at the moment. I ask, "How's Angel?"

"Not well," Rosie says. "I stopped to see her on my way back from my mother's. They put her in Ad Seg." Ad Seg, or administrative segregation, refers to a special area for prisoners who are believed to be in danger. It's still the county jail, but it's an upgrade. Rosie swallows hard and says, "Her behavior is becoming erratic. Midlevel hysterics followed by twenty minutes of silence. She stopped taking her medication a few weeks ago."

"For what?"

"Depression. We're trying to get a doctor to prescribe more Prozac. It's going to take some time and it will be weeks before it really kicks in. For the moment, all I can do is try to keep her calm."

Not good.

Rosie changes the subject. "Rolanda told me what happened with Tony."

"What would you do if you were in his shoes?"

"It's a mess. I think he's going to have to cut a deal."

"Probably. If he doesn't, somebody else will. Then he'll really be in deep."

"They got him." She scratches her chin and says, "I think I'll spend some time with Rolanda. Then I'd better get over to my mother's to get Grace." She stands and heads for the door. I notice her stride seems labored.

EIGHT O'CLOCK. The card table in the corner of Madame Lena's old séance studio is covered with empty Styrofoam boxes that held burritos an hour ago. At Fernandez and Daley, our idea of haute cuisine is a little different than our contemporaries' at the big downtown firms. Rolanda, Carolyn and I are studying the development proposal for the China Basin project. Carolyn got a copy from a friend at the redevelopment agency. She has a mole in every corner of the bureaucracy. The glossy document looks like one of those fancy annual reports for a public company and is filled with photos and graphs. The text, however, is decidedly dry reading.

"It's pretty straightforward," Rolanda says. "They formed a limited-liability company in which Ellis Construction and Millennium Studios each owns a thirty-five percent interest. MacArthur Films owns ten percent."

"That leaves twenty percent," I observe. I ask who got the rest.

"Big Dick, Dominic Petrillo, Carl Ellis and Martin Kent each got five percent."

Interesting. "Have they put any money up?" I ask.

"So far, the group has put up ten million dollars to cover startup costs," she says.

"What happens when they need more money to start construction?"

"There's a capital call. Everybody has to pony up cash in proportion to their respective percentage interests. The total investment is a hundred million. Ellis Construction and Millennium Studios will each have to put up thirty-five, MacArthur Films will have to put up ten and each of the individuals will have to put up five. They plan to borrow another two hundred million from Bank of America."

"Big Dick had already put up half a million dollars of his own money?" I ask.

"Yes."

"Where did he get the money?"

"He borrowed it from Citibank. MacArthur Films put up another million. The company borrowed its share from the same bank."

Citibank had more faith in Big Dick's creditworthiness than I would have thought. I ask, "What if they don't get the approvals or the outside financing and the deal goes south?"

"The entity will liquidate, and the investors will lose what they've put up so far. If creditors are unpaid, the company will file for bankruptcy."

"What if somebody can't come up with his share?"

"The other members have the right to buy out the defaulting party."

"And if somebody dies?"

"Same deal. The other investors can buy him out at a formula price based upon the book value of the company at the time of the buyout. The buying parties would get a substantial discount on the true value of the company, assuming the deal moves forward."

We look at each other. All the investors were at the MacArthur home on Friday night. Two are dead. The others now have the right to buy out the interests of MacArthur Films, Big Dick and Marty Kent at bargain prices. Somebody is going to make out on this deal. It could be Dominic Petrillo and Millennium Studios. It could be Carl Ellis and Ellis Construction. It could be both of them.

The phone rings. It's Pete. He's still at Little Richard's house. I ask, "Anything interesting?"

"Maybe."

"Like what?" My head is throbbing. I'm not in the mood to play cat-and-mouse tonight.

"A limo just pulled up."

I put him on the speakerphone. "What's the license number?"

"ALLURE1."

## Chapter 17

# "Don't Let Them Out of Your Sight"

Some people are content to make little movies. Not at Millennium Studios. We're in the dream business. We think people should have big dreams.

—Dominic Petrillo
Profile in *Daily Variety*

We're still on the speakerphone. "Who's in the limo?" I ask Pete.

"Wait a minute." The phone goes silent for a moment. I can barely make out his voice above the static when he whispers, "The studio guy—Petrillo."

"He went back to L.A."

"No, he didn't, Mick. He just walked into Little Richard's house."

"Anybody else?"

"No."

I glance at my watch. Eight-fifteen. "Where are you?"

He gives me an address on El Camino Del Mar.

"Do they know you're there?"

"I'm a professional, Mick."

"Sorry."

"Do you want me to talk to them?" he asks.

My mind races. "No."

"What if they leave?"

"Call me on my cell and don't let them out of your sight. We're on our way." I hang up and look at Rosie. I say, "Feel like going for a ride?"

Her eyes light up. "You bet."

I reflect for an instant and ask, "Should we call Little Richard?"

"That would be the polite thing to do." She gives me a melodramatic frown and adds, "Of course, then they'd know we're coming." She adds with a wry grin, "We're all family. I'm his stepmother's aunt, for God's sake. That makes him my step-grand-nephew."

"Something like that."

"In any event, I'm sure he won't mind having a couple of drop-in guests. He's always welcome at our house, right?"

"Absolutely." I add, "Call your mother and tell her you're going to be late picking up Grace. I'll get the car."

I HAVE TO adjust some plans, too. "I'm going to be late," I tell Leslie. I'm talking to her on my cell as I'm walking toward my car.

Judge Shapiro is unamused. "Not again. I was making you an elegant dinner."

"I'll be there as soon as I can."

"When?"

I don't know. "I'll call you with a status report in a little while."

There's a pause. "Business relationships have status reports," she says. "Personal relationships don't." She corrects my wording and grammar when she's annoyed. Her language in casual conversation is as precise as her legal opinions. I can't live up to such a high standard.

"I'm sorry, Leslie. I'm in a hurry."

"What's causing you to change our plans this time?"

A murder investigation. "We're trying to talk to Petrillo."

"I thought you said he went back to L.A."

"He lied."

"What makes you think he'll talk to you?"

"My powers of persuasion are magical."

This gets a chuckle. "I forgot about that," she says. "It's more fun being a judge. People return my calls. It's easy to get their attention if you can throw them in jail for contempt."

I'll bet. "I'll call you as soon as I can."

She lets me off the hook. "I know you aren't doing this on purpose,

Michael. You didn't get up this morning and try to think of another new and unique way to tick me off."

"That's true."

She turns serious. "I would really like to see you tonight," she says. "And not just because I'd like to sleep with you."

Uh-oh. "You *do* still want to sleep with me, right?"

"Definitely. But I want to talk to you, too. I've been thinking about our conversation the other night about our . . ." She clears her throat as she searches for the right word. Finally, she selects "situation."

"I'm glad." At least I think I am. I get into the car and put the key in the ignition. I brace myself and ask, "Do you want to give me a little preview?"

"We'll talk about it when you get here, Michael."

EIGHT TWENTY-FIVE. Rosie is in the passenger seat of my Corolla. There are no freeways between downtown and Sea Cliff. Back in the fifties, there were plans to build a highway through the center of town. The neighborhood groups screamed, and construction was halted. Pine Street is our best bet, and we've taken the wide one-way street from downtown past Chinatown. My Corolla does its best to struggle up Nob Hill. Then we barrel through Polk Gulch and the Western Addition or, as the developers now call it, Lower Pacific Heights.

As always, Rosie is offering helpful driving suggestions. She says, "Can't you get this wreck to go any faster?"

I don't answer. My car is semiretired. I can take it up hills only twice a week. "What are we going to tell Little Richard when we get there?" I ask.

"I'll come up with something. We'll have to sweet-talk your friend Eve to get into the house. Then we'll wing it."

We cross Presidio Boulevard and veer left onto Masonic, then take a right onto Geary, the main thoroughfare out to the Richmond district. Traffic is heavy and I have to slow down as we cross the numbered avenues.

Eight-forty. We're a mile from Little Richard's house. My cell phone rings as I'm turning right onto Twenty-fifth. "Petrillo's leaving," Pete says. "He just got into the limo."

Dammit. "Is Little Richard with him?"

"No."

"Can you stop him?"

"Only if I ram his car."

"Don't do that. Can you follow him?"

"Yeah. Where are you?"

"Twenty-fifth, just north of Geary."

The line crackles. "He's moving," he says. "I'm with him. We're coming south on Twenty-fifth, straight toward you. You want to try to block the road?"

Are you out of your mind? "No. I'm not a trained stunt driver."

"Fine," he says. I can hear the agitation in his voice. "Can you put on your turn signal and make a very careful U-turn and try to follow us?"

"Yeah." I hand the phone to Rosie. "You talk to Pete. I've got to drive."

I make a quick U-turn, much to the chagrin of the Lexus SUV behind me. I look in my rearview mirror and wait. The third car to pass us is a black Lincoln with license ALLURE1. Although it's almost dark outside, I can make out the silhouette of the driver. I can't see anybody in the backseat through the tinted windows. My engine is running and my adrenaline is pumping. Two more cars pass us. Then Pete goes flying by us in his old unmarked police car. He gives us a wave, and I can hear his voice as Rosie holds the cell phone to her ear. "Come on," he says. "Let's go."

I turn to Rosie and say, "You in the mood for playing cops and robbers tonight?"

"I didn't have any plans. It would be nice to get Grace to bed at a decent hour." Then she turns serious and says, "Let's see where they're going."

We head south on Twenty-fifth and keep our distance as we pass through Golden Gate Park. We pick up Nineteenth Avenue, the main thoroughfare on the south side of the park. Traffic gets heavier as we roll through my old neighborhood and past Stern Grove, Stonestown Mall and San Francisco State. Rosie is still on the phone with Pete. We're crossing Brotherhood Way and getting onto the 280 freeway when Rosie hands me the cell and says Pete wants to talk to me.

"Check your mirror," he says. "There's a black Suburban two cars behind you."

He has eyes in the back of his head. "So?" We're now going sixty.

"Keep me in view," Pete says. "Now change lanes."

I do as he says. The Suburban also changes lanes.

"Change back," Pete says.

I switch lanes. So does the Suburban. "We've got company," I say. Rosie gives me a puzzled look, and I gesture behind us with my thumb. I ask Pete, "What am I supposed to do?"

"Lose him."

Yeah, right. I give Rosie a helpless look. "This isn't a James Bond movie," I say.

"And you're definitely not Sean Connery," she says.

I'm trying to keep Pete in sight while I switch lanes to try to lose the van. I'm able to keep Pete in view, but I can't shake the van.

Our convoy is doing the limit as we drive through the fog past the Serramonte Mall. I edge closer to Pete, who still has the Lincoln in sight. "The limo driver doesn't seem to be in any hurry," Rosie observes.

"They don't want to draw attention to themselves," I say. "We're the ones who decided to turn this into the Daytona Five Hundred."

"Just drive." She looks ahead toward Pete and adds, "And be careful."

I shut up and drive. Pete's about a quarter of a mile ahead of us. The limo is about three car lengths in front of him. The Suburban is right behind us. I glance at my rearview mirror, and I can make out a light-skinned man with a mustache in the driver's seat. I think I can see somebody in the backseat. He's making no effort to conceal the fact that he's following us. The limo exits 280 onto the 380 cutoff, which connects to the airport. When we get onto 380, I can see Pete, but I've lost the limo. "Do you see him?" I ask Rosie.

"Over on the right," she says.

The limo is heading toward the airport. "We've been reenacting our own pathetic version of the chase scene in *Bullitt* just to follow a guy who is catching a plane?"

"Looks that way," Rosie says, "except you're no Steve McQueen, either."

Thanks. "Rosie, I did it in one take—McQueen took a week."

We follow Pete under the international terminal and up the ramp to the departure level. The Lincoln is just ahead of us. Pete tells Rosie he's going to drop back. I tell him to try to stay with the Suburban, because I'd like to know who's been following us. We circle the parking structure and pull in behind the limo, which is double-parked in front of the United terminal. A traffic-control cop tells us we have to keep moving. Rosie assures him we'll be gone in a moment.

We watch Petrillo get out of the limo. A female driver in a dark suit with a matching hat pulls his overnight bag out of the trunk. Petrillo glances in our direction and gives us a sarcastic wave. A moment later, the Suburban goes by us without stopping. I try to catch a look at the driver, but can't see him through the tinted windows. I look for a license plate, but there is none. Pete's Plymouth is three cars behind the Suburban. They roll out into the night.

Rosie and I get out of the car and approach Petrillo, who is standing on the sidewalk. The roar is deafening as the cars, buses and limos barrel around the departure level. Petrillo pretends he doesn't see us. He's cupping a hand against his left ear and holding his cell phone against his right. Then he snaps his phone shut. His voice drips with sarcasm when he turns to me and says, "Isn't this a pleasant coincidence, Mr. Daley? You didn't mention you were leaving town tonight."

I ignore the quip and say, "I thought you left this afternoon."

"Change of plans. Business."

"What sort of business?"

He looks at Rosie and says, "We've invested a lot of money in your niece." Then he turns to me and adds in a measured tone, "She's making our lives very complicated."

"We wanted to talk to you for a few minutes."

He rolls his eyes. "You could have called. You didn't have to chase me down here."

"We were in the neighborhood," I say.

"You followed us all the way from Sea Cliff." The right corner of his mouth turns up when he says, "So, who was he?" His offhand tone suggests he could be asking about the score in today's Giants' game.

I try to sound innocent. "Who?"

This gets a half grin. "The guy in the Plymouth."

"What Plymouth?"

"The one that followed us here."

I ask, "Who was in the Suburban?"

"What Suburban?"

"The one that followed *us* here."

"I have no idea what you're talking about."

Gimme a break. I try again. "Who was in the Suburban?"

His tone becomes more adamant. "I don't know anything about it. Who was in the Plymouth?"

We're starting to sound like Abbott and Costello. "A friend," I say. "Who was in the Suburban?"

His irritation is beginning to show. "It seems *your* friend decided to follow us here."

"He was showing *your* friend the way."

He holds up his hands and says, "We took the license number. We'll find out who it was. It doesn't take a rocket scientist to figure out you hired a P.I. to watch us. Obviously, he saw me at Richard's house and called you."

I don't respond.

"I don't appreciate being followed, Mr. Daley."

"Neither do I."

His tone becomes more strident. "We didn't hire anybody to follow you."

I glance at Rosie. "We still want to talk to you," I tell him.

"I asked you to call my office."

"I can get impatient."

He tries to take the offensive. "Was your P.I. watching me?"

"No."

"That means he was watching Richard."

"That's right. What about *your* P.I.?"

He gives me a bewildered look. "What P.I.?"

Enough. I fold my arms and say, "Look, Mr. Petrillo—"

He interrupts me. "It's Dom."

"Fine. I'll tell you what, Dom. I'll promise to stop bullshitting you if you'll do the same for me. Deal?"

"Look, Mr. Daley—"

"It's Mike."

A crooked grin cuts across his face, and he starts talking faster. "Okay, Mike. Let's cut the crap. We know your P.I. was following us. I don't know anything about a Suburban."

"You didn't hire a P.I. to help you with this case?"

"Of course we did. Ours is still parked down the street from Richard's house."

Rosie attempts to strike a conciliatory tone. "So you don't know who was in the Suburban?"

"No. Maybe Richard hired a P.I. to watch me."

It's nice to see there is such a high level of trust among the parties involved in the China Basin deal. I ask, "What's your P.I.'s name?"

"That's confidential. What's yours?"

"That's confidential."

Stalemate. We say nothing for a moment. Then he decides to play poker. "I'll tell you the name of mine if you'll tell me the name of yours," he says.

It's a variation of "I'll show you mine if you show me yours." Pete and I used to do it all the time when we were kids. We used to play with baseball equipment, then it involved car accessories when we got older. Rosie taught me a different version. It still involved equipment and accessories, but it had nothing to do with baseball or cars. I extend the olive branch. "My brother," I say.

Petrillo gives me a knowing nod. "We figured."

"And your guy?"

"It's not a guy. Her name is Kaela Joy Gullion."

I glance at Rosie, whose face breaks out into a broad smile. "The cheerleader?" I ask.

Petrillo doesn't return my smile. "She came very highly recommended."

Indeed. Kaela Joy Gullion is a statuesque blonde who once played professional volleyball, became a Niners cheerleader and got married to an offensive guard. When she became suspicious of his fidelity, she started taking road trips with him—without his knowledge. She caught him red-handed in a strip club in New Orleans, and put him on waivers around the same time the Niners did. Her highly publicized efforts as an amateur P.I. led to a big divorce settlement and a new career. She moved her operations to L.A. a few years ago. Now she plays in the big leagues of P.I.'s.

"How long has she been working for you?" I ask

"About six months. Our security guys found her. We needed somebody to help us check out the MacArthurs. It's a standard part of our due diligence."

It begs the question. "Was she watching Big Dick's house for you on Friday night?"

He hesitates almost imperceptibly and then says, "Yes."

Whoa. This is news. "Did she see anything?"

"I don't know. We've traded calls. I haven't talked to her yet."

"Has she talked to the police?"

"Not as far as I know."

We have to talk to her. "Did she come up with any dirt about the MacArthurs?"

"Not much. The company was clean. Marty Kent kept them out of trouble. It was a full-time job."

"And their personal lives?"

"The stories about the divorces, the drugs and the financial troubles are all true."

"Was Dick cheating on our client?"

He nods.

"Was he planning to file divorce papers?"

"I don't know."

"And now she's watching Little Richard?"

"Yes."

"You told us you weren't going to get involved in Angelina's case."

"As far as the media and the public are concerned, we're not. We can't be perceived as condoning the actions of a murderer."

"Accused murderer," I correct him.

"Whatever. We're trying to protect our investment. We can't ignore it."

I ask, "Do you think Richard had anything to do with his father's death?"

"That's what we're trying to find out."

"Did he and his father get along?"

"At times. And at times they fought like angry little children. They were fighting the other night."

"About what?"

"The movie and the China Basin project. It didn't take much to set the two of them off."

He is trying to appear forthcoming. "Why are you telling me this?" I ask him.

"Dick MacArthur's life was an open book."

It was more like an open soap opera.

"Besides," he continues, "if you think about it, we're on the same side. We want Angelina to get off just as much as you do. We're trying to release a movie in less than a week. We're going to lose millions if there's a delay. Angelina's promotional appearances will be canceled if she's in jail. Not to mention the beating we'll take in the press if we release a movie with a star who has been charged with murder."

"What are you suggesting?" Rosie asks.

"Let's help each other out."

This elicits a cautious glance from Rosie. Trusting Dominic Petrillo is probably as precarious as forming an alliance on *Survivor*. On the other hand, he may have some information that could help us. "We'd like to talk to your P.I.," I tell him.

"I'll see what I can do."

"And we'd like to talk to you."

"I have nothing to hide."

In my experience, when somebody says they have nothing to hide, they always do.

"My plane leaves in forty-five minutes," he says. "Let's get a drink."

# Chapter 18

# "Making Movies Is Like Playing Craps"

Members only. Kindly present identification to the attendant.

—Entrance to United Airlines Ambassador's Club
San Francisco International Airport

"Where are you?" I ask Pete. I've parked my car and I'm walking across the overpass from the parking lot to the United Terminal. Rosie is at the Ambassador's Club with Petrillo. I have no idea how we ever existed without cell phones.

"One-oh-one north at Army," he says. "The Suburban is two cars ahead of me. I don't know where he's going."

Neither do I. They aren't heading back toward Sea Cliff. I ask him if he's ever heard of a P.I. named Kaela Joy Gullion.

"Of course. The cheerleader."

"Do you know her?" I tell him Petrillo hired her to watch the MacArthurs.

"I've met her."

"Is she as good as they say?"

"Better."

I ask him if he can find her.

"Sure."

"Any chance she's in the Suburban?"

"Not unless she's had a sex change." Then he adds, "I don't think the guy in the Suburban is a P.I., Mick. And I don't think he's interested in us."

"How do you figure?"

"He doesn't drive like a P.I. And he drove right by you at the airport."

That leaves Petrillo, who may have been telling the truth when he said he didn't know who was in the Suburban.

I ask, "Where are you now?"

"Getting off at the Seventh Street exit by the Hall."

"Do you think he's a cop?"

"He doesn't drive like one. Cops don't drive Suburbans without plates."

I arrive at the Ambassador's Club. "I've got to talk to Petrillo," I say. "I'll call you later."

"I'M IN AN IMPOSSIBLE SITUATION," Petrillo laments.

I give him my best empathetic nod. The man has problems, dammit.

For those of us who fly with the great unwashed masses in coach, the Ambassador's Club is not as opulent as I would have expected. I've always thought there was a miniature Playboy mansion tucked behind the locked door, complete with flowing liquor and scantily clad waitresses. Not true. It looks more like the lounge at the student union at Cal. The bustling room is full of modular furniture and harried business travelers. There isn't a single Playboy bunny. We have twenty minutes until Petrillo has to go to his gate. He's drinking Scotch and munching pretzels.

I ask him, "Why did you stay in town?"

"We have a serious problem with the China Basin project. MacArthur Films is supposed to be one of our anchor tenants and a major investor."

I knew that much. "It's a big operation," I suggest. "They aren't going anywhere."

"Dick's death changes the economics of our deal."

I try to sound nonchalant. "Not necessarily. His son will run the business."

"It isn't the same," he insists. "He's a decent young man, but he doesn't have his father's credibility in the industry."

I disagree. He's an *asshole* who doesn't have his father's credibility in the industry.

Petrillo is still talking. "Try to imagine Lucasfilm without George or DreamWorks without Spielberg. Young Richard is a competent line producer, but I don't think he has the ability to run a production company. I know for sure he can't write and direct. If this film doesn't do well, they may not be able to fulfill their obligations. Frankly, even if the movie is successful, I'm not sure MacArthur Films will have the resources to remain viable."

I wonder if the same can be said about Millennium Studios. "I'd imagine you have a lot riding on this movie, too," I say.

"We do."

"And where does it leave you if it doesn't meet your box office expectations?"

He chews on a pretzel. "We'll be fine. We have other projects and access to other funding sources."

I'm not convinced. "Have you heard from the lender?" I ask.

"We're going to meet with the bank tomorrow. Not surprisingly, they've expressed some concerns about the financial stability of the project."

If I were in B of A's shoes, I'd be worried sick. "I understand Dick and Marty were going to invest in the project."

"That's true."

Now they're dead.

His tone remains measured when he says, "We may have to find some other investors."

I try to sound innocent when I ask, "Can't you buy out their positions?" I'm looking for a reaction. I don't want him to know we've been studying the entity's operating agreement.

He plays his cards close to the vest. "Our attorneys are looking into it."

I catch Rosie's eye. "Where does Little Richard fit into all of this?" she asks.

"For obvious reasons, our deal will change. He's borrowing the bulk of the money for his investment. At a minimum, we'll expect him to assume full responsibility for his father's and Kent's funding commitments. The bank wants him to personally guarantee the rental payments of MacArthur Films under the lease. The other investors want him to personally guarantee his obligations to make capital contributions to the company. The bank wants a first deed of trust on some of his assets to secure the lease. We'll need a second on the same property to secure his funding obligations."

I ask, "I take it no such requirements were being imposed on his father?"

"For all of his shortcomings, his father was a better credit risk. He had access to funding sources that may not be available to his son."

Where I grew up, we used to call such funding sources loan sharks. Young Richard is getting squeezed. I can't tell if Petrillo wants to rework the deal or take him out altogether. I ask, "Which property does the bank want him to pledge?"

"The winery is the only asset of any substantial value that he owns free and clear. Everything else is mortgaged to the hilt."

MacArthur Cellars is located on eight hundred pristine acres in the north end of the Napa Valley. Big Dick purchased it twenty years ago to keep up with his friend and competitor Francis Ford Coppola, who bought and lovingly restored the Niebaum estate and the Inglenook winery near Oakville. MacArthur once told Barbara Walters that he would never—ever—sell the winery or use it as collateral to fund a film project. He said he'd give up the house at Sea Cliff and the condo in Beverly Hills before he would hand over the keys to the winery.

"How did Richard respond?" I ask

"Unenthusiastically."

No surprise. "Can't you restructure the deal? Maybe he'd be willing to take a smaller interest if you dropped the guarantee and the mortgage. Maybe you could buy him out."

"It's not that simple," Petrillo says. "The deal will pencil out only if we have reliable long-term tenants. If MacArthur Films goes under, we'll have an empty building. We have a timing problem, too. We're scheduled to have a final hearing before the redevelopment agency next Friday. We've tinkered with the deal a dozen times. It's never been popular among the neighborhood groups."

"Can't you get an extension?"

"Not likely. We've already gotten three. If they don't like the revisions to the plans, they may open up the process to other proposals. Then we're back to square one."

And they'll lose the millions they've already invested. I think about my conversations with Tony. "Have you heard anything about a competing plan?" I ask.

His expression suddenly becomes guarded. "Why do you ask?"

I begin evasive maneuvers. "I saw something about it in the *Chronicle*."

"Jerry Edwards has been against the project from the beginning. The redevelopment agency has assured us it won't consider other proposals unless they turn us down."

"What are your chances of approval?"

"Before Dick died, I'd say ninety-nine percent."

"And now?"

"Assuming we can get our finances reordered, about fifty-fifty."

"And if you don't get the approvals?"

"That's not an option. We've spent millions on start-up costs, environmental impact reports, design expenses and attorneys' fees. The redevelopment agency isn't unreasonable. They know about Dick's death. They won't say it out loud, but they'll let us rework our finances. They'll approve it. You'll see."

I'm not sure if he's trying to convince me or himself.

"I appreciate your forthrightness," I tell him.

"The details of the studio project are no secret," he says. "Any changes will become a matter of public record. It would serve no useful purpose to lie or be disingenuous."

I don't know if he's lying, but I'm sure he's being disingenuous. I notice a change in Rosie's expression. Her bullshit detector just went off.

"Besides," he adds, "we'll piss off the redevelopment agency if we screw around."

That they will. I understand why somebody wanted to get the support of the businesses in the Mission—not that I expect him to admit he's making payoffs. I say, "I understand you're trying to get some help from the local businesses."

He says in a carefully measured tone, "We're doing everything we can."

"I heard you might be willing to make it worth their while."

He eyes me up and down. "Who said anything about that?"

I try to keep my tone conversational. "I saw that in the paper, too. They said you might be willing to give the locals first crack at jobs." I leave out the fact that they're also blatantly trying to buy their support in cold, hard cash.

He relaxes a bit. "We really want their backing," he says.

Time to spin the roulette wheel. "It said you might give them more than jobs."

He tenses again. "What are you suggesting?"

I keep my tone even as I repeat, "You might be willing to make it worth their while."

His tone changes to one of tempered annoyance. "Are you accusing me of something?"

"Absolutely not. It's not uncommon for developers to provide incentives to the neighborhood. Maybe you promised to build a park or donate money to a community group." Maybe you're doing it the more traditional way and just offering bribes to the local politicians.

"What does that have to do with Dick's death?"

I want to find out who authorized the payments to Tony and his neighbors. "Maybe nothing. Somebody who was trying to screw up your deal would have put a big monkey wrench in the works by arranging for Dick's death."

He keeps his tone level as he says, "I trust my partners, and I'm not aware of any competing proposals."

I won't get more from him unless I want to accuse him of bribery. I glance at my watch. I need to get what I can. "Maybe you could tell us what you saw Friday night," I say.

"It's in the police reports."

It's an evasive response from a guy who keeps promising to do everything in his power to help us. "We'll study them," I say. This may be my only chance to hear him tell his story in his own words. "Maybe you can give me the abbreviated version."

His demeanor remains businesslike as he tells his story. It jibes with what we've heard so far. He arrived at the MacArthur house by limo at eight, and they watched the movie and drank champagne. "I left with Carl Ellis by limo at one forty-five," he says. "We went to the Ritz."

Your alibi is duly noted. "Were you at the hotel the rest of the night?"

"Yes."

"Ellis, too?"

"I can't imagine he went out for a walk at two in the morning."

I ask, "How was the movie?"

He answers too quickly, "It was fine."

I press him. "You were happy with the way it turned out?"

He repeats, "It was fine."

"But there were some things you didn't like?"

He shows a hint of irritation. "There are always some things you'd do differently."

It's an opening. "Like what?"

"We might have tweaked the script or tinkered with the ending. We might have cast a few characters differently."

"Were you happy with the cast?" I ask.

"Happy enough."

"Were you happy with Angelina's performance?"

He gives us a halfhearted "Yeah."

"And Daniel Crown?"

"He was fine."

Everything was fine. I don't have time for finesse. "It sounds to me like you were unhappy about the movie."

"Not true," he says. "It's perfectly fine."

There's that word again.

"Like all movies," he continues, "it has some problems. We didn't set out to make *Citizen Kane*. Dick MacArthur was no Scorcese. And believe me, Angelina is no Meryl Streep."

Got it. "So you're prepared to release the movie in its current form?"

"Of course." His face reddens and his jowls shake. "Look," he says, "making movies is like playing craps. Everybody thinks they have a winning system. In reality, you roll the dice and hope for the best. It may be a blockbuster or a bomb. It will probably end up somewhere in between. A lot of it is completely out of your control. If you have bad weather in certain parts of the country, your numbers may go down. If Roger Ebert has a lousy dinner the night before the preview, you may be in trouble. You never know until you put it out there."

Not exactly a ringing endorsement from a man who has been described as a master of movie marketing. His tone suggests he has nothing more to say about it. I decide to shift gears. "How was Dick acting the other night?" I ask.

"He was all right."

At least he didn't say fine. He's answering my questions without telling me anything. "Was he happy with the movie?"

He gives me a noncommittal shrug. "There were some holes in the script. He was still tinkering with the editing."

"What about the cast?"

"What about it?"

"Was he happy with their performances?"

"Overall, yes."

"But he would have made some changes?"

"You always think about things you might have done differently."

"What did he think of Angelina's performance?"

He wiggles his fingers, but doesn't say anything. Another unenlightening response.

I attack from another direction. "How was Angelina acting the other night?"

He gulps his Scotch and says, "She isn't the only temperamental actress in the world. At times she was the perfect hostess. Later in the evening, she was stressed out and angry."

"Anything out of the ordinary?

"Not really."

"Was there a problem the other night?"

His expression changes to one of feigned sadness. "She'd had too much to drink. She may have been high."

"On what?"

His tone remains level. "Probably coke."

"Daniel Crown's fingerprints were found on a Baggie of coke in the car."

"I don't know anything about that. If it's true, we have another problem."

"You said she was angry."

"Yes." He doesn't elaborate.

"Why?"

He strokes his beard and sighs. "All right. This is just between us, okay? Because I can't afford for it to get out before the movie opens. You asked me about Angelina's performance. She's very pretty. Her smile lights up the screen. But she has limitations. She can handle romantic comedy. She could probably do action adventure. *The Return of the Master* is a serious drama. She was miscast."

"And?"

"Some of us may have been a little too forthcoming about her limitations."

They probably humiliated her. "Who?" I ask.

The corners of his mouth turn down. "Her husband was an immensely talented man who had many virtues," he says. "Diplomacy wasn't one of them. He told her if he had a chance to do it again, he would have cast somebody else in the lead. This did not sit well with her."

Rosie and I share a quick glance. I ask, "Did she say something to him?"

Petrillo frowns. "I believe she said he was a lying, backstabbing asshole."

I get a stern look from Rosie. Petrillo's version of the events on Friday night is considerably different than the story Angel told us. "What did she do?" I ask.

"She stormed upstairs."

"Did Dick go up to talk to her?" Rosie asks.

"No."

Sensitive guy. "Why not?"

"Look," he says, "there was a lot of tension. She was upset. He wasn't good at apologies. He wanted to let her sleep it off."

"And then you decided to leave?"

"It seemed like an appropriate time to call it an evening."

I ask him who was still there when they left.

"Dick and Angelina. Dick's son. Danny Crown and Cheryl Springer. Marty Kent."

This jibes with what we've heard so far. "What was Little Richard's temperature?"

"He didn't like Angelina's performance, either."

"Did he inform his father of his opinion?"

"Every day for eight months. They both had egos and opinions they were not afraid to express. They both had tempers."

"Did Richard make his views about Angelina's performance known to his father on Friday night?"

"In minute detail. He handled himself with his usual finesse."

"What was his father's reaction?"

"It precipitated another shouting match of rather epic proportions. Never underestimate the level of venom that parents and children are capable of inflicting upon each other." He gets a faraway look in his eyes and asks, "Do you have children, Mike?"

His question takes me by surprise. I guess I've always assumed guys like Petrillo don't have families. I tell him about Grace.

He tells me he has three grown children and six grandchildren. He says, "I have never uttered the words *fuck you* to my children. Even when they did drugs and wrecked the cars. Likewise, my kids never used those words to me." He holds up his hands and says, "The same cannot be said for the MacArthurs. They were still going at it at full tilt when I left."

In some respects, the Daleys weren't as dysfunctional as I'd always believed. "Where was Angelina when all of this was happening?" I ask.

"Upstairs."

"Did she hear any of it?"

"She must have."

I ask him about her reaction.

"I don't know. She didn't come back downstairs."

It must have been a memorable night. "How was Kent acting?"

"To all outward appearances, he was acting pretty normally. But if you'd spent some time with him, you'd have known he was really pissed off."

"How could you tell?"

"He was twitching."

"Excuse me?"

"The corner of his mouth twitched when he was mad." He holds his index finger a quarter of an inch from his thumb and says, "Just a little. That's when you knew the explosion was coming."

"What kind of explosion?"

"Yelling. Throwing things. A moment later, he'd stop." He arches his eyebrows and adds, "They were always directed at Dick."

I ask him if there was an explosion on Friday night.

"Not while we were there," Petrillo says. "Just twitching."

"Why?"

"He didn't like the movie. And then there was the whole matter of the China Basin project. Marty put up some of his own money. He didn't like it from the start."

"It was business," I say. "He was a big boy. He knew what he was getting into."

Petrillo's voice takes on a sharp edge. "That doesn't mean he was happy about it. Dick and I understood the risks. Carl Ellis knows any development project can go south. You put up your money and you hope for the best. I've made and lost fortunes over the last thirty years. Marty never liked taking risks."

"Then he shouldn't have put up his own money," I observe.

"Dick strong-armed him into it."

Then he has nobody to blame but himself. Maybe that's why he was twitching. "Surely he could have afforded to have lost his investment," I say. "He must have been worth millions."

"I'm not so sure," Petrillo says. "His wife's illness ate up a lot of their resources."

"Do you think he was mad enough at Dick to have killed him?"

Petrillo shrugs. "He was really ticked off. He was having some financial difficulties, and he was wound tighter than a drum. That's all I know."

Seems like Petrillo is more than happy to point a finger at Marty Kent.

Rosie asks, "Do you think he was the kind of guy who would have killed a man with whom he had worked for more than three decades?"

Petrillo doesn't hesitate. "Absolutely not." Then he ponders for a moment and adds, "People do strange things sometimes."

"Was he desperate enough to have jumped off the Golden Gate Bridge?"

"I don't know."

I ask him about Daniel Crown and Cheryl Springer.

"Have you ever met Crown?" Petrillo asks. "*Real* good-looking guy. Billion-dollar smile. Twenty-cent brain. Life is unfair. You point a camera at schmucks like us, we look like, well, schmucks. You point a camera at Danny, read him his lines a couple of dozen times and tell him to smile, and people will pay nine bucks a head to see him." He winks at Rosie and says, "You'd like to sleep with him, wouldn't you?"

"He's not my type."

"And I subscribe to *Playboy* just to read the articles. Come on. Just between us."

"Is this sexual harassment?"

Enough. "How was he acting the other night?" I ask.

"To Danny, life is an ongoing frat party. He had a few beers and loved the movie. He was the only person who was laughing in the screening room."

"I thought you said it's a drama."

"It is. Danny thinks everything is funny."

I ask, "What about his wife?"

"She wasn't laughing." He holds up a menacing index finger and says, "There is nothing funny about Cheryl Springer. All business. An ice queen."

Do I sense hostility?

"She made Danny Crown. She has only two things on her mind: keeping Danny off drugs and making sure his movies are released on time. She's prepared to do anything to get *The Return of the Master* into the theaters."

I'll keep that in mind. "How did she like the movie?"

"She said she loved it."

"Do you believe her?"

"It doesn't matter. We still owe Danny some of his money." He glances at his watch and stands up.

"What are you going to do about the movie?" I ask.

"I'm going to do everything in my power to release it on time. Then I'll be able to focus on the China Basin project." He gives me a knowing look and adds, "If you can get the right result, there will be a modest gratuity in it for you."

I catch Rosie's eye. She says, "We'll just bill our client by the hour. We'll leave it up to you whether you'd like to make a contribution to her defense fund."

"Fine. I'll let you know. I hope you're successful. It's a lot easier to fix real-estate deals than murder trials."

Interesting choice of words. Coincidentally, he's absolutely right.

# Chapter 19

## "Never Let the Truth Get in the Way of a Perfectly Good Story"

> Insiders reported serious problems on the set of *Return of the Master.*
>
> —*Los Angeles Times*
> Sunday, June 6

"What did you think?" I ask Rosie. It's a few minutes after ten. We're on the Army Street off-ramp heading toward Sylvia's house to pick up Grace. Summer vacation will be starting soon. This will help. The practice of law often presents unique challenges for your parenting skills. It would be nice to coach Grace's Little League team before she goes to college. I may need to make some lifestyle adjustments before I'll have the chance.

Rosie yawns. "I think it's past Grace's bedtime," she says. "She's going to be crabby."

"So will I." I turn onto Bryant and try again. "What about Dom?"

"He seems like a pleasant enough fellow. Especially if you like arrogant weasels who talk out of both sides of their mouths."

Don't sugarcoat it, Rosie. "I can see how he became the head of a movie studio. Actually, I thought he was pretty forthright at times."

"When was that?"

"When he wasn't talking."

Rosie smiles. "Maybe we're being unfair to him. He was nice enough to tell us about his warm and fuzzy relationship with his grandchildren."

Papa Dom. "And he admitted he hired Kaela Joe Gullion to watch the MacArthurs."

She turns serious and says, "We should get to her right away."

"He's probably already written a script for her."

"I don't think so. She kicked the crap out of her ex-husband in the middle of Bourbon Street. He outweighed her by two hundred pounds. I don't think anybody tells her what to say."

"You may be right, but we shouldn't underestimate Petrillo. You can be sure he has his own agenda."

"Indeed. He wouldn't have talked to us unless he thought there was something in it for him. The hard part is sorting through the bullshit."

"He told us more about the studio than I would have thought."

"It was a good performance, but he didn't tell us anything that won't become a matter of public record. The redevelopment agency will get to approve any changes in the deal. I'm sure there were elements of truth in everything he said. On a scale of one to ten, I'd probably give him about a seven." She reflects and adds, "I wouldn't want to be in Little Richard's shoes."

"Why?"

"If he wants to stay in the deal, he's going to take a big haircut. He's going to have to put up more money and collateral. It wouldn't surprise me if they try to squeeze him out. It was one thing for Petrillo to get in bed with Big Dick, who had some legitimate directing talent. It's another thing to deal with his son. MacArthur Films is bringing a lot less to the party."

"Do you think they'll be able to get approval?"

Rosie is practical. "The redevelopment agency has been working on this for years. They don't want to start over. At the end of the day, if Petrillo and Ellis can come up with a restructured deal that makes economic sense, they'll get the approvals." She looks out her window and asks, "What did you think of his version of the screening the other night?"

"It was a lot different from Angel's. I thought it was an Oscar-winning performance."

"How so?"

"He covered all the bases. First, he took care of himself. He made it clear that he and Ellis can alibi each other. Then he swore he'd like to see Angel exonerated. Then he gave us motives for Kent and Little Richard."

"You didn't expect him to point the finger at himself, did you?"

"No. I take it Angel never mentioned any of the outbursts he described?"

"Nope. She spun the story away from her."

Just like everybody else who was there. "Whom do you believe?"

"I'm not sure." She thinks and says, "Parts of Petrillo's story may help us. Kent and Little Richard were both still there after Petrillo and Ellis left. Now we know they were angry."

"You don't think they would have killed him over a real estate deal, do you? "

"I don't know. It's all we have for now. Kent isn't around to defend himself."

No, he isn't. We cross Twenty-sixth and head north past the tightly packed bungalows not far from where my parents grew up. I say, "I noticed he didn't point a finger at Daniel Crown."

"It's bad publicity if either of the stars is in jail. It's better for him if they find a way to blame it all on Little Richard or Kent."

"Unless he wants to take advantage of the publicity that would follow from his arrest."

Rosie grins. "Cynic."

"Guilty." I glance out the window and say, "What about the China Basin project? If they pin the murder on Little Richard, the deal is dead."

"Not necessarily. They can find another tenant and get another investor. Maybe Petrillo *wants* to kill the China Basin project. Maybe he's decided it doesn't pencil out. You can bet he'll figure out a way to rearrange the financing if he has to."

"Are you suggesting Petrillo might have killed Big Dick so he could restructure or maybe even terminate the China Basin project?"

"Maybe that was the whole idea," Rosie says.

Seems like a stretch. "There isn't a shred of evidence pointing in Petrillo's direction. Big Dick was still alive when he left with Ellis at one forty-five."

"So he says. Maybe he went back."

"There is no evidence that he did."

"That's why we have to talk to the limo driver and the people at the Ritz."

"And his P.I.," I add.

Rosie nods. "*Especially* his P.I. She may have been the only person who was there when everything happened—other than Little Richard and Kent."

I add, "And Angel." We're still grasping. I ask, "If you're Petrillo and you want to try to blame somebody else, whom do you like the best?"

"I think Marty Kent is Petrillo's best choice. He can release the movie on time and still build the studio. He gets everything he wants. So does Ellis. For that matter, so do Angel and Little Richard. She gets to star in a movie, and he gets to run a production company. It's the perfect result for everybody—a complete win-win."

"You seem to have this all worked out."

She gives me a serious look and says, "Petrillo makes movies. He gets people to invest large sums to finance productions that are often little more than a concept. He's sunk a ton of money into a movie that may not be released and a studio that may not be built. He's doing exactly what you'd expect: damage control. First he made sure Ellis would alibi him. Now he's going to try to salvage the movie and the business park, along with his ass. Somebody involved in the China Basin project has already demonstrated a willingness to dole out a few selectively placed bribes to grease the approval process."

"We don't know if it was Petrillo," I interject.

"That's true. It could have been Kent or Ellis. It could have been the MacArthurs. Either way, somebody is worried about this project and wants it to move forward. If Petrillo needs to bend the truth a little bit to obtain the approvals he needs or to point the finger toward Marty Kent—or anybody else, for that matter—you can bet he'll do it. Never let the truth get in the way of a perfectly good story—especially if your money and your ass are on the line."

"Have you always been this cynical?"

She smiles. "Only since I started working with you."

"Let's assume you're right. Play it out. Pretend you're Petrillo and you want to finger Kent. How do you explain it? Tell me how Kent would have done it."

"Easy. You take Little Richard at his word that he left before Kent. That means Kent was the only one still there. He killed Big Dick with the Oscar, put it in the trunk of the car, put Angel in the car and drove over to the bridge. They even found his fingerprints on the steering wheel. Maybe he drugged Angel."

"You forgot about the nightgown."

"That's easy, too. He changed her clothes before he put her in the car. He took the nightgown with him. He parked at the bridge, moved Angel into the driver's seat, and then jumped off the bridge, nightgown and all."

"Come on. Why did he change her clothes?"

"There was no blood on the nightgown. It would have been obvious to the police that she hadn't hit him."

I don't know about that. "Why didn't he get rid of the Oscar, too?"

"Then there would have been nothing to connect Angel to the murder weapon."

"And his motive for killing Dick?"

"Financial problems. Stress. Disagreements about the movie and the China Basin project."

"You think he was pissed off enough to kill him?"

"Why not? Work with me on this, Mike."

I'm not buying it just yet. "Nope. Why go to all the trouble of framing her just so he could jump off the bridge a few minutes later?"

"Guilt. Maybe he didn't decide to jump until after he got to the bridge."

"You're stretching."

"You got any better ideas?"

"Not at the moment. Have you concocted a similar scenario for Little Richard?"

"Of course. Let's assume he lied about his departure and Kent left first."

"I'm listening."

"Little Richard was the last one there. He killed his father. He changed

Angel's clothes and put her in the car. He drove her to the bridge. Then he went up to Napa."

"Where was Kent while all of this was happening?"

"He'd already left. He went to the bridge."

I point out that Kent's car was still parked at Big Dick's house. "How did he get to the bridge?"

"The old-fashioned way: he walked. It's less than a mile."

"And why did he jump?"

"Same reasons. Stress. Financial problems. He was unhappy about the deal."

"We have no hard evidence of any stress or financial problems."

"We have Petrillo's word."

"You believe him?"

"It's just a theory. That's why we need to talk to Kent's son."

I'm not convinced. "Have you concocted a motive for Little Richard?"

"Money. He stood to inherit half of his father's money. If he could have shifted the blame to Angel, he might have been able to get even more—maybe the whole thing. Besides, he and his father didn't get along. He was mad about the movie and the studio. He was tired of playing second fiddle. The casting of Angel in the lead was the final straw."

"Are you serious?"

"Why not? It's possible."

"You haven't connected him to the Oscar or his father's car," I say.

"We will." She reminds me that Nicole Ward told us earlier they found four unidentified sets of fingerprints on the Oscar.

"You still haven't shown he was in his father's car."

"That's tougher. We'll have to find something in the police reports."

We'll see. "And the nightgown?"

"There was no blood on it. He changed Angel's clothes when he put her in the car. He got rid of it on the way to the bridge."

"You think young Richard was smart enough to think of that?"

She doesn't hesitate. "Yes."

There are too many holes. It's all speculation. I ask, "How did he get to Napa?"

"He drove his own car."

He couldn't have driven two cars at once. "How did he get his car if he drove Angel to the bridge in his father's car?"

"The same way Kent got to the bridge. He walked back home and got the car."

"You think he had the presence of mind to do this in the middle of the night after he had just murdered his father?"

"Sure. It was dark. Nobody would have seen him. The drive to Napa was an attempt to create a better alibi."

We have no evidence that any of this happened.

Rosie's wheels are still turning. "There's another possibility," she says. "Somebody could have picked him up at the bridge."

"Who?

"Maybe Kent. Maybe Ellis. Maybe Crown and/or his wife."

"You think there was a conspiracy? There's no way they could have planned it all out."

"I don't think we should rule out the possibility."

"I don't think we should count on it."

"You got any other ideas?"

I pull into Rosie's mother's narrow driveway and pause to think. Who else was there? Who else would have known that Little Richard was at his father's house? Who else might he have called? Rosie and I look at each other and say simultaneously: "Eve."

I say, "He said he went to Napa by himself."

"Why should we believe him?"

"We shouldn't."

"She could have picked him up," she says.

"There's no evidence that she did."

"We need to subpoena his cell phone records."

"And Eve's," I say. "We need to talk to her."

"And Kent's son," Rosie says. "We need to find out if his father was the cool cucumber Angel described or the depressed psychotic Petrillo said he was."

I see Grace come out the front door. She walks down the steps and knocks on the window. "Are you going to stay in the car all night?" she asks.

Rosie opens her door and says, "Go get your things together, honey. We'll be right up."

As we get out of the car, I look over at Rosie and ask, "How are you holding up?"

"Fair."

"Any word from Dr. Urbach?"

A shrug. "Later this week." She leans back and says, "What's up with you and Leslie?"

"I'll find out in a little while."

"You got a date?"

"I hope so."

"I WANT TO go to the arraignment," Theresa tells us. She's sitting on her mother's sofa with her arms folded. Her mother, Sylvia, is sitting next to her. Tony is leaning against the fireplace.

Grace is standing by the door holding her backpack. "Can we go now, Mommy?" she asks.

"Soon, honey," Rosie says. "Why don't you wait out on the porch with Uncle Tony?"

Grace sighs. It's tough being ten and tired. "Okay." She heads outside. Tony follows her. Rosie mouths her thanks to him.

Rosie turns back to Theresa and says, "We'll talk about it in the morning."

"Why can't we talk about it now?"

"Grace has school and is very tired," Rosie says. "So am I."

This doesn't stop Theresa. "Why won't you let me go to my daughter's arraignment?"

Rosie's exhaustion is reflected in her tone. "We've been over this."

"Don't talk to me like I'm a ten-year-old."

Rosie's patience runs out. "Then don't act like one," she tells her sister.

"Dammit," Theresa says, "I want to talk now."

Sylvia takes Theresa's hand and says, "Rosita is right. Let's talk about it in the morning."

Theresa's eyes flare and her voice goes up a half octave. "'Rosita is right.' I've been hearing that my entire life." She takes a deep breath and says, "Rosita is not always right."

"Now is not the time for this," Sylvia says.

Theresa points a finger at her mother and says, "*Your* daughter isn't in jail."

Sylvia points a finger right back at her and snaps, "*My* granddaughter is."

"It's not my fault."

"This isn't about fault."

"Around here, *everything* is about fault."

"That's not true."

"Yes, it is."

Rosie holds up her hands. Her eyes are red as she says in a voice that is barely a whisper, "All that matters right now is what's best for Angel. She's the one in jail. The two of you have the rest of your lives to work out your other issues. The arraignment is tomorrow. The preliminary hearing will be in a week. If we don't get her out by then, she'll be spending the next six months in jail waiting for her trial to start. I'm not sure she'll make it." She stands and starts to head toward the door.

As she reaches for the handle, Theresa calls out to her in a broken voice,"What about the arraignment? Can I sit in the back? I promise I won't say anything."

Rosie heaves a long sigh. She walks over to her sister and takes her hand. Then she lays it on the line. "Honey," she says, "I'm not going to pretend I know how you're feeling. If I were in your shoes, I would want to be there. On the other hand, I'm not sure how Angel will react if she sees you. There's a good chance she'll become very upset—too upset for her own good. I'm going to need her to act respectful. We're going to ask the judge to grant her bail. The chances that she'll agree aren't very good. If Angel loses her composure, whatever those chances are will become nonexistent. This judge is very strict. She likes order in her courtroom. I need Angel's full attention tomorrow. Do you understand? This is about Angel—not you."

"Yes."

"I know this sounds harsh," Rosie continues, "but this is the reality. We have to deal with now. Our feelings have to stay out of it."

Theresa nods. "If you think it's better for Angel, I'll stay home."

"I do, Theresa."

"I TALKED TO DENNIS ALVAREZ this afternoon," Tony tells me. We're still standing on Sylvia's front porch. He stopped me as we were leaving. Rosie and Grace are waiting in the car.

"What did he have to say?"

"Good news and bad news."

I wait.

"The good news is he's talked to a couple of other business owners in the neighborhood. It seems they received similar propositions from Armando Rios."

At least there are others who are in the same boat. "Did they take the money?"

"I think so."

I ask him if Alvarez gave him any names.

"No."

It's understandable. He doesn't want Tony to get together with the others and try to negotiate a group deal. "Can you find out who they are?"

"I'll try."

"What's the bad news?"

"One of them is prepared to cut an immunity deal."

"Any chance Alvarez is bluffing?"

"No."

"When is the deal coming down?"

"Tomorrow. No later than two o'clock."

"He told you he'd keep your offer open until Tuesday."

"My deadline just got shorter. He gave me until tomorrow at two to make up my mind."

It's the same time as Angel's arraignment. "What are you going to do?"

"Sleep on it."

"Tony," I say, "I still have to talk to a couple of witnesses in Angel's case in the morning. And Angel's arraignment is at two."

"I understand. I'll call Rolanda."

"WHERE ARE YOU, Mick?" Pete asks. I'm talking to him on my cell phone. It's a few minutes after eleven. I've taken Rosie and Grace back to Rosie's car, which is parked by our office. They're on their way home. Grace may sleep through social studies tomorrow morning. I postpone this line of parental concern because I know it's not going to change anything now.

"I'm in my car," I say. I don't mention I'm heading to Leslie's for a little heart-to-heart.

"I think you've got another problem," he tells me. "The Suburban ended up at Fifth and Mission."

It's the headquarters of the *Chronicle*. "Did you see anybody get out of the car?"

"Jerry Edwards and a guy with a fancy camera."

He doesn't need to tell me the obvious. Our rendezvous with Dominic Petrillo is going to be front-page news tomorrow morning.

## Chapter 20

# "I Want You to Turn Off Your Cell Phone for a Few Minutes"

My father is a Supreme Court justice. There was an expectation that I would follow in his footsteps.

—Judge Leslie Shapiro
*San Francisco Chronicle*
Sunday, June 6

"You're late again, Michael," Leslie says. Her arms are folded. In her courtroom and personal life, Judge Shapiro places a high value on punctuality.

I'm standing in the doorway to her flat. It's just after midnight. I've had about three hours of sleep in the last two days, and things aren't likely to get better any time soon. I do my best to sound contrite. "I'm sorry, Leslie. It's been a long day."

She's wearing a light blouse and jeans. Her contacts have given way to a pair of Calvin Klein wire rims. She invites me in. We walk through her narrow living room, which is sparsely furnished with a brown leather sofa and a matching chair that are positioned to take advantage of the view. It's a clear night, and I can see the beacon on Alcatraz. The wall opposite the fireplace has two built-in bookcases that are overstuffed with law books and classics. The photo of her parents on the mantel reminds me that Leslie is an only child. There are no pictures of nieces or nephews. The room is immaculate. She's lived by herself for a long time.

We walk into the small kitchen where we're greeted by the aroma of tomato sauce, oregano and Parmesan. The marble countertops are spotless. I come from a family of many generations of abysmal housekeepers.

If we ever move in together, Leslie may find my living habits to be a significant annoyance. Her tone softens when she says, "I made you a nice dinner. Vegetable lasagna." It's a kind gesture. She doesn't like to cook. "I'll heat it up for you."

"Thanks, Les. I know you went to a lot of trouble."

"Forget it. I'll have the leftovers for lunch for a few days. The food at the Hall has never been the same since the old cafeteria went out of business. The ambience isn't there."

A number of years ago, a McDonald's took away much of the clientele of the cafeteria in the basement of the Hall. Although it felt like the lunchroom at St. Ignatius, the cafeteria was the Hall's demilitarized zone, where cops, prosecutors, defense attorneys and even a few judges could mingle. My dad used to take me there for lunch when I was a kid. When I was a P.D., I cut a few deals with the D.A.'s while we were waiting for our grilled-cheese sandwiches.

We exchange small talk as she heats up the lasagna and pours us each a glass of Merlot. Then we sit in the two chairs at her butcher-block kitchen table. The CD player is on, and I can hear the crystal voice of Judy Collins singing "Both Sides Now." I had a crush on her when I was in college. Seems like a long time ago. The last line of the second verse seems eerily appropriate as she sings, "I really don't know love at all."

A tired smile crosses Leslie's face. She plants her tongue firmly in her cheek and asks, "So, how was your day, Ozzie?"

I play along. "Just fine, Harriet. And yours?"

"Just wonderful, dear." Her tone remains upbeat. "Is your client a murderer, honey?"

"Oh no, sweetie." I can't keep a straight face any longer. I start to laugh as I say, "She didn't hit her husband with his Oscar. That would have been wrong."

She starts to laugh. She picks up her glass and clinks mine. "Here's to you, Ozzie."

"And to you, Harriet. And to us." I take a sip of wine and say, "Leslie, I'm sorry I'm late."

"Never mind. I knew you kept irregular hours when we started this little adventure." She winks and adds, "You'll make it up to me."

"Soon, I hope."

"We'll see about that." She swirls her wine and says, "How did things go today?"

"Not well." I give her an abbreviated version of the blow-by-blow, starting with the discovery of Martin Kent's body at five this morning and ending with the events at the Ambassador's Club tonight. I leave out any mention of Tony's problems or the blowup with Theresa at Sylvia's house. Some things should stay within the family.

She takes it in without comment. After I finish, she observes, "You've had a full day."

"It isn't going to get any better." I glance at my watch. I tell her about my plan to rendezvous with Daniel Crown seven hours from now. "I may get to meet a movie star."

Her smile broadens. "Would you give him a message? Tell him he can have me—anytime, anyplace. I would sleep with him in the witness box of my courtroom in broad daylight."

"I'll pass that along. Does the same go for me?"

She gives me a wry grin and says, "If you want to sleep with Daniel Crown in my courtroom, you'll have to work out your own arrangements with him."

I chuckle. "That wasn't quite what I meant."

"I know."

"So?"

"So what?"

She isn't making this easy. "If Crown isn't available, do I get the same deal?"

She turns serious. "Not just yet."

Uh-oh. I try for a hopeful tone. "Maybe someday?"

"Maybe."

Here it comes. "But?"

"It's complicated."

My cell phone rings and I cringe. I should have turned the damn thing off. Leslie's face rearranges itself into an icy stare. "I'd better answer it," I say. "It's probably Rosie."

"As usual."

I flip open the phone, but I don't recognize the incoming number on the display. "Michael Daley speaking."

"Jerry Edwards, *San Francisco Chronicle*." He sounds like Walter Matthau.

Christ. "I'm a great admirer of your work, Jerry. This really isn't a good time."

This doesn't stop him. "We've been spending a lot of time on the China Basin project."

"I've read your articles."

"And the death of Richard MacArthur."

"It's a big story."

"One of our sources told us you met with Dominic Petrillo at the airport tonight."

Like a good reporter, he isn't going to ask questions. He's going to make statements and hope I'll confirm his conclusions. I try to buy some time by responding with a question.

"Who's your source?" I ask.

"That's confidential."

"I understand your reluctance to reveal your sources. On the other hand, I'm not comfortable confirming or denying statements that may be nothing more than rumors."

"Does that mean you're denying the meeting ever took place?"

Nice try. "I'm neither confirming nor denying anything."

"Mr. Daley," he says, "we have this information from a very reliable source."

I decide to try again. "And who would that be?"

"Me."

"Does that mean you were in the Suburban that followed Petrillo down to the airport?"

He gives me a phony laugh. "You got me, Mr. Daley."

He wants information. So do I. I ask him, "Why were you watching Petrillo?"

"We weren't. We were watching Richard MacArthur. When Petrillo left his house, we decided to see where he was going."

"So you followed him to the airport?"

"So did you."

Touché. "I assume you have photos?"

"Indeed. We have a nice shot of the two of you standing outside the United terminal. We're planning to put it on page one of tomorrow morning's paper."

Hell.

"Look on the bright side," he says. "In a few hours, you're going to be famous."

I was hoping to reserve my fifteen minutes for another time.

"So," he says,"do you have any comment about your meeting with Mr. Petrillo?"

The last thing I want to do is start answering open-ended questions. He'll give me just enough rope to hang myself. "And if I say no comment?"

"We'll publish the facts as we know them." He clears his throat and adds, "Of course, that would give us a little more wiggle room to speculate."

I give Leslie a helpless look, and I try to choose my words carefully. "I'll confirm I met with Petrillo in connection with our investigation in the Angelina Chavez case. He may be a witness. For obvious confidentiality reasons, I can't reveal what he said."

This doesn't stop him. "Did he reveal any details on MacArthur's murder? We know he was there Friday night."

"You know I can't comment on that."

"Is he still planning to release *The Return of the Master* next week?"

"You'll have to ask him."

"Did you talk about the China Basin project?"

I repeat my mantra. I tell him I have no comment.

He pretends he's frustrated. In reality, he knows he won't get much from me. "He issued a statement earlier today saying Millennium Studios wasn't going to get involved in Angelina Chavez's defense. Does his meeting with you represent a change of policy?"

"No comment, Jerry."

"Are you and Petrillo trying to work out a deal?"

"No."

"He was at Richard MacArthur's house tonight. What were they talking about?"

"I don't know. I wasn't there."

"Are you trying to cut a deal with Richard MacArthur?"

"Obviously, we'd like his cooperation."

He sighs. "You aren't making my job any easier, Mr. Daley."

It isn't *my* job to make *your* job easier. I can be sanctimonious, too. "We want to find out what really happened just as much as you do, Jerry. My client is innocent, and we'd like to find out who really killed her husband."

There is silence on the other end. Then he asks, "Have you spoken with Carl Ellis?"

"Not yet."

He feigns exasperation. "You have to give me something, Mr. Daley."

"My client is innocent."

"Come on, Mr. Daley."

"I've told you everything I can for now, Jerry."

"Have it your way. We'll go with what we've got." He hangs up without saying good-bye. I'm going to get nailed in the morning paper.

I finish my wine and set my glass on the table. Leslie says, "The *Chronicle*?"

"Yeah."

"When?"

"Tomorrow morning. Front page."

She tries to sound upbeat. "You'll become a media darling. Your phone will be ringing off the hook. Who knows? Maybe they'll ask you to be the new spokesman for Viagra."

"I wouldn't count on that."

Her expression turns serious. "What lies is he going to write about you?"

"I don't know what angle he'll take. You can bet it won't be anything good."

She tries to downplay it. "I'm second-guessed in the media all the time. It isn't a big deal. Most people barely glance at the paper."

"He'll be talking about it on *Mornings on Two*."

"Nobody pays any attention to that stuff."

It's kind of her to try to make me feel better. I replay my conversation with Edwards in my head. I wonder what bombs I might have detonated.

She gives me a concerned look and asks, "Is there anything I can do?"

"Can you throw Jerry Edwards in jail for a few weeks?"

"Sure. Anything else?"

A back rub would be nice. "Nah. You said you wanted to talk."

"I do."

"Is this a good time?"

"As good as any." She brushes her fingers against her lips and says, "I want you to turn off your cell phone for a few minutes."

*Bad vibes.* I do as she asks. "Are you sure you want to talk about this now?"

There's a hesitation. She bites her lip and says, "Yes."

I steel myself. We sit in silence for what seems like an hour, but is probably only a few uncomfortable seconds. She leans back in her chair. I lean forward in mine. She swallows. I cough. She scratches her ear. I look at her. She looks away. It's the mating ritual of desperate, middle-aged people in the early twenty-first century.

It's put-up time. I take a deep breath and say, "Do you want to go first?"

She answers quickly, "No." Then she adds, "You're the media star. You go first."

What does this mean? I feel like I'm back in high school trying to get up the courage to ask Carolyn to the prom. Does this ever get easier? I take her hand. At first she pulls it away. Then she sees the look in my eyes and reconsiders. She wraps her hands around mine. "Look," I say, "I know the last few days have been difficult—"

"This has nothing to do with the last few days. This has to do with where we're going."

I hit a defensive lob. "Where would you like us to go?"

She hits it right back to me. "Where would *you* like us to go?" It's a lawyerly maneuver. See what the other side has to say. Then you can react. It's another reason why lawyers shouldn't date each other. Somebody will write a dissertation about it someday.

Here we go. "Okay," I say, "here's where I'm at." Her eyes open wide. I lower my voice. "I like you, Leslie—a lot."

"I like you, too."

I look in her eyes for a hint. Nothing. Judges get a lot of practice at hiding their feelings. It would be fun to watch a group of them play poker. I decide to turn my cards up. "I'm falling in love with you Leslie, and I want to make our situation more permanent."

Her eyes are open wide. "How permanent?"

I was hoping for something a little more enthusiastic. Here goes. "Very."

A look of genuine alarm crosses her face. "Do you want to get married?"

Air raid! Begin evasive maneuvers! I start backtracking. "No. No. Not yet, anyway. It's too soon." I berate myself for sounding defensive. There are kids with acne who have more polish than I do.

"Then what are you saying?"

What *am* I saying? "I'd like us to be a couple—a *real* couple—for the world to see. I want to give ourselves a chance to have a successful long-term relationship—a permanent one."

She's still holding my hand. Her eyes twinkle as she says, "Are you asking me if I want to go steady?"

I guess so. "Essentially, yes."

"You're remarkable, Michael Daley."

Is this good or bad? In my experience, it's usually a bad sign when someone calls you by your first and last names. It's even worse if they use your middle name, too. I knew I was in serious trouble when my mom called me Michael Joseph Daley when I was a kid. I lean back and remain quiet. Don't say anything. Let her talk.

Her eyes lock into mine. "Michael Daley, I think about you all the time. Even when I'm on the bench. I want to be with you. I want to see your smile. I want to read the paper and drink coffee with you at Caffé Trieste on Sundays."

This is starting to sound pretty hopeful.

She swallows hard and says, "And I want you to be there in the mornings to hold me when I'm lonely and scared."

She's never opened up this way before. I squeeze her hands and whisper, "You'll never be lonely as long as I'm around. And you never have to be scared."

"Even judges get scared, Michael. And everybody gets lonely."

"What are you scared of, Leslie?"

She thinks about it for a moment and says, "Being alone for the rest of my life. It's great to be independent, but it's better to have someone special to share it with."

We're on the same page. "I want you to share it with me, Leslie."

"And I want to share it with you."

There's still a sense of reservation in her tone. "Is there a *but* coming?"

"It's complicated."

Dammit. With Leslie, everything is complicated. I strain to keep my voice measured. "What is it?"

"There are just so many issues."

"We aren't kids. We both have baggage. It isn't going to magically go away if we decide to be together. The real issue is whether being with each other is important enough to us that we're willing to deal with the baggage. For the record, it's important enough for me."

She looks down.

I ask, "What's really bugging you, Leslie?"

She shifts in her chair and says, "I don't want to compete with Rosie."

We've covered this territory. "You don't have to."

"I think I do."

I hold my hands up and say, "What more can I tell you? We're business partners. She's free to go out with anybody she wants."

"There's a lot more to it."

She's right. "It's time for both of us to move on with our lives. For what it's worth, I'd like to move on with you."

"And Grace?"

This one's nonnegotiable. Grace trumps Leslie. "You're going to have to deal with her. She's part of the package. If you force me to make a choice, she's going to win."

She becomes defensive. "I would never put you in that position, Michael. I know how much your daughter means to you."

"Then what is it?"

She takes another sip of wine and says, "What if she doesn't want to be with me?"

"She isn't going to move in with you."

"I know. But we'll be spending time together. What if she doesn't like me?"

"It won't happen."

"It could. What if she resents me? What if she thinks I'm trying to take her mother's place?"

It's an unpredictable risk. "I've gone out with other people. She's been good about it."

"So far. But you never know how she'll react."

"No, we don't. We never will unless we try."

"I have a lot riding on this too, Michael. There's a huge risk when a relationship will be impacted to a substantial degree by the feelings of a ten-year-old."

"I can't control her feelings, Leslie. I can only try to make it easier for her—and for us. We'll just have to do the best we can. You're going to have to accept some risk."

"It may be more than I can handle."

"I'll understand if that's what you decide." I reflect for a moment and add, "I'll be disappointed as hell, however." We might as well get everything out on the table. "What else is troubling you?"

"If we stay together, I'll have a host of interesting issues to deal with at work."

"We can work around them."

"It isn't that easy. Being a judge is like being a priest."

Not quite. "How's that?"

"You live under a magnifying glass. You have to think about potential conflicts of interest twenty-four hours a day. You have to pick your friends carefully. You can't be seen with certain people." She adds, "And you have to be very careful whom you sleep with. Sometimes I think it's better not to sleep with anybody at all."

"As I recall, the celibacy rules for judges are a little more relaxed than those for priests."

"I realize that. On the other hand, I can do serious damage to my career if there is even the appearance of impropriety. If I'm seeing somebody and a conflict of interest arises, my career could be over. My judgment and impartiality will be brought into question. There are political issues to consider, too. If I want a realistic shot at the federal bench, I have to be sure nothing unseemly will appear on my résumé."

It's a legitimate concern. "It hasn't been a problem so far," I say.

"I know. But that can change at any time." She walks over to her briefcase, which is sitting on her small desk in the corner of the kitchen. She takes out a manila folder and hands it to me. She tells me to turn to the second page. "Look at the last item."

I study the court papers. It's her docket for the upcoming week. The case she's noted is *The People v. Benjamin Taylor*. The charge is possession of a controlled substance. The preliminary hearing is Thursday.

"It's Carolyn's son," I say.

"Right. Your firm is listed as attorneys of record. It's a conflict of interest."

"I know. I talked to Carolyn about it. We're going to refer it to somebody else."

A look of alarm crosses her eyes. "Carolyn knows about us?"

"She does now. I had to tell her."

"Has she told anybody else?"

"No."

"Have you?"

"Just Rosie." I think for a moment and add, "And Grace."

She sighs. "This won't be the last time your firm will have matters in my courtroom."

"No, it won't."

"And how do you plan to deal with the conflict?"

"We're prepared to withdraw from any case where we might appear before you."

"I can't let you do that."

"Yes, you can."

"I *won't* let you."

"Then we'll have to find another way to handle it."

"What would you suggest?"

"You can recuse yourself from our cases."

"That's not always going to be feasible."

"It *is* always feasible. It isn't always going to be easy. You can find a way to get out of hearing almost anything if you really want to." I realize it sounds harsh as I say it.

"I'll need a reason."

I've barely slept or eaten in two days. I'm overwhelmed and exhausted. I'm not going to play games. I lay the cards out. "The reason is that you're sleeping with me. If we make our situation a matter of public record, everybody will understand."

Silence. She swirls her wine and looks out at the beacon on Alcatraz. I rest my chin in my hands. The ball is in her court. I'm not going to give her an easy way out.

Finally, she says, "I need to think about it. I'm in the middle of discussions with my colleagues. I may be put up for presiding judge later this year. There's also the federal bench."

I'm not going to put my life on hold. "You're going to have to tell them about me sooner or later. They'll find out about us. It's better to be upfront."

"I know. The timing is bad. The people who make these decisions don't want to deal with a judge who has a relationship with a defense attorney. It's hard enough being a Democrat. I don't want to give them a chance to say I lack the moral character to be a federal judge."

"Everybody knows you're a Democrat. The fact that you have a boyfriend has nothing to do with your qualifications as a judge."

"This has nothing to do with my qualifications, Michael. It has to do with politics. I'm going to have enough trouble getting an appointment to the federal bench. Getting a reputation as a woman with questionable morals won't help."

"Is that what this is really about? You think being seen with me is bad for your career?"

She retreats slightly. "No. There are other factors. I'm trying to weigh the risks against the potential benefits."

She sounds like she's deciding a case. "Look," I say, "this isn't a civil trial where you look at the merits and assess damages. This isn't a criminal case where you try to determine whether the prosecutors have proven their case beyond a reasonable doubt. Dating a defense attorney won't be a gold star on your résumé. On the other hand, we're talking about my feelings, too. I just opened a vein for you, Leslie. I'm willing to withdraw from any case where it might create a conflict for you. You seem hesitant to do the same for me."

"I need to think about it."

"You've been thinking about it for weeks."

"I need to think about it a little longer."

It would be a mistake to press her for an answer. In my experience, it is usually counterproductive to issue ultimatums. I try to find a middle ground. "I'd like to know soon, Leslie."

"How soon?"

"Pretty soon."

"How soon is pretty soon?"

I hate arguments over semantics— especially with other lawyers. "I won't wait six months to see if you get the appointment as presiding judge. And I won't wait a year to see if you're nominated for the Northern District. I'm not that patient."

"That's fair." She pauses and says, "I'm sorry, Michael. This is hard on me, too. It's the best I can do tonight."

It's as far as I can go. I say without conviction, "I understand."

She finishes her wine and says, "Do you want to stick around for a little while and listen to some music? You can have another glass of wine."

I hear Judy Collins singing "Send in the Clowns." "I think I'd better take a rain check. I have a busy day tomorrow. I think it might be better if I went home."

"HEY, MICK," Pete's voice whispers. "Where are you?"

"The Waldo Grade." It's almost two in the morning. The reception on my cell phone isn't good as I churn up the embankment toward the tunnel just north of the Golden Gate Bridge. The fog has come in, and I can barely see past the end of my headlights. "Where are you?" I ask.

"In the alley down the block from Little Richard's house."

"You're a fun guy, Pete."

"Wait until you get my bill." Notwithstanding his incessant complaining, he's having a ball. He loves the chase.

I tell him about my conversation with Jerry Edwards.

"I'll look for you in the paper in the morning. It should be a beaut."

"Any sign of Kaela Joy Gullion?"

"No. If she's got this place staked out, she's well hidden."

"Any visitors at Little Richard's place since you got back?"

"Just one. Cheryl Springer."

"What was Daniel Crown's wife doing at Little Richard's house?"

"I don't know. Maybe she was offering a few suggestions for the edits on the movie."

"How long did she stay?"

"About twenty minutes. She looked unhappy when she left."

I hope her husband is having his regular cup of coffee when I go looking for him at Willie's less than six hours from now.

# Chapter 21

# "Life Is All about Dealing with Complications"

> Studio Head Holds Secret Meeting with Movie Star's Attorneys.
>
> —*San Francisco Chronicle*
> Monday, June 7

"DID YOU SEE the paper?" I ask Rosie. She's in her kitchen pouring water into the coffee maker at six o'clock the same morning. Grace is still asleep.

She ignores my question and asks, "How was your date last night?"

First things first.

I reply honestly. "Fair."

I had a horrible night. I tossed and turned for a couple of hours, then gave up at five thirty and came over here. Rosie was already up and dressed when I arrived. Her small TV is tuned to Channel Two. A copy of the *Chronicle* is on the kitchen table. I'm studying the photo of Petrillo, Rosie and me standing on the sidewalk in front of the United terminal. Petrillo's eyes are bulging. I'm looking down. Rosie's arms are folded. The headline reads, STUDIO HEAD HOLDS SECRET MEETING WITH MOVIE STAR'S ATTORNEYS. There is a smaller photo of Petrillo leaving Little Richard's house.

"So," Rosie says, "is Leslie prepared to step up to the plate?"

Not exactly. "She's still weighing her options."

"She's been doing that for weeks."

"She's very methodical."

Rosie scowls. "She should have been able to figure it out by now. She's stalling."

"It's complicated."

"It isn't that complicated. Life is all about dealing with complications. Anybody can handle the easy stuff."

So true. "There are issues on many levels."

"Such as?"

"Her career. It doesn't look nice for a potential federal court nominee to be intimate with a criminal defense attorney."

"Whom she chooses to sleep with has nothing to do with her qualifications as a judge."

"It may be viewed as a lapse of judgment."

"I didn't view it as a lapse in judgment when I was sleeping with you."

"You weren't being considered for the federal bench."

She gives me a half smile. "Tell her to grow up and get over it."

"I may have suggested that to her."

"I assume this was not met with resounding enthusiasm?"

"That would be correct."

She sighs. "What else?"

I explain that Leslie has concerns about Grace. "She thinks Grace may resent her."

Rosie's tone softens. "It's a risk. I'll do what I can to help."

"Thanks." I pause for a moment and add, "She's also worried about you."

This gets a discernible reaction. "Me? Why?"

"She thinks we still have feelings for each other."

"Do we?"

"I can only speak for myself."

"And speaking only for yourself, what have you decided?"

"Come on, Rosie. I thought we agreed that it was time to move on. I thought that was what you wanted."

Her eyes flare. "Don't lay this on me. And don't tell me what I want. What do you want?"

It's too early for this. I swallow hard and say, "I will always have feelings for you, Rosita, but I don't think we're meant to live with each other. I think it would be better if we tried to move on with our lives in some positive direction."

"And you want to move on with Leslie?"

"I think so."

She nods. "Do you love her?"

"I'm pretty sure."

"Does she love you?"

"She's trying."

"Tell her to try a little harder."

"What about you, Rosita?"

"What about me?"

"Are you ready to move on?"

"I think so." She pauses and adds, "I have a lot of stuff going."

"I know."

"Do you have any idea how big my sacrifice has been?"

"How's that?"

She smiles and says, "I gave up my personal sex toy so you could roll around together. The least she can do is pay me the courtesy of being serious about you so that my self-control hasn't been in vain."

Ever the pragmatist. "Where do I fit in? You seem to think of me as some sort of a functionary in all of this."

Her eyes dance. "Essentially."

I chuckle. "Do you think I'll ever be in a story where I actually get the girl in the end?"

"It happened once," she says. "Then we got married and ruined everything."

"Not everything," I say. "We still have Grace."

"That's true."

"And we have each other."

"Yes, we do."

I say, "Do you think other divorced couples have conversations like this?"

"We aren't like other divorced couples."

That's for sure. It's one of the reasons we weren't good at marriage counseling. Rosie says neither of us reacts well to conventional stimuli. I came over here to talk about Angel's case and the *Chronicle* article. So far,

I've gotten ten minutes of advice on my love life. She has a unique ability to make me feel better while she's telling me I'm acting like an idiot.

She's ready to talk business. "So," she says, "that was a nice picture in the paper."

"We look bad."

"It could have been worse." She arches her eyebrows. "They got your right side."

"So?"

"That's always been your good side."

I'm a basket case, and she's making wisecracks. I wish I had her ability to keep things in perspective—and to sleep at night.

She takes a sip of orange juice and says, "This headline about a secret meeting is preposterous. There was nothing secret about it. We were in a public place. They took our picture in a crowded airport. They could have followed us to the Ambassador's Club."

"It doesn't help. The article suggests we were trying to cut a deal."

"That's bullshit. We were talking to the wrong guy. Last time I checked, the president of Millennium Studios has no authority to approve a plea bargain for an accused felon. Did Edwards consider that Petrillo's company invested millions in this movie? Does he expect him to walk away from Angel? He's trying to protect his investment."

I start to respond when she holds up her hand and points to the TV. "Looks like they're talking to your new buddy."

The anchorman with the impeccable hair furrows his brow and tells us in his best melodramatic voice that there have been significant developments in the MacArthur case. He says, "*Chronicle* political correspondent Jerry Edwards has joined us." His tone suggests Edwards just happened to be driving by the studio and decided to drop in for a chat.

Edwards looks as if he slept in his rumpled gray suit. His narrow tie is loosened and his collar is open. He bears an uncanny resemblance to a bulldog. "Big developments overnight," he growls to the camera. His delivery is a cross between Walter Winchell's and Paul Harvey's. "One of our camera crews was at SFO last night."

"What a coincidence," Rosie says.

Edwards cocks his head and starts talking faster. "Lo and behold, guess who drove up?" He pauses and says, "None other than Dominic Petrillo, the head of Millennium Studios, which is financing *The Return of the Master* and the controversial China Basin project."

I find it annoying when people ask questions of themselves on TV and answer them as if they're imparting oraclelike wisdom. I prefer to talk to myself in the privacy of my own home.

Edwards continues his conversation with himself. "Guess who else was there? None other than Michael Daley and Rosita Fernandez, the attorneys for Angelina Chavez."

Before I realize I'm talking to a television, I say, "It doesn't mean a thing."

"There's more," Edwards says. His eyes open wide. "Guess where Mr. Petrillo was earlier yesterday evening?"

The anchorman gets into the act. He sounds like Ed McMahon feeding straight lines to Johnny Carson when he asks, "Where?"

"The home of Richard MacArthur, Jr. Coincidence? I think not."

Rosie asks, "Do you think this guy talks to his wife that way?"

"Yeah. They're in bed and she says, 'Sex tonight?' Then he says, 'I think not.'"

This elicits the hint of a grin.

Edwards is still going strong. "Who was Mr. Petrillo dining with at Postrio yesterday evening? None other than Carl Ellis, the construction contractor for the China Basin project."

I say, "I thought Ellis went back to Vegas."

Rosie can't resist. She smiles and says, "I think not."

Edwards explains that the studio project is up for final approval next week. "Where does this leave the people of San Francisco?" he asks. "Why are secret meetings being held at the airport?"

The camera flashes back to the anchorman. He takes the cue and asks, "Why, Jerry?"

Edwards jabs an index finger at the camera and says, "We don't know."

I say, "There's insight for you. Don't you just love live TV?"

Rosie puts a finger to her lips.

Edwards isn't finished. "Something smells," he says. "We *will* continue to monitor this situation. We *will* talk to Dominic Petrillo. We *will* talk to

Michael Daley and Rosita Fernandez. We *will* talk to Angelina Chavez. We *will* talk to Richard MacArthur and Carl Ellis. We *will* make sure the China Basin project does not move forward without a full hearing."

Rosie adds, "We *will* make noise just to hear the sound of our own voices."

I glance at the TV a moment later. They're showing a video of flames shooting out the roof of a liquor store. "Isn't that down near Tony's market?" I ask.

Rosie looks at the TV and nods. She turns up the sound. The announcer says a three-alarm fire destroyed a liquor store on Twenty-fourth. Nobody was injured. Fire department officials are investigating the possibility of arson.

Rosie's phone rings, and I pick it up. It's Tony. He asks, "Did you see what they did to Roberto Peña's store?"

I put it together. "Yeah. Who did it?"

"I don't know." His breathing is heavy. "It's three blocks from the market. I'll bet you I'm next."

"Stay calm, Tony."

"Easy for you to say. Roberto's store is gone. He could have been killed."

"We don't know if this has anything to do with you."

"Let me talk to Rosita."

I hand her the phone. Rosie's family speaks Spanish only when there's a serious problem. She hangs up a few minutes later. "I need to get down there right away," she says. "I want to talk to Sergeant Alvarez." She reflects for a moment and says, "Are you still planning to intercept Daniel Crown?"

"Yes. Do you still want to come with me?"

"No. I have to see Tony. Let me know if you find out anything from Crown."

"DO YOU REALLY THINK Crown is going to show up?" I'm talking to the young woman who has turned the operation of the espresso machine at Willie's Café into a higher art form.

Her name is Becky. Most of her customers think of her simply as the woman who runs the coffee machine. If they spent a minute with her, they would discover she's a single mom who attends College of Marin. Trying to make ends meet on her modest income with a four year-old isn't easy. Her blonde hair cascades down her shoulders. Her eyes look older than twenty-four.

"He'll be here," she assures me. "He hasn't missed a day since his son started first grade, except when he was out of town working on movies."

When I was a kid, people used to get their morning coffee at coffee shops and donut stores. In Marin County, people hang out at places like Willie's, an upscale café on the edge of Kent Woodlands, an affluent community set in a tree-lined canyon adjacent to the Mt. Tam watershed. A two-bedroom fixer-upper in this part of the woods will set you back at least two million dollars. My car looks lonely among the SUVs in the parking lot. The oak tables in the restaurant are covered with checked cloths. The sweet aroma of freshly brewed coffee and home-baked muffins wafts through the cheerful room. A harried young man with piercings on various parts of his anatomy operates the grill behind the counter. Everybody in the line outside the door seems to be wearing a designer sweatsuit or a cycling jersey. Attractive young au pairs rock infants in souped-up jogging strollers. The atmosphere is friendly, almost festive.

I'm sitting at the counter at the end of the coffee bar, not far from the windows. It's a few minutes before eight. I dropped Grace off at school. Rosie went to see Tony. Then she's going to the Hall to see Angel. I'm picking at my scrambled eggs and drinking coffee. It's warm this morning and I wish I had a seat out on the deck. A steady stream of joggers and cyclists kibbitz at the coffee bar. It seems everybody knows everybody else—except me. I have more in common with Becky than anybody else in this restaurant. I'm trying to hide behind the sports section. My picture is on the front page.

The minutes tick. I finish my eggs. I ask Becky for another cup of coffee. I pay the bill. Still no sign of Crown. Finally, at eight-thirty, Becky gives me a nod. I glance toward the door. Crown walks in and takes a seat at an open table in the corner near the windows. He looks more like the guy who grew up in a comfortable Chicago suburb than a budding movie star. He's wearing a University of Illinois T-shirt and a pair of cutoffs. His golden hair is slicked back and his eyes are covered by sunglasses. Becky leaves her post at the espresso machine to pour him a cup of coffee. He talks to her for a moment. It seems he's ordering the usual, whatever that may be. On her way back to the counter, she walks by me and says, "Here's your chance."

I stick out like a sore thumb as I start walking toward Crown. I'm due in court later today and I'm wearing a business suit. I'm the only person who isn't wearing spandex. I sense every eye in Willie's is upon me.

Crown looks up when I reach him. A few months ago, I went to a seminar on criminal procedure given by a flamboyant criminal defense attorney named Mort Goldberg, who said that if you want to get somebody talking, you should act like you know them and start with sugar. If flattery doesn't work, you can try something else. I extend my hand and say, "Danny, I'm Mike Daley. Our kids played soccer together."

I get the reaction I want. His face breaks into a broad smile, and he seems at ease. "Tell me your daughter's name again," he says.

"Grace."

"I remember Grace," he lies. Then he backtracks. "Well, maybe. I spend a lot of time on the road. I don't always remember all the kids on my son's teams."

He starts to open his newspaper. We aren't bonding yet. I try another softball question: I ask him how he likes living in Marin.

He's a little more forthcoming. "It's very nice," he says. "The whole scene in L.A. was bad news. People respect our privacy here. I can come into a place like this, and they treat me like I'm one of the neighbors. We live down the street from Sean and Robin. We can have them over to our house for a barbeque without helicopters flying overhead."

I try to remain nonchalant as I quickly slide into the chair across from him. It's considered bad form to act awestruck when someone mentions one of our local celebrities. Sean and Robin are the Penns, who live about a mile from here. They caused a bit of a stir when they moved in because they wanted to put up a new fence that was a little taller than permitted by code. The town fathers ultimately concluded the fence would discourage gawkers and tabloid photographers. Notwithstanding the height of their fence, they're good neighbors. I've seen them at Little League games.

We exchange small talk. He doesn't seem to mind my company. "Look, Danny," I say, "there's something I was hoping I could talk to you about."

His demeanor changes abruptly. He picks up his newspaper, but doesn't open it. When you're a budding movie star, you always have to keep your defenses up.

"I have to make a confession," I tell him. "I'm Angelina Chavez's lawyer."

The warm glow in his eyes quickly disappears. He doesn't say a word.

It's better to come clean. I point toward his newspaper and say, "You'll see my picture there along with my partner and Dominic Petrillo."

He looks at the front page. Then he looks at me, but doesn't say a word.

I tell him, "It would really help me if I could ask you a few questions."

He leans back in this chair and sighs. "My lawyers told me not to talk to anyone."

"Just a few questions. It would help Angelina."

This gets a grimace. "I've already told my story to the police. My people have told me not to talk to anybody else."

I wish I had people. "I'm not looking to get you or anybody else in trouble. I'm just trying to figure out who was there and what time everybody left." Of course, if you want to give me a detailed blow-by-blow of everything that happened, I'd be more than happy to listen.

He considers for a moment and says, "Cheryl and I left a few minutes before two."

It's a start. "Did you drive straight home?"

"Yes."

"Who was still there when you left?"

He looks up toward the counter and thinks for a moment. "Dick MacArthur, his son and Marty Kent." He nods to reassure himself that he hasn't left anybody out.

"What about Angelina?"

"She was there, too. She went upstairs early."

"And Dom Petrillo and Carl Ellis?"

He waves his hands and says, "They left a few minutes before we did."

He's starting to warm up again. "How was the movie?" I ask.

He gives me the golden smile. "Terrific. It turned out better than I thought. Dick MacArthur was a great director."

"And everybody liked it?" I ask.

"Oh, yes. Dom Petrillo said he thought the movie would do at least a hundred million in domestic box office." He winks at me and says, "I think it will do better than that."

Petrillo's impression of the film was decidedly more reserved when he talked to me. I guess everybody hears what he wants to hear. "The early buzz has been very hot," I lie.

His eyes light up. "They might even increase the advertising budget," he says.

I search for an innocent tone. "Danny," I say, "is there a chance Dick's death will delay the release?"

"No. Everything's in motion. They can't stop it now." He glances down at the paper.

"Did you see anything out of the ordinary on Friday night? Was anybody acting funny? Was anybody upset?"

He doesn't look up as he says, "Nope."

"Was Angelina okay?"

"Yeah." His eyes are still down. He's trying to disengage.

"She wasn't stressed out or upset?

Finally, he looks at me and says, "She was a little stressed out, but she wasn't upset."

"Between you and me, the police said she may have had a little too much to drink."

"That's possible. And she may have taken some coke."

He hesitates for an instant. "I don't know anything about that."

The hell you don't. On the other hand, I'll lose him if I push too hard. I ask him how Little Richard and Kent were feeling on Friday night.

"They had a great time." He looks over my shoulder and waves.

I glance outside and see Cheryl Springer walking forcefully toward the restaurant. He motions her toward us. There is a pronounced grimace on her face. He starts to introduce me as she approaches our table. She interrupts him midsentence. She says to him in a tone that leaves no doubt, "Daniel, I need to talk to you right away."

The last vestiges of warmth in Crown's eyes disappear. "This is Mike," he tells her. "His daughter knows Jason. We were just having coffee."

She gives me a firm, but perfunctory, handshake. Her jaw tightens. My guess is that she's a little older than Crown, although it is sometimes difficult to judge the age of someone who has had her hair, eyes, nose and breasts redone. "Cheryl Springer," she says through clenched teeth. "You'll have to excuse us. I need to talk to my husband."

"Sure thing." I don't move.

Her scowl becomes more pronounced. Her voice dips a half octave when she adds, "Alone." She takes off her oversized orange sunglasses and says, "Right now."

"Actually," I say, "I was hoping I could talk to you for a few minutes, too."

She shakes her mane of painfully bleached, frizzy hair. A look of recognition crosses her face. She points a finger at me and says, "You're Angelina's attorney."

It will serve no useful purpose to try to deny it. "Yes."

Her grimace changes into an expression that is somewhere between anger and panic. She glares at her husband and snaps, "What were you talking about?"

"I was just telling Mike a little bit about what I saw the other night."

Her voice takes on a tone that might be used by a grammar school principal speaking to an ill-behaved second grader. "Daniel," she says, "you've already talked to the police. You aren't supposed to talk to anybody else."

He pleads his case. "I was trying to help Angelina."

"She's an adult. She can take care of herself. That's why she's hired Mr. Daley."

I come to my new pal's defense. "Danny was trying to help us find out what happened," I say. "We want to know the truth about Dick's death." I pause for a beat and add, "And we were discussing the release of *The Return of the Master*."

Her eyes bore in on mine. "What about it?"

"I was just asking Danny whether the movie will be released on time."

She gives me an incredulous look. "Of course the movie will be released on time." She looks at her husband and says, "You didn't suggest to him that there might be a delay, did you?"

He looks like he's going to curl up into a ball. His voice is barely a whisper when he says, "No."

I don't want her to stop. I ask, "Are you happy with the way the movie turned out?"

"Of course."

"And so was everybody else?"

"Yes."

"And Dom Petrillo and Richard MacArthur are prepared to proceed?"

"Absolutely."

"When was the last time you talked to Richard about it?" I ask.

She gives me a circumspect look. "Why do you ask?"

"Just curious. He told me he thought Angelina's situation might be bad publicity."

"There is no question about the release, Mr. Daley. I talked to him last night."

This explains their meeting. I ask, "Was anybody acting unusually on Friday night?"

"No. It was a nice party."

"And you left around two?"

"Yes. We came straight home." She sighs. "Mr. Daley, Danny and I have already given our stories to the police. We don't have time to repeat them to you. We have to be downtown."

"Where can I reach you?" I ask.

She hands me a card with a post-office box and a phone number. "Call this number," she tells me. "We'll get back to you." With that, she points to the parking lot and practically lifts her husband off his chair.

"DID CROWN SHOW UP at Willie's?" Rosie asks me. She's at Tony's market. We seem to conduct about 90 percent of our communications via cell phone these days.

"You bet." I'm fighting traffic on the Golden Gate Bridge as I'm heading for the city. "He seems like a nice enough guy."

"Is he as gorgeous in person as he is in his movies?"

Why burst her bubble? "He's even better looking in person. I didn't ask him if he wanted to meet you. I thought that might have been a little presumptuous in our first meeting."

"I'll come with you next time."

"I got a bonus. I met his wife."

"What's she like?"

"A holy terror."

"Did they tell you anything that might be helpful?"

"No. They stayed with the party line. Everybody loved the movie. Everybody had a great time. They're going to proceed with the release on schedule."

"Do you think they were telling the truth?"

"I doubt it. Something is going on. His wife was pissed off at him for talking to me. She practically pulled him out of the restaurant. I don't know what it means." I ask about the fire at the liquor store.

"It looks like arson."

"Can they tell whether it had anything to do with the studio project?"

"Too soon to tell. We're going to see Sergeant Alvarez after the arraignment. In the meantime, I'm going down to see Angel. Then I've been promised a brief audience with Marty Kent's son at eleven at Nicole Ward's office."

"I'll meet you there."

# Chapter 22

## "My Father Did Not Commit Suicide"

> KENT, Martin H. Died June 5 at age 62. Beloved husband of the late Marilyn, father of Scott and Michelle. A respected film executive and retired Marine. Services will be private. Donations in his memory may be made to the American Cancer Society.
>
> —*San Francisco Chronicle*
> Monday, June 7

"I STOPPED at bridge headquarters and talked to the guard who found Angel," I tell Rosie. "He saw her while he was making his rounds. He didn't know how long she'd been there."

We're waiting outside Nicole Ward's office at eleven o'clock. The D.A. is inside with Marty Kent's son. I'm dreading the moment the door opens. We'll have to ask him some sensitive questions. It will be difficult for us, but could be excruciating for him. To her credit, Ward facilitated the process by letting us talk to him. We agreed not to disturb him at home.

Rosie asks, "Did the guard see anyone else?"

"No." I tell her he confirmed Angel was in the driver's seat and the ignition was on. "He called the cops. I talked to the head of security and everybody else who was working on the bridge Friday night and Saturday morning. Nobody saw Angel arrive."

Rosie asks if there are security cameras.

"Yes, but not in the parking lot." I tell her there are cameras at the tollbooths to catch cheaters and on the walkways to look for jumpers. "The guard who was monitoring them on Saturday morning didn't see anything suspicious. It was foggy, and he couldn't see much. He promised to get us copies of the videotapes."

She asks about traffic cameras.

"There's one mounted on the administration building. It shows all six lanes and the walkways at the south end of the bridge."

"Was it turned on at three o'clock Saturday morning?"

"It's always on. The TV stations tap into it to broadcast live traffic updates on their websites. They've promised the videos from the traffic camera, too."

The door opens. Nicole Ward joins us and closes the door behind her. She whispers, "Keep it short. He has to catch a flight to L.A. to make funeral arrangements."

Rosie asks, "Did Rod Beckert determine cause of death?"

"Technically, he drowned. It was a suicide. He jumped off the bridge. He probably lost consciousness when he hit the water. He had other trauma-related injuries."

"Is Rod sure?"

Ward folds her arms. "Rod Beckert has been the chief medical examiner for more than thirty years. There have been over a thousand documented suicides on the bridge. He has the unenviable record of having performed more autopsies on bridge victims than anybody else on the face of the earth. The answer to your question therefore is yes, he's sure."

We'll still want to talk to Beckert about it. "Did anybody see him jump?"

"No."

"Did any of the security cameras catch him in the act?"

"We're waiting for the videotapes."

"Do you have any idea why he did it?"

Ward shrugs. "His wife died about a year ago. He was having financial problems. He was under a lot of pressure. I suspect he was depressed."

"His son acknowledged all of this?"

Ward closes her eyes and says, "No. He's still dealing with the shock. He's in a state of denial. It's understandable under the circumstances."

Rosie darts a glance in my direction. Then she turns back toward Ward and says, "We'd like to talk to him now."

"Fine. Bear in mind his father committed suicide two days ago."

Rosie says, "We'll keep it short, Nicole."

---

"MR. KENT," Rosie begins, "we're terribly sorry about your father."

Scott Kent nods, but doesn't say anything. Marty Kent's only son is a younger, taller and less robust version of his father. He's with one of the big brokerage firms downtown and looks the part. His gray business suit matches his hair. His skin has a pasty pallor. The bags under his eyes suggest he hasn't gotten much sleep in the last couple of days. Nicole Ward is sitting at her desk with her hands folded.

Rosie starts gently. "Were you and your father close?"

Kent looks down. "Yes, we were."

She leans forward and says, "We understand your mother recently passed away."

Kent takes a sip of water and says, "It was almost a year ago."

"I'm sorry."

"So am I."

"It must have been a terrible loss for him."

"They were married for forty years. She was sick for the last three. Cancer."

Rosie looks at me. "Mr. Kent," I say, "did you notice any changes in your father's behavior after your mother's death?"

"He was grief stricken for several months."

"That's entirely understandable. I'm sorry if this sounds terribly personal."

"I want to find out what happened to my father just as much as you do, Mr. Daley."

He's showing extraordinary grace. "Did you notice any signs of depression?"

Kent swallows. "No."

"Did he have counseling? If not from a therapist, perhaps from a clergy person?"

"He went through counseling with our priest. He bounced back, Mr. Daley. His energy was good. He was looking forward to the release of the movie. He was particularly excited about the studio. He and Dick MacArthur had talked about building a facility up here for years."

"Did you notice any changes in his behavior in the last few months? Stress? Fatigue?"

"He was always under a lot of stress, Mr. Daley. He was involved in the planning for the release of *The Return of the Master*. He was trying to line up the final approvals for the China Basin project. He had a full plate, but he was very excited about what he was doing."

I ask him if he noticed any changes in his father's behavior in the last few weeks.

"None."

"How was he getting along with Dick MacArthur?"

"They were like brothers. They were two grumpy old men who screamed and yelled and cursed. They were always pissed off at each other about something. Then they'd hug and make up. Most of the time, Dick listened to what my dad said."

"Did your father get along with Angelina?"

"He dealt with her in a professional manner. Frankly, my father thought it was inappropriate for a man of Dick's age to marry a woman who was so much younger. He made his view known to Dick, who ignored him."

"And did he get along with Dick's son?"

"Let's just say he recognized that young Richard has a talent for producing movies."

"We've heard rumors your father may have been experiencing financial difficulties. It's been suggested in the papers that he was unhappy about the arrangements for the studio project."

He becomes indignant. "Not true. He was unhappy about the studio because he thought Dominic Petrillo and Carl Ellis railroaded Dick MacArthur into taking a smaller piece of the deal."

"He wasn't trying to get out of it?"

"Absolutely not."

"And he didn't want to renegotiate?"

"A deal's a deal, Mr. Daley."

I glance at Rosie. "Mr. Kent," she says, "did Ms. Ward explain that the chief medical examiner has come to a conclusion about the cause of your father's death?"

His voice is barely audible when he says, "Yes."

She lowers her voice. "And do you understand that Dr. Beckert believes it was suicide?"

"Yes, I do."

"Look," she says, "I know it isn't going to change anything, but I have to ask—"

Scott Kent holds up his hand. His eyes turn the color of cobalt. He looks at Rosie and says in a tone that leaves no doubt, "I've seen Dr. Beckert's report. My father was an All-American football player at UCLA and an officer in the Marines. He got a Purple Heart in Vietnam after he rescued three men from a burning village. He always believed the mark of a true man was his ability to handle adversity with dignity." His voice is starting to crack. "My father was a lawyer, a businessman, a soldier and a hero. He never panicked. I don't care what Dr. Beckert says. He never met him. My father did not commit suicide. And there is nothing that he—or you—can do to convince me that he did."

ROSIE AND I are still in Ward's office. Scott Kent has left to catch his flight. Ward is still sitting behind her desk, and Lisa Yee has joined us. She drops a box of manila file folders on the table in front of me and says, "We made copies of everything we have: autopsy reports on MacArthur and Kent; police reports; crime-scene photos; fingerprint analysis on the house, the car and the Oscar; information about the film and the studio project; background materials." She shrugs and says, "See you at the arraignment."

"Can we talk about this for a few minutes?" Rosie asks.

Ward responds for her. "There's nothing to talk about. We'll play out our respective roles the way we always do. Your client will plead not guilty and you'll ask for bail. We'll oppose it. The judge will set a date for a preliminary hearing. It will be over in fifteen minutes. Then we'll go downstairs and plead our cases to the media. In my seven-second sound bite, I'll tell everybody we have an airtight case. You'll proclaim your client's innocence. The TV stations will try the case on the front steps of the Hall. We'll get to see ourselves on the news. If it's a slow night, we might even make CNN or *Entertainment Tonight*."

I'm not sure if I'm more disturbed by Ward's self-confidence, her cynicism or the fact that her description of what is likely to happen is probably dead accurate.

Rosie lowers her voice and says, "You didn't mention the charge."

"First-degree murder." She hesitates and adds, "We're thinking about special circumstances."

Rosie scowls. "The death penalty?"

The posturing begins. "Absolutely."

Rosie's tone turns incredulous. "In a circumstantial case? On what basis?"

Ward remains defiant. "The old standby: one ninety-point-two-A-one."

I've never been impressed by people who memorize and recite penal code sections. Ward's triumphant expression suggests she's hoping I'll ask her for an explanation of the cite. She won't get the satisfaction. Section 190.2(a) of the penal code contains a list of "special circumstances" where the death penalty may be imposed. It includes multiple murders, murders of judges or police officers and murders in connection with a robbery, kidnaping or rape. Section 190.2(a)(1) says the death penalty may be imposed if the murder was intentional and carried out for financial gain. I say, "This isn't a murder for hire."

"Maybe not, but the courts are willing to apply the statute to cases that involve other types of financial gains."

It's an aggressive interpretation. She may be bluffing. I won't be able to talk her out of it, so I start fishing. "What financial gain?"

"I already told you. The proceeds of a million-dollar life insurance policy and a substantial inheritance under her husband's will. His death voided the terms of her prenuptial agreement. His assets must now be distributed under his will. She gets half of everything except the winery."

I know, I know. Time to try a diversion. I ask, "What about MacArthur's son?"

"What about him?"

"He had a huge financial stake. Under the will, he gets half of his father's cash and securities, including half of the stock in MacArthur Films. He gets the winery."

"So?"

"If you're looking for people with financial motives, you shouldn't rule him out."

Ward feigns disbelief. "You think he killed his own father?"

"You should consider the possibility."

"No way. Play it out. All he had to do was wait a few months for his father to divorce Angel. His father would have reworked his will to reinstate his son as the sole beneficiary. He could have just waited, and he would have gotten everything when his father died."

"Maybe he needed the money. Maybe his father had other ideas."

"Like what?"

"I don't know. There was no guarantee he would have made Richard the sole beneficiary." I don't want to mention the mistress in L.A. who might have gotten a piece of the action. It might suggest Angel had a motive to kill her husband in a jealous rage.

Ward is defiant. "Get real, Mike. Look at the facts before you start trying to deflect blame. Do you think any jury will believe Richard had this figured out? He couldn't possibly have planned it. He didn't know when everybody was going to leave. He couldn't have known Angelina would pass out—if she did. We have no evidence that he drove her to the bridge."

"I'm only suggesting you consider all the possibilities. For that matter, you certainly shouldn't rule out Marty Kent."

"He committed suicide."

"I'm not convinced. Neither is his son."

"Rod Beckert is. You're not the chief medical examiner."

"He never met Marty Kent."

She still isn't persuaded. "He was depressed and under a lot of pressure."

"He was a lawyer and ex-Marine who knew how to handle it. Just because he may have killed himself doesn't rule him out as a suspect."

"There isn't a shred of evidence."

I feel the back of my neck getting red hot. "Sure there is. His fingerprints were on the steering wheel of MacArthur's car. He could have hit him, put Angelina in the car and driven to the bridge."

"Just because he touched the steering wheel doesn't mean he was involved. It was a new car. Maybe MacArthur let him take it out for a drive."

I'm not giving up. "And maybe he killed him and drove Angelina to the bridge."

"Get us some evidence and we'll look into it."

"What about the other fingerprints on the Oscar?" I say. "You told us earlier they were still trying to identify them. Did you find Kent's?"

She hesitates for an instant before she answers, "Yes."

This helps. "So his fingerprints were on the murder weapon. That should be enough to consider him a suspect."

"Not unless you find some other evidence."

This gets a glance from Rosie, who says, "Whose fingerprints did you find on the Oscar?"

Ward locates the file containing the fingerprint analysis and opens it to page four. She hands it to Rosie and says, "There."

Rosie's eyes get wider. "It says here you've identified eight people whose fingerprints were found on the Oscar." In addition to Big Dick and Angel, she rattles off the names of Kent, Little Richard, Petrillo, Ellis, Crown and Springer.

"So?"

"You've identified Kent's fingerprints on the murder weapon and the car. You've identified Little Richard's fingerprints on the murder weapon. How can you rule them out?"

Ward points a finger at me and says, "Everybody—including your client—confirmed they passed the Oscar around while they were drinking champagne. That's how they got their fingerprints on the statue. There isn't another shred of evidence to connect anybody else to the attack on Big Dick MacArthur." She taps the desk with her pencil and adds, "No fingerprints, no footprints, no blood—nothing." Ward holds up her hands and begins to stand up.

Rosie isn't finished. "Come on, Nicole," she says. "Your case has a lot of holes. You're going to be embarrassed if we start pointing them out in open court."

Ward acts unimpressed. It's her turn to probe. "Like what?"

"There wasn't any blood on Angelina's arms or clothing. How could she have hit her husband with an Oscar and not been covered with blood?"

"She washed the blood off her hands. Then she got rid of her bloody clothing."

"Where?"

"Somewhere between the house and the bridge."

"Have you found it?"

"No."

"Why didn't she get rid of the Oscar at the same time?"

"I don't know."

We act out our respective roles for a few more intense minutes. Ward remains firm. Rosie rifles through the file folders. She points out that Angel, Little Richard, Petrillo, Ellis, Crown, Springer and Kent were all at the house late into the night. "Surely," she says, "you must have considered the possibility that somebody may have come back?"

"Of course. There is no evidence to connect anybody to MacArthur's death."

It's a standoff. We aren't going to get the charges dropped in Ward's office. I'm about to respond when I see Rosie lift her hand slightly. It's time to regroup.

As we're leaving, I look at Lisa Yee and say, "Can I see you for a minute?"

She darts a quick glance toward her boss and says, "I think Nicole should be there if it involves this case."

"It involves a drug charge against a young man named Benjamin Taylor."

Yee steals another look at Ward, who nods. Yee says, "I'll meet you in my office in five minutes."

# Chapter 23

## "My Hands Are Tied"

> Our office has put a high priority on prosecuting drug dealers. We intend to take a hard line to try to stem the flow of the hallucinogenic known as Ecstasy.
>
> —A.D.A. Lisa Yee
> *San Francisco Chronicle*. Monday, June 7

Rosie asks, "So, what did you think?"

We're standing in the hallway just outside Lisa Yee's office a few minutes later. Yee is still with Ward. "About what?" I ask.

"Scott Kent."

"I think he's a decent guy who is going through a tough time. I'd like to believe him. It must be difficult to consider the possibility that his father committed suicide."

Rosie nods. "But?"

"We have to take what he says with a certain amount of skepticism. Put yourself in his shoes. Your father's body was found the day before yesterday. You're having enough trouble dealing with his sudden death. The last thing you want to do is try to come to grips with the fact that he may have killed himself." I reflect and add, "I saw it when I was a priest. People won't acknowledge that possibility until they're confronted with solid evidence. It's human nature."

She nods, but doesn't say anything.

I ask, "What about Little Richard? He had a material financial stake."

"He would have been entitled to more if he had waited for his father to get divorced."

"Maybe he has some pressing obligations. And it wasn't a particularly warm and fuzzy father-son relationship."

"You and your father didn't have a particularly warm and fuzzy relationship, either. That doesn't mean you would have killed him."

"This is different. We should be looking at every possibility. At the very least, I think we should pay him another visit."

Rosie agrees with me.

I ask, "What did you think about Nicole's decision to ask for special circumstances?"

"I expected it."

"Do you think she's serious?"

"Probably. It's also a negotiating ploy. She's trying to put more pressure on Angel. We'll have to deal with it."

I see Lisa Yee coming toward us. I turn back to Rosie and say, "I'm going to talk to her about Ben's case. Do you have time to sit in with us?"

"No. I have to make a couple of calls. Then I need to talk to Angel."

"BENJAMIN TAYLOR is a drug dealer," Lisa Yee says to me. She's sitting behind a beat-up metal desk in the windowless office that she shares with another young A.D.A. She adds, "I get paid to prosecute drug dealers."

"He's a kid, Lisa. He's never been arrested. He's never even had a traffic ticket."

Mountains of paper cover her desk and her mismatched file cabinet. Her dry cleaning hangs in a cellophane bag on a nail hammered into the back of her heavy wooden door. An overworked fan is losing the battle against the eighty-five-degree heat. A brown-bag lunch sits in her open briefcase on the linoleum floor. Her diploma from Hastings hangs on the wall just above her desk. She graduated with highest honors and could have landed a job with any firm in town. She's sitting in this stuffy office because she wants to put the bad guys away. She tugs at the cotton blouse that is sticking to her skin and says, "He was selling Ecstasy, Mike."

"You don't know that for sure."

"We have an eyewitness."

"Whom you've granted immunity to testify against him."

"It's part of the process. We're trying to slow the distribution channels. Do you have any idea what a serious problem we have with this drug?"

"As a matter of fact, I do. It's dangerous stuff." I opt for a tone of reason. "Look," I say, "he's prepared to admit he had some in his possession, but he wasn't selling. You've got a shaky case. A wobbler at best." In the vernacular of the Hall, a "wobbler" is a case that falls in the gray area between a misdemeanor and a felony. The D.A.'s make the final call. "You'll never get a felony charge to stick."

Yee isn't buying. "He was carrying a plastic bag with a hundred tablets."

"They were in a backpack somebody handed to him right before the police arrived."

She smirks. "Promise me you're going to come up with something better than the old line about your client having been left holding the bag."

This isn't going well. "If he was selling, why did he have only twelve dollars in his pocket?"

"He wasn't a good salesman. Besides, it was early."

"It was three in the morning."

The corner of her mouth turns up. "That's when most raves are getting started."

I feel old.

"Besides," she adds, "Ecstasy is cheap. You have to sell a lot of it to make real money."

It's true. That's one of the attractions of the drug. I try again. "And you really intend to charge a nineteen-year-old kid with a felony?"

"Yes."

I take a deep breath. I hold up my hands and say, "Lisa, how are we going to fix this?"

She strokes her chin and says, "We can't."

"Be reasonable. Charge him with possession. Put him on probation. I'll convince him to do some community service."

She repeats, "We can't."

I don't like her tone. "What's this all about?"

She's less than convincing when she repeats, "It's our job to put away drug dealers."

"Lisa," I say, "this is just between us. You must have more interesting things to do with your time than to prosecute first-timers. What's really going on here?"

She points toward her door and says, "Shut it."

I do as I'm told. The room can't possibly get any stuffier. I wait.

Her eyes turn serious. "This stays in this room."

"Understood."

She points toward the ceiling and says, "This comes from above."

"Nicole?"

"Higher."

There is nobody higher in the Hall. "Who?"

"The mayor."

What? "Since when does he get involved in prosecutorial decisions?"

"He did in this case."

"Why?"

"He's taking a lot of heat. The *Chronicle* did a series about how we're supposedly soft on drugs. They said we're running a halfway house and not a prosecutor's office. It's an election year. The mayor got all hot and bothered and called the chief. He called Nicole and told her to tighten the screws—particularly in cases involving raves and late-night parties. Anything involving coke, heroin and Ecstasy is getting prime-time play. The kids who were picked up last weekend are going to get their chops busted."

This is bad news. The chance that reason will prevail goes down tenfold where the politicians try to use a case to make political capital. "What else is going on here?"

"Nothing."

I'm not so sure. "Come on, Lisa. We've always been straight with each other. Does it have anything to do with old grudges between Nicole and Carolyn?"

She gives me an indignant look. "Absolutely not." Her eyes lock onto mine. "Their personal history has no bearing on this case."

I believe her. I try once more. "How can we fix this, Lisa? Some decent people are going to get hurt. Lives are going to get ruined."

"My hands are tied, Mike."

"What would you do if it were your kid?"

"Try to encourage him not to deal drugs."

I deserved that. "What's it going to take to make this go away?"

Her frustration seems genuine when she says, "Have him plead guilty to a felony. I'll recommend a light sentence."

"He'll end up in jail with a bunch of real drug dealers."

"It's the best I can do."

"It's insane."

"Tell that to the mayor."

Dammit. Tell that to Ben. And to Carolyn.

# Chapter 24

## "Say It Like You Mean It"

I expect civility in my courtroom.

—Superior Court Judge Elizabeth McDaniel
Remarks to new admittees to the California Bar

Judge Elizabeth McDaniel peers over the top of her reading glasses at Angel and asks, "Do you understand the charges against you, Ms. Chavez?"

The temperature in the hushed courtroom is only slightly lower than it was in Lisa Yee's office, and it smells like the locker room at the Embarcadero YMCA. Reporters jockey for position in the jury box. Jerry Edwards is in the front row, wearing the same suit he had on during *Mornings on Two*. Little Richard is in the first row of the packed gallery. Nicole Ward is sitting at the prosecution table along with Lisa Yee.

Rosie is at the lectern. I'm standing at the defense table next to Angel, who is wearing an orange jumpsuit. She looks like any other accused felon. Her lifeless eyes turn to Rosie, who nods. Angel whispers, "Yes."

Judge McDaniel is a gregarious woman in her mid-fifties who came to the law after her children were grown. She jettisoned her husband, finished first in her class at Hastings and took a job with a big law firm. Bored with the endless paperwork in civil cases, she moved to the D.A.'s office and worked her way up to the head of the narcotics division. She was appointed to the bench about five years ago. She seems to enjoy her work as much as anybody in this building. She's also something of a mother hen. In a tradition she started when she was a D.A., she throws a holiday party every year to introduce the young prosecutors to the judges and other members of the legal community. It's considered an honor for a defense attorney to get an invitation. I got to go once. Rosie gets invited every year.

Judge McDaniel's round face takes on a serious cast. "Ms. Chavez," she says, "I'm going to have to ask you to speak up so our court reporter and I can hear you." Even though she's lived in the Bay Area for more than three decades, you can still catch the hint of a southern accent in her voice. If you ply her with a couple of double Scotches, she'll regale you with stories of her proper upbringing in rural Alabama. She gives Angel a sympathetic smile and adds, "I'm not as young as I was when I woke up this morning."

There's a smattering of chuckles in the gallery. The reporters who cover the legal beat consider it a perk to be assigned to Judge McDaniel's courtroom.

I whisper to Angel, "You'll have to talk a little louder."

Angel turns to the judge and says in a voice that is now too loud, "Yes, Your Honor."

"Thank you, Ms. Chavez. And your attorneys have explained to you that the charges include special circumstances?"

At least she didn't say death penalty. Angel closes her eyes. She looks as if she's in a trance. I take her by the arm and whisper, "You have to answer her, honey."

Angel's eyes are still closed as she whispers, "Yes, Your Honor."

Judge McDaniel leans forward and gives me an inquisitive look. "Your Honor," I say, "Ms. Chavez understands the nature of the charges."

The judge nods and says to Angel, "Ms. Chavez, I need you to enter a plea."

Silence. All eyes turn toward Angel. I can hear the buzz of the clock at the back of the courtroom. Angel swallows and gives Rosie a desperate look. Rosie nods and Angel faces the judge. Her lips form the words, "Not guilty," but no sound comes out of her mouth.

Judge McDaniel takes off her reading glasses and gives Angel a patient smile. "I'm sorry, Ms. Chavez," she says. "I need you to talk a little louder."

Angel's eyes are filled with unrelenting fear. She shoots a helpless glance at Rosie, who comes back to the defense table. I hear her whisper into Angel's ear, "Say it like you mean it."

Angel is struggling to fight back tears. She's wiping her eyes with a tissue when she says in a broken voice, "Not guilty, Your Honor."

I take Angel's hand and gently assist her into her seat.

Judge McDaniel nods. "Thank you, Ms. Chavez." She makes a note and then recites for the record that a plea of not guilty has been entered. She puts her reading glasses back on and studies her calendar. Without looking up, she says, "If there is no other business, we should set a date for a preliminary hearing."

Rosie interrupts her. "There are a couple of items we'd like to discuss, Your Honor."

The reading glasses come off. "Yes, Ms. Fernandez?"

Rosie walks to the lectern. "We would ask that the prosecution be ordered to comply with discovery before the preliminary hearing, and preferably by the end of this week."

The judge looks at Ward and says, "Any problem, Ms. Ward?"

"That's tight," she says.

Rosie says, "They're talking about a capital offense, Your Honor."

Judge McDaniel doesn't hesitate. "Sounds fair to me. So ordered. What else, Ms. Fernandez?"

"We'd like to request bail."

"I understand my colleague Judge Vanden Heuvel wasn't really excited by the idea."

"That's true," Rosie says. "In fact, she denied our request."

The judge smiles. This is a bad sign. The scouting report says you're in trouble if Judge McDaniel does it. You're in *serious* trouble if she starts to use the royal we. She says, "We have a great deal of respect for Judge Vanden Heuvel's judgment."

Rosie reads the tea leaves. I catch a tiny grimace in the corner of her mouth. "So do we. But we were hoping you might reconsider in this case."

Ward leaps to her feet and says, "Objection, Your Honor."

Judge McDaniel motions Ward to sit down. "We'll hear from you in a moment." Her smile gets wider. It's almost impossible to engage her in meaningful debate while she's giving you that grandmotherly grin. You feel like an ass and look like a fool. The reporters eat it up. "Ms. Fernandez," she says, "we understand Ms. Chavez was arrested at the parking lot at the Golden Gate Bridge. This suggests she was attempting to flee."

"There are serious questions about exactly how Ms. Fernandez got to the bridge," Rosie says. "We believe the evidence will ultimately demonstrate she was driven there."

Ward's up again. The judge tells her to sit down. Judge McDaniel leans back in her chair and says, "We understand your position, Ms. Fernandez. Nevertheless, one of the issues we're required to consider is whether the accused is likely to flee. We must tell you that based upon what we've seen so far, it seems Ms. Chavez has a propensity for flight."

"Your Honor," Rosie says, "my client is willing to surrender her passport and submit to regular status checks. She's prepared to wear an electronic wrist or ankle bracelet so the police can monitor her whereabouts. She'll abide by limitations on her movement and a curfew. Ms. Chavez can't possibly leave town without being recognized. You have her word—and mine—that she'll appear in court when called upon."

Judge McDaniel points to Ward and says, "Your turn."

Ward stands and says, "Your Honor, the defendant was actively fleeing when she was picked up. She was driving under the influence of alcohol and drugs at three in the morning. If she hadn't passed out at the bridge, she might have left the country. She may have cash or other assets in bank accounts in other parts of the world. She's already attempted to run. If you let her leave again, we may not be able to find her."

Rosie reiterates that Angel will cooperate with the authorities and will not flee.

The judge leans forward and folds her hands. Her smile disappears. "Ms. Fernandez," she says, "we've known each other for a long time, haven't we?"

"Yes."

"And you've appeared in our courtroom regularly over the last few years, haven't you?"

Rosie nods.

"And we've given you the benefit of the doubt on more than one occasion, haven't we?"

"Your Honor has been very fair."

Judge McDaniel points a finger at Rosie and says, "I'd like to be able to give you the benefit of the doubt in this case. But I have to weigh the interests of your client against the possibility that she might flee. In addition, I have to consider the seriousness of the charges. As you know, Ms. Fernandez, I'm not supposed to grant bail in a capital case."

It's true. The penal code says a judge can't grant bail in a capital case where the proof of guilt is evident or the presumption thereof is great. As a practical matter, this means judges don't do it. I've seen a judge grant bail in a death penalty case only once, and it was subject to strict limitations.

Rosie gives the correct response. "Your Honor," she says, "in the interest of justice, you always have the discretion to grant bail. We believe you can make a legitimate determination that the proof of Ms. Chavez's guilt is not evident and the presumption thereof is not great." Rosie then launches into a discussion of why the evidence against Angel is shaky.

Judge McDaniel takes in Rosie's argument without saying a word. Then she looks at Rosie and ends it by saying, "With all due respect to you and your client, Ms. Fernandez, it is the judgment of this court that the proof of guilt is evident enough and the presumption thereof is great. Bail is denied."

The air leaves Angel's lungs. I hold her hand as she struggles to catch her breath. Then her head drops down into her chest and she starts to cry.

"Your Honor," Rosie implores, "Ms. Chavez is not a flight risk."

"I've ruled, Ms. Fernandez."

The first big call goes against us. Strike one.

Angel is shaking. Her breaths are coming in gasps. I put my arms around her shoulders. Rosie gives me a troubled look. Then Angel lifts her head, looks straight at the judge and shouts, "Judge McDaniel, if you leave me in jail, they're going to kill me!"

The gallery erupts. Judge McDaniel bangs her gavel only once. The courtroom becomes completely silent, except for the sound of Angel's muffled sobs. The judge points her gavel at Angel. There is no maternal grin now. "Ms. Chavez," she says, "if you want to remain in my courtroom, you're going to have to address us through counsel. Do you understand?"

Tears stream down Angel's face as she whispers, "Yes, Your Honor."

The judge points her gavel first at me and then at Rosie. "I trust the two of you will ensure that we won't see another outburst of this nature?"

"Yes, Your Honor," we say in unison.

Rosie is still standing at the lectern. "Your Honor," she says, "as a precautionary measure and in the interest of my client's safety, I would ask you to instruct the deputies to keep Ms. Chavez in administrative segregation. She needs her own cell."

Ward jumps up again. "Your Honor," she says, "while we always have concerns about the safety of the prisoners in our facilities, we believe the defendant should not be afforded any special privileges simply because she is famous."

"Your Honor," Rosie says, "Ms. Chavez was attacked before she was placed in her own cell. Surely, you can order that she be kept outside the general prison population."

Judge McDaniel is unhappy. "We are concerned about Ms. Chavez's safety. I will discuss this matter in chambers with the deputies."

Rosie asks, "Does that mean you'll arrange for Ms. Chavez to stay in her own cell?"

The judge isn't giving an inch. "That means I'll talk to the prison authorities to make arrangements to ensure her safety."

Although she remains outwardly calm, I can see the frustration building in Rosie's eyes. This is not going well. She keeps pushing forward. "Your Honor," she says, "we have one other issue."

"And that would be?"

"There will be a private memorial service for my client's husband tomorrow. His ashes will be scattered at sea." She leaves out the part about the fireworks.

"And?"

"We would request that Your Honor permit Ms. Chavez to attend the service."

Ward won't hear of it. "Objection, Your Honor. Bail has been denied. There is no authority to permit such an action. There are no standards for accommodating such a request."

"Your Honor," Rosie says, "we aren't challenging the court's ruling on bail. On the other hand, in the interest of fundamental decency and fairness, we would ask you to make arrangements to accommodate this request."

If you have no real authority, you cite fundamental decency and fairness.

"Your Honor," Ward says, "this is an extraordinary request. It's outside the realm of accepted procedure. We would have to make special arrangements with the police and sheriff's deputies. Surely Your Honor cannot expect us to go to such extraordinary means."

Judge McDaniel takes in Ward's diatribe with measured stoicism. Then her wide mouth rearranges itself into a subdued frown. The judge turns to Angel and says, "Ms. Chavez, do you have anything to say about this?"

Angel had been staring straight at the table in front of her. She looks up at the judge and says in a cracking voice, "He was my husband, Your Honor. I want to say good-bye."

"Are you willing to pay for the cost of police overtime to allow you to do so?"

"Yes, Your Honor."

Ward can barely contain herself. "Your Honor," she says, "this is highly irregular. At the very least, I believe you should hear from members of the victim's immediate family to determine whether they feel it is appropriate for the defendant to attend this memorial service."

Judge McDaniel's head swings back to look at Ward. She says, "Ms. Chavez *is* the victim's immediate family."

"I think we should hear from other family members—those who are not accused of murder."

Rosie leaps back in. "Your Honor—"

Judge McDaniel holds up her hand. She looks at Ward and says, "Is there a family member available to address this issue?"

"Mr. MacArthur's son is in the courtroom."

Judge McDaniel ponders for a moment and says, "Well, this is unusual, but in the interest of fairness, I guess we should hear what he has to say." She looks at the gallery and says, "Would Mr. MacArthur please identify himself?"

All eyes turn to the front row of the gallery. Little Richard stands slowly. He's dressed in a dark suit. In a measured voice, he says, "Your Honor, under the circumstances, the MacArthur family believes it would be inappropriate to include the defendant at the memorial service. We believe it would not be respectful of my father's memory."

Angel leaps to her feet. She points her finger at Little Richard, who is only a couple of feet from her. "You have no right to judge me," she hisses. "Everything you have you owe to your father. You never showed the slightest respect. You were just trying to get his money."

Judge McDaniel bangs her gavel and calls for order. Young MacArthur looks at Angel and says in a tone that drips with contempt, "Everything *you* have you owe to my father. He found you on the street. He gave you a place to live. He gave you money and he put you in his movies. And you turned around and killed him."

"That's not true," Angel cries.

Ward shouts, "Your Honor!"

I step between Angel and Little Richard. The courtroom buzzes. Judge McDaniel bangs her gavel. Angel is sobbing.

Order returns a moment later. Little Richard is sitting with his arms crossed, a smug look on his face. Angel is at the defense table, her hands clutching a tissue. Judge McDaniel turns to Rosie and says, "Do you wish to add anything further at this time?"

"Your Honor," Rosie says, "in the interest of fundamental decency, we respectfully request that arrangements be made to allow Ms. Chavez to attend her husband's service."

Judge McDaniel stops to think. The stifling courtroom is silent. The good-natured smile is long gone. After a few long moments, she turns to Angel and says, "Ms. Chavez, I believe it would impose an undue burden on the authorities to permit you to attend your husband's memorial. In addition, I think it would be in everybody's best interests if you focused on your defense. As a result, I'm ruling that you may not attend your husband's service."

Rosie tries once more. "Your Honor—" she says.

Judge McDaniel holds up a large hand and says, "I've ruled, Ms. Fernandez."

Strike two.

Angel is starting to shake. Then she starts breathing heavily. Rosie comes over from the lectern and holds her. "Everything's going to be all right," she repeats. Then she turns to the judge and says, "Can we take a brief recess?"

Judge McDaniel holds up an index finger and says, "I think we can finish our business in another thirty seconds." She studies her calendar for a moment and says, "Preliminary hearing one week from today at two o'clock." She looks at Ward and says, "I assume you'll be ready to move forward next week, Ms. Ward?"

"Yes, Your Honor."

Judge McDaniel turns to Rosie and says, "Is that acceptable to you, Ms. Fernandez?"

Rosie gives her a halfhearted nod. "Yes, Your Honor."

Judge McDaniel looks at her calendar and adds,"Judge Leslie Shapiro will be presiding."

*Shit.* I catch Rosie's eye. She doesn't acknowledge me. She is whispering to Angel as she's led from the courtroom.

Judge McDaniel bangs her gavel and says, "We're adjourned."

Strike three. The disaster is now complete.

## Chapter 25

# "I'm Never Going to Get Out of Here Alive"

Angelina Chavez pled not guilty to first-degree-murder charges this afternoon. A preliminary hearing has been set for next week before Judge Leslie Shapiro.

—KGO Radio
Monday, June 7, 4:00 p.m.

"We have to talk," I say to Rosie.

We're standing in the crowded corridor just outside Judge McDaniel's courtroom. Angel is being taken back to the jail wing.

Rosie doesn't look at me when she says, "Later."

The media throng surrounds us. I catch a glimpse of Nicole Ward standing on the other side of the hallway. I hear her tell a reporter that Judge McDaniel acted with great prudence. Rosie and I express mild disappointment about the decision on bail. Then we offer the usual platitudes about the strength of our client's case. We assure the cameras that we'll be ready for the preliminary hearing. "We expect Ms. Chavez to be fully exonerated," I say.

A reporter from Channel Five shouts, "What do you know about Judge Shapiro?"

More than you could imagine. "We've had several cases in her courtroom over the years," I say. "We have great respect for her. She's a conscientious and thoughtful judge." She's also beautiful and terrific in bed. And there isn't a snowball's chance in hell she'll be handling Angel's prelim next week.

"Is your client willing to consider a plea bargain?"

Rosie answers, "No." Then she grabs my arm and adds, "We have no further comment."

We push our way through the mob and open the heavy door to the stairway. It's quiet inside, and we stop at the landing. I ask, "What about Leslie?"

"I'm sure you'll be hearing from her."

"What do you want me to do?"

Rosie shoots me a stern look. "The two of you created this problem. You're going to have to figure out a way to fix it."

ANGEL'S VOICE is lifeless when she says, "I'm going to die in here, Aunt Rosie." Her panic-stricken look in the courtroom has given way to an air of resignation. Dried tears cover her face. Her shoulders slump. The windowless cell is barely ten feet by four. The Plexiglas door reminds me of a fishbowl. There're a built-in cot, a sink and a toilet without a seat. A deputy walks by to check on her every ten minutes.

Rosie takes Angel's hands and says, "We'll get you out of here."

"No, you won't."

"Yes, we will. You'll have to be patient."

"It doesn't matter anymore. The deck's stacked. I'm going to take the fall."

Rosie repeats, "No you won't."

"Yes, I will. My life is over. Even if you get me off, they're going to kill me."

"Who?"

"I don't know. Dick's son. Petrillo. Ellis."

"They can't get to you."

"Yes, they can—if somebody here doesn't get to me first."

"Nobody will hurt you."

"I can't hide in this cell forever. Eventually, they'll put somebody in here with me. That will be the end."

"That won't happen."

"Yes, it will."

Rosie tries to encourage her, but loses the battle. Finally, Rosie says, "Angel, you've been through difficult situations before."

"Nothing like this."

"That's true. But I need you to be strong. I need you to call on everything you have inside. You have to stay smart and see this through."

"I can't."

"You have to. You're going to make it."

Her demeanor takes on an eerie calm. She's almost serene as she says, "It's nice of you and Mike to help. But you know it as well as I do. I'm never going to get out of here alive."

"SHE'S GIVING UP, Rosie," I say. We're standing just outside the intake center.

Rosie's eyes turn to steel. "She's stronger than you think. She made it through her mother's problems. She'll rally. You'll see."

"I hope so."

"I know so." She reflects for a moment and asks, "Were you able to reach Leslie?"

"Not yet. I left a message."

"What are you going to do?"

"It's a conflict of interest. One of us is going to have to withdraw from the case."

She turns to me and says in her best lawyer-voice, "It isn't going to be us. There's too much riding on it, and Angel won't trust anybody else."

She's right, of course. "I know."

"That leaves you with only two options. Leslie can do the right thing and withdraw or you two are going to have to stop seeing each other."

She's trying to let me down easy. "Actually," I say, "you know as well as I do that even if we break up today, there is no way she'll hear this case. We can argue till we're blue about whether it's a technical conflict of interest under the rules of professional conduct. At the end of the day, it doesn't matter. It smells. It has the appearance of a conflict. It gives us grounds to challenge the validity of the prelim. She knows it. She has to recuse herself."

Rosie swallows hard and says, "Do you think she will?"

"Yes."

"What's the best-case scenario for her?"

"Nobody will find out we've been seeing each other."

"And for you?"

I reflect for a moment and say, "We'll continue seeing each other."

Rosie gives me a skeptical look. "What do you think will happen?"

"She'll withdraw."

"I was referring to your relationship."

"So was I."

The corners of her mouth turn down. "I'm sorry, Mike."

"Me, too."

"It's an unusual situation."

"That it is." I pause and tell her, "You should give me some credit."

She gives me a puzzled look. "How's that?"

"I've come up with a new and unique way to screw up a relationship. I should get some points for creativity."

"You may have outdone yourself." She puts her hand on my arm and smiles. "Are you going to be all right?"

Same old story. There are a few things in life you can count on: death, taxes and Mike Daley never gets the girl. "I'll be fine."

We're about to open the door to leave the intake center when I see Rolanda walking in our direction. There's an unmistakable look of determination in her eyes when she says, "I've been trying to find you for the last hour. We have to get down to my father's market."

"We were going to meet with Dennis Alvarez at five," I tell her.

"We need to go now. My dad called. He said he thought somebody was watching him. And he said he couldn't talk about it on the phone."

# Chapter 26

## "Work with Us"

We haven't ruled out arson as the cause of a suspicious fire at Peña's Liquors in the Mission District.

— Sergeant Dennis Alvarez, KGO Radio
Monday, June 7, 4:00 p.m.

Tony takes a toothpick out of his mouth and says, "Everything's changed." He, Rolanda, Rosie and I are sitting on wooden crates by the loading dock at the back of his market at four o'clock. The aroma of fresh vegetables surrounds us. Rosie is eating an apple. I'm studying a photo of the burnt-out liquor store two blocks from here on the front page of the afternoon paper.

I ask Tony, "Did they figure out what happened down the street?"

"Arson. It went up like a sheet."

"Who did it?"

"It was a professional job. They'll never catch anybody." He scowls and adds, "Roberto's family has run the store for thirty years. Now they'll have to start from scratch."

I hope they had insurance. "Who paid for the hit?"

"I'm not sure."

"Did you talk to Armando Rios?"

"He told me everything would be fine and to keep my mouth shut."

No surprise. I ask, "Was Roberto talking to the cops?"

"Probably. Where do you think this leaves me?"

In serious trouble.

Rolanda asks, "Have you talked to Sergeant Alvarez?"

"Not yet. I wanted to talk to you first."

"You said there was something else."

"There is." He opens a manila envelope and removes a stack of Polaroids. He hands them to Rolanda and says, "Don't get scared, honey."

She studies the photos for a moment, and her face turns ashen. "Where did you get these?" she asks her father.

"Somebody dropped them in the mail slot earlier today. I didn't see who it was."

I ask to see the pictures. Rosie and I study them together. The first is a photo of the liquor store. The second shows Rolanda leaving our office. In the third, she's entering her apartment. Next she's getting into her car. The last is most disturbing. It shows her walking into Tony's store. There is a red circle around her face with a line drawn through it. There's a computer-generated note that says, "Smart people know when to keep their mouths shut."

Rolanda looks at us, but doesn't say a word. Tony heaves a sigh and says, "You see why I didn't want to talk about this by phone."

I ask, "Have you seen anybody around? Have you noticed anything suspicious?"

Tony shakes his head.

Rosie turns to Rolanda and asks, "Have you?"

She swallows hard and says, "No."

Rosie chews on her lip. "We need to be careful."

I'll say. If I were in their shoes, I'd be a basket case.

Tony asks, "You're the legal geniuses. What do we do now?"

Rosie and I exchange glances. "Call the cops," Rosie says. "We need to talk to Dennis Alvarez. We don't have the firepower to deal with this on our own."

Tony tosses his toothpick into the trash. "They've torched one store," he says. He looks at his daughter and adds, "They're watching us. What makes you think they can protect us?"

I say, "It comes down to a matter of whom you trust."

"I don't trust anybody."

Rolanda sounds just like Rosie when she says, "Mike's right. You've known Dennis since you were kids, Dad. Do you trust him or the thugs who burned down Roberto's store?"

Tony puts his hand on his daughter's cheek. "You're all I have left, honey," he says.

Her voice cracks as she says, "Everything's going to be fine, Dad."

"From your lips to God's ear."

"Let's go see Dennis."

ALVAREZ STUDIES the photos of Rolanda. He asks Tony, "Any idea who took these?"

"No."

We're in the consultation room at Mission Station. Tony is sitting in a wooden chair. Rolanda is next to him. Rosie is standing by the door.

Alvarez looks at Rolanda and says, "Have you noticed anything unusual?"

"No."

Alvarez sighs. "We'll check the photos for prints. They're Polaroids, so we won't be able to track them through the photo-development shops. I assume you touched them?"

We nod in unison. Alvarez tells us we may have smudged any usable prints.

Tony folds his arms and says, "What are we going to do about this, Dennis?"

"I'll arrange for police protection for both of you," he says. He pauses and adds, "I still need you to help us."

Rolanda isn't impressed. "I assume that's the same deal you offered to Roberto Peña."

Alvarez's mustache twitches as he does a quick internal calculus of what and how much he should tell us. "Yes, it is," he says.

Rolanda is visibly upset. "His store is smoldering, and we've been threatened."

"We'll protect you."

"Just like you protected Roberto?" Rolanda points a finger at Alvarez and says, "Those are photos of *me*."

Alvarez's hands ball up into fists. "His situation was different. He has a big mouth. He must have said something to the wrong person. Word got out that he was going to cut a deal."

Tony's face takes on an air of resignation. "How do you know he didn't give them my name? What makes you think they didn't follow us here?"

"It won't happen to you," Alvarez says.

"How can you be sure?" Tony asks. "They didn't just pull my name out of a hat. They sent me the pictures of Rolanda. They must know I'm talking to you."

"I won't let you or Rolanda leave this building without a police guard."

Tony says, "I can't walk around with an army. I have a business to run."

Rolanda adds, "And I have a law practice. Why don't you guys haul in Armando Rios for questioning?"

"We did."

"And?"

"He called his lawyers and didn't say a word. He was back on the street in an hour."

I offer, "Why didn't you arrest him?"

"We don't have enough evidence."

Rolanda is indignant. "Sure you do. You have my father's testimony. Now you have these pictures."

Alvarez shakes his head. "Your father hasn't agreed to testify yet. And we have no way to connect him to the photos."

Tony says, "What if I'm willing to testify that he offered me money?"

"It isn't enough. He didn't deliver the money himself. He used an intermediary."

Tony's irritation is showing. He says, "So you won't arrest him unless you catch him in the act of handing me a bag of cash?"

"We need more than your word against his. And we want to pressure him to give us the name of the bankroll."

"You want me to run and hide?"

"We want to protect you." He turns to Rolanda and says, "And you."

Tony turns stone-cold silent. We wait. Alvarez looks at his watch. Rosie and I glance at each other.

Alvarez grimaces. "I'm running out of time, Tony. They've already taken a shot at one of your neighbors. I want to nail these guys before they hurt somebody."

Tony holds up his hands and says, "What do you want me to do?"

"Work with us. Tell us what you know. Find out who's bankrolling Armando Rios."

"How?"

"Tell Rios you want to talk. You're unhappy about the fire at Peña's store. You don't like being threatened and you want assurances."

"And if he won't meet with me?"

"He will."

"And you'll want to record our conversation."

"Ideally, yes."

Tony eyes Alvarez and says, "Forget it. I won't wear a wire."

"You don't have to."

"And where will you be?"

"We'll have a dozen people outside. We'll protect you."

"And if he doesn't tell me anything?"

"We'll have to come up with something else."

Rosie asks, "Are you prepared to offer a deal to Rios?"

Alvarez hesitates for a moment. "Maybe."

Rosie points a finger at him and says, "That's not good enough. You have to give Rios something. He's going to want immunity before he points the finger at anybody."

"I can't make any promises."

Tony picks up the cue and says, "Then I'm not going to talk to him. I don't have a death wish." He points a thumb toward Rolanda and adds, "If you arrest me, my lawyer here will instruct me not to say anything to you. Then I'll give an exclusive interview to Jerry Edwards at the *Chronicle*. I'll tell him you're busy harassing small-business owners in the Mission. Wait till that finds its way onto page one."

The airless room is completely silent. Dennis Alvarez folds his arms and looks up at the ceiling. Finally, he says, "I may be able to get immunity for Rios if he's willing to tell us who bankrolled the bribes." He pauses for a moment and adds, "I'll have to clear this with my captain and the D.A.'s office."

We're starting to make progress. I hand him my cell phone. "We can wait," I say.

Tony stops to think. He looks at Rolanda. "I have some other conditions," he says.

Alvarez frowns. "What are they?"

"I get full immunity. Rolanda will negotiate the terms of my agreement. I want a cop sitting in my market and a squad car in front of my apartment twenty-four hours a day until this is over. I need a squad car sitting in front of Rolanda's apartment and in front of her office. I want to know the names of the other businesses you've talked to. I don't want any of them to sell me out without my knowing about it."

Alvarez hesitates for an instant and says, "Done. Anything else?"

Tony says, "I want a squad car in front of my mother's house." He looks at Rosie and adds, "And I want the Larkspur police to put a black-and-white in front of my sister's house."

Alvarez shakes his head. "You're asking for a lot."

"I'm giving a lot."

"Is that it?"

"That's it."

Alvarez nods. "How soon can you talk to Armando Rios?"

"I'll call him as soon as you tell me your captain has approved my conditions and I see that black-and-white parked in front of my market."

"DO YOU THINK Tony's doing the right thing?" Rosie asks. We're crawling through traffic up Mission Street toward the office. Rolanda stayed with Tony to work out the details of his immunity agreement. The captain at Mission Station feigned great reluctance before he agreed to give immunity to Armando Rios. So did Nicole Ward. It was an act. There are bigger fish to fry than Tony and Armando.

"He had no choice," I say. "Now he has something to offer Rios. They can walk together or they can both get arrested. I'd be inclined to do what Tony did."

Rosie sighs. "I don't want anything to happen to Tony or Rolanda."

"Neither do I."

"I'm not sure they can protect them."

"I know. The sooner he cuts a deal with Rios, the better. We'll make sure it gets into the *Chronicle* right away. Jerry Edwards will start asking a lot of questions. They'll be watching everybody who may have been involved. Between the cops and the press, somebody will be watching Tony twenty-four hours a day. It's not a perfect shield, but it's as good as we can do, short of putting Tony and Rolanda into the federal witness protection program."

"I still don't like it."

"Neither do I, but it's the best we can do for now, Rosie."

She nods.

My cell phone rings and I answer. "I heard you had a busy day," Pete says. The reception fades out as we pass under the freeway. Then he fades back in.

"Where are you?" I ask.

"Camped out near Little Richard's house. I've moved down the street. I'm up in a tree."

It's better than being up a creek, I suppose. "What can you see?"

"The front door of his house."

I ask him if Little Richard had any visitors today.

"Armando Rios stopped by a few minutes ago."

Really. "Sounds like he's reporting in. Who else?"

"Cheryl Springer."

"She's spending a lot of time over there."

"They're bonding. I presume she wanted to talk about the release of the movie."

"Who else?"

"Eve."

The omnipresent Eve. "Any idea why she was there?"

"She comes by every day. That seems to be her job."

I ask Pete if he found out anything else.

"I talked to the caterers. There's good news and bad news."

I hate it when he plays these games. "What's the good news?"

"Nobody saw Angel kill Big Dick."

"Good work, Pete. What's the bad news?"

"Nobody saw anybody else kill Big Dick, either."

Helpful. "Anything else?"

"One of the caterers was out in the garage when Marty Kent arrived. The door was open. She said Big Dick met Kent on the driveway and let him go out for a drive in his new Jaguar. That means—"

"The prosecution has an explanation for Kent's fingerprints on the steering wheel."

"Right."

This doesn't help. "What else?"

"I tracked down Kaela Joy Gullion."

I can't resist. "How does she look in person?"

"Even better than she looked on the sidelines."

"Where did you find her?"

"In a tree."

"Excuse me?"

"You heard me."

I hope he's kidding. "The same tree you're sitting in?"

"As a matter of fact."

I ask what she's doing there.

"Same thing I'm doing—watching Little Richard. She wasn't really happy to see me at first, but then I offered her a beer and she was more receptive."

I picture my brother sitting in an old oak tree pounding Buds with the ex-cheerleader. "Is she willing to talk to us?"

"Yeah."

"When?"

The phone goes silent for a moment. Then he gets back on the line and says, "Tonight. After we're sure Little Richard and his teddy bear are in bed." He hesitates for an instant and adds, "I'd guess that would be around one."

Another long night. "Deal."

"Meet us at the Edinburgh Castle."

It's an old pub just north of City Hall. "I'll see you there." I pause for a moment and ask, "Did you find out anything else about the memorial service?"

"The boat from the Neptune Society is leaving at one o'clock tomorrow."

"Do you have any idea who will have the privilege of seeing the remains of Richard MacArthur Senior get shot up in fireworks?"

"We'll find out tomorrow. Joey D'Augustino said he'd take us out on his boat."

Perfect. Joey is a retired cop who bought a fishing boat a few years ago. It's always nice to know somebody with connections at the wharf.

# Chapter 27

## "Do You Really Think There's a Heaven?"

Richard MacArthur died from a blow to the head. Martin Kent drowned. His injuries are consistent with those of a person who had jumped from the Golden Gate Bridge.

—San Francisco Chief Medical Examiner Roderick Beckert
KGO Radio. Monday, June 7. 7:00 p.m.

"What are you doing?" Rosie asks me.

"Looking at the crime-scene photos. I thought it would be a nice break after I finished reading the police and autopsy reports."

We're back in the office. It's almost eight o'clock Monday night. My head is starting to throb. I can't believe we've been working on this case for less than seventy-two hours. The first few days after an arrest are critical. Memories fade quickly.

She tries to cheer me up. "You're a fun guy."

"It was this or the Giants' game. And you know how much I love the gruesome stuff."

This gets the hint of a smile. "We're cranky tonight, aren't we?"

"I'm just tired."

She turns serious. "So am I."

Something's wrong. "What is it, Rosie?"

She tries for an offhand tone. "Test results."

Uh-oh. "And?"

Her lips form a tight ball. Then she says quickly, "Not great news."

My stomach begins to churn. "Bad news?"

Her tone remains flat. "Not necessarily. You know the drill. More tests."

She's holding something back. "When?"

"Soon."

"I'll come with you."

"I might take you up on that."

"Rosie, if you don't have time to deal with Angel's case right now—"

"I'll be fine. It's better to stay busy. It takes my mind off . . ." She hesitates and adds, ". . . the other stuff."

Beautiful Rosie. I remember the day they found the first little spot on the X ray, and how she calmly described it in clinical terms. She told me she'd be fine. She was going out with the guy from the D.A.'s office at the time, and she wouldn't let me stay with her that night. Grace told me later Rosie stayed up and cried all night. "If we need to get more help—"

"Not yet."

I try once more. "Rosie, you really need to take good care of yourself right now."

"Please don't lecture me."

"It's been a long day. Why don't you go home?"

"In a little while. I have some work to do. It's going to be a busy week."

Tell me about it. "Do you want to talk about it?"

"Angel's case?"

"Yours."

She scrunches her face and says, "Not right now."

I've learned not to push. She'll tell me when she's ready. "Maybe tomorrow?"

"Maybe." She looks out the window at First Street. The night law-school classes are in session at Golden Gate University around the corner. A few of the students are out for a break. She gets a faraway look and says, "I may need to take a break after we finish Angel's case."

She may need one a little sooner. The concept of slowing down is very difficult for her. Me, too. "That's a good idea."

"I don't look anything like those young and eager law students across the street. I've been doing this for almost twenty years. Maybe it's time to recharge my batteries."

"Maybe." She turns back to me and I see tears in her eyes. "What is it, Rosie?"

"I'm starting to feel old. I don't like it."

"I started to feel old ten years ago."

She gives me a weak smile. "I don't mean this in a negative way, Mike, but you have an old soul. It's something I've always loved. Maybe it was the years as a priest. You've always seemed older and wiser than your chronological age."

"I feel much older than I look. And you'll always be young and beautiful to me."

Her eyes take on a melancholy cast. "You're sweet," she says. "And you're a lousy liar."

"You just said I have wisdom beyond my years."

"You do. But you're still a lousy liar." She reflects for a moment and says, "So, is it okay with you if I take a break after Angel's case is done?"

"Sure."

"I promise I won't break up Fernandez and Daley."

"Whatever you decide will be fine with me."

"You could take a break, too. Have you given any more thought to the dean's offer?"

"Some."

"And?"

"It might be fun to be a professor for a while."

"You're seriously thinking about it?"

"Yes."

She smiles. Then she changes the subject. "What did you find in the pictures?"

"About what you'd expect." I give her the highlights. Somebody attacked MacArthur from behind, and he fell off the deck. The autopsy results are exactly as Nicole Ward described them. He died from a blow to the back of the head. Kent was a suicide.

"Any chance Dr. Beckert might reconsider his conclusion on Kent?"

"I doubt it. I've known him for twenty years. He's never changed his mind. Not once."

"What else?"

"The neighbor's story checked out. And the interviews with the caterers confirmed that MacArthur let Kent take his car for a test drive. The blood analysis and the prints on the Oscar checked out, too."

"We aren't getting to reasonable doubt at lightning speed," she observes.

"No, we're not."

"What about Eve?"

"The police talked to her. She said she was at Little Richard's house early in the evening. Then she went home. She lives in the Marina, not far from Kent."

Rosie asks, "And the security tapes from the Golden Gate Bridge?"

"We'll go through them as soon as we get them. Where's Rolanda?"

"With Tony. They've agreed on his immunity agreement."

"Good. What happens next?"

"Tony is meeting with Armando Rios tomorrow morning at Rios's office."

"I assume it will be surrounded by police?"

"Enough to bring down a small third-world country."

"What if Rios has his own militia?"

"World War Three will break out." Rosie considers and says, "I don't think he'll bring soldiers. It's not his style. He's a manipulator, not a fighter. Besides, he knows Tony has been talking to the cops. He isn't an idiot. He knows he's being watched."

"What angle do you think he's playing?" I ask.

"We'll find out tomorrow."

"Where's Tony staying tonight?"

"His house. Rolanda is with him. There's a squad car in front and another in the back."

"Sounds like Dennis is being true to his word."

"I hope so. I told Tony we'd go with him to see Rios."

"Sounds like fun."

"He seemed to appreciate the offer." She says, "You'd better watch your backside."

"You, too."

She gives me a sardonic grin. "That's the beauty of having a serious illness, Mike. It simplifies your life. You spend so much of your time and energy worrying about getting well that you don't have a chance to fret about other things."

She has a unique perspective on every element of life. It shouldn't surprise me that she would have an interesting angle on cancer. "Tell you what," I say. "I'll worry for you. I got a lot of practice. We spent a whole semester on it at the seminary."

Her grin broadens. "I thought priests were supposed to get all excited about going to heaven."

"Maybe that's why I'm not a priest anymore. Let's just say I may not have had quite as much enthusiasm about the concept as some of my former colleagues. Just because you're a priest doesn't mean you have to go looking for trouble."

She turns serious and says, "Do you really think there's a heaven, Mike?"

I pause to think about it. Then I say, "Yes."

"Are you sure?"

"Pretty sure."

"What if you're wrong?"

"A lot of people are going to be very disappointed after they die. I'll be one of them."

She isn't letting it go. "What's the first thing you want to do when you get there?"

"I'd like to spend some time with my dad. There were a few things we didn't get around to talking about."

"What sorts of things?"

"I'd like to thank him for trying so hard. We had our ups and downs, but as I get older, I realize he gave it everything he had." I think for a moment and add, "And I want to yell at him because he didn't take better care of himself and he never quit smoking."

"Anybody else?"

"I'd like to let my mom know that Grace is doing okay. She worried. I'd like to spend some time with my older brother. It would have been nice to have seen what he would have done with his life."

"He must have been special," Rosie says.

"He was." I can still picture Tommy in his football uniform at Cal. I'll never forget the way he pitched the ball into the stands when he scored the winning touchdown in his last big game against Stanford. He was gone a year later. He could have played in the NFL. "You would have liked him. He was good-looking, athletic and very funny."

"Was he better looking than you?"

"Maybe a little."

"You miss him, don't you?"

"Yes, I do. He was only a year older."

We sit in silence for a few minutes. Then Rosie asks, "Did you talk to Leslie?"

"Not yet. She hasn't returned my call."

"Why is she waiting?"

"She's probably considering her options."

"No doubt."

I look at my watch. Eight o'clock. "Gotta run," I say.

"Where are you going?"

"To interview a witness."

"Who?"

I point through the windows down to First Street. Rosie gives me a confused look. "They sent a limo to pick you up?"

"I wish. The witness *drives* the limo."

"You're going to interview him in the limo?"

"It's a her. And why not? I asked her if she would show me where she took Petrillo and Ellis. Besides, she promised to stock the bar."

"She agreed to do this for free?"

"No, I had to rent the limo."

"How much?"

"Ninety bucks an hour. I figured she might be more willing to talk if I paid her."

"You're a marvel."

I wink and ask, "Want to come along for the ride?"

"I don't think so."

"Come on, Rosie. There's no charge for an extra passenger. When was the last time you were in a limo?"

"When we got married."

"Well, it's time to do it again. It's in the line of duty. Grace is staying with Melanie and Jack. Besides, I'll bet there's a bottle of champagne in the fridge. Let's go down and toast the glorious day we've had today."

Her smile broadens. "Why the hell not?"

## Chapter 28

# ALLURE1

A Touch of Luxury. A Reflection of Good Taste.

—PROMOTIONAL BROCHURE
FOR ALLURE LIMOUSINE SERVICE

THE LIMO DRIVER points toward Big Dick's house and says, "That's where I picked up Mr. Petrillo and Mr. Ellis."

Rosie and I are sitting in the back of a black Lincoln with livery license ALLURE1. The sun is setting. The gates are locked and the house is dark.

"What time did you pick them up?" I ask.

Her name is Bridget. She's a wiry woman who speaks with the hint of a lilting Irish brogue. She told us her parents started the limo service about ten years ago. She and her brother run the operations now. She turns around and says, "It was about one forty-five."

This jibes with Petrillo's timeline. "Did you take them straight to the Ritz?"

"No."

Rosie's eyes get bigger. She asks, "Where did you go?"

"First we went to the Golden Gate Bridge."

Really. "Why?"

"It was on the way, and Mr. Ellis wanted to see it. First I took them down to Fort Point. Then I took them to the lot by the toll plaza.

"Would you mind showing us how you got there?"

"Sure." She starts the car and drives down North Twenty-fifth. She turns left onto Lincoln Boulevard, and it takes us only a couple of minutes to drive up the winding hill through the Presidio. We head past the entrance to Baker Beach and Battery Chamberlin. Then we go by the administration building and swing under Doyle Drive. She follows the narrow access road down to Fort Point and stops near the spot where Marty Kent's body was found Saturday morning.

I ask, "Did Mr. Ellis or Mr. Petrillo get out and walk around down here?"

"No. They just took a look from the car."

"Where did you go from here?"

"Up to the parking lot at the bridge."

We retrace our route back up the hill. She turns onto Lincoln Boulevard and then makes a quick right into the parking lot. It's dark now and the fog is rolling in. She pulls in next to the spot where Angel was found on Saturday morning. "Where did you park?" I ask.

She turns off the ignition and gestures toward the snack shop. "Over there," she says.

"Was anybody else around?"

"A couple of cars. It was late."

I ask if either Ellis or Petrillo got out of the car.

"Both. They took a walk." She points toward the south tower. "They went past the souvenir shop. Then they came back. The gate to the pedestrian walkway was locked. They couldn't get out onto the deck." She says they were at the bridge for only about five minutes.

"And then you took them both back to the Ritz?"

"Yes." She confirms they both got out of the car there.

"And as far as you know, did they both stay at the hotel the rest of the night?"

The young woman tugs at the black bow tie that hangs loosely around her neck. "Mr. Petrillo went upstairs," she says. "Mr. Ellis stayed in the lobby."

"How do you know?"

"I went inside to use the bathroom. I know the doorman. It was late and he lets me leave the car in the driveway."

"And?"

"I saw Mr. Ellis as I was leaving. He asked me if I had time to take him somewhere. I told him I had to pick up a client at the airport and I was already running late. I offered to call another one of our drivers, but he said he'd take a cab."

"Do you know where he wanted to go?"

"Back to Mr. MacArthur's house."

*What?* "Did he say why?"

"No."

Seems decidedly odd. "Did he make it back to Mr. MacArthur's house?"

"I don't know."

"Do you know the name of the doorman who was working Friday night?"

"Graham Morrow."

I ask if he's working tonight.

"I think so."

"Maybe you could take us over to the hotel so we can have a word with him."

MORROW IS A BLOND Adonis with wide shoulders that look as if they could support the Golden Gate Bridge. He studies Ellis's photo and says in a congenial Australian accent, "Sorry, mate. I'm not allowed to talk about our guests. Company policy."

I try to keep my tone patient. "We're not asking you to reveal any secrets. We just want to know whether he left the hotel after Bridget dropped him off on Saturday morning."

He holds up his gloved hands. "I can't help you, mate. Company policy."

"Let me talk to the manager."

He returns a few minutes later with an officious young woman who looks like she got her M.B.A. about three weeks ago. She reminds me of Sister Karen Marie Franks, my third-grade teacher at St. Peter's. Her name tag says Sally Todd. "I'm sorry," she tells us. "We don't discuss our guests unless we have permission to do so. Company policy."

We have a company policy at Fernandez and Daley. If you won't talk to us when we ask nicely, we come back with a subpoena. I try sugar. "Ms. Todd," I say, "we simply want some information from Mr. Morrow. We really don't want to come back with a subpoena."

"I'm sorry, Mr. Daley. I have no choice."

I give her a melodramatic sigh. "Have it your way." I flip my cell phone open and punch in the number for the office. When Carolyn answers, I say, "Could you put together two subpoenas for me, please? And could you run the standard background checks on a Sally Todd and a Graham Morrow?"

I get the response that I expect. "What the hell are you talking about, Mike?"

I put my hand over the mouthpiece. I turn to Graham and Sally and say, "May I have your exact legal names please?"

The manager turns white. The Aussie gives her a panicked look. "Look, mate—"

I stop him. Then I catch the hint of a grin on Rosie's face. She decides to get into the act. She lays it on thicker when she tells them, "We'll need your social security numbers, too."

Sally Todd freezes. If she tries to explain this to her corporate superiors, she'll be working nights for twenty years. She asks,"What do you need to know, Mr. Daley?"

It's nice to know you can still get away with a bald-faced bluff every once in a while. "We'd like to know whether Mr. Ellis left the hotel after he was dropped off a few minutes after one o'clock on Saturday morning."

The manager looks at Morrow and says, "Did you see him?"

"Yes."

"Tell Mr. Daley what you know."

I hold the phone back up to my ear and say, "Carolyn, I don't think we'll need those subpoenas after all."

"You're completely full of shit," she says.

"Yes, I am." I snap the phone shut. Rosie's eyes are gleaming. I turn back to my new buddy and say, "Did Ellis leave the building?"

Young Crocodile Dundee squints into the evening air. The congenial tone returns when he says, "Yeah, mate."

I ask, "Do you know where he went?"

He scratches his chin and decides, "No, mate."

"Do you happen to recall the cab company that picked him up?"

"Same one we always use. Veterans."

Now for a shot in the dark. "Do you know the name of the cabdriver?"

"I know every cabdriver in town. It was Joe Lynch."

Another lead. "And were you here when he got back?"

"Yes. It was a few minutes after three."

"Did he return in the same cab?"

He hesitates for just an instant. "No. He wasn't in a cab."

Really? "How did he get here?"

"Somebody gave him a ride in one of those fancy SUVs, mate."

"What make?"

"I think it was a Lexus."

I ask him if he remembered who was driving.

"I'm not sure, mate."

I'm going to throttle him if he says the word *mate* one more time. "Do you recall if it was a man or a woman?"

"A woman."

"What did she look like?"

"Young. Pretty. Long dark hair. Kind of exotic-looking."

I steal a glance at Rosie. Her eyes catch mine. She mouths the name, "Eve."

I look at Graham Morrow and say, "Thanks, mate."

## Chapter 29

## Joe Lynch

> Driving a cab is just a temporary gig.
>
> —Veterans cabdriver Joe Lynch

Rosie and I are standing in the lobby of the Ritz a few minutes later. I take out my cell and call four-one-one to get the number of Veterans Cab. Then I punch in the number and wait. A guttural voice answers, "Veterans. Please hold."

Rosie gives me an inquisitive look. I tell her, "The guy who answers the phone sounds just like Louie from *Taxi*." She smiles.

The voice returns a moment later. "Veterans."

I ask, "Is Joe Lynch driving tonight?"

I hear him clear his throat. Then he shouts to somebody, "Did Lynch check in?"

"Yeah."

He says to me, "He's driving. You want him?"

"Yes please. The Ritz."

"Name?"

"Mike."

"Five minutes."

Unlike his dispatcher, Joe Lynch speaks in a lush baritone with an elegant British accent. "I drive the cab to pay the bills," he says. "I'm studying to do radio voice-over work."

Rosie and I are in the back seat of Veterans cab 714. We're heading up Pine Street for our second trip to Sea Cliff in the last hour. I miss Bridget's limo. Listening to Lynch's lyrical inflections is a small consolation for the tired shocks and the bumpy ride. He's a talker. It doesn't take much to get him started.

"How long have you been driving?" I ask.

We're doing almost fifty in a thirty zone, and he turns around to look at me through dark brown eyes. His closely cropped gray hair and trim mustache contrast with his ebony skin. "Sixteen years," he says. Thankfully, he turns back to look at the road just before we barrel into a double-parked delivery truck.

He reminds me of people in New York and L.A. who describe themselves as actors or actresses, even though they've been working for the phone company "temporarily" for twenty years. "Where are you from, Joe?"

"The British Virgin Islands."

That explains the accent. "You have a very distinctive voice."

"We were poor, but my mother insisted that we learn to speak properly." Without prompting, he tells us with enormous pride that his daughter is in medical school at USC.

We're heading west on Geary through the Richmond District when I try to ease him into a discussion of business. "Do you recall what time you picked up Mr. Ellis at the Ritz?"

"Around two."

"Where did you take him?"

"A house in Sea Cliff. I'll show you." He turns right onto Twenty-fifth Avenue and heads north for a few blocks. Then he takes a left onto El Camino del Mar, just before Twenty-fifth Avenue turns into the North Twenty-fifth Avenue cul-de-sac.

Rosie asks, "Wasn't the house on North Twenty-fifth?"

"No. It was on El Camino del Mar." He drives west for a couple of blocks and stops in front of Little Richard's house. "That's it," he says.

Rosie and I exchange glances. What the hell was Ellis doing here? I ask, "What time did you get here?"

"A quarter after two."

"Was anybody still awake?"

He pulls into a no-parking zone across the street and turns off the ignition. "The lights were on. He didn't ask me to wait for him."

"So you didn't drive him back to the hotel?"

"No."

"Are you pretty sure about those times, Joe?"

"I remember it clearly" He smiles. "I was hoping he was going to ask me to wait."

"Why?"

"He gave me a twenty-dollar tip on a twelve-dollar fare. I was hoping I'd pick up another twenty on the way back."

WE'RE BACK in my office at ten o'clock. Joe Lynch dropped us off a few minutes ago and in a moment of whimsy, I gave him a twenty-dollar tip. He gave me his private number. Rosie is stationed in her favorite spot on the corner of my desk. "Listen to this," I tell her.

I punch in the buttons to summon my voice mail. After skipping ten messages from TV and newspapers, I get to the one I want. "Michael," Leslie's voice says, "call me as soon as you can. I'll be waiting up for you." She leaves her cell phone number.

I look at Rosie and say, "So? What do you think?"

"Tough to tell. It's pretty cryptic."

"Care to make a prediction?"

"No way."

"I'm not optimistic," I tell her.

"You never know," she says. We sit in silence for a moment. Then she gets back to business. "Okay, Sherlock, why did Ellis go to Little Richard's house at two in the morning?"

"I assume they wanted to talk about the China Basin project."

"And was it really Eve who took him back to the Ritz?"

"Probably. Who else would Little Richard have called?"

"How soon can you get down to Vegas?"

"Tomorrow or Wednesday."

"What are you going to do now?"

"I need to talk to Carolyn. Then I'm meeting Pete at the Edinburgh Castle."

"Isn't that a little late for a drink?"

"I'd stay up all night for a chance to meet Kaela Joy Gullion in person."

# Chapter 30

## Kaela Joy

I didn't set out to become a private investigator. It just worked out that way.

—Kaela Joy Gullion
Profile in *San Francisco Chronicle*

First, I have to deal with Leslie. I punch in her number and wait. The next thing I hear is, "Hello, Michael."

*Bad vibes.* "How did you know it was me?"

"Intuition." She hesitates and says, "You know I've been assigned to Angelina's prelim. It's a conflict of interest." She pauses for another beat and adds, "We need to talk."

"Yes, we do."

"I can't do it tonight, and I don't want to do it by phone."

*Really bad vibes.* "Neither do I."

"How about tomorrow night? It might be better if we get together someplace where we aren't likely to be seen."

I suggest her place. She says that isn't a good idea. I feel like a teenager trying to sneak out of my parents' house. We settle on a sushi place in the outer Richmond.

I ask, "Is there anything we should talk about now?"

"We'll talk tomorrow, Michael."

"Thanks for talking to Ben," Carolyn says to me a few minutes later.

"Everything will get worked out."

"I hope so. I talked to Lisa Yee again. She's still planning to file felony charges."

So much for my impassioned plea for leniency. While Rosie and I have been running around trying to gather information, Carolyn has been doing the real legal work on Angel's case. She's spent the last two days preparing subpoenas and document requests. It's a tedious but vitally important job. We're sitting in Rosie's office at eleven o'clock.

"I'll talk to her again," I say.

"The prelim is Thursday."

"I talked to Randy Short. He's up to speed if we need him."

She exhales.

I take her hand and say, "We're going to fix this, Caro."

KAELA JOY GULLION could pass for a professional basketball player. The former Niners' pompom girl's sculpted, six foot two inch frame reflects a lot of time at the gym. Black jeans hug her endless legs. The onetime model has a creamy complexion, with full lips and high cheekbones. You would have to look closely to figure out she's in her mid-forties. Her shoulder-length auburn hair is covered by a black stocking cap. She and Pete look like cat burglars. She takes a draw from her Guinness and says, "The late Richard MacArthur was an asshole."

That covers it. I catch Pete's eye. He smiles and says, "Tell us what you really think."

Her face rearranges itself into the smile that graced the covers of glamor magazines twenty years ago. She pulls off her hat and shakes her long locks. If Dominic Petrillo thinks Angel's smile lights up a room, he ought to see Kaela Joy's.

We're hunkered down near the dartboards in the back of the Edinburgh Castle, an old pub on Geary between Larkin and Polk, in what was a fashionable neighborhood a century ago. Now the area is called the Tenderloin, and the Castle is surrounded by peep shows. It isn't fancy, but it has, well, ambiance. A long bar runs the length of the narrow room, which smells like Guinness. Although there is no kitchen, they'll send somebody around the corner to fetch some fish and chips if you're hungry. In what passes for entertainment in this part of town, they used to bring in a guy who played his bagpipe on Saturday nights. He retired a few years ago, and they haven't found a replacement. It's just as well. It was noisier than the disco bowling that Grace inflicts upon me every once in awhile.

"How did you hook up with Millennium Studios?" I ask.

"The head of security was on the Niners' practice squad for a few years. I helped him with his divorce. He hired me to do some work in Southern California."

I like her already. "What did you find out about Dick MacArthur?"

"Those horror stories are true." Her tone is businesslike. She orders a second Guinness and fills us in on the gory details. "He was a creep," she says. "He had illegitimate children all over the world. He got what he deserved." She takes a sip of her beer and adds, "Your client was getting royally screwed. He made her sign a one-sided prenup. She'll never see a penny of his money." She holds up her hands and says, "She's just a kid. He was using her. I know what it's like to be married to an asshole." The venom in her voice is striking. Although it seemed funny when Kaela Joy dropped her ex-husband with one punch in a Bourbon Street bar after she caught him with another woman, the episode must have been very difficult for her.

She's just warming up. "MacArthur's son is a bigger schmuck than his father," she says.

The schmuck genes run in the MacArthur DNA. I ask, "Why are you talking to us?"

She smiles at Pete and says, "I like your brother. Our jobs will be a lot easier if we help each other. Your client's a sweetie and somebody's setting her up to take the fall. It isn't right."

I'd like to believe her.

"Look," she says, "I'm not doing this out of the goodness of my heart. You seem like nice-enough guys, but I'm also looking out for my client's interests. Her arrest fouls up the marketing plan for the movie." She turns dead serious when she says, "Petrillo knows I'm here. He told me to cooperate. I wouldn't be talking to you if he didn't say it was okay."

I ask, "What can you tell us about Petrillo?"

"I can't reveal anything confidential."

"What can you tell us that isn't confidential?"

She grins. "He's an asshole, too—a very smart one."

"Why did he get in bed with MacArthur?"

"He's good at making movies."

"There are other good people who are lower maintenance."

She gives me a knowing grin. "Have you spent much time in L.A.?"

"Some."

"In the movie business, they expect you to be an asshole. It's in the job description. You get slaughtered if you aren't. MacArthur was no worse than most people in the industry. Petrillo looked at the bottom line. The script worked, and he had a director who could do it. So he green-lighted the movie."

"And all that stuff about problems on the set?"

"All true. And completely irrelevant. Movie stars don't need to get along with their directors. Petrillo wanted to get the movie in the can. Everything else was window dressing. He didn't give a rat's ass if Dick and Angelina were screaming at each other every day."

Such a delicate way with words. "Is he going to release the movie on time?"

"Of course."

"He told us he might delay because of Big Dick's death."

Her eyes open wide. "Oh, bullshit. They'll get a lot of free publicity and play it for all it's worth. They'll ramp up the marketing budget and issue a press release saying it would be a fitting tribute. They'll put Richard Junior on the *Today* show and take out ads in *Daily Variety*. Even if the movie is a dog, it will gross fifty million its first weekend."

"And the rumors about reworking the script and recasting some roles?"

"That was never going to happen. The movie was over budget. Do you really think they were going to go back and shoot the damned thing again?"

Got it. "Is Petrillo still planning to proceed with the studio?"

"As far as I know."

"Were he and MacArthur getting along?"

"Are you asking me whether my client was pissed off enough at MacArthur to have him murdered?"

I like her style. "Essentially."

"Get real. Petrillo can be as offensive as MacArthur was. They both had huge egos and treated everybody like crap. But there's a difference between being a jerk and being a murderer. Petrillo is vicious and greedy, but he operates within the law—at least as it applies to the movie business." She gives me a wink and adds, "Besides, I don't represent murderers."

A pasty-faced bartender who looks as if he just got off the boat from Glasgow comes over and tells us it's last call. I pay him for the beers. Except for a couple of guys playing darts, we're the only people here.

I ask Kaela Joy, "What about MacArthur's son?"

"He's a twit."

"I know. What's his angle?"

"Money. He's going through another divorce. He has a lot of overhead. He's already paying alimony to his first ex-wife, he has a couple of fancy vacation homes and he likes to refurbish classic sports cars. He's a decent producer, but he fancies himself a movie director. He didn't want to see his father's fortune get tied up in what he called the 'Pipedream by the Bay.'"

"He wants to kill the China Basin project?"

"Absolutely. As they say in the real estate business, the numbers don't pencil out. He didn't want to blow his inheritance on a money-losing deal."

"He can back out."

"It will cost him millions. There is a side letter to the development agreement that makes it very expensive for anybody to pull out. He'll get back pennies on the money his father put up and have to ante up a five-million-dollar penalty to the other investors."

"He's stuck."

"Maybe not. He won't have to pay the penalty if the deal isn't approved."

"Are Ellis and Petrillo prepared to buy him out?"

"They'd do it in a nanosecond, but they'll have a problem. They won't be able to find another tenant for two hundred thousand square feet before the hearing on Friday. The redevelopment agency may decide to withhold the approvals. They're looking for a backup tenant. In the meantime, they want to get the approvals and move forward."

"And if young Richard pulls out after they get the approvals?"

"They'll deal with it when the time comes."

It's more complicated than I thought. "What are the chances they'll get the approvals?"

"Fifty-fifty."

That's why somebody was paying gratuities to the businesses in the Mission. I ask, "Does Angelina have some say in any of this?"

"She might. Under the will, she gets half of MacArthur's assets, including half of the stock of MacArthur Films. They may not be able to rework the deal without her approval."

Sounds as though Angel may have a lever. "Do you think MacArthur's son could have killed his father?"

"He certainly had financial motive, and they didn't get along."

"Is there any evidence?"

"He was there late, and his fingerprints were on the Oscar."

I tell her about his visit from Carl Ellis later that night. She says she wasn't aware of it. I ask her about Kent.

"He was a very unhappy man. Apparently, he was never the same after his wife died. And he was pissed off about the China Basin project. He thought Ellis and Petrillo got a much better deal than they deserved. He didn't think MacArthur Films was going to be able to meet its financial commitments. And he had personal assets at risk."

"Is it possible something set him off on Friday night?"

She grins. "You never stop trying, do you? Why don't you just come right out and ask me whether he was mad enough to have killed Dick MacArthur?"

I bite. "Okay. I'm asking."

"You left out the part where he framed your client and committed suicide."

"That, too."

She rests her perfect chin on her right hand and leans across the table. She leaves no doubt when she says, "No."

"Why not?"

"Why would he have framed Angelina if he was going to kill himself?"

Why, indeed? I pause to regroup. Then I ask, "Was Kent trying to squelch the deal?"

"No. He wanted to make sure it went forward."

This runs against everything we've heard so far. I ask why.

"They had already signed the development agreement. But there was a silver lining in it for him. He had negotiated a success fee for himself. He was promised a three-million-dollar bonus for obtaining the approvals."

"I didn't see anything about it in the development agreement."

"There was nothing in writing. It was a handshake. Evidently, Kent had drained most of his assets on bad investments and experimental treatments for his wife. He needed the money. There were rumors he was paying off local businesses to buy their support."

I play dumb. "Are the rumors true?"

She gives me a coy look. "I don't know. Jerry Edwards seems to think they are."

"And Petrillo and Ellis had nothing to do with this?"

"Petrillo didn't. I don't know about Ellis."

It's unrealistic to think she'd implicate her client. Yet I find it hard to believe Kent was doing this all on his own—especially if he was running low on cash. "Is it possible MacArthur's son was involved?"

"Maybe, although if you believe he was against the deal, I don't think he would have been paying people off to ensure that it moved forward."

I'm not sure I accept the premise that Little Richard was working against the deal, although her explanation of his financial situation suggests she may be right. I ask her about Daniel Crown and Cheryl Springer.

"Springer cares about only one thing: getting the movie released on time. She doesn't want her husband's money to be used to fund the China Basin project."

"Do you think it's possible she may have had something to do with MacArthur's death?"

"They found her fingerprints on the Oscar. She and her airhead husband left the party and drove home. Otherwise, I can't connect her to MacArthur or to Angelina."

Another loose end. She looks at her watch. It's almost two. She says, "I understand Rod Beckert decided Kent killed himself."

"That's true."

"What do you think?"

"I don't know."

She says, "Surely you must have a theory."

"Not yet. I'd like to think he killed MacArthur, framed Angelina and jumped off the bridge, but I can't prove any of it. Until we can come up with some evidence, the police and the D.A. will call it a suicide." I pause for an instant and then go fishing. "What do you think?"

"I don't know."

I put it right back to her. "Surely, *you* must have a theory."

"I might." She finishes her beer and answers with a question. "Guess where I was Friday night?"

I already know. "The MacArthur house."

"Who told you?"

"Petrillo."

She smiles. "He wanted me to keep an eye on Ellis. There were rumors that Big Dick and Ellis were going to try an end run on the China Basin project to squeeze out Millennium."

Sounds as though everybody was trying to screw everybody else. I ask her what she saw on Friday night.

"Ellis left with Petrillo in the limo. I assume they went back to the hotel together."

"Did you follow them?"

"I couldn't get to my car soon enough. It was parked a couple of blocks away."

I ask, "Where were you hiding? Down on the beach?"

"No. I would have been too easy to spot. I was in the bushes on the east side of the house, next to the path leading to the beach." She assures us that nobody could have seen her.

I ask her if she could see the deck.

"No. I couldn't see much of the front of the house or the driveway, either."

"Do you know when everybody left?"

"For the most part." She says Ellis and Petrillo left in the limo at one forty-five and Springer and Crown left around two. "I'm not sure when Kent or Richard Junior left."

I think about my conversation with Joe Lynch. I wonder if Little Richard and Ellis went back to Big Dick's house. If they walked, Kaela Joy probably wouldn't have seen them and may not have heard them. I ask her if anyone else came over to Big Dick's house after Springer and Crown left.

"Not that I'm aware of."

"Did you hear any cars after Springer and Crown left?"

"I heard a car pull up around two-fifty. I think somebody was picked up, but I don't know who. I heard another car pull out about twenty after three. I don't know who was in it."

Now we have two cars that are unaccounted for. Angel or Kent or even Little Richard or Ellis could have been in either one. "Was the second car MacArthur's new Jag?"

"I don't know."

So close. "Have you talked to the police?"

"I told Inspector O'Brien everything I know. By the way, he said your client is guilty."

"Do you agree with him?"

"If I did, I wouldn't be here trying to help you."

I finish my Guinness and say, "You said you had a theory about Kent."

"I heard footsteps around three. Somebody walked down the path to the beach."

"Could you see who it was?"

"I didn't get a good look."

"Man or woman?"

"Man."

"Do you have any idea who it was?"

"I'd guess it was Kent."

"WHAT DID YOU THINK?" I ask Pete. We're standing outside the Edinburgh Castle watching Kaela Joy Gullion saunter down Geary. The homeless people and night owls give her a wide berth. She's the embodiment of the term "Don't mess with me."

Pete tugs at his mustache. "I believe her."

So do I. "Sounds like the movie is going to be released on time. That leaves the studio project. If she's right, Big Dick and Kent wanted in and Little Richard wanted out."

"Yep. And it seems Ellis and Petrillo are in, but it's hard to tell whose side they're on. Maybe they're in together and they're trying to screw everybody else."

"Maybe." I'm struggling to fight the fatigue. I ask, "What about the cars?"

"The first one may have been a cab. The second one was probably the Jag."

"Who was in them?"

He smiles and says, "If we knew the answer, we'd have this case solved, wouldn't we?"

True enough. "Do you think it was Kent who walked by Kaela Joy?"

"Probably."

"Where was he going?"

"To the bridge to commit suicide."

I'm inclined to think he's right. And you can bet that's the argument Nicole Ward will make. Pete's cell phone rings. He answers it and hands it to me. "Rosie," he says.

Why is she calling on Pete's phone? I grab it and ask, "Are you and Grace all right?"

"Yeah." She sounds exhausted. "I've been trying to reach you."

I pull my cell phone out of my pocket and realize the battery is dead. "It's after two."

"I know. Where are you?"

"Polk and Geary," I say. I tell her we were talking to Kaela Joy.

"You can tell me about it later. How soon can you meet me at San Francisco General?"

"Right away. Is your mother okay?"

"She's fine."

My mind races. "Tony? Rolanda? Theresa?"

I hear her take a deep breath before she says, "Angel tried to commit suicide."

Oh God. "Is she going to be all right?"

"I don't know."

"They were supposed to be watching her. How could they have let this happen?"

Rosie keeps her composure. "I'll meet you at the hospital."

"I'm on my way."

## Chapter 31

# "She Really Wanted to Die"

> Angelina Chavez has been admitted for treatment. We will provide additional information as it becomes available.
>
> —Spokesman for San Francisco General Hospital
> Tuesday, June 8. 3:00 a.m.

I hear Rosie telling Theresa that she'll call her as soon as she can. Then she snaps her cell phone shut and gives me an exhausted frown.

"How is Angel?" I ask.

We're standing next to a police guard outside the intensive-care unit at San Francisco General. The drab corridor at the public hospital smells of industrial-strength disinfectant and brims with activity.

Rosie's eyes are red, and her voice is barely a whisper. "She really wanted to die. She lost some blood, but they think she's going to be okay."

Thank God. "Do they know how she did it?"

"She cut her wrist. I don't know how she got her hands on something sharp."

"Somebody was supposed to have been watching her."

"They were. She was under a blanket. The guard saw blood after she passed out."

I ask if she left a note.

"They found a scrap of toilet paper." Rosie's voice cracks. "There were only five words: I didn't kill my husband." She buries her head in my shoulder. I hold her tightly. My arms are still around her as we walk into the waiting area. I help her into a seat and give her a drink of water. The television is tuned to Channel Four, but the sound is off. I see a headline that says Angel attempted suicide. Rosie slowly regains her composure. We sit in silence.

A short time later, a young resident in a white coat approaches us and says, "Your niece is conscious, Ms. Fernandez. She's going to be all right. She lost some blood, but her injuries were relatively minor. She was very fortunate."

"Can we see her?"

"For a few minutes, but please keep it short. She's very tired." The doctor hesitates and says, "Ms. Fernandez, we discovered some slight irregularities in her blood work."

Rosie darts a glance in my direction. "What sort?"

"At first we thought she was pregnant, so we ran a few more tests. Then she told us she had terminated a pregnancy about two weeks ago."

"An abortion?"

"No, Ms. Fernandez. A miscarriage."

Rosie closes her eyes. She reopens them slowly and asks, "Will she be able to have children?"

"We think so. There doesn't seem to be any permanent damage. We'll need to run more tests. So far, everything appears to be within normal ranges."

Under the circumstances, normal ranges are good. I ask, "How far along was she?"

"Early. No more than six to eight weeks."

Rosie tells the doctor she'll be in to see Angel in a moment. She turns to me and says, "What am I supposed to tell Angel? What do I tell my sister?" She looks away for a moment and adds, "I can't begin to think about all the potential legal issues. The papers are going to go crazy."

I take her hand and say, "We have to focus on Angel. She needs to know that we're with her—and we always will be—no matter what. That's what we have to tell her now. As for your sister, we'll have to try to keep her calm. We'll need a lot of help from your mother and your brother. You're going to have to look after Angel—and probably Theresa. You're the only family they have. Carolyn and Pete and I will worry about the legal maneuvering and the investigation. Somehow, we'll get through this."

"Easy for you to say."

"It's the best we can do." I look into her eyes and ask, "Do you want me to come with you to see Angel?"

"It might help. Thanks."

ANGEL'S once-vibrant eyes are now a dull gray. She's wearing a hospital gown. An IV is connected to her arm. She whispers, "I really screwed up this time."

I'm standing by the door. Rosie is holding Angel's free hand. "Everything's going to be okay," Rosie tells her.

Angel looks like a teenager. Her eyes are filled with tears. "My husband is dead, Aunt Rosie," she says. "So is my baby. I'm going to rot in jail for the rest of my life."

"We'll get you out of there, honey. You have your whole life ahead of you."

"My life is over."

Rosie brushes the hair out of Angel's eyes. She kisses her forehead and says, "Why didn't you tell us you were pregnant?"

"It didn't matter anymore. The baby was gone."

"How far along were you?"

"Only a few weeks. I missed two periods."

"Did anybody else know you were pregnant?"

"Dick knew."

Rosie swallows hard and asks, "Was he pleased?"

Angel takes a sip of water. She takes a deep breath and answers, "No."

A look of alarm crosses Rosie's face. "Why not?"

Angel starts to cry. She looks at me through her tears and says, "Uncle Mike, are you still permitted to listen to confessions?"

What do I say? I can't send her down to St. Peter's. "Sure, honey."

Angel looks at me and recites, "Bless me, Father, for I have sinned."

"How long has it been since your last confession?"

"About two years."

I catch Rosie's eye. She's still holding her niece's hand. I turn to Angel and say, "What is it, honey?"

"I lost my baby, Uncle Mike."

"These things happen. It isn't a sin, and you mustn't blame yourself."

"Yes, I should."

Rosie squeezes her hand and says, "No, you shouldn't. It wasn't your fault."

"Yes, it was."

I try again. "It wasn't anybody's fault."

"But it *was* my fault, Uncle Mike. I didn't take care of myself. I didn't take care of my baby. I took drugs. I drank alcohol. God decided I wasn't fit to be a mother."

I say to her, "No, Angel. Everybody makes mistakes. You shouldn't blame yourself."

"I do. And it wasn't my only mistake."

This gets a troubled look from Rosie. She turns to Angel and says, "What is it, honey?"

Angel bites her lip, and the tears flow freely. She tries to hug Rosie, but the IV gets in the way. Finally, she blurts out, "Dick wasn't the father."

# Chapter 32

## "I Have to Ask"

> We were very saddened to hear about the suicide attempt by Angelina Chavez. We wish her a speedy and full recovery.
>
> —Cheryl Springer, KGO Radio
> Tuesday, June 8, 3:30 a.m.

It all comes pouring out. "I knew Dick was having an affair with an actress in L.A.," Angel tells us. "So I slept with another man. That's why God is punishing me. I deserved to lose my husband. And my baby." She dissolves into a torrent of tears. She sobs uncontrollably into Rosie's shoulder. Rosie rocks her tightly and whispers into her ear. I stand helplessly at the foot of the bed.

Fatigue finally overcomes Angel, and Rosie manages to calm her down. Angel drinks water and closes her eyes. Rosie leans over to her and says, "Did Dick know he wasn't the father?"

"Yes. He told me I had to get an abortion. When I told him I wouldn't, he said he'd file for divorce. He said he'd make sure I would never work in the film business again—ever." She swallows hard and adds, "Then he hit me."

Christ. I ask, "Where?"

"In the stomach. I started bleeding. I called an ambulance. The baby was gone by the time I got to the hospital."

I can feel a burning in the back of my throat. The vile bastard.

Angel lowers her eyes and says, "He didn't even come to the hospital. He said I got what I deserved. He told me I wouldn't get a cent because of the prenup. I was an idiot. I should have hired a lawyer."

Rosie's eyes are on fire. She says to Angel, "It wasn't your fault."

"Yes, it was." Angel turns to me and says, "Is there any way God will forgive me?"

One of the reasons I left the priesthood was because I felt unqualified to act as God's spokesperson. I pause with hopes that God will give me a sign. Then I quietly say, "God loves you, Angel. God will forgive you."

"Are you sure, Uncle Mike?"

"I'm sure, honey."

She nods submissively and buries her face in Rosie's shoulder. Then the doctor comes in and tells us that Angel needs to rest. Rosie negotiates a few extra minutes. She turns back to Angel and says, "Honey, I have to ask. Who was the father?"

Angel's voice is barely a whisper when she says, "Danny Crown."

My God. "Does he know?"

"Yes."

"Did you tell him about the miscarriage?"

"Yes."

"When?"

"Friday night. He was furious at Dick."

## Chapter 33

# "Crown Is Back in the Mix"

> Our sources have reported that the father of Angelina Chavez's baby was her costar in *The Return of the Master*, Daniel Crown.
>
> —Jerry Edwards, KGO Radio
> Tuesday, June 8, 4:00 a.m.

FOUR A.M. A combination of heavy sedatives and exhaustion finally caused Angel to doze off. Rosie and I are in the corridor outside the ICU where Jack O'Brien is chatting with one of the uniforms. Nicole Ward stopped by to check on Angel's condition. She informed us that the preliminary hearing will proceed as scheduled.

We told O'Brien that Angel had recently suffered a miscarriage and that Crown was the father. We explained that he was irate at Big Dick. There is no reason to hide the ball. They'll find out eventually, and it gives them another suspect. The flip side is that they'll argue the miscarriage gave Angel greater motive. The tabloids are going to love this.

Rosie and I shove our way through the reporters on the front steps of the hospital. The morning news shows will treat their viewers to my shouts of "No comment." We sit in stark silence in the car. Rosie leans back against the headrest and closes her eyes.

Things get infinitely worse when we arrive at Sylvia's house ten minutes later. Sylvia is trying to put on a good front, but Theresa is a basket case. She loses what little composure she has left as soon as we walk in the door. "Is Angel going to be okay?" she asks repeatedly. It takes Rosie an hour to calm her down. Theresa insists she has to go to the hospital to see Angel.

Rosie convinces her that she should wait until morning when Angel is awake.

Rosie and I don't sleep at all. We sit at her mother's kitchen table drinking coffee and playing out the scenarios in Angel's case. In our exhaustion, our analytical skills are substantially diminished. We discuss Daniel Crown. We talk about my conversation with Kaela Joy Gullion.

"Ward will argue she killed him because she was upset about the miscarriage," Rosie says. "The will, the prenup and the life insurance may be irrelevant."

"Do you think she did it?"

"No, I don't." Her eyes turn to brown steel. "You can bet Nicole Ward does."

I try to offer some hope. "Crown is back in the mix. He was angry about the miscarriage."

"Angry enough to kill?"

"Maybe. What about his wife? She was there. Maybe she helped him."

Rosie is still skeptical. "You think they did it together?"

"I don't know. Maybe he did it by himself, and she helped him clean up the mess. It wouldn't have been the first time."

She isn't buying it. "They left before Little Richard and Kent."

"So they say. Maybe they went back."

"There's no evidence that they did."

"Kaela Joy said a car came to the house a few minutes before three."

"We have no evidence that it was Crown and his wife. And even if they did, why would they have framed Angel?"

"Maybe she was the only one around."

"If one or both of them drove Angel to the bridge in Big Dick's car, how did they get back to the house to get their car?"

"Maybe he drove her to the bridge and she picked him up. Maybe he walked back."

Rosie is exasperated. "Our client just admitted that her husband hit her in the stomach and caused her to have a miscarriage. It doesn't just give Crown motive. It gives *her* motive, too." We finish our coffee in silence.

We leave Sylvia's house at six. I take Rosie back to the hospital and then head for home to change clothes. I'm working on my second consecutive all-nighter and my hands are shaking as I'm driving across the Golden Gate Bridge. Angel's attempted suicide is the lead story on the radio. I hear Nicole Ward say she plans to proceed with the prosecution as expeditiously as possible, notwithstanding the circumstances. She just lost my vote.

I walk into my apartment at six forty-five. I hop into the shower and try to wash away the exhaustion. The room is spinning when I get out. I notice the flashing light on the answering machine in my bedroom. I punch the button and listen to a familiar voice. "Mr. Daley, Jerry Edwards of the *San Francisco Chronicle*. We were looking for a comment on your client's suicide attempt." He pauses and adds, "We understand she was pregnant and that the father of the baby was Daniel Crown." He leaves a phone number.

The next voice I hear is Tony's. "I just wanted to be sure you're coming to my meeting with Armando Rios at nine." I walk into the kitchen and start pouring water into my coffeepot. On top of everything else, I have to be at Rios's office less than three hours from now.

# Chapter 34

## "I Want to Be Sure the Same Thing Doesn't Happen to Me"

> I'm a respected businessman in this community. I provide legitimate services to my clients.
>
> —Armando Rios. *Mornings on Two*
> Tuesday, June 8. 7:00 a.m.

"What's this all about?" Armando Rios asks Tony. Rios's self-confidence turns into measured incredulity when he adds, "First you tell me you want to see me privately. Then you bring along a crowd that could fill Pac-Bell Park."

It's nine A.M. Rosie decided to stay at San Francisco General with Angel. Tony, Rolanda and I are standing in a semicircle in Rios's office on the second floor of a restored turn-of-the-century Victorian at Eighteenth and Guerrero. Rios is a slight man in his late forties with a gleaming tan and beautifully coiffed silver hair that matches his three-piece Wilkes-Bashford suit. Business casual is not appropriate attire for political operatives. We accept his offer of coffee. Then he takes a seat behind his antique mahogany desk. Tony sits in the chair across from him. Rolanda and I find spots on the soft leather sofa.

Tony folds his arms and says, "We need to talk."

Rios scans our faces. "With all due respect, why are your relatives here?"

"They're my lawyers."

Rios studies a photo of his grandchildren on his credenza. Then he gives Tony a melodramatic frown and says, "You have a lot of lawyers."

"I like to avoid legal problems."

"And why is Dennis Alvarez sitting in a police car outside my front door?"

"He has an interest in this, too." Tony leans forward and says, "We need to discuss what happened at Roberto Peña's store."

Rios answers quickly, "It was a terrible accident. I've asked some people in the neighborhood to help him out." Although he has lived in the U.S. since he was a child, he still has the trace of an accent.

"It was arson," Tony says.

"I don't know anything about it. I understand they've initiated an investigation."

Tony's voice stays perfectly even when he says, "I want to be sure the same thing doesn't happen to me."

Rios's feigned indignation gives way to the polished politician's smile. He glances at a photo of a Little League team that he sponsored and says, "Tony, we go back a long way." His accent may be Hispanic, but his inflection is straight out of *The Godfather*. "I gave you the respect of inviting you to my office. You are not returning it. You are treating me as if I'm some sort of criminal."

Tony hasn't moved. His arms remain folded tightly against his chest. His eyes are fixed on Rios. They've known each other for four decades. Tony knows when he's being bullshitted. He lowers his voice and asks, "Are you, Armando?"

The phony smile disappears. "No."

Their eyes lock. Tony says, "We had a deal, Armando."

"I don't know what you're talking about."

"You know exactly what I'm talking about. You paid me twenty grand, and I agreed to support the China Basin project. I paid half of it to the Democratic steering committee. You were supposed to make sure nobody got in trouble. I kept my side of the bargain. You didn't keep yours."

Rios's grin makes another appearance. He gives me a quick glance and then returns his gaze toward Tony. His voice is soothing when he says, "My recollection is a little different, Tony. One of my clients asked for assistance in obtaining support for the studio project. I called upon you to help us. My client agreed to reimburse you for your time in an amount equal to ten thousand dollars. The reimbursement was paid. Our business is now concluded."

Tony doesn't like being patronized. "No, it isn't!" he snaps. "The cops came to see me. You were supposed to make sure *that* didn't happen. They know all about it, Armando. They knew all about *you*."

Rios doesn't flinch. He says in a measured tone, "I've given my statement to the police. They've made some baseless accusations about illegal political contributions."

"Which you denied."

"Of course I did, Tony. They weren't true." His face turns serious when he adds, "I'm a reputable businessman. Everything I do is subject to scrutiny. My reputation will be ruined if I break the rules. I can't afford to let that happen." He pulls a long Cuban cigar out of a humidor and caresses it with his fingers. "If the accusations were true, I would have been arrested."

I can feel my heart start to beat faster. It's one thing to arrange bribes. It's another to look your lifelong friend in the eye and taunt him. It's as if he's saying, "Catch me if you can."

Rolanda gives him an icy stare. Then she says, "Your luck is going to run out, Armando. You can't burn down every store to cover your tracks. You can't intimidate every business in the neighborhood. Somebody is going to point the finger at you."

His tone remains patronizing. "I provide services to my clients," he says. "They pay me to make sure they don't get in trouble."

"You didn't do a very good job in my case," Tony says.

Rios doesn't respond.

Rolanda shakes her head. "Work with us," she says. "Work with the police."

"I haven't done anything illegal," Rios insists.

Rolanda isn't letting up. "Dennis Alvarez says they'll give you immunity. They want to know who's bankrolling this deal."

Rios remains adamant. "I have no idea what you're talking about."

"Armando," Tony says, "I came to you because we've been friends since we were kids. You can stop this before somebody gets hurt." He pauses and emphasizes every syllable when he adds, "Next time, somebody is going to get killed."

"There won't be a next time. I regret there was a fire at Roberto's store. I hope it wasn't arson. In any event, I had nothing to do with it."

Rolanda can't contain herself any longer. "That's bullshit," she says. "Next you'll say you had nothing to do with the pictures that were delivered to my father's store."

Rios glances at Rolanda and then shoots a confused look at Tony. "What pictures?"

Rolanda answers for him. "Pictures of me. Somebody has been following me, Armando. Somebody is threatening us. We need you to tell us who it is."

Tony shows Rios copies of the photos. Rios is visibly troubled. His smug demeanor transforms into one of ashen seriousness. "Do you have any idea who took these?" he asks.

Tony's eyes are equally somber. "We were hoping you could tell us."

Rios swallows hard. "I can't."

Rolanda's patience has run out. "You mean you won't," she says.

Rios puts down the cigar and says, "I mean I don't know."

Rolanda's voice goes up a half octave when she says, "What are you talking about?"

The posturing is over. Rios's face turns deathly serious. "I don't know who is responsible for the fire at Roberto's store. And I don't know who took these pictures."

"Why should we believe you?" she asks.

"I've known your father since we were children. I was at your baptism." He lowers his voice and adds, "I was a pallbearer at your mother's funeral." He lets out a large sigh and adds, "And because it's the truth."

"Then you'll have to find out who's responsible."

"I can't."

Tony stands up and thunders, "So you expect us to take the risk? These people are following us, Armando. Whoever is doing this is going to kill someone."

"There's nothing I can do."

Tony jabs a finger straight into his face and says, "Do you remember what Coach Nava used to tell us when we played basketball at the Y?"

"He told us a lot of things."

"But do you remember what he told us to do when somebody started fucking with us?"

"I don't recall."

"He said to give them a hard elbow right in the middle of their chest. If they did it again, they knew they were going to get something coming back at them."

"I'm not fucking with you, Tony."

"Yes, you are, Armando. You wear your fancy suit and your gold cuff links. You sit in your big office and drink your cappuccinos. You get favors from your buddy the mayor, and you arrange for kickbacks from Vegas developers." Tony takes a deep breath and says, "To me, you're still just another asshole from the neighborhood. If you fuck with me and my family, I'll nail you right in the chest. I want you to give your thugs a message. The police are going to follow them everywhere they go. We have protection—they don't. If your animals come after us, we're going to nail them—and you. Do you understand?"

"I had nothing to do with these photos," Rios says.

"I don't believe you. And even if I did, I'm holding you personally responsible. If anything happens to Rolanda or me, the same thing is going to happen to you."

"Is that a threat?"

"It's a promise." Tony lowers his voice and says, "I can't believe this, Armando. When we were growing up, this neighborhood was like a big family. People looked after one another. They didn't threaten their friends' children. They didn't burn down their neighbors' businesses." Tony points a long finger at Rios. "I don't know you anymore. You used to be a stand-up guy. I used to look up to you because you became a lawyer and made something of yourself. You used to say you fought for the little guy. Now you're part of the problem. You're as corrupt as the system you used to fight. I'm glad your parents are not alive to see what you've become, Armando."

Rios takes in Tony's diatribe with stoicism. He fingers his cigar and looks out the windows at the traffic on Guerrero Street. Then he looks at his old friend and says in a barely audible whisper, "What would you have me do?"

Tony glances at Rolanda, who says, "Work with us. Tell the police who is funding the payoffs. Tell them to call off the thugs."

"What's in it for me?"

"Immunity from prosecution and an opportunity to spin the story any way you'd like."

Tony glances at the pictures of Rios's grandchildren on the credenza and adds, "And you may be able to reclaim your self-respect."

Rios frowns. "And if I choose not to cooperate?"

Tony turns somber. "You'd better have eyes in the back of your head, because I won't let you sleep until I find out who threatened us. Dennis Alvarez will give me a police escort to the Hall of Justice, where I'll swear out a complaint that you've solicited bribes and arranged for the fire at Roberto's store."

"You have no proof. I have lawyers. The cases will be dismissed within hours."

"Maybe. Maybe not. I'll call Jerry Edwards at the *Chronicle* and give him an exclusive interview. I'll tell him everything I know, Armando. I may even bring him over here, and we'll tape an interview for *Mornings on Two* right in front of this building."

Rios remains stoic. "You'll make a fool of yourself, and I'll be exonerated."

"And you can kiss your career good-bye. The mayor will distance himself from you. Nobody at city hall will speak to you. An expediter without connections is worthless. You may have to go out and get a real job."

Rios sits in irate silence. Tony's face is red with anger. Rolanda clenches and unclenches her fist.

I observed the dynamics for a few moments. Then I try to strike a conciliatory tone. "The cops aren't after you, Armando," I say. "They'll protect you if you cut a deal now. Things could change in a hurry if you wait."

"My lawyers will protect me."

I fire right back, "They can't protect you from the people who burned down Roberto's store."

Silence. Rios puts the cigar into the humidor. I look at Tony, who is still leaning forward. I turn to Rios and say, "Armando, you know the bottom line. Somebody is going to get hurt. Somebody is going to go to jail. If you work with us, you can cut a deal. You can try to control the spin. You might even look like a hero." I lean back to give him a moment to think. Then I add, "It all comes down to a matter of trust."

Rios ponders for a moment. He punches a button on his phone and tells his secretary to hold his calls. He goes over to his wet bar and pours himself a cup of coffee. Then he returns to his chair and sits down. We wait. He stares out the window. He tugs at his neatly trimmed mustache. Finally, he measures his words carefully when he says, "I want you to understand something. The arrangements I made to obtain support for the China Basin project involved an exchange of rather modest sums. They did not at any time include the possibility of violence or intimidation. I do not condone such tactics or threats directed at my friends or their children. I don't do business that way, and I never will."

His attempt at self-exoneration is heartfelt—and completely irrelevant. I say, "We need more than an apology. We need information. Who ordered the fire at the liquor store?"

The corners of his mouth turn down. "I don't know."

"Who sent the photos to Tony?"

"I told you. I—don't—know."

"That's bullshit, Armando"

Rolanda leans forward and says, "Somebody is going to get killed, Armando. You can stop this now or you can take your chances with Carl Ellis or Dominic Petrillo or young Richard MacArthur or whomever else is calling the shots. I wouldn't want to be in your shoes if you decide to play ball with them."

"I have no control over the people who are involved in this matter," he says. "I have no idea who arranged for the fire at Roberto's store."

"How is that possible?" I ask.

"I've only been dealing with one person on this matter."

"Who?"

"I won't reveal any names unless and until I have an immunity agreement in place."

"Fine," I say. "Get your lawyer up here." I pull out my cell phone.

"Who are you calling?" he asks.

"Sergeant Alvarez."

# Chapter 35

## "He Told Me the Situation Was under Control"

> The reports that I was involved with the recent fire at a Mission District liquor store are completely false. I would never condone such activity.
>
> —Armando Rios. KGO Radio
> Tuesday, June 8. 11:00 a.m.

Rios is still scowling two hours later. The modest gathering in his office has expanded into a full-blown summit conference that now includes Sergeant Alvarez, the captain from Mission Station, Lisa Yee and Rios's attorney. We've worked through the terms of an immunity deal. Rios's morose downtown lawyer has asked him a dozen times whether he really wants to proceed. Rios keeps repeating his mantra that he has no choice. Political consultants lose a substantial amount of influence after they've been indicted.

Alvarez takes the lead. He asks Rios, "Who approached you to obtain the support of the local businesses for the China Basin project?"

"Martin Kent."

"He's dead."

"I know."

"Do you know what happened to him?"

"I understand from the news reports that he committed suicide."

"Did you deal with anybody else?"

"All my contacts were through Mr. Kent. He was representing a group that included MacArthur Films, Millennium Studios and Ellis Construction."

Sounds as though Rios is trying to put some distance between himself and Ellis and Petrillo.

Alvarez asks, "What were you asked to do?"

Rios's explanation jibes with Tony's. About a dozen businesses in the Mission were offered twenty thousand each to sign a letter supporting the China Basin project. Each of them got to keep ten grand. The balance went to the Mission Democratic Organization. The money changed hands, and the letters were signed.

Alvarez says, "I assume you are to be paid a fee for your services?"

"Yes."

"How much?"

Rios scowls. He glances at his lawyer, who tells him he has to answer. "Fifty thousand dollars up front," he says, "and another two hundred thousand when the permits are issued."

Not bad. A quarter of a million bucks for a few days of influence peddling. I'm in the wrong line of work. I ask, "Have you been paid?"

"Just the first installment. I'll get the rest when we get the approvals next Friday. There is nothing illegal about accepting a fee for consulting services."

No, there isn't. Paying bribes to public officials is another matter. Give him credit. He remains self-confident even when he's being questioned by the cops.

Sergeant Alvarez is not so easily impressed. He asks, "What went wrong?"

He remains defiant. "Nothing. Then the press somehow got wind of it. Jerry Edwards started asking questions. A number of participants got nervous."

"Did you report the problems to Mr. Kent?"

"Yes."

"When?"

"We called him last week."

Rios has suddenly shifted to the royal we.

Alvarez pushes forward. "Where did you leave it with Kent?"

"He said he'd deal with it."

"Did he?"

"I don't know."

Alvarez chews on a toothpick. Then he asks Rios about the fire at Roberto Peña's store.

"I don't know anything about it."

"Did Mr. Peña accept money to support the studio project?"

"Yes." He hesitates and adds, "I told Mr. Kent I thought Mr. Peña had been approached by the police."

Alvarez bores in. "Coincidentally," he says, "there was a fire at his store just before we finalized his immunity agreement. Did you have anything to do with it?"

"Absolutely not." He says he deals in influence and money. He leaves muscle to others.

They volley back and forth for more than an hour. Rios implicates Kent in the payoffs, but claims he has no idea who provided the funding. He insists the entire scheme was legal. He disavows any knowledge of who ordered the fire at the liquor store or the photos of Rolanda. Without further evidence, it will be difficult, if not impossible, to figure out if Big Dick, Little Richard, Ellis or Petrillo, or, for that matter, anyone else, had any direct involvement.

Alvarez tries another angle. "After Mr. Kent's death," he says, "to whom did you report developments on the studio project?"

Rios tries to evade the question. "He died only a couple of days ago."

I decide to offer a little help. "Our investigator saw you at Richard MacArthur's house last night. Did you talk to him about it?"

Rios appears flustered by the news that he was being watched. Then he says in an even tone, "I explained the situation to Mr. MacArthur."

"Was he aware of the arrangements you had made with Mr. Kent?"

"He certainly was after I talked to him last night."

"Did he know about it before you told him?"

"I don't know."

"Did he still want to proceed with the China Basin project?"

"Yes."

Not according to Kaela Joy Gullion.

Alvarez asks, "Did he give you any further instructions?"

"He told me the situation was under control and I should not take any further action."

WE REGROUP in the back of Tony's market a little while later. I say to Tony, "At least your immunity agreement is in place."

"I hope I live long enough to enjoy it. If Rios is telling the truth, the only guy we know was involved was Kent."

"The other investors in the China Basin project must have known," I say.

"We don't know that for sure. And we have no way of proving it."

"Somebody put up the money," I say. "Maybe Little Richard knew more than he let on."

"Maybe."

I'm frustrated. "We can connect the dots from Rios to Kent," I say, "but that's as far as we can go. Dennis Alvarez said he had someone talk to Little Richard about his conversation with Rios. Not surprisingly, he said it was the first he'd heard about the arrangements Kent had made to grease the approvals. He said he was surprised Kent had gotten involved in something so sordid. He also denied any knowledge of the fire at the liquor store."

Tony shrugs and says, "Big surprise."

I look at Rolanda and Tony and say, "I think we should make Rios nervous."

Rolanda gives me a puzzled look. "What do you have in mind?"

"Let's fight back. Let's keep *him* under surveillance. Maybe he'll lead us to his source. Let's see how he likes being watched."

Rolanda's eyes light up. She says, "I'm in. Let me watch him. See how he likes it."

Tony gives me a concerned look and says, "I don't like it."

Rolanda replies, "I won't do anything stupid."

Tony says, "I still don't like it."

Rolanda is adamant. "I'll stay out of anything dangerous. I'll call Dennis Alvarez if it looks like anything is going to happen."

Tony strokes his chin. Then he says, "Maybe it isn't a bad idea."

I CALL ROSIE at the hospital and tell her about our visit with Rios.

"At least Tony's off the hook," she says.

"If they can protect him." I tell her about our plan to keep Rios under watch.

Her voice turns somber. "Is it safe?"

"Rolanda is cautious. She'll be careful." I ask, "How's Angel?"

"Physically, she's going to be fine. Emotionally, she's a train wreck."

"Are you going to stay there for a little while?"

"Yeah. Then I need to get to the office." She pauses and says, "Did you see Jerry Edwards on the news this morning?"

"Yeah."

"He left a message for you. Apparently, Crown denied he was the father. He wants to interview Angel."

"Forget it. Maybe this will light a fire under Ward and O'Brien to consider Crown as a suspect."

I hear Rosie sigh. "This is a disaster," she says. "Angel is going to be hysterical when she sees the papers. My sister will be beside herself."

"We'll just have to take it one step at a time," I tell her. The tired cliché rings hollow as I hear myself say it.

"Can you imagine the headlines, Mike?"

"Angelina Chavez was carrying Daniel Crown's love child," I say.

"Something like that. She's going to be absolutely devastated by this."

"We'll deal with it, Rosie."

"Yeah." The line goes silent. The wheels are already starting to turn. "We need to talk to Daniel Crown," she says. "And Little Richard."

"I'll get to them as soon as I can."

"Where are you going now?"

"I'm going for a boat ride with Pete. We're going to see who got invited to Big Dick's funeral."

# Chapter 36

# A Fitting Tribute

> The Northern California Neptune Society offers a variety of services to accommodate all needs. Our trained specialists will ensure that arrangements are handled in a supportive and dignified manner. Special services, scatterings at sea and pre-need arrangements are available.
>
> —Brochure for the Northern California Neptune Society

"Are you all right?" Joey D'Augustino asks me. The retired-cop-turned-fisherman's weather-worn face breaks into a wide grin, exposing deep crevasses in his leathery skin. He gives me a fatherly pat on the shoulder and says, "Did you take the Dramamine like I told you?"

"Yeah."

"How much?"

"Not enough."

"You'll be all right, Mikey."

I hope so. I look up at Pete, who is doing his Captain Ahab imitation. He's trained his binoculars on the Neptune Society's yacht, the *Naiad*, which is about a half mile ahead of us. We're trying to remain inconspicuous, but it's hard to hide a twenty-foot fishing boat in the middle of the bay. We've just passed under the Golden Gate Bridge at one-thirty on Tuesday afternoon. It's a beautiful day for a funeral. The sun is shining and my head is splitting. The water is calm, but my stomach feels as if I'm reliving the climactic scene in *The Perfect Storm*. I could have let Pete come out here alone with Joey, but I thought the fresh air would do me good. Bad idea. The saltwater spray and the diesel fumes are making me sick.

I ask Pete, "Can you see them?"

"Yeah. The captain is at the wheel. There are a couple of deck hands. Gilligan, Ginger, MaryAnn and the professor are sitting in the stern. The Howells are drinking mint juleps."

"Come on, Pete."

"Your stomach will feel better if you lighten up, Mick. There are only four other people on the boat. Little Richard is wearing his sailor costume."

My brother doesn't make jokes on dry land. Why he's chosen to do his Jay Leno imitation escapes me. "Who else is with him?"

He studies the *Naiad* for a few seconds. He says to Joey, "Can you get us a little closer?"

"Sure." He guns the motor and we head toward the Point Bonita lighthouse on the Marin side. I can see Big Dick's house perched on the bluff above Baker Beach to the south. We make a wide semicircle around the *Naiad*, which is about halfway between the bridge and the ocean.

Pete stares intently through his binoculars. "One of the deckhands is giving MacArthur a container," he says. "It must be his father's ashes."

"Who else is there?" I ask.

"Two men and a woman with long hair and dark skin."

Eve. I throw caution to the wind. I stand tenuously and take the binoculars. My legs feel like silly putty. I focus on the *Naiad* and see Little Richard standing next to Eve. Then I look straight into the eyes of Dominic Petrillo, who must have flown up from L.A. I adjust the focus and can't believe my eyes. Daniel Crown is standing next to Petrillo. The father of Angel's unborn child is one of four guests at her husband's memorial service.

I feel Pete's hand on my arm. "You okay, Mick? You look like you just saw a ghost."

I tell him about Crown.

He gives me an incredulous look and says, "What the hell is he doing there?"

My mind races. "Either he hasn't the slightest sense of decency, or Angel's lying."

I see a flash and hear an explosion. The passengers and the crew of the *Naiad* flinch and then look up at the sky. The Pacific provides a spectacular backdrop as we watch Big Dick's ashes explode. It's a fitting tribute for a man who spent his life making fireworks.

"ARE YOU SICK?" Nicole Ward asks. "You look awful."

Thanks. "I was out on a boat," I tell her.

It's three-thirty the same afternoon. Rosie and I are meeting with Ward in her office. Jack O'Brien is sitting at the end of the long conference table, his hands wrapped around a cup of coffee. Lisa Yee is next to Ward, who summoned us to get an update on Angel's condition. In the spirit of cooperation, she's also promised us some new information.

The D.A. gives me a puzzled look. "You thought it might be a nice day to go sailing?"

"I went to see who was at MacArthur's funeral." I tell her I saw his son, Eve, Petrillo and Crown.

Her eyebrows go up. "Crown was there?"

Rosie interjects, "It's disgusting."

Ward gives Rosie a suspect look and says, "That assumes your client is telling the truth about the baby."

Rosie lowers her voice and says, "Crown's the father. He was furious at Dick MacArthur for causing the miscarriage. That makes him a suspect."

"We don't know who the father was," Ward says. "Your client admitted she was angry at her husband about the miscarriage. Maybe that's what motivated her to kill him. You don't think Crown would have shown up at the funeral if he was the father, do you?"

I catch Rosie's eye. She tells Ward, "You should ask him about it."

"We did. He denied it."

"Of course he did. Why did you take his word for it?"

"Until we have some evidence to the contrary, his word is better than your client's. She's desperate. She made the whole thing up to try to deflect blame."

"You don't know that," Rosie says.

"We take everything your client says with a healthy dose of skepticism."

"We'll ask for DNA testing."

"So will we." Ward tells us it's unclear whether there are any tissue samples from the fetus. She says they're checking the records at Saint Francis Hospital.

Rosie glares at her and says, "You said you had some new information."

"We do." Ward nods to O'Brien, who cues the VCR. The picture on the TV is fuzzy. I see a black-and-white video that looks like something from *America's Most Wanted*.

"This is a tape from the traffic camera that's mounted on the administration building at the bridge," O'Brien explains.

It's the view that I see every day on *Mornings on Two*. We study the grainy footage. The date and time are stamped in the lower left corner in white block letters and numerals. We're looking at Saturday morning at three-thirty A.M. The screen is dark gray. "Are you sure it was working?" I ask.

"It's hard to see," O'Brien acknowledges. "It was foggy."

I can make out a few cars coming southbound. A sign on the northbound side that says two lanes are open.

A few minutes pass. I'm getting anxious. Rosie's eyes are fixed on the picture. I'm inching closer to the TV when Ward suddenly points at the screen and says, "There!"

I look at the fog-shrouded bridge. "What?"

O'Brien stops the tape and rewinds it. Ward moves closer to the screen. So do I. I can smell her cologne as we're both sitting within a couple of feet of the nineteen-inch Zenith.

I glance at Rosie, whose eyes are still on the screen. "What is it?" I say.

Ward points toward the walkway on the east side of the bridge and says, "Right there."

O'Brien reruns the tape in super slow motion. The headlights of a few cars coming southbound reflect off the fog. Ward moves her right index finger along the footpath leading to the locking gate at the south end of the bridge. "There he is," she says.

"It's a shadow," I say.

"It's Martin Kent."

I'm not sure. "Run it again."

She does. This time Ward uses her pen as a pointer. I can make out the silhouette of a man walking on the paved path toward the entrance to the bridge. "No doubt about it," Ward insists. "Look at him stop at the gate. He's trying to decide what to do."

Rosie gives me a troubled look. We watch the shadow staring at the locked gate. He ponders for a moment and glances at the roadway. Then he turns around and faces the camera for an instant. He's wearing a suit and a tie. His hands are empty.

Ward starts doing play-by-play. "He's climbing over the guardrail onto the roadway." She gestures emphatically at the screen. "That's how he got around the locked gate and the barbed wire." She taps her pen on the screen. The shadow hustles up the roadway and into the fog. Not even Ward's eagle eyes can tell what happened next.

"What time was that?" Rosie asks.

"Three-fifty A.M. It's right after they found your client and about twenty minutes after they found her husband's body."

"You don't know for sure it was Kent," I say. "And even if it was, there was still plenty of time for him to have driven Angelina to the bridge."

"Or walked," Ward says. She tells us about her interview with Kaela Joy. "She said she saw Kent walking toward the bridge early Saturday morning."

"She told us she said she couldn't identify him."

Ward hesitates. Then she says, "She told me it was Kent."

She's bluffing. I asked Kaela Joy specifically about this issue. She wasn't sure. We debate our recollections of our respective conversations with Kaela Joy. It ends up a draw.

We sit in silence. It's becoming clear that Marty Kent jumped off the bridge a few minutes before four on Saturday morning. It is decidedly unclear what happened in the minutes leading up to his death.

Rosie tries to smoke out as much information as she can when she asks, "Assuming for the moment that you're right, why did Kent kill himself?"

Ward says, "His son said he was despondent about his wife's death. He had lost a lot of money in the market and spent a fortune on his wife's treatment." She gives us a knowing look and adds, "We talked to Dennis Alvarez at Mission Station. Kent was involved in a scheme to make illegal payments to obtain the approvals for the studio project. Dennis says he would have been indicted. His reputation would have been ruined."

Rosie and I exchange glances, but we don't say anything.

"There's more," Ward says. She takes a thin document out of a file folder and slides it across the desk to me. "This is an amendment of MacArthur's will," she says.

I place the brief document between Rosie and me and we start to read. Ward directs us to Article Third, which says, "I give to my son, Richard Andrew MacArthur, Jr., if he survives me, all my interest in any and all cash, securities, individual retirement accounts, pension plans, profit-sharing plans, stock-bonus plans, other qualified retirement plans, real and personal property of any nature, furniture, fixtures, automobiles and all other tangible articles of a household or personal nature, together with all insurance policies thereon." I look for Angel's name, but I can't find it.

Rosie says, "Angel's been written out of the will. Everything goes to MacArthur's son."

Ward nods and says, "Exactly."

"Where did you get this?"

"MacArthur's probate attorney."

I ask, "Have you talked to his son about it?"

"Yes. He doesn't plan to contest the will."

No kidding. "Did he know about it?"

"Not until the probate attorney called him. It turns out his father also canceled the life insurance policy. Your client is no longer entitled to the million-dollar proceeds."

What? "When?"

"About two weeks ago."

"Obviously he didn't tell Angel."

"He was under no obligation to do so."

Rosie tries to keep her tone measured when she says, "I appreciate the fact that you've brought this information to our attention."

"You're entitled to it under the rules of discovery."

Rosie thinks about it and says, "You realize this creates a huge hole in your case."

Ward tries to keep her tone nonchalant. "How do you figure?"

"Our client had no motive to kill her husband. If he had canceled the life insurance and amended his will, she wasn't going to get a cent."

Ward corrects her. "Your client may have had no *financial* motive to have killed him," she says, "but she didn't know he had canceled the life insurance and amended the will. As far as she knew, she was still entitled to the insurance proceeds and half of his assets. She knew the will trumped the prenup. She figured she could get her hands on his fortune by killing him before he divorced her."

Rosie's eyes light up. "Their marriage was imploding," she says. "She must have known he was going to file for divorce."

Ward takes it in without visible reaction. Then she says, "She had other motives."

Rosie decides to play cat-and-mouse with her. "Such as?"

"She was furious at her husband because he humiliated her at the screening. Then there's the entire situation with her pregnancy. Your client believed her husband killed her baby."

"You'll never be able to prove it," Rosie says.

"You'll have to put her on the stand to tell her side of the story," Ward replies.

"No, we won't. And you won't want us to put a vulnerable-looking young woman whose husband beat her in front of a jury."

Ward strokes her delicate chin. She glances at O'Brien and then turns back to us. "Juries are smarter than you think," she says. "I'm not out for your client's blood. She almost killed herself last night. It looks to me like financial concerns may not have been her most important motivating factor. Based on her relationship with Crown, I think she may have acted in a rage. I think she may have killed her husband on an angry impulse."

"That argues against a charge of first-degree murder," Rosie says.

Ward nods. "Perhaps."

"Are you prepared to suggest something?"

"I may be willing to go down to second degree. I'll take a lot of heat for it, but it will take the death penalty off the table."

Rosie seizes the offensive. "You want her to plead to second degree in a case that shouldn't even have been charged as manslaughter?"

Ward leans across the table and says, "I'll catch hell for it. Your client could be out within fifteen years. She's young. It's a good deal."

It's bogus. "I'll take it to my client," Rosie says.

"Will you recommend it?"

"I'll think about it."

---

"WHAT DO YOU MAKE of Nicole's offer to plead to second degree?" I ask Rosie. We're in the car heading back to the office.

"She knows she has a problem. The cancellation of the life insurance and the change in the will leave Angel without a financial motive."

"There's still the miscarriage and the Daniel Crown situation," I argue. "Ward might be able to show premeditation."

"True," Rosie says, "but Angel will appear more sympathetic. Juries don't like to convict people they perceive as victims. Ward is running for office. It won't play well to her female voters if she tears apart a vulnerable young woman who just had a miscarriage. I think she may go down to manslaughter."

I don't share her confidence. We don't know whether Angel is telling the truth about Crown.

Rosie asks, "What are you going to do now?"

"I have to go to a Little League game."

She gives me a puzzled look. "Grace doesn't play until Thursday."

"I know, but Daniel Crown's son has a game at five o'clock."

## Chapter 37

# "It Starts with the First Lie"

> Heartthrob Daniel Crown has issued a vehement denial of accusations that he was the father of Angelina Chavez's unborn baby.
>
> —*Entertainment Tonight*
> Tuesday, June 8

Daniel Crown's face rearranges itself into an emphatic frown as soon as he sees me. "What makes you think I have anything to say to you?" he mutters to me. He's standing next to the backstop in the bucolic Ross Common, a tree-lined park in a community of multimillion-dollar homes nestled in a grove of oaks on the north side of Mount Tam. Crown throws a baseball to his son, who is standing on the pitcher's mound.

I take a deep breath of the forest-scented cool air and say in my best priest-voice, "I really need your help, Danny."

"Talk to my lawyer."

"Please, Danny."

He catches a toss from his son and holds the ball. He turns to me and says in a voice that is too low for his son to hear, "Let's cut the crap, okay? The first time we met was at Willie's yesterday. I asked Jason about you. He doesn't know your daughter. She never played on his soccer team. You were just yanking my chain to get information."

"I'm sorry, Danny."

"Go to hell."

"Look—"

He gives me the tough-guy look he almost perfected in his soap opera days. "No, *you* look. You guys are spreading lies. You're trying to ruin my marriage. And my career." He glances at his son and says, "How do you think Jason feels when the kids ask him if his dad is sleeping with Angelina Chavez? You aren't going to destroy my family to get your client off."

I feel bad for his son. The kids always seem to get hurt the most. "I'm sorry, Danny."

He gives me a melodramatic look and tosses the ball back to his son. "You should have thought of that before you started talking to the press."

I try again. "I was hoping I could prevail upon you to help my client."

He gives me a sarcastic grin. "There was never anything between us. You'll be hearing from my lawyer."

I try for a measured tone. "I'd rather talk to you."

"I wasn't sleeping with her. She's lying."

"Help us find out what really happened."

"I tried to help you yesterday. Today my wife and I have had to endure phone calls from idiots who think I was sleeping with Angelina. Send me a subpoena if you want to talk to me. My lawyers will tie you up in litigation for years."

"Danny," I say, "they're going to be able to confirm that you were the father of the baby. We've agreed with the prosecutors to do DNA testing."

This stops him for an instant. He faces me and says, "Come back with a subpoena."

I decide to up the stakes. "They kept samples of the tissue of the fetus at the hospital to run some tests." I have no idea if this is true or not. I'm turning on the smoke machine full blast. "It's a standard procedure."

He searches my face to try to determine if I'm bluffing. I stare him down. His eyes never leave mine.

Jason's coach summons the players to home plate. His father and I watch the team take a lap around the bases. Crown stands with his arms folded as he encourages his son. Finally, he turns to me and says, "I have nothing else to say to you."

"It's going to look worse if you lie."

"How much worse can it possibly look? You've already accused me of being an adulterer. Why don't you accuse me of murdering Dick MacArthur while you're at it?"

Maybe we will. "I didn't say that, Danny."

He jabs a finger into my face and says, "You're full of shit. Dick MacArthur was a tremendous director and my friend. His son invited me to his funeral because we're friends and he knew how much I respected his father."

Except, of course, for the times when you were doing the hokeypokey with his wife.

He isn't finished. "Do you really think I would have gone to his memorial service if I was sleeping with Angelina? Give me a little credit."

I try once more. "You'll be better off if you come clean."

He juts his perfect chin forward and says, "I'll take my chances."

"You aren't a suspect. If they catch you in a lie, they'll come after you."

"I have nothing to hide."

It's the answer I expect. "Let me give you some free advice."

"Is there any way I can stop you?"

"No." I reach down and pick up a baseball and toss it to him. "I've been a lawyer for a long time," I say. "In my experience, once you start lying, it gets harder to keep track of your story. Eventually, the cops will catch a minor inconsistency. Then another. Pretty soon, you'll start trying to improve your story. That's a mistake. You won't remember the details. That's when they'll nail you, Danny. It starts with the first lie. Then it mushrooms." I smile and add, "My old secretary used to say that when a house of cards falls down, it's a problem. But when a house of bullshit falls down, it's a mess."

Crown is unmoved. He throws the ball to his son. Then he turns to me and says in an even tone, "Let me give *you* some free advice, Mike. Your client is lying. Eventually, the cops will catch a minor inconsistency. Then another. She told her first lie when she said she didn't kill her husband. She told her second when she said I was the father. That means she's already two lies ahead of me. You may be a good lawyer, but she's going to get nailed."

"They're going to come looking for you," I say. "They know you and Angelina were doing coke the other night. Your parole officer will be very interested in that discussion."

He hesitates. Then he says, "I've already talked to the cops about it."

"They found your fingerprints on the Baggie."

"Angelina handed it to me, and I gave it back to her. She's the one with the drug problem."

"How did the Baggie find its way into the front seat of her husband's car?"

"She must have put it there."

It's a glib explanation. It's also a standoff. I look him in the eye and say, "What really happened?"

He doesn't hesitate. "Cheryl and I had dinner and watched the movie. We drank some champagne. We drove home around two. Dick was still very much alive when we left."

It's his story, and he's sticking to it. If I didn't know any better, I'd swear he's telling me the truth.

"WHERE ARE YOU?" Rosie asks. She's in the office.

"The Golden Gate Bridge." I'm stuck in traffic at the south tower as I try to drive back into the city at six-thirty the same evening. I look out at the walkway on the east side where we saw Marty Kent on the videotape. I glance at the east-view lot as I crawl toward the tollbooth.

"How did things go with Crown?"

"Not well." I describe our conversation.

"You mean he didn't break down and confess right there at his son's Little League game? That's the way it always happened on *Perry Mason*."

"Sometimes it doesn't work that way in real life."

"Did he admit that he's the father of Angel's baby?"

"Absolutely not."

"So you struck out completely."

"Looks that way."

"Maybe I should talk to him next time."

"Fine with me." I ask if she's heard anything from Tony.

"Everything seems to be quiet at the market."

"And Armando Rios?"

"Rolanda called in. He's left town."

"Where did he go?"

"Vegas. I assume he was going to see Carl Ellis. Rolanda is on his tail."

Interesting. "Has Pete called?"

"Yes. He said Petrillo flew to L.A. and Little Richard and Eve went up to the winery. He wants us to meet him there first thing tomorrow morning."

"I'm in. Do you feel like taking a ride with me?"

"Sure. The drive will do me good." She hesitates for a moment and asks, "Where are you going now?"

"I'm going over to Baker Beach to check in with Pete's people. Then I have to be out in the Richmond later to take care of another pressing matter."

"And that would be?"

"I'm having a little heart-to-heart talk with Leslie."

# Chapter 38

## "It Doesn't Have to Be That Complicated"

> A judge must avoid conflicts of interest and remain true to her principles.
>
> —Judge Leslie Shapiro
> *California State Bar Journal*

Kabuto Sushi is an unpretentious little place on Geary at Fifteenth. Although it has zero ambience, the offerings prepared by its sushi maestro are among the best in town. The regulars are chatting with the chef. Leslie and I are sitting at a table near the back of the sparsely furnished room at ten o'clock. She's nibbling on one of the exotic creations. I'm not hungry.

"We really shouldn't be talking to each other," Leslie says. "It's *ex parte* communication. You could lose your license."

I got tired of people talking to me in Latin when I was a priest. Although I know she's right, I have no patience for a lecture on ethics right now. I realize I'm not helping matters as I say, "And you could lose your gavel."

She swallows her sushi and washes it down with a sip of tea. She puts her cup on the table and looks into my eyes. "I'm sorry I snapped at you."

"I'm sorry, too."

She's wearing a nonjudicial outfit: faded jeans, beat-up Nikes and a fuzzy blue Cal sweatshirt. "We've gotten ourselves into a classic no-win situation," she tells me.

I nod. Let her talk.

Her lips curl up into a tight ball. Then, she says, "I told the presiding judge I can't handle Angelina's prelim."

I'm relieved. "I'm sorry, Leslie."

"So am I."

"You did the right thing."

"I'm planning to celebrate my great moral victory."

"Did he ask you why?"

"I told him it was personal. When he probed, I said it involved a situation that may generate a potential conflict. That was all he needed to hear. He reassigned it to Judge McDaniel. She's familiar with the case, and her calendar is open."

Not a great deal. We get to do an encore performance in the courtroom of a pro-prosecution judge. "You would have been a better draw for us."

"You're right." She hesitates and adds, "She'll give you a fair shake."

That she will. "I guess that leaves us."

She takes a quick sip of tea and says, "Yes, it does."

I never know if I'm supposed to lead or follow. My gut tells me to talk. My mind tells me to listen. My gut wins. "Leslie," I say, "I still have the same feelings for you."

The telltale sigh. She makes eye contact with me for an instant, then looks away. She's looking down when she says, "You're a dear, sweet, bright, kind man, Michael Daley."

They always start with a flowery compliment just before they hit you with the sledgehammer. I steel myself for the big "But."

She looks up and says, "But this relationship is too complicated for me."

I've heard this before. "It doesn't have to be that complicated," I tell her.

"Yes, it does." She swallows hard, and I think I can see a tear in her eye. "Michael," she says, "I don't think it's a good idea for us to continue seeing each other."

Don't react. Let her keep talking.

Her tone becomes more judicial when she says, "It isn't going to work. It creates all sorts of potential conflicts—at work and at home." She hesitates and adds, "I don't think it has a long-term future."

I hate when people use the term *it* in referring to a relationship. It's better not to quibble about semantics with her. I can feel a burning in the back of my throat and a knot in my stomach. In my head I can hear the plaintive voice of Bonnie Raitt singing, "I can't make you love me if you don't." I put my chin in my hand and look her in the eye. I don't know what to say, so I remain silent.

She's uncomfortable. She nibbles at her sushi and then throws it down on her plate. She looks at me with tearstained eyes and says, "Say something, dammit. Yell at me if you want to. Get angry. Get sad. Cry. But don't just sit there and look at me."

I reach across the table and put my finger to her lips. "You don't have to say anything else," I tell her. "We've been to this movie. Deep down, we knew how it was probably going to end." I wipe the tears from her cheeks. "It's going to be okay. It was a long shot from the start." I remind her of the line she quoted to me when we first started seeing each other: "Judges aren't supposed to cry."

She gives me a weak smile. "I'm going to miss you."

"I'll miss you, too."

"I hope we can be friends."

It's a kind thought and the right thing to say. There is virtually no chance it will happen. "I'd like that," I tell her.

We make strained small talk for a few minutes. I insist on picking up the check. In what appears to be a modest offer of conciliation, she takes my hand and says, "Now that we're officially just friends, would you mind if I gave you a friendly suggestion?"

"Sure. Something about Angelina's case?"

"We're not allowed to talk about that."

"Then what?"

"Something about you."

Uh-oh. I'm prepared for a lengthy recitation of my shortcomings. "Did I do something?"

"No."

"Something in bed?"

She chuckles. "Not that, either. It's about you and Rosie."

"What about us?"

She bites her lip and says, "I know this may not be the right time."

Probably not.

"But I think the two of you should consider getting back together."

I haven't slept in three days. My ex-wife, law partner and best friend has cancer. My girlfriend broke up with me less than ten minutes ago. Now she feels compelled to offer me counseling on my love life. "I appreciate your concern," I say, "but our situation is also very complicated."

"It doesn't have to be that complicated."

I hate it when people do my lines back to me. "We weren't good at living together."

"You could be."

"You aren't the first person who's suggested it. We gave it a shot. It didn't work out." And I endured five years of therapy to get through the depression and guilt after the divorce. "I don't want to talk about it." More precisely, I don't want to talk about it with *you*.

"Hear me out."

I have no choice. "I'm listening."

"She's your soul mate, Michael. I've been trying to find mine for forty-six years. Everybody sees it—except you and Rosie."

Why does everybody feel the need to give me advice on my love life? I go with an old standby. "That's easy for you to say."

"Yes, it is." She swallows and says, "Don't wait too long. You're going to wake up one of these days and realize it was staring you right in the face."

I don't respond.

"Look," she says, "I don't mean to butt in—"

"You already have."

"If you would just look at the big picture—"

"I'm a little-picture person."

She's exasperated. "Dammit, Michael, if you would just put aside your pride—"

"Tell that to her."

She hesitates for an instant and whispers, "I did."

What? "When?"

"About a month ago. We had a talk."

Now it's my turn for exasperation. "About what?"

"About you."

Oh, hell. "Why?"

"I wanted to be sure I wasn't moving in on her territory."

I never realized my life was such an open book. Next they'll create one of those reality-based TV shows about me. The woman who can stand me the longest will win a million bucks. "And what did you decide?"

"She said you'd agreed to move on. She didn't want to stand in your way."

I don't say anything.

She gives me an uncomfortable nod and says, "Take my advice for what it's worth."

"I appreciate your judicial wisdom."

"I'm a pretty good judge of people."

If that truly were the case, you wouldn't be breaking up with me. I try to bring the conversation to a close when I tell her, "I'm going to miss you, Leslie."

"I'll miss you, too. Is there anything I can do to make this easier for you?"

I think for a moment. Then I say, "There may be something you can do for me. Would you be offended if I asked you for a favor?"

"You name it."

Here goes. "There's a preliminary hearing for Carolyn's son in your courtroom on Thursday morning."

She eyes me cautiously. She knows I'm about to cross the line. "I'm familiar with it."

"I want you to make the charges go away."

She gives me an icy look and says, "Are you serious?"

"Yes."

"You're trying to get me to fix a case?"

"It's a bogus charge. Nicole Ward is looking for TV time." I give her a half grin and say, "And *fix* is such a harsh word. Let's just say I'm trying to encourage you to resolve it in the interest of justice. Besides, you have plenty of other cases to keep you busy. If Angel's case moves forward, the Hall is going to be swarming with media people for months. It's going to be a three-ring circus. Do you know how bad the traffic is around there?"

"I'm familiar with the problem."

"I'm trying to help you get to work every morning. More important, I'm helping you do a public service. You can prevent gridlock."

"I can't believe you're asking me to do this."

"Neither can I."

She gives me a judicial look and says, "Is he really a good kid?"

"Yes."

"Is this one of Nicole Ward's publicity stunts?"

"Uh-huh."

Her face rearranges itself into a smile. "What's in it for me?"

I give her a melodramatic sigh. "In light of our conversation a few minutes ago, I'm afraid I can no longer offer you sexual favors. I guess you'll have to settle for the knowledge that you'll be doing the right thing and giving a good kid another chance." I decide this may not be the right time to point out that she will also be violating a series of ethical rules for which she could be sanctioned and I could be disbarred.

"That's it?"

"That's it."

Her grin disappears. "No promises," she says.

"Understood."

"HOW ARE YOU holding up?" I ask Rosie.

It's just after midnight and I'm at home. It's the first time in four days that I may get to spend a few hours of quality time in my own bed. As we talk on the phone, I'm tired, but strangely content with the resolution of things with Leslie. Maybe I'm getting older and wiser. Maybe we weren't that far along in the relationship. Maybe I'm numb.

"Another glorious day," she says.

The sound of her voice concerns me. She isn't just tired. Something's wrong. "What is it, Rosita?"

A sigh. "The principal called. There was a problem at school."

Uh-oh. In spite of our unconventional family situation, Grace is a very good student, and she never gets into trouble. "What happened?" I ask.

"One of her Neanderthal classmates started giving her grief about Angel. Some of the other kids joined in."

Ten-year-olds can be nasty. I ask how Grace reacted.

"She held her ground and defended her cousin. Then she told her teacher about it."

It's exactly what Rosie would have done.

Rosie hesitates and adds, "When she got back to her classroom, she started to cry. Her teacher was able to calm her down. That's when the principal called me. She said Grace was holding up okay, but we need to keep a close eye on her."

A less enlightened school wouldn't have called. "What did Grace have to say about it?"

"She put up a good front. She said it wasn't a big deal. I pushed a little, but not too hard." Her voice cracks when she adds, "She has a lot on her plate, Mike."

"I'll do everything I can."

"Thanks." We talk for a few more minutes. Then she asks, "How did it go with Leslie?"

"Not particularly well."

"Did she recuse herself from Angel's case?"

"Yes." I hesitate for a moment and add, "And from our relationship."

The phone is silent. Then she says, "I'm sorry, Mike."

"Me, too. It's a new cast, but the movie always ends the same way."

"Do you want to come over for a few minutes?"

The old temptations are there, but my brain overrules my urges. "No, thanks. I'll pick you up in the morning."

"Whatever you want, Mike."

"Give Grace a kiss for me."

# Chapter 39

# Little Richard—The Sequel

> We are going to proceed with the release of *The Return of the Master* as scheduled. It's what my father would have wanted.
>
> —Richard MacArthur, Jr. *Daily Variety*
> Wednesday, June 9

"Are you sure he's in there?" I ask Pete.

"Yeah."

Pete, Rosie and I are standing just outside the imposing stone gate to the MacArthur Cellars compound at eight o'clock the next morning. An inviting breeze is blowing through the eight hundred acres of carefully tended vines, and the sweet aroma of grapes and jasmine envelops us. I understand why Big Dick became a gentleman farmer.

Zinfandel Lane was a dirt path when the first vines were planted on this site just south of St. Helena in the 1880s. If you believe the marketing propaganda on the MacArthur Cellars label, the climate and soil here are superb for producing Cabernet and, of course, Zinfandel grapes. The original owners laid out the rows of vines and built a modest house and a small stone winery. In the forties, one of the pioneer families of the modern Napa wine industry acquired the property and restored the historical buildings. It inspired Francis Coppola to undertake a similar project at the Inglenook winery on the Niebaum estate just south of here at Oakville.

Dick MacArthur had grand plans when he bought much of the Zinfandel Lane property twenty years ago. To the chagrin of his neighbors, he tore down the stone winery and replaced it with an enormous wine-making facility and tasting room. The modern structure looks like a Home Depot. The old house is gone, too. He put up a ten-thousand-square-foot faux château, complete with a screening room, an Olympic-sized pool, a fully equipped gym and six guest cottages. It looks like a Club Med.

Pete tells us he spent an uneventful night in his car just down the road near the entrance to Highway 29 at the west end of Zinfandel Lane. His occasional tree-climbing companion, Kaela Joy Gullion, kept watch at the intersection of Zinfandel and the Silverado Trail on the east side of the valley. They've compared notes over an elegant breakfast of doughnuts and coffee. He tells us Little Richard and Eve arrived at the winery last night. They dined at TraVigne and skinny-dipped in the pool until two. Richard seems to have bounced back from his father's funeral. Eve was last seen driving toward St. Helena this morning. Kaela Joy followed her.

The sign on the locked iron gate says the tasting room is closed. Rosie and I walk up to the adjacent kiosk, where a uniformed security guard is watching a small black-and-white TV. The clean-cut kid can't be much older than nineteen. His window is open, and he looks up as we approach him. Rosie says, "We have an appointment with Mr. MacArthur."

"The winery is closed. Mr. MacArthur isn't seeing guests. His father passed away."

Rosie gives him a maternal look and says, "We're relatives." She pauses and adds, "And we're the attorneys for his father's wife."

The word *attorney* seems to get his attention. He picks up the phone and punches in four numbers. I hear him say "uh-huh" a couple of times. His head bobs. He gives us a helpless look. Finally, he cups his hand over the receiver and says, "Is he expecting you?"

"Yes."

"One sec." He explains to whomever that Rosie and I have an appointment. He emphasizes that we're Angel's attorneys. He says "uh-huh" a few more times. Then he hangs up and gives us a relieved smile. I think he's about to blow us off when he says, "They're sending somebody up here to escort you inside."

---

"I DON'T UNDERSTAND why you wasted your time coming up here," Little Richard tells us a few minutes later. "I've given my statement to the police and told you everything I know. "

I expected to find him drinking coffee on the patio and perhaps talking on his cell phone. Instead, the guard escorted us past the house and straight to the eight-car garage, which resembles an elegant, if somewhat surreal, auto-repair shop and classic-car museum. It's nicer than Phil Menzio's shop in San Rafael, where I take my Corolla for oil changes and periodic life support. There are six vintage cars in various stages of restoration. Only one of the doors is open, and the garage smells of a rank combination of gasoline, paint fumes and motor oil. Little Richard is wearing faded jeans and a MacArthur Cellars T-shirt. He's putting a new finish on a '57 Ferrari.

"We're sorry to trouble you again," Rosie tells him.

His tone is subdued. "You're just doing your job," he says.

I shoot a quick glance at Rosie. "Richard," I say, "I had no idea you were so interested in classic cars."

His eyes light up. He pours some thinner into a bucket and says, "There are three things in life that excite me: beautiful women, fine wine and old cars." He points toward two perfectly restored Lamborghinis and a pristine Tucker. There is great pride in his voice when he tells me, "The Tucker is for Francis Coppola. He's going to display it at his winery."

Although his demeanor remains circumspect, the acrimony that we saw on Saturday is gone. He takes us on a tour of a separate building, where he gives us a detailed history of a dozen restored cars. His favorite is a '38 Jaguar that would fetch over a million dollars today.

We return to the garage, and Little Richard starts mixing paint. Rosie asks him, "Aren't you supposed to be doing something related to the promotion of the movie?"

"The studio can handle it."

I'm surprised by his lackadaisical attitude. "Are you going to release the film on time?"

"Yes." He ponders for a moment and adds, "I'm going on the *Today* show tomorrow to say it's what my father would have wanted."

"Is it?" I ask.

His demeanor takes on an air of resignation. "Probably. It's what Dom Petrillo wanted."

Rosie asks him, "Are you going to make another movie anytime soon?"

"I hope so. I like making movies." He shrugs and adds, "But not nearly as much as my father did. To be perfectly honest, I'm not as good at it as he was—at least not yet. Besides, if the China Basin project moves forward, we won't have any money to make movies."

Rosie gives him a puzzled look. She scans the rows of grapevines just outside the garage and says, "Looks to me like money shouldn't be any object."

"I know how it looks," he says, "but it isn't that simple. My father always operated right on the edge. The company has a lot of debts. The new movie was supposed to pay some of our bills. He liked to build things. He was planning to tie up the bulk of his assets in the studio."

I look around the garage and say, "It looks like you like to build things, too."

"I'm a helluva lot more practical than he was. Movies cost a lot. Intellectually, my father understood it. In real life, however, he chose to ignore the economic realities—or maybe he just didn't want to deal with them. He left the business side up to me and Marty Kent. We were in charge of trying to keep his films close to budget. It wasn't easy." His tone turns somber when he says, "If Marty and I hadn't watched him like a hawk, he would have been bankrupt years ago." He shrugs and adds, "I like to build cars and make movies. If you ask me, we would have been better off directing our resources toward making movies than putting up a fancy new building."

I ask, "Why did you go along with the plan?"

"I didn't have any choice. I told my father I thought it wasn't a good idea. He disagreed." He asks, "Did you and your father agree on everything when you were growing up?"

"Of course not."

"Who usually won the arguments?"

"My dad."

He gives me a knowing smile. "Same here. My father wanted to build his dream studio. It was his money. Do you think my opinion on the economic viability of the project carried any weight? He spent his life being told he was a genius. That word isn't generally used when people talk about me. Now it's going to cost us a fortune to get out."

Families. Rosie keeps her eye on the ball. "Richard," she says, "you told us you left your father's house around two. Who was still there?"

"My dad, Angelina and Marty Kent."

"Do you know what time Kent left?"

"No."

"Do you have any idea what happened to him?"

"I understand he jumped."

Rosie lays the cards on the table. "Do you think he killed your father?"

He starts mixing paint again. Without looking at us, he says, "I think Angelina killed my father. Then again, nothing Marty did would have surprised me. He was a self-righteous ass. He thought he was the brains behind the operation and my dad and I were just pawns. And he was really ticked off." The venom in his tone surprises me. He tells us Kent and his father had been fighting about the China Basin project. "Marty thought he was getting screwed," he says. "My dad went to the other investors to try to negotiate a bonus for him."

"Did something happen on Friday night?"

"Yes. My dad told him that the other investors had vetoed the bonus."

This jibes with the information we received from Nicole Ward.

He adds, "There was something else. Marty decided to try to pull some strings at city hall. He hired a consultant to help him get the approvals for the China Basin project."

I decide to play coy. "Do you know his name?"

"Armando Rios. Some money may have changed hands. Marty never told me about it." He reflects for a moment and adds, "Marty never told me much of anything."

"How would your father have reacted if he knew Marty was arranging bribes?"

"He would have fired him."

"Richard," I say, "how did you find out about Kent's deal with Rios?"

He eyes me warily and says, "Rios called me Sunday night. It was the first I'd heard about it."

I'm not sure about that. "Do you have any idea who was providing the money?"

"It wasn't us."

"Could it have been Marty Kent?"

"I doubt it. He was in a tough spot financially. He lost a lot of money in the market and spent a ton of dough on his wife's treatments." His demeanor remains calm. This suggests he's telling the truth. Or he may be a very good liar. "The only realistic possibilities," he says, "are Carl Ellis and Dom Petrillo."

My mind races. I ask, "Do you have any reason to suspect either one?"

"If you're smart, you should suspect both of them. They both have a lot of money, and they have a lot riding on the studio project. Ellis probably has more to lose than Petrillo."

"Why?"

"It's an important project for his firm. They've turned down other work to make people available. The deal isn't as important to Petrillo, except to massage his ego. His company can use the money to make a couple of movies."

Probably true. I look at Rosie for an instant. I turn back to Little Richard and ask, "Have you talked to the police about it?"

"I told them everything I just told you."

The good news is that he seems to be coming clean and acknowledging the sordid activities involving Rios. The bad news is that he's undoubtedly given the police an ironclad alibi for himself. "Richard," I say, "what time did you drive up to Napa?"

"Shortly after I got home."

Not so fast. "Did you have any visitors before you left?"

He puts his brush down, and his eyes dance. "Just one," he says.

"Who?"

"Ellis."

"You didn't mention it the other day."

His left eye twitches. "I don't remember what I told you."

He's lying. "What time did Ellis get back to your house?"

He looks up and thinks for a moment. Then he decides, "Probably around two-twenty."

"He showed up unannounced in the middle of the night?"

"It wasn't the first time."

"What did he want?"

"To renegotiate the terms of the China Basin project. He wanted us to take a smaller piece of the deal and to put up the vineyard as security for our financial obligations."

"And if you refused?"

"He said he would pull the plug on the deal and sue us."

"Why did he come to see you instead of your father?"

"I got along with him better than my father did." The corner of his mouth turns up slightly when he says, "My father was a bit opinionated."

"So I'm told. What did you tell Ellis?"

"That I'd talk to my father in the morning. He insisted that we go to his house. I agreed, but I told him I wasn't going to wake him up in the middle of the night. The lights were on when we got there. We went inside and talked."

"Was anybody else there?"

"Marty was still there. I assume Angelina was upstairs."

"Did you stay for the entire conversation?"

"Just the beginning. Then Ellis told me he wanted to talk to my father and Marty privately. That's when I walked home."

"What time was that?"

"Around three."

"What happened to Ellis?"

"He went back to his hotel."

"How did he get there?"

He pauses for an instant and says, "I called Eve and asked her to pick him up at my father's house. She drove him back to the Ritz."

That may have been the car that Kaela Joy heard at three. "Why didn't you drive him yourself?"

"I'd had too much to drink."

Really? "Yet you drove up to the winery?"

"Yes."

No. I glance at Rosie, who asks, "If you thought you'd had too much to drink, why did you feel comfortable driving yourself to Napa?"

He pauses for a beat. He gives me a sheepish look and says, "Eve drove me."

This contradicts the story he told us on Saturday. I ask, "Why didn't you tell us about it the other day?"

"Look," he says, "I'm getting divorced. My soon-to-be ex-wife is making all sorts of accusations. Eve and I started seeing each other about six months ago. It won't enhance my leverage in the divorce negotiations if my wife finds out I'm having an affair."

"Why are you telling us this now?" And why should we believe you?

"Eve told the police," he says. "They got her phone records. They identified the call I made to ask her to take Ellis back to the hotel. They also identified a call from her cell phone here at the winery on Saturday. They confronted her, and she admitted it. Inspector O'Brien told me about it yesterday."

Little Richard and Eve both lied to the cops and to us about their whereabouts and their relationship. What else? "What's going to happen to the studio?"

Another shrug. "Petrillo told me they're going to push ahead."

"Are you going to stay in?"

"No. My father may have been willing to pledge the winery as security for our financial obligations. I'm not. I'm out. It's going to cost me something—probably millions."

I ask him who was still at his father's house when he left for the second time early Saturday morning.

"Marty Kent and Carl Ellis."

"Anybody else?"

"Just my father and Angelina."

If he's telling the truth, that means Kent and Ellis should become suspects. "Richard," I say, "I understand your father made some changes in his will."

His tone becomes guarded. "That's none of your business."

"The district attorney showed me a copy of the amendment."

He swallows hard. "What do you want me to say? He decided to change his will."

"I'm told you're going to do pretty well."

He can't hide a smirk. "It's like winning the lottery."

"Do you have any idea why he decided to change his will?"

"He didn't tell me. I assume he was planning to file divorce papers."

He's so casual about it. I ask him if he knows anything about a fight that may have led to Angel's miscarriage. He feigns ignorance.

I say, "I understand you invited Daniel Crown to your father's memorial."

"We're friends. He respected my father. I thought it was the right thing to do."

"Crown is the father of Angelina's baby."

"I don't believe it." He picks up his thinner and starts stirring again. His voice drips with sarcasm when he says, "Danny and Angelina didn't get along. They were fighting on the set for six months. Do you think I would have invited him to my father's memorial service if I thought he was the father? Give me a little credit for having some sense of respect. Your client pointed the finger at Danny to deflect blame away from herself."

"Who was the father?"

"My dad. I'm prepared to testify to that effect if I have to."

Somebody's lying. I give him a cold stare. Then I put the cards on the table. "What happened on Saturday morning?"

"Angelina was upset. The marriage and her career were over. She killed my dad and got to the bridge before the drugs and booze stopped her."

It shouldn't surprise me that he's trying to point the finger elsewhere. For now, Angel is the easiest target. "And Marty Kent?"

"I think he committed suicide."

I don't say it out loud, but I think so, too. "And Petrillo and Ellis?"

"They were just in it for the ride. I'll bet you they'll have the entire studio project reworked by the end of the week. Danny Crown will be starring in Petrillo's next movie."

"Where does that leave you?"

"I may make another movie one of these days. In the meantime, I get to refurbish old cars, make some exquisite Merlot and count the money I'm going to inherit from my father." He winks and adds, "And I get to go skinny-dipping with Eve. Not a bad deal, if you ask me."

Not bad at all. "And *The Return of the Master*?"

He smiles. "The show must go on."

# Chapter 40

## All about Eve

> *The Return of the Master* will ensure Richard MacArthur's place as one of the great American filmmakers of his generation.
>
> —Dominic Petrillo, *Daily Variety*
> Wednesday, June 9

We give Pete a quick debriefing after we leave the MacArthur property. He stays behind to keep an eye on Little Richard.

Rosie's in a reflective mood as we're driving south toward Oakville. "Little Richard is a jerk," she says, "but in some respects, I feel sorry for him. Left to his own devices, I think he'd be content to manage the winery and tinker with his cars. It doesn't excuse his boorish behavior, but it couldn't have been easy working with his father."

She's far more understanding than I am. I ask, "Do you believe him?"

Her thoughtful look turns into a scornful smile. "No." She looks out at the carefully tended rows of vines as we head down Highway 29 and says to me, "He was too cooperative. I'd like to know why. He lied to us on Saturday. He's probably lying to us now. He said he drove to Napa with Eve. That means his girlfriend can alibi him. He pointed the finger at Angel. If that doesn't pan out, he's also suggested Kent may have been involved. If all else fails, he can blame Ellis."

"Ellis may have something to say about that," I say.

"I'll bet he will. In any event, he's constructed a neat little package that points to everybody but himself. It's too tidy."

"Do you really think he killed his father?"

"I don't know. They didn't get along. He has a financial motive."

"It's all the more reason to keep an eye on him—and Eve."

Rosie nods. "I think he's holding something back. I just don't know what it is."

I trust her instincts. We drive in silence for a few minutes. Rosie calls the office and gets a report from Carolyn on the phone records from Friday night. Then she snaps her cell phone shut and tells me that there were no calls placed from Big Dick's home phone or cell after ten o'clock on Friday night.

I ask, "What about Angel's cell?"

"They found it in her car. No calls were placed after eight o'clock Friday night."

I ask her about calls that may have been placed from Little Richard's house.

"There were outgoing calls to a cell phone belonging to Eve. That's it."

"And his cell phone?"

"Two calls to Eve's cell. The first was at two-forty. The second was at three-thirty."

Presumably, the first was to arrange a ride for Ellis to the Ritz and the second was to ask for a ride to Napa. I ask her about Petrillo and Ellis.

"There was a call from Petrillo's cell to the limo service around one-twenty. Nothing else. No outgoing calls from their rooms at the Ritz after the screening."

"I suppose we should see if there are any pay phones in the area."

"Yes, we should."

"Did she talk to Rolanda?"

"Yes. Armando Rios checked into the Tuscany last night and met with Ellis today. She had no idea what they talked about. You can bet it had something to do with the China Basin project. Carolyn made reservations for you and Pete. You're leaving for Vegas at six tonight."

"Would you like to join us?"

"I'd better stay with Angel and prepare for the prelim on Monday."

Sounds right. I ask her about Angel.

"Carolyn and my mother went to see her this morning. It didn't go well. The injuries from the suicide attempt are healing. The emotional scars are just starting." Carolyn reported that Angel was becoming distant. At times she wouldn't talk.

My cell phone rings. It's Kaela Joy. "Where are you?" she asks.

"Heading south on Twenty-nine."

"Turn around. I found Eve."

Yes! "Is she willing to talk to us?"

"I think so."

"Where are you?"

"Gillwood's."

It's a coffee shop on Main Street in St. Helena. "I can find it."

"We'll wait for you."

EVE'S LONG EYELASHES flutter. "Nice to see you again, Mike," she tells me. She's wearing tight jeans, and her dark hair cascades down her white cotton blouse. Even without makeup, she's an intriguing presence. "What a pleasant coincidence."

Kaela Joy gives us a sideways look and says, "Very pleasant, indeed."

Gillwood's is the anti-Starbucks. It's been a fixture in the center of St. Helena's historic two-block business district for decades. Although the name has changed several times, the storefront restaurant has been serving honest American food as long as I can remember. A dozen tables are scattered around the small room. There is a larger community table in the middle bearing a sign that says people are encouraged to share. The kitchen is down a hallway in the rear, just behind a modest coffee bar. The ambience is workmanlike. The aroma is inviting. Vineyard workers mingle with young mothers. I'm devouring a cholesterol-laden concoction called the Gillwood's special scramble — a combination of eggs, cheese, bacon, spinach, mushrooms and onions. My doctor would be appalled, but it's the first real food I've eaten in a couple of days. Kaela Joy ordered scrambled eggs. Rosie is eating a bagel.

"Eve," I say, "we talked to Richard."

She caresses her coffee mug, but doesn't say a word.

"I understand you drove Richard to the winery on Saturday morning."

She hesitates slightly before she says, "Yes, I did."

"You didn't mention it to me the other day."

Her eyes turn down. "I didn't mean to mislead you. I was trying to be discreet about our relationship. Richard is going through a difficult time."

Indeed. "I understand you also drove Mr. Ellis back to the Ritz on Saturday morning."

She nods.

"What time was that?"

"A few minutes before three."

"Where did you pick him up?"

"Mr. MacArthur's house."

I give Kaela Joy a glance and ask, "*Which* Mr. MacArthur?"

Eve's lips form a full-blown pout. "The senior Mr. MacArthur."

So far, her story jibes with Little Richard's. "Did you pick up Richard *and* Mr. Ellis?"

"Just Mr. Ellis."

"Why not Richard?"

"He was still inside with his father and Mr. Kent. Only Mr. Ellis was waiting for me outside the house."

Rosie puts down her coffee mug. Eve is contradicting Little Richard's story. He said he went home while Ellis and Kent were still talking to his father. Eve just said Little Richard was still there after Ellis left. I want to be sure I heard her right. I try to keep my tone even as I ask, "Are you sure he was still meeting with his father while you took Mr. Ellis to the Ritz?"

I can see a slight discomfort in her eyes when she says, "Yes."

"Then you came back and picked up Richard at his father's house?"

"No. I picked him up at *his* house." She says Little Richard walked home from his father's house while Eve was driving Ellis to the Ritz. He called her on his cell and told her to meet him at his house. "We left for the winery around three-thirty."

"And why didn't you tell us about this on Saturday?"

"I was trying to be discreet."

Right. Rosie gives me a knowing look. I decide it would be best to leave out any mention of the skinny-dipping under the Napa Valley moon. After all, she's trying to be discreet. We finish our breakfast, and I pick up the check. Eve heads out onto Main Street.

We regroup in the doorway to Gillwood's. I tell Kaela Joy about the inconsistencies in Little Richard's and Eve's respective accounts.

Her eyes light up. "Who's lying?" she asks.

"I'm not sure. Little Richard didn't want to admit he was the last person to see his father alive. He blamed Angel. And just to be safe, he told us Kent and Ellis were there, too."

"We have to talk to Ellis right away."

"Pete and I are flying down to Vegas tonight," I tell her.

"I'm coming with—" She's stopped midsentence by blaring sirens. We see two fire engines go charging down Main Street. "What is it?" she asks.

I feel my cell phone vibrating in my pocket. I snap it open and I can barely make out Pete's voice shouting, "MacArthur's house is on fire! There was an explosion in the garage."

My God. "Where's Little Richard?"

"I'm not sure."

I flash back to the cans of thinner. I think of his proud look when he showed me his restored autos and the sound of his voice as he told me about his car collection. I tell Pete we'll be there as soon as we can. I realize I'm already starting to walk up the street when Rosie grabs my arm. Kaela Joy is standing next to her.

"There was an explosion at the winery," I say.

Kaela Joy's dark brown eyes turn serious. "I'll meet you there."

Rosie and I start walking toward my car. She pulls the keys out of my hand as I'm about to open the door. "I'll drive," she says.

# Chapter 41

## "One of His Damned Cars Must Have Blown Up"

There has been an explosion at MacArthur Cellars just south of St. Helena.

—KGO Radio
Wednesday, June 9. Noon

Highway 29 is clogged with emergency vehicles. Rosie and I abandon our car a half mile north of Zinfandel Lane and we hike the rest of the way. We find Pete standing by a roadblock near the gate to the MacArthur estate, where pandemonium reigns. Fire trucks surround the garage. A rescue helicopter hovers overhead. Billows of black smoke pour into the acrid air, and the usually pristine valley is shrouded in a thick haze.

"One of his damned cars must have blown up," Pete shouts above the roar. He says he was in his car near the main gate when he heard the explosion. He called 911. "Eve came back just after the fire started," he says. "I tried to get to the garage, but the fire was too intense. Then the fire trucks arrived, and I got the hell out of the way."

Rosie asks, "Did you see anything before the fire started?"

"I saw a farm worker drive by the garage on a tractor, then I saw him running toward the house after the explosion. I don't know what happened to him."

I ask, "Did anybody else come to see Little Richard after we left?"

"No." He reflects and says, "You may have been the last people to have seen him alive."

The cops will have some questions for us. We gaze at the fire in silence.

We watch vineyard workers scurrying to protect the precious vines. The employees of MacArthur Cellars are standing in small groups outside the gate. The parking lot near the tasting room is jammed with police cars. The unsightly winery building is still intact.

An officious young woman with trim hair and sensible clothing approaches us and flashes a badge. She looks at Pete and says, "We'd like to take your statement now, Mr. Daley."

I interject, "And you would be?"

"Inspector Julie Hart. St. Helena Police. And you would be?"

Pete replies, "He's my brother." He pauses and adds, "And my lawyer."

Inspector Hart looks me up and down. Then she glances at Pete and notices the resemblance. I say to her in a measured tone, "I'm Michael Daley." I introduce Rosie and say, "We're Angelina Chavez's attorneys."

A look of recognition crosses her face. "We need to talk to your brother. Then we'd like to ask you some questions."

OVER THE COURSE of my long and illustrious career, I have been present at hundreds of interrogations. Most have taken place at crime scenes, in police stations or in the bowels of the Hall of Justice. The setting is therefore a bit unusual as I answer Inspector Hart's questions at a picnic table at the edge of a hundred pastoral acres of vines along Zinfandel Lane while Little Richard's garage is still engulfed in flames a quarter of a mile away.

Inspector Hart just finished an unproductive half hour with Pete, who told her very little. He isn't a chatty guy, and he knows you have to be careful about what you say to the police. At one point she threatened to detain him, whereupon he asked me to sit in on the conversation. Then things moved along more quickly. Inspector Hart was taken aback when she found out that Pete and Kaela Joy had been keeping Little Richard under surveillance. This sort of thing doesn't happen in the Napa Valley. Rosie and Kaela Joy are going through a similar exercise at adjacent picnic tables with Inspector Hart's colleagues.

I'm not used to being on the receiving end in this procedure. It's a little unnerving when a police officer starts asking you questions. Inspector

Hart is doing her interrogation by the book. She isn't going to get much more out of me than she got from Pete. I'm not trying to be difficult, but I don't want to say anything that might adversely impact Angel's case. She takes meticulous notes as I give her the thirty-second version of my story: Rosie and I talked to Little Richard. He was working on a car in the garage where there were flammable materials. He was cooperative. We didn't see anything suspicious. Then we left and had breakfast with Eve and Kaela Joy at Gillwood's. We came back when Pete called.

Inspector Hart isn't going to accept my explanation without additional discussion. She asks, "How well did you know Mr. MacArthur?"

"I'd met him once before today."

"Did you notice anything unusual in his behavior?"

"No."

"Did he mention anything about threats or other problems?"

"No." You might consider the fact that his father was murdered less than a week ago.

"What was your brother doing here?"

"We were keeping Mr. MacArthur under surveillance. We were trying to figure out if he had any involvement in his father's death."

"Did he?"

I want to plant a seed. "We think so," I say. "His father changed his will to make him the sole beneficiary. He was one of the last people at his father's house early Saturday morning." I tell her there were some inconsistencies between his story and Eve's. I suggest that she talk to Jack O'Brien. Maybe she can convince him to consider Little Richard as a suspect.

She furrows her brow. We parry for twenty minutes. She says she'll talk to O'Brien. "I'll need to ask you and your colleagues to let us know if you're planning to leave the vicinity."

"No problem," I say as I hand her a card. I tell her that Pete and I plan to go to Vegas to interview a couple of witnesses. I promise to keep her informed of our whereabouts. I glance at the medical helicopter that is lifting off from the parking lot. I turn back to Inspector Hart and ask, "Is that Mr. MacArthur?"

"Yes."

"Is he going to be all right?"

"No, Mr. Daley. He's dead."

PETE IS SITTING on a picnic table, arms folded. "Inspector Hart was pushy," he says.

I'll bet he was at least as pushy when he was a cop. "She was just doing her job."

"She could have been polite."

"At least she didn't haul your ass into jail."

He gives me a sideways grin and says, "When she heard I was represented by Fernandez and Daley, she folded up like a tent. Besides, she knew I didn't have anything to do with Little Richard's death. She finally told me the guy who was driving the tractor admitted he started the fire. He said he was dragging a chain that scraped the ground and caused a spark. It set off a chain reaction when it hit the fumes. It's going to be ruled an accident."

He's good. "How did you get her to tell you about it?"

"Just because a cop is asking questions doesn't mean you can't ask a few of your own."

"She volunteered the information?"

"Professional courtesy. Besides, I can be very charming when I want to be."

Maybe *he* should have been the lawyer.

# Chapter 42

## "This Case Has Been Getting Round-the-Clock Coverage"

You call them as you see them. You do your best to get it right.

—Superior Court Judge Elizabeth McDaniel
*San Francisco Daily Legal Journal*
Wednesday, June 9

We're back in Judge McDaniel's courtroom later the same afternoon. She's giving me an icy stare over the top of her reading glasses. The motherly voice that we heard on Monday has given way to a more judicial tone. She says to me, "I didn't expect to see you again, Mr. Daley."

Neither did I. When Leslie withdrew from the case, Judge McDaniel was drafted to hear some motions that we filed yesterday. This is more than an academic exercise. The decisions she makes today will have a substantial bearing on the direction of Angel's case.

I try to sound respectful. "We appreciate the fact that you were able to make yourself available on short notice."

This gets a quick glance from Rosie. We got back from Napa ten minutes ago. We hadn't anticipated the events at the winery when we scheduled this hearing. I changed into my suit in the bathroom down the hall. After Monday's debacle, Rosie decided to let me try to work my magic today. Perhaps Judge McDaniel will be more receptive to a fresh voice.

The judge leans back in her chair and scans her crowded courtroom. She looks at Nicole Ward and holds up her hands in the universal gesture of frustration. Then she turns to me and says in an even tone, "I've read your papers. Where do you want to start?"

To her credit, at least she's going to give us a chance—however brief—to tell our story. I jump right in. "Your Honor," I say, "our first issue relates to the production of evidence by the prosecution. On Monday, you ordered Ms. Ward's office to comply with discovery as expeditiously as possible."

Ward is still seated when she interjects, "We're complying, Your Honor."

Judge McDaniel turns to me and says, "What's the problem, Mr. Daley?"

"The prosecution has not been forthcoming with police records and other evidence."

Ward is now on her feet. She strains to keep her tone even when she says, "That's completely false, Your Honor. We've been providing everything as fast as we can process it."

It's the reaction I wanted. I'm trying to put Ward on the defensive. We'll have more important issues to discuss in a minute.

Judge McDaniel tells Ward to sit down. Then she turns back to me and says, "You'll have to be more specific."

Carolyn hands a list to Rosie, who passes it over to me. "Police reports, Your Honor. Inspector O'Brien informed us that he filed his first report on Monday. We still haven't seen it."

Ward leaps in. "We haven't had time to inventory it, Your Honor. We'll provide it to Mr. Daley within twenty-four hours."

"Your Honor," I say, "we're already seeing a pattern of delay."

The judge sets down her reading glasses. She points to Ward and says, "I expect you to make every effort to catalogue evidence right away and provide it to the defense. Understood?"

Ward is seething. "Understood."

Judge McDaniel turns back to me and says, "As for you, Mr. Daley, two days isn't a pattern of delay. Let's try to be realistic here."

It's a fair response. "Yes, Your Honor."

"What else?"

On to the main events. "Your Honor," I say, "we have some serious issues to consider. My client's constitutional rights have been violated."

This elicits an arched eyebrow from Judge McDaniel, but she says nothing.

"In particular," I continue, "my client was not properly Mirandized until well after she was taken into custody. Anything she said prior to that time is clearly inadmissible. The fact that she was given the Miranda warnings so late means that she was not afforded her fundamental protections."

Judge McDaniel interrupts me. "And so, Mr. Daley, I take it you're suggesting that I dismiss the charges?"

She certainly cuts right to the chase. "Yes."

The corner of Judge McDaniel's mouth turns up in a sardonic half smile. She looks at Ward and says, "What do you have to say about this, Ms. Ward?"

"Your Honor," Ward begins, "the defendant was properly Mirandized at the Hall of Justice before she was questioned about her husband's death."

"Your Honor," I say, "the Miranda warnings are required prior to questioning. The officer who found Ms. Chavez informed her of her husband's death. How can Ms. Ward possibly suggest that Ms. Chavez wasn't questioned at the bridge? Ms. Ward's argument completely undercuts the purpose of the Miranda warnings. My client was stopped, given a breath test and taken into custody. She was not read her rights until an hour later at the Hall of Justice. If you accept Ms. Ward's interpretation of the law, it makes the Miranda rules meaningless."

Ward comes right back. "Your Honor," she says, "Mr. Daley is correct in that the Miranda warnings must be given prior to questioning. However, the events at the bridge and the subsequent ride to the Hall did not constitute questioning. It's well established that voluntary statements made by defendants who are not being questioned are admissible even in the absence of the Miranda warnings. The defendant's rights were respected at all times."

I search for an incredulous tone. "So," I say, "you're suggesting that Ms. Chavez and the police officers were just chatting?"

"I'm saying that her statements were voluntary."

Hell. The answer to the question of whether certain statements were made voluntarily or in the course of questioning is often an elusive one. That's why criminal defense attorneys tell their clients not to talk to the cops. We joust over the latest Supreme Court rulings on the Miranda warnings. Ward doesn't give an inch. Neither do I.

Finally, the judge says, "I am not going to drop the charges. I'll take it under advisement and issue a written ruling if I determine that any of Ms. Chavez's statements should be excluded."

It's less than I had hoped for, but it's about what I had expected. I didn't think she'd drop the charges, although she may still limit the admissibility of some of the statements Angel made at the bridge. Overall, her ruling doesn't help us.

Judge McDaniel is becoming impatient. She gives me a sharp look and says, "Anything else, Mr. Daley?"

Now for the main event. "Your Honor," I say, "the prosecution proposes to introduce a significant piece of evidence that was obtained as a result of an illegal search. An Academy Award statue was found in the trunk of the car. Ms. Ward thinks it's the murder weapon. We believe that it was obtained illegally and should be excluded."

I glimpse Ward out of the corner of my eye. She stands for an instant, then reconsiders and sits down.

Judge McDaniel gives me a serious look. "How was the search illegal?"

"Ms. Chavez was stopped for driving on an expired license and a DUI charge. The officer at the scene opened the trunk. There was no probable cause to have searched the trunk."

The judge turns to Ward and says, "Why did the officer open the trunk, Ms. Ward?"

"The officer found a Baggie containing a suspicious substance on the front seat of the defendant's car. It turns out it was cocaine."

The judge isn't going to make it easy. "Where's the probable cause to open the trunk?"

Ward pauses to regroup. She understands the gravity of the situation. If Judge McDaniel rules against her, she won't be able to produce the murder weapon and her case will probably collapse. She searches for a tone of reason when she says, "Your Honor, the officer faced a situation where the driver of the car was intoxicated and perhaps high. The Breathalyzer test clearly bore out the fact that Ms. Chavez was driving under the influence. He found illegal drugs in plain view. The defendant's behavior was erratic. Under the circumstances, it is not unreasonable to suggest that the officer had probable cause to search the trunk of the car for other illegal substances."

I interject, "He didn't know the substance he found in the car was illegal."

"He was experienced," Ward replies. "He knew exactly what was going on."

Judge McDaniel looks at me and says, "Does your client dispute the fact that the Oscar was found in the trunk of the car?"

"She doesn't know how it got there," I say.

"Answer my question, Mr. Daley. Does she dispute the fact that it was in the trunk?"

I have no choice. "No, Your Honor."

"And you recognize that a decision was made to take Ms. Chavez into custody."

"That's true."

"As a result," the judge continues, "the car was impounded."

"Yes."

"And you know that as part of the process of impounding a car, it is standard procedure to inventory its contents, including the trunk. Correct?"

I give Rosie a helpless look. "Yes, Your Honor."

"So, you're asking me to exclude the Oscar even though you freely admit your client does not dispute that it was in the trunk and that it would have been found anyway in connection with a legitimate impoundment of the vehicle."

I have no choice. "Yes, Your Honor."

Judge McDaniel heaves a sigh. "I'm not going to exclude this evidence, Mr. Daley."

"But, Your Honor..."

"I've ruled, Mr. Daley."

Hell.

Judge McDaniel gives me the grandmotherly grin and says, "Anything else, Mr. Daley?"

I'm not quite finished. "Your Honor," I say, "this case has received extensive press coverage and publicity." I shoot a quick glance at Jerry Edwards, who is sitting in the front row. "It will be impossible for our client to empanel an impartial and unbiased jury here in San Francisco. We would therefore request a change of venue."

It's a standard request. Judges are usually pretty willing to comply, although the costs of moving a full-blown trial to another town are substantial.

Ward is up again. "Your Honor," she says, "it's too early to discuss this issue. We haven't completed the prelim. Surely, this is something we can address later."

Ward doesn't want to move the trial. It will create logistical issues she'd rather not deal with, and she may end up in a tiny media market. It's a mixed bag for us. The media scrutiny will be just as intense if we move the trial to Chico. Moreover, San Francisco juries are usually well educated and pretty liberal. On the other hand, Rosie and I decided that the wall-to-wall coverage and the small potential juror pool in San Francisco will make it difficult to empanel twelve people who aren't predisposed to convict Angel.

The judge reflects for a moment and says, "I'll take it under advisement. We can discuss the venue for the trial after the prelim."

Not good enough. "Your Honor," I say, "this case has been getting round-the-clock coverage on all of the local TV stations and has been the lead story on page one of all of the major newspapers. Surely, this is an issue that bears discussion sooner rather than later."

"Mr. Daley," the judge says, "I understand your concerns about the potential effect of pretrial publicity on the juror pool. We'll discuss it after the preliminary hearing next week."

"Your Honor," I say, "the location of the trial will have a material impact on our strategic decisions. In fairness to our client, I believe we should resolve this issue as soon as we can."

I'm not just blowing smoke. San Francisco juries are different from those in other parts of California. The location of the trial will have a significant impact on the tone of our case.

Judge McDaniel gives me a thoughtful look. While she isn't buying my argument entirely, she seems receptive to continuing the discussion. "Do you have any empirical evidence that the media coverage in this case has already tainted the potential juror pool?"

"Yes, Your Honor. We'd like to submit a study prepared by Professor Stephen Harris of the University of California." I explain that Harris is an authority on statistical analysis and one of the leading political pollsters in California. "We have asked Professor Harris to join us to explain his conclusions."

Ward rolls her eyes. Judge McDaniel says, "Let's hear what the professor has to say."

It takes just a moment to run Steve Harris through his credentials. Although he's a full professor of mathematics at UC Berkeley with an expertise in statistical sampling, the bulk of his income comes from political consulting. He's done polling on every major statewide campaign for thirty years. Although he's a millionaire many times over, he still looks the part of a college professor. He's barely five feet tall, with a full head of hair, a bushy gray beard, John Lennon spectacles and a chatty demeanor. Carolyn bought him a new striped tie to go along with his ancient sport jacket. Ward doesn't challenge his qualifications.

I want to keep this short and sweet. "Professor Harris," I begin, "did you conduct a telephone survey yesterday concerning the ongoing case involving Angelina Chavez?"

"Yes."

"And could you briefly describe the methodology of your survey?"

"Yes." Harris explains that he took a poll of four hundred randomly selected registered voters in San Francisco. He is completely disarming as he talks in mathematical and layman's terms about such esoterica as sample size, standard deviations and margins of error. Judge McDaniel's stern look softened as soon as he started talking. She seems intrigued and amused.

I ask Harris, "How many questions did you ask?"

"Just one."

"What was that?"

"Do you think Angelina Chavez is guilty of murdering her husband?"

I glance at Nicole Ward for an instant. Then I turn back to the professor and say, "What was the response?"

"Seventy-eight percent said yes."

Perfect. "No further questions."

Ward is up immediately. "Professor Harris," she says, "you'd be the first to admit that informal polls such as the one you took have certain inherent limitations, wouldn't you?"

Harris remains congenial. "That's true."

"In fact, they have varying margins for error, don't they?"

"Of course."

"So, it would be fair to say that the results of your poll may not be reliable."

Harris pauses. His gentle smile disappears. "No, Ms. Ward," he says, "my methods are statistically very reliable. The only limitations are the size of the sample and the time we have to ask the questions and compile the data."

Ward isn't ready to concede. "But you would acknowledge that the results could be flawed if the sample size was too small or the respondents were not telling you the truth."

"That is theoretically possible," he says. "However, it is highly unlikely."

They joust for ten minutes. Harris holds his ground. Finally, Ward says to Judge McDaniel, "Your Honor, before you make a final decision on this issue, we would request the opportunity to retain our own expert and conduct our own poll."

"Objection," I say. "Ms. Ward has already stipulated to Professor Harris's expertise."

Judge McDaniel ponders for a moment and says, "Overruled." She looks at Ward and says, "I'll withhold judgement on this issue until the end of the week. I'm going to give you until Friday to find your own expert."

Then she turns to me and adds, "No matter what my findings on this issue, Mr. Daley, the preliminary hearing for this matter will be held in this courtroom as scheduled next week. Understood?"

It isn't a day for great victories, but it's the best we can do for now. "Yes, Your Honor."

"Anything else, Mr. Daley?"

"Yes, Your Honor. In an effort to prevent further tainting of the potential juror pool, we request that you impose a gag order on everyone involved in this matter."

It's an easy call for her. "So ordered," she says. She raises her gavel and adds, "We're adjourned."

ROSIE IS DRIVING ME to the airport a short time later. We're sitting in traffic on 101 at Hospital Curve as the radio announcer confirms that Little Richard died instantly and three others were injured in the ensuing explosion and fire. Little Richard's prized car collection was destroyed, and there was three million dollars' worth of damage. The newsman concludes by saying, "Authorities believe the fire was started when a spark ignited some flammable materials in the garage. Although the final results of the investigation are pending, it is anticipated that MacArthur's death will be ruled accidental and no charges will be filed."

As usual, Pete was right.

I ask, "What did you think about the judge's ruling on the Oscar?"

"It didn't surprise me. We knew it was a long shot. If she ruled in our favor, it would have undercut Ward's case. Judge McDaniel wasn't going to do that. She's a good judge, but she still has the mentality of a prosecutor. She doesn't want to be perceived as soft." She reflects and adds, "If this case goes to trial, we're going to have to deal with the Oscar."

Rosie's instincts are usually dead-on. I move on to another delicate subject. "How are you feeling, Rosita?"

Her stoic expression doesn't change. "I'm exhausted. I'm sick. My niece has been accused of murder, and she tried to kill herself. Everybody involved in the China Basin project is either crooked or dead. We're going to have to try Angel's case before a pro-prosecution judge." She hesitates and says, "And how are you?"

"I'm fine. I get to go to Vegas tonight. What more could a person want?"

This gets the hint of a grin.

We sit in silence for a moment. Then I say, "So?"

"So what?"

"Are you ready to talk about it?"

"Angel's case?"

"Your test results."

A heavy sigh. She tugs on her ear. She swallows. Her eyes are still on the road when she says, "It isn't so good." Then she turns to me and says, "They found another lump."

"Where?"

"Right breast."

"How bad?"

"Worse than last time."

"How much worse?"

"Enough to make things interesting. I've graduated to stage three-A."

Dammit. "What are the options?"

Her tone remains clinical when she says, "They're suggesting a total mastectomy." It means the removal of the entire breast, but not the muscle tissue beneath it or lymph nodes under the arm. "Maybe some radiation," she adds. "The good news is that I didn't have a lot of terrible side effects from the radiation last time. The bad news is that it didn't seem to work." She bites her lower lip and says, "In case you're wondering, the average five-year survival rate for this stage is fifty-six percent." She gives me a wry half smile and adds, "You could say my chances of being here five years from now are a little better than tossing a coin."

"You're going to be fine, Rosie."

"Yeah. I want to have it taken care of as soon as I can. I'm supposed to call in the morning." She says she'll schedule the surgery at the UCSF cancer center at the old Mt. Zion Hospital. She adds, "I may need a little help with this."

"I'll be there."

"Thanks. I want to keep working until the prelim next week. Then we'll have to see how it goes. I need to take care of this."

"Have you told Grace?"

"Yeah. She was okay. She's strong."

So are you. "And your mother?"

"She's strong, too."

It runs in the family. I tell her, "Whatever you need, Rosie."

"I'll let you know." She gives me a tired smile. "It would be nice if you could find Richard's murderer in the next few days. I don't think I'll be able to take Angel's case beyond the prelim."

"I'll take care of it."

"Thanks." She forces a chuckle and says, "Look on the bright side. Except for my diagnosis and the explosion at the winery, it's been a pretty good day."

"How do you figure?"

"Nobody in our family got arrested today."

The voice of perspective. I can't help myself, and I laugh. "We're in trouble if that's our new benchmark. Inspector Hart was ready to haul in Pete. He wasn't especially cooperative."

"He can be difficult."

"He's stubborn."

"How did he persuade them not to take him down to the station?"

"He told her he was represented by Fernandez and Daley. She cut him loose right away."

"Our reputation precedes us."

We drive in silence for a moment. Our windows are open, and the fog is rolling in. I take a deep breath of the cool sea breeze. "Where does this leave Angel's case?" I ask.

Her demeanor becomes lawyerly again. "I'm not sure. Eve and Little Richard contradicted each other about who left Big Dick's house. If we give them the benefit of the doubt, it seems one of them was mistaken." She gives me a skeptical look and says, "The more likely explanation is that one of them was lying. It may give us an opening." She adds, "And now young Mr. MacArthur can't defend himself."

Ever the pragmatist. "What about Eve?" I ask.

"Kaela Joy is going to keep an eye on her while you and Pete are down in Vegas."

So many possibilities. I ask, "Are you going to stop at the hospital on your way home?"

"Yeah. Somehow, I'm going to have to figure out a way to explain everything that happened today to Angel."

# Chapter 43

## "This Is America"

We set out to build the most elegant resort and casino in the world.

—Carl Ellis, Opening of the Tuscany Hotel Casino
*Las Vegas Sun*

"The Tuscany looks nice, Mick," Pete says. He's looking out the window of our United 737 as we are beginning our descent into McCarran Airport just south of the Vegas strip. Our plane was late flying out of San Francisco, and it's almost midnight. I look down upon the oasis of wretched excess in the middle of the desert. My dad used to say Vegas isn't a city; it's a state of mind.

I wink at Pete and say, "This is America."

"We live in a great country."

I was only six when I saw the twinkling lights of Vegas for the first time. Pete was still a baby and our younger sister, Mary, wasn't born. My mom and dad used to take us down here for long weekends a couple of times a year. Reno was closer, but my dad insisted the real action was in Vegas. They'd pile us kids in the backseat and we'd go speeding down the central valley. It was a big treat for us, and my dad loved to gamble. He knew some retired SFPD cops who worked in casino security. We got to stay in some of the nicer hotels for a cut rate. We'd sit by the pool all day with my mom while my dad played blackjack. He used to take us out for steak dinners when he won. We got hamburgers when he lost. Although I have no official statistics on his winning percentage, in my recollection, we ate more steak than hamburger. Nowadays, the hotels and casinos are bigger and nicer. The focus on bringing in conventions and families has taken a bit of the edge off the city's tawdry image. Every new hotel comes with its own ersatz theme park. In some ways, it looks more like a bad Disneyland knockoff than a gambling mecca.

Everything in Vegas is designed to get you and your money into the casinos as efficiently as possible. It takes us twenty-five minutes to breeze through McCarran and get a cab to the Tuscany. It's ninety-eight degrees as we enter the grounds through the sculpted gardens and the huge man-made lake. The marketing materials boast that the hotel has over a thousand fountains. Waterfalls are cascading in the middle of the desert, and there is an expertly choreographed water show a couple of times a day. The Tuscany has the usual assortment of upscale restaurants, pools, health clubs and spas, as well as the obligatory roller coasters. There's even a private botanical garden and an art gallery. Most important, you can always gamble.

There are no clocks in Vegas. Even though it's after midnight, the lobby is jammed. Although the Tuscany attempts to portray an upscale image, the ever-present tour groups, businessmen, cocktail waitresses, casino workers and security guards are milling around. Mercifully, the check-in line is relatively short. Our room is in the "deluxe" category, which is at the low end of the scale. It runs over two hundred bucks a night.

The attractive young woman behind the counter is wearing a badge that says her name is Penny Warner. She looks at her computer screen, and her eyes open wide. I expect her to tell me they've lost our reservation when she says, "Mr. Daley, you've been upgraded to a suite."

"Really?" I'll bet we're up to two thousand bucks a night. I turn around and look at Pete, who is scanning the lobby area. "Looks like we're moving up to a nicer room," I tell him.

He nods as if he expected it. I turn to the clerk, who hands me my credit card and says, "This won't be necessary. Your accommodations are complimentary. Everything has been taken care of by your host."

"My host?"

"Yes."

My mind races. "There must be some mistake."

"No," she says. "Mr. Ellis made the arrangements."

Welcome to Vegas. Pete taps me on the shoulder and says, "We'll need to figure out a way to find Ellis."

"Looks like he found us."

"NOT BAD, MICK," Pete says as he flicks on the light in our two-bedroom suite on the eighteenth floor. We take a quick look out at the lake. Then we check out the plush furnishings in our sitting room. The bathrooms are larger than my bedroom at home. "It reminds me of the time we stayed in that suite."

My dad's former partner knew somebody whose brother was the night manager at the old Flamingo. On one of our last trips down here, he was able to get us a suite that was bigger than our house. We felt like high rollers. We spent most of the weekend in the room watching TV. We wanted to savor the experience. In retrospect, I'm sure the accommodations were on a par with your average Embassy Suites. It made an impression on me. "This is nicer," I tell him.

He looks around the room and smiles. "Carl Ellis put us up in nice digs."

"That he did. He knows we're here. We need to contact him."

"He'll contact us. He wants to talk. He wouldn't have paid for the room if he didn't."

I pick up the phone and call Rolanda's room. No answer. I try her cell. I get voice mail.

"Sit tight," Pete says. "He must know we're here by now."

The phone rings five minutes later. I glance at my watch. A quarter to one. An unfamiliar baritone says, "Mr. Daley?"

"Yes."

"Carl Ellis."

"Good evening. What can I do for you?"

"Armando Rios and I are dining with your associate. We were hoping you'd join us."

"We'd love to."

"Excellent."

"Where should we meet you?"

"Firenze."

"When?"

"Now."

# Chapter 44

## "We Have Found It Necessary to Reevaluate the Project"

I run a successful and completely legitimate business.

—Carl Ellis, *Las Vegas Sun*

Carl Ellis bears an uncanny resemblance to Edward G. Robinson. He sounds like him, too. "Welcome to Las Vegas, Mr. Daley," he says.

Firenze is the Tuscany's culinary crown jewel. The luxuriously appointed Italian restaurant overlooks the lake. In typical Vegas fashion, the hotel imported an expensive facsimile of an acclaimed restaurant from New York. It's a far cry from the pizza-and-pasta places in North Beach or the Tuscan villas in Florence. The posh room is an elegantly crafted combination of red velvet chairs, starched white tablecloths and colorful murals. Except for the staff and two ominous-looking security guards, Carl Ellis, Armando Rios, Rolanda and a gnomelike man whom I don't recognize were the only people in the restaurant when Pete and I walked in a moment ago. We're sitting at one of the round tables in the corner under a mural. The restaurant is completely silent. The effect is unnerving.

Ellis's slicked-back silver hair contrasts with his black Armani suit and matching silk shirt. He isn't wearing a tie. He's one of the few people in Vegas with the clout to turn the Tuscany's finest restaurant into his private dining room. "I trust you found your accommodations satisfactory?" he says.

"Indeed. Thank your for your hospitality."

"You're quite welcome." He motions us to sit down. "Our firm was the contractor on this hotel. The management allows me to host private parties from time to time. I've asked the chef to prepare something for the table. I hope that will meet with your approval."

"Absolutely."

He motions to the waiter, who points toward a colleague standing near the entrance to the kitchen. Looks like we're getting the works. I glance at Rolanda, who never takes her eyes off Ellis. Armando Rios is frowning, but says nothing.

I look at Ellis and say, "I don't believe we've met your colleague."

Ellis looks at the studious man and says, "He's my attorney. He wanted to be here when I spoke to you."

That's understandable. The morose man extends a chubby hand, which I shake. Then he sits down without a word. Ellis's self-confident grin vanishes, and he takes the offensive. "I assume you came down here because you wanted to talk to us about your client's case."

"That's true."

"I have been a respected businessman in this community for many years. I believe in telling the truth. It's the right thing to do. And it's good business."

It's good bullshit, too.

He uses a sterling-silver knife to dab butter on a piece of bread. He says in an offhand tone, "I've given my statement to the police. I've been told I may have to make myself available to testify at your client's preliminary hearing. I assumed you were going to contact me sooner or later. When I found out you were coming, I thought it would be better to talk in civilized surroundings."

It also gives him an opportunity to put a favorable spin on his story. "How did you know I was coming?"

"The studio project is a major matter for our company. Your client's situation is a substantial and unnecessary complication. So are the untimely deaths of Dick MacArthur and his son. We're monitoring the situation. In all honesty, as part of the process, we decided to monitor you."

"You've been following us?"

"Yes." He hesitates and adds in an accusatory tone, "Turnabout is fair play, Mr. Daley. You were following Mr. Rios."

"How did you know?"

He looks at Armando and says, "We've been following him, too."

Rios's frown becomes more pronounced. I look at Ellis and say, "We understand you met with Mr. Rios earlier today."

"We did." He glances at Rolanda. Then he turns to me and says, "I asked Mr. Rios to provide a status report on the China Basin project." He turns to Rios and says, "Tell him what you told me, Armando."

Rios is unhappy about being addressed as if he were a trained seal. Nonetheless, he says in an even tone, "There are serious complications in our attempts to obtain the approvals for the China Basin project."

Ellis leans back in his chair and answers for him. "Mr. Daley," he says, "in light of this week's events, we have found it necessary to reevaluate the project."

"Are you still planning to move forward?"

"Yes." He pauses and says, "But the project will have a revised investor group and a new major tenant. Dom Petrillo and I believe MacArthur Films is no longer a viable partner. We instructed our attorneys to submit a new proposal to the redevelopment agency." He glances at Rios and says, "It does not involve MacArthur Films."

Presumably, it won't involve Armando Rios, either. "Will you be calling upon Mr. Rios for his assistance with the new proposal?"

"No."

The squeeze-out is now complete. Big Dick didn't get his studio. Little Richard didn't get his inheritance. Marty Kent didn't get his bonus. Armando Rios didn't get his payoff.

"Mr. Ellis," I say, "how long have you known Mr. Rios?"

"We met for the first time earlier today."

"Did you know that he had been hired to assist with the approval process?"

"Yes. It's customary to hire a consultant. His reputation is very good."

The corner of Rios's mouth turns up slightly.

I say, "Are you aware of the fact that there have been allegations of money changing hands in order to facilitate the approval process?"

"So I'm told."

"Did you have any knowledge of any such payments?" I sit back and wait for the denial.

He points an emphatic finger at me and says in an even tone, "I want to assure you that I knew nothing about any alleged payoffs and I wouldn't have condoned them if I did."

I'm assured. Armando Rios must be burning inside. I ask Ellis, "I don't suppose you might know who was bankrolling this activity?"

"Absolutely not."

"It wasn't Dominic Petrillo, was it?"

This elicits an emphatic head shake. "No. It could have been Martin Kent or somebody from the MacArthur organization. I simply don't know."

And it's certainly convenient that Kent and the MacArthurs are no longer alive to tell their side of the story. I turn to Rios and say, "Can you shed any light on this, Armando?"

He glances quickly toward Ellis. Then he looks back at me and says, "All the arrangements were made by Mr. Kent. I don't know where the money came from."

And I don't know how much Ellis is paying him to keep his mouth shut. I'm frustrated, but I try not to let it show. I turn back to Ellis and ask him about the events of Friday night and Saturday morning. He shows no signs of defensiveness when I ask him why he returned to Little Richard's house. He says he wanted to talk about the China Basin project. He claims he was concerned about the success of the movie and the economic viability of MacArthur Films. "In all honesty," he says, "I told young Richard that we were going to need some additional security before we were going to move forward with the deal."

It's the second time he's used the phrase "In all honesty" in the last five minutes. "What did you ask for?"

"A first-priority deed of trust on MacArthur Cellars."

This is consistent with Little Richard's description of their conversation. I ask him why he talked to Little Richard instead of his father.

"He was more businesslike and reasonable." He gives me a quick wink and says, "And more pliable. I wanted to warm him up to the idea before I talked to his father."

I ask him about Little Richard's reaction.

"He was against it. Then I told him I wanted to talk to his father."

"Which you did a short time later."

"Yes."

"What was his father's response?"

"He agreed to it. We shook hands. We had a deal. In all honesty, I was surprised."

There's that phrase again. "That's it?"

"That's it. I asked young Richard to call me a cab. He called his assistant instead."

"Eve?"

"Yes. She drove me back to the Ritz." He assures us that Big Dick was very much alive when Eve came to pick him up.

I ask him, "Who was there when you left?"

"Young Richard and Martin Kent." He pretends to ponder for a moment. Then he adds, "I assume Angelina was upstairs."

He can't corroborate any of this. I ask, "How did Kent and Little Richard react to the new deal?"

"Kent was irate because we told him he wasn't going to receive the bonus that he had expected. Young Richard was even angrier. He thought his father was putting his family's most valuable asset at risk. You know how families can be. They were out on the balcony screaming at each other as I was leaving."

That might explain the shouting that Robert Neils heard from his bedroom. I ask him what he thought really happened on Saturday morning.

"I don't know, Mr. Daley. I do know that Angelina, young Richard and Marty Kent were all very upset at Dick."

THREE A.M. We've regrouped upstairs in our suite. Rolanda is sitting on the couch. Pete is standing by the windows. Armando Rios is sitting in the armchair.

Rolanda is seething. "Ellis gave us nothing on the payoffs," she says. "He constructed a perfect alibi for himself. Now I understand why he wanted to talk to us. He was setting us up. He's pointed the finger at Angel. If that doesn't work, he can still point the finger at MacArthur's son and Marty Kent. There's nobody else around to corroborate his story."

I look at Rios and say, "Is there anything you can give us? Is there any way we can trace the money?"

Rios stares out the window for a moment. His jacket is off and his tie is loosened. Even political operatives look ragged at this hour. He addresses Rolanda: "You and your father are no longer in any danger. You will not be followed. You will not be intimidated. Your father's market will not be vandalized. Nobody else in our community will be harmed."

Rolanda remains skeptical. "How do you know?"

Rios's expression takes on a cast of deathlike seriousness. "You have my word."

"How do we know it's good?"

Rios folds his arms and says, "You must trust me."

Rolanda ponders for a moment, then nods. I try in vain to pry additional information out of Rios, who doesn't budge. We'll never know what deal he made with Ellis to ensure that Tony and Rolanda won't be harassed. We won't find out how much money, if any, changed hands. They'll never be able to trace it. I hope Dennis Alvarez will be able to find some evidence that might implicate Ellis or Rios in the payoff scheme, but I'll bet he won't. We have what we want for Tony and Rolanda. That's enough. Dennis Alvarez can chase Carl Ellis and Armando Rios.

I'M DOZING OFF a few minutes after four when the phone rings. For an instant, I think I'm dreaming. Then I recognize Rosie's voice. "How soon can you get to L.A.?" she asks.

"We can probably catch a plane in a few hours. Why?"

"Kaela Joy called. Eve flew down to L.A."

"Why?"

"I don't know."

"Did she know where Eve is staying?"

"The Beverly Hills Hotel."

How elegant. "We'll get there as soon as we can."

She tells me she's on her way to the airport. She says, "I'll meet you there."

I realize Pete's standing in my doorway. "Who?" he asks.

"Rosie." I tell him Eve's in L.A. "I'll call the airline."

"Forget it. Get us a car. It's only three hundred miles. It'll be faster to drive."

# Chapter 45

# "It's Worth Taking a Chance"

Death Valley National Park—85 miles.

—Road sign on Interstate 15

PETE'S SITTING behind the wheel of our white Ford Taurus two hours later. "Beautiful, Mick," he says.

He's referring to the sunrise over the mountains surrounding the barren area south of Death Valley known as Devil's Playground. The temperature is already in the low nineties. It will be a hundred and fifteen in an hour.

"Yes, it is," I tell him. My eyes are closed. I'm leaning back in the passenger seat. The air-conditioning is hitting my face. I'm trying to shut out the world until we get to L.A.

"What did you think about Carl Ellis?" he asks.

I open my eyes and say, "He's an asshole."

"Tell me something I didn't know. He's also smart. Did you believe him?"

"Parts of what he said may have had some basis in truth."

"They can't get anything past you, can they?"

"Nope. He only talked to us so he could spin his story. You can bet he was involved in the payoff scheme with Armando. He probably set up the fire at the liquor store. The only question is how he was involved in Big Dick's death."

"What makes you think he wasn't involved in Little Richard's death, too?"

"It was an accident."

"So they say."

"You think he was murdered?"

"We shouldn't take anything for granted. There are too many coincidences. And I think Ellis's alibi on Big Dick is too clean. He told us Angel, Little Richard and Kent were still there when he left. Angel's already been arrested, so the cops will consider anything she says as suspect. Little Richard and Kent are dead. Unless the cops come up with some other evidence, Ellis is off the hook. End of story. They're going to blame Angel or one of the dead guys."

"What about Eve?"

"What about her? If anything, she corroborated Ellis's story."

"Maybe we should consider her as a suspect."

"What evidence?"

I reflect for a moment and conclude there is none.

"I'll tell you something else," Pete says. "Eve and Petrillo and Ellis have this all worked out. They've compared stories, and they're getting ready to point the finger at somebody. I just hope for our sake it isn't Angel."

"You think there's a conspiracy?"

"The timing is convenient. They're going to release the movie and ask for approval of the China Basin project tomorrow. Do you really think it was a coincidence that Ellis agreed to see us—in fact, welcomed us—in the middle of the night? Do you think it's just coincidence that Eve flew down to L.A.? Do you think Petrillo's P.I. would have told us about it if he didn't want us to know? Grow up, Mick. The fix is in."

He still has the instincts of a cop. "What do you think really happened?"

He sets his jaw and says, "I don't know, but I plan to find out."

We drive in silence for another half hour. I'm starting to doze off as we're approaching Barstow. Pete turns to me and says, "So, let me ask you something else, Mick."

Now what? "Shoot."

"Who was she?"

"Who?"

"The woman you were in bed with when I called you about Marty Kent."

Not now. "Long story. Besides, it doesn't matter anymore. It's over."

"That was quick."

"Yeah."

"So who was she?"

"Nobody you know."

"Come on, Mick."

"Somebody I shouldn't have been seeing in the first place."

"You should stay away from married women, Mick."

"She isn't married."

He chuckles and says, "How about a hint?"

"Nope."

He sounds like Grace when he says, "Pretty please? I won't tell anyone."

He isn't going to give up, and we have another three and a half hours to L.A. "You promise?"

"Pinky swear."

He's my brother. "She's a judge."

This stops him cold. "Bad idea, Mick."

"Yeah."

He spends fifteen minutes trying to pry Leslie's name from me. He isn't going to get it.

We drive in silence for what seems a long time. Then he asks, "How's Rosie?"

"Not great." I tell him about the latest test results and the prognosis.

He takes it in and says, "What is it with you two?"

"What do you mean?"

"I've never seen two people who spend so much time tweaking each other and trying to deny their feelings. Why don't you just admit you love each other instead of pretending you're waiting for something better to come along?"

Give him credit for being direct. "I can't deal with this right now."

"Maybe you should start dealing with it soon." He regrets it as soon as he says it.

"We weren't good at being married, Pete."

"I didn't say you had to get married."

"It's more complicated than you think."

"No, it isn't."

"Dammit, Pete. This isn't your issue."

He swallows hard and says, "Let me give you some free brotherly advice."

"I didn't ask for it."

"Unless you want to walk two hundred miles through the desert to L.A., I'm going to give it to you anyway."

I fold my arms and say, "Fine."

He grabs the steering wheel tightly with his left hand and points his right index finger at me. "That's another thing I don't need. You've been giving me attitude for forty years. On good days, you're just patronizing. On bad days, you're condescending. Let me give you a news flash, Mick: You're not as smart as you think. I know you think I'm an idiot, but I'm not."

"That's not true, Pete."

"Don't patronize me."

"I'm not."

"Yes, you are. Maybe I didn't graduate from Cal. Maybe I didn't get to be a priest or a hotshot lawyer. My bachelor's in criminal justice from State is worth something. I had to work a lot harder for it than you did for your law degree."

This is true. School never came easily for him. "I never said you weren't smart, Pete."

"You never said it out loud."

"Don't tell me what I was thinking."

"Then don't treat me like I'm a moron. I was a good cop before they took it away from me. I'm a good P.I."

I never said you weren't. "Look, Pete—"

His face becomes more animated. "No, you look, Mick. Do you think I had it easy? I was the third of four kids. I wasn't a star football player like Tommy. I wasn't at the top of my class like you. And I wasn't the baby—and a girl—like Mary. Nothing I did was good enough. Nothing ever measured up to you and Tommy. Not to my teachers. Not to Mom. And certainly not to Dad. My biggest problem when we were growing up was that I wasn't Tommy and I wasn't you. Nobody ever talked about me."

This isn't the first time we've had this discussion. It is, however, the first time he's been so frank about it. It must not have been easy to have had two superachieving older brothers. I don't know what to say. "I'm sorry, Pete. Maybe it's a little late, but I think you're good at what you do. I respect and admire you for it."

He's unpersuaded. "You could have mentioned it once or twice in the last four decades."

"I'll try to remember to do it more frequently." I add, "For what it's worth, if I ever get in trouble, you're the first person I would call."

This seems to mollify him a bit. "No kidding?"

"No kidding."

He thinks about it for a moment. Then he guns the engine and we barrel down the 15 in silence toward the City of Angels.

WE'RE PASSING the thriving metropolis of Victorville about twenty minutes later when I turn to him and say, "So, what was the advice you were going to give me?"

"Forget it, Mick."

"Come on, Pete. I'm listening."

"Fine." He turns to me and says, "For what it's worth, I was going to tell you I think you and Rosie should try to work something out."

Christ. "You know all the history."

"Maybe you don't have to be married. You don't even have to move in together. Maybe it's enough to decide you're going to stop looking for somebody else. You're going to drive yourselves nuts if you think you're going to find somebody better."

"We've tried, Pete."

"Maybe you ought to try harder." He sighs. "Look, Mick," he says, "When Wendy and I got married, we both knew it was a long shot. We had very little in common, but we loved each other and we had a great time together. It was worth taking the chance. People who say they'd rather be alone are kidding themselves or just lying. You found yours, Mick. You know it and she knows it."

"We aren't compatible."

"You could be if you worked at it."

"We're too stubborn."

"Yes, you are." He lowers his voice and says, "Don't be a schmuck this time, Mick. Talk to her about it. You need each other. You're going to wake up all by yourself one of these days, and you won't remember what the hell you spent so much time fighting about."

I take a deep breath of the air-conditioned air. I look at my younger brother—my very wise younger brother—and say, "I don't know if she would be interested."

"Yes, she would."

"How do you know?"

"Because I asked her."

It seems Rosie and I are getting a lot of coaching on our love life these days. "When?"

"A couple of months ago. I was curious. And both of you seemed unhappy."

"What did she say?"

"She wouldn't rule anything out."

"That's it?"

"That's it."

I look up and see the San Gabriel Mountains in the distance. Then I look at Pete and say, "What if it doesn't work out?"

"It's worth taking a chance. You can either win or break even."

# Chapter 46

## "It's Hot! I Love It!"

Based in Beverly Hills and serving clients all over the world, the Endeavor Talent Agency provides a full range of services to the biggest names in the entertainment industry.

—WEBSITE FOR
THE ENDEAVOR TALENT AGENCY

MY CELL PHONE crackles. "Where are you?" Carolyn asks.

"Sunset Boulevard," I reply. "A few blocks from the Beverly Hills Hotel."

I've always liked L.A. It's a city of dreams. I almost took a job in the public defender's office down here when I got out of law school. I thought the change of scenery might have done me some good. Then an offer came through up north, and I decided to stay home. The sun is out, and a warm Southern California breeze is blowing. Pete is guiding us around a double-parked Hummer. People down here love their cars. Those who drive Hummers have a lot of car to love.

Carolyn says, "I was calling about Ben's case."

Uh-oh. I glance at my watch. It's almost noon. Ben's preliminary hearing should be in full swing. "Aren't you supposed to be in court?"

"Yes." She hesitates and says, "I mean no. The prelim was canceled."

"Prelims don't get canceled."

"This one did."

"Why?"

"I got a fax from Lisa Yee this morning. They've agreed to reduce the charges to a misdemeanor if Ben does six months of probation and some community service."

It's a slap on the wrist. The deal has Leslie's fingerprints. She couldn't get Yee and Ward to drop the charges completely, but she was able to persuade them to teach Ben a lesson without ruining his life. "I trust this is acceptable to you and Ben?"

"Indeed. I'm not sure what you said to them, but it seems to have worked."

"That's great news."

I hear a relieved sigh. "How can I thank you?"

You might send a nice note to Leslie. "Don't worry about it, Caro. I'm glad everything worked out."

"Can Ben and I buy you a nice dinner when you get home?"

"I'd like that."

THE BEVERLY HILLS HOTEL is an icon. Whether you love it or hate it, the revival style "Pink Palace" that was used as the backdrop for the original *A Star Is Born* is a classic. Built in 1912 when much of the area was still covered with lima-bean fields, the place where Marilyn Monroe and Humphrey Bogart used to hang out is now owned by the sultan of Brunei, who plunked down a hundred and eighty-five million bucks to buy it in the mid-nineties. Then he dropped another hundred million to spruce it up. Hollywood's most expensive face-lift has worked. The landmark stucco building on twelve lush acres is once again one of the great hotels of Southern California. Although the movie moguls now spend more time at the Four Seasons and the Peninsula, the legendary Polo Lounge is still a place to be seen.

We find Rosie in the lobby near the Fountain Coffee Shop, which is still decked out in the hotel's trademark banana-leaf wallpaper. "Where's Eve?" I ask her.

"Cabana number eight. She got here around three this morning. You can bet the tabloids will get wind of it by the end of the day."

"Is anybody with her?"

"Her lawyer."

Figures. "Were you able to talk to her?"

"No. There is security everywhere. I couldn't get close."

"Where's Kaela Joy?"

"Watching the cabana."

I pause to consider how a beautiful, statuesque blonde can remain inconspicuous in the middle of a crowded hotel. Then I look around the lobby and realize that everybody here seems to be a beautiful, statuesque blonde. "Did you recognize anybody else?"

"No."

Pete nudges me. His eyes dart toward the corner of the lobby. He nods toward a thin, well-dressed man who is talking on his cell phone. "That's Tom Eisenmann," he says. "He's an investigator for the D.A.'s office. He's good."

"Ward must know Eve is here."

"Yeah. Now she knows we're here, too."

Rosie and I glance at each other. She says to me, "We sit tight and don't let Eve out of our sight. And we wait to see who else shows up."

Her question is answered twenty minutes later when we see Jack O'Brien walk into the lobby and nod toward Eisenmann. He presents his badge to the desk clerk, who immediately gets on the phone. A moment later, an impeccably coiffed man in a dark suit appears from behind the counter and shakes hands with O'Brien. He nods several times and gestures toward the entrance to the pool and the cabana area.

The manager is leading O'Brien toward the back door of the lobby when he sees us. We approach him and he stops. Rosie says, "We weren't expecting to see you here today, Jack."

"I wasn't expecting to see you, either."

"What brings you to the Beverly Hills Hotel?"

"The same thing that brings you here. A material witness is staying in one of the cabanas. We'd like to talk to her."

"So would we."

O'Brien's face breaks out into a wry smile. "I get to talk to her first." He takes out his badge and says, "That's the prize when you carry one of these."

"Look, Jack," I say, "if she has information that's relevant to Angelina's case, we're entitled to know about it."

"You *will* know about it," he says. "I get to know about it first."

"Come on, Jack—"

He holds up his hand and says, "Be patient. Her lawyer said she wants to tell us something. I'll give you a status report in a few minutes."

It's the best we can do. We follow him out past the pool. The security guards part like the Red Sea. We watch him knock on the door of cabana eight. A man whom I don't recognize answers and lets him in. I assume this is Eve's lawyer. The door closes. I turn to Rosie and ask, "What do we do now?"

"We wait." Then she points toward the pool and says, "Who knows? Maybe one of those hotshot producers will ask you to star in a movie."

WE'RE SITTING at a table by the pool almost two hours later. The afternoon sun is beating down on us. Kaela Joy has joined us. Jack O'Brien is still inside with Eve and her lawyer. We've been observing a well-dressed, hyperactive young man at the next table who has been screaming into a cell phone since we sat down. I suspect he's an agent. For at least the fifth time, I hear him shout, "It's hot! I love it!"

Pete rolls his eyes.

Rosie looks at me and deadpans, "Can you imagine what he must be like when he doesn't take his medication?"

I smile. I'm glad she's making jokes.

We sit by the pool for another hour. Killing time at the Beverly Hills Hotel isn't a tremendous hardship. Finally, I look at Rosie and say, "What do you make of it?"

"Something's coming down."

As she says the word *down*, the door to the cabana opens. Jack O'Brien is the first one out. Eve is wearing sunglasses and a huge hat as she follows him. Her lawyer is bringing up the rear. His expression is grim, but his starched shirt and Italian suit still look perfect.

We intercept O'Brien as he starts toward the lobby area. "We have some new and interesting developments in Angelina Chavez's case," he tells us.

"We're entitled to know about any such information," Rosie says.

"We're going to issue a statement later today."

"Why can't you tell us about it now?"

"We need to work out some details," he says. "And we have to go down to Burbank."

"Why?"

"It's the headquarters of Millennium Studios. We need to talk to Dominic Petrillo."

"We'll come with you," Rosie says.

"Suit yourselves," O'Brien replies. "I can't stop you. We'll bring you up-to-date after we talk to Petrillo." He leads Eve toward the front of the hotel.

As soon as he's out of earshot, I turn to Rosie and say, "I don't like it."

"Neither do I."

"What do you think?"

"I'm not sure."

Pete is more sanguine. "They made a deal," he says.

"How do you know?"

He glances around the bucolic gardens and says, "This is the Beverly Hills Hotel. It's where everybody in Hollywood makes deals."

## Chapter 47

# The Two Faces of Eve

> I've always dreamed of making an acceptance speech at the Academy Awards. I'd do anything for the chance.
>
> —Aspiring Actress Evelyn ("Eve") LaCuesta
> *People* magazine

"Mr. Petrillo will see you now," we're told by a receptionist who looks like a *Playboy* model. Rosie, Pete and I are sitting in the sleek waiting area outside Dominic Petrillo's office. He's inside with Jack O'Brien, Eve and her lawyer.

It's a few minutes after four. An unusual caravan made the drive from the Beverly Hills Hotel to the Millennium Studios complex in Burbank. An LAPD cruiser took the lead, followed by a limo carrying Eve and her lawyer and O'Brien. Tom Eisenmann's rented Ford Escort was next in line. I guess the SFPD has a limited budget for car rentals. Then came Kaela Joy in a Jeep Cherokee. Pete, Rosie and I were next in our white Taurus. Another LAPD car brought up the rear.

I expected something more opulent when we pulled up to the main gate of Millennium Studios. The converted business park is in an industrial area just off the Golden State Freeway, not far from the Disney complex on Buena Vista. The old warehouses need paint. Petrillo's office is in a nondescript three-story building that looks like it was put up in a hurry a few years ago. It hardly seems fitting for a man of his enormous stature. I can see why he wants to build a new facility up north.

The door to the inner sanctum opens. I feel as if I'm entering the gate to the Emerald City. I'm not prepared for what I see. Petrillo's office is about the size of a basketball court and is a museum of movie memorabilia. The bright red walls are covered with movie posters dating back almost a hundred years. An assortment of historic movie cameras is on display next to the wet bar. One corner is devoted to *Star Wars*. There is a tribute to the work of Francis Ford Coppola. A pool table from *The Hustler* sits next to a chariot from *Ben-Hur*. Kaela Joy is perched on a director's chair just inside the door. She nods as we walk by.

Petrillo is sitting behind a huge desk made of hand-carved oak. His hands are templed in front of his face. His tone is subdued as he stands to greet us. Eve is sitting in an armchair next to the desk. She nods to us. Petrillo introduces Eve's attorney, a silver-haired sage named George Hauer, who works for one of the Century City firms and bears an uncanny resemblance to Dan Rather. His grip is firm. His tone is measured. Jack O'Brien is standing next to Petrillo's desk. His expression is stern.

We stand in silence for a moment. Then we hear a familiar female voice from the *Star Wars* corner. Nicole Ward makes her grand Hollywood entrance from stage left. "Hello, Mr. Daley," she says.

Rosie looks at me for an instant. Then she turns to Ward and says, "We didn't know you were in town, Nicole."

Ward eyes us and says, "We have some new information about your client's case."

Rosie is still standing. She folds her arms and says, "We're listening."

Ward stares at Hauer for a moment. Then she turns to Rosie and says, "Eve—er, Ms. LaCuesta—came forward today and has agreed to sign a declaration under oath with respect to the circumstances surrounding the death of Richard MacArthur Senior."

Eve nods.

Rosie never takes her eyes off Ward. She asks, "What is Eve prepared to tell us?"

Ward looks at Hauer and says, "Perhaps it would be better if you spoke on behalf of your client."

Hauer nods solemnly as he gets out of his chair. Lawyers are trained to stand when they have something important to say. "Ms. LaCuesta is demonstrating great courage to come forward at this time," he says.

Duly noted.

"She believes it is important that the truth be told."

I think I see a look of disbelief on Pete's face.

Rosie's arms are still folded. She says, "Can we cut to the chase, Mr. Hauer?"

"Yes. Ms. LaCuesta is prepared to admit that she has not been entirely forthcoming about certain statements she made to the police with respect to Mr. MacArthur's death."

When my clients say something that isn't true, I call it lying. When Hauer's clients do the same thing, they're not entirely forthcoming. "What statements?"

"Those pertaining to Mr. MacArthur's son."

This gets a reaction from Rosie. I don't say anything. Let him talk.

"As you may know," Hauer continues, "Ms. LaCuesta told the police that young Mr. MacArthur went to the winery by himself early Saturday morning. That wasn't entirely true. Ms. LaCuesta accompanied him to the winery. In fact, she drove him."

By my reckoning, it wasn't anywhere close to the truth. I look at Rosie, who holds up a hand. Let him talk.

Hauer explains that Eve lied about her trip to the winery because Little Richard didn't want his soon-to-be ex-wife to know about it.

Rosie gives him a half grin. "We already knew she went to the winery, Mr. Hauer. Your client admitted it." Her tone remains measured when she asks, "What else did your client lie about?"

Hauer takes off his glasses and puts them back on. He chooses his words carefully when he says, "She also made a misstatement about the circumstances surrounding her drive to the winery."

A moment ago, she was not entirely forthcoming. Now she's making misstatements. It will be interesting to see how many euphemisms he can come up with for the concept of lying. I ask, "What was her misstatement?"

He clears his throat. "It had to do with where she picked up Mr. MacArthur."

I say, "She told us she picked him up at his house. In fact, *he* told us she picked him up at his house."

He clears his throat again. He fiddles with his glasses. Then he uses them to gesture. "That was incorrect. She didn't pick him up at his house, Mr. Daley. She picked him up at the east-view lot at the south end of the Golden Gate Bridge."

Rosie and I look at each other in stone-cold silence for what seems like an eternity. She unfolds her arms. Finally, she asks, "What time was that?"

"Around three-forty A.M."

It was just a few minutes before the security guard found Angel. Rosie faces Eve as she asks, "Did Mr. MacArthur give you any indication as to how he got the to bridge at that hour?"

Hauer glances at Eve, who nods. Then she turns back to us and says in an even tone, "He drove to the bridge in his father's car."

Rosie's jaws clench as she asks, "What was he doing there?"

Eve gives Hauer a helpless look. He answers for her. "Mr. MacArthur told my client that there had been an accident at the house. He said he and his father had fought and he had lost his temper." He nods melodramatically and says, "He struck his father with the Oscar statue and killed him."

Jesus. Rosie and I look at each other for a couple of beats. Then she says to him, "And he tried to frame our client?"

"It appears that way. Ms. Chavez was unconscious. He loaded her and the Oscar into the car and drove to the bridge. Ms. LaCuesta gave Mr. MacArthur a ride from the bridge to the winery. He asked her not to tell anyone where she picked him up."

"And your client is prepared to testify to that effect under oath if we need her to do so?"

He pauses for an instant before he says, "Yes."

I glance at Rosie, who doesn't move a muscle. I ask Hauer, "If Mr. MacArthur hit his father with the Oscar, there would have been traces of blood on his clothing. What happened to his clothes?"

Hauer hesitates. Then he looks at Eve, who says, "I don't know. Richard must have dumped them somewhere on the way to the bridge."

Rosie shoots me a stern look. The elusive bloody clothes are still a gaping hole in the story. On the other hand, it's in our client's best interests to take Eve's word at face value.

Rosie turns to Ward and says, "Are you planning to press charges against Ms. LaCuesta?"

"No. We believe she was merely an unwitting participant after the fact. We appreciate the fact that she came forward. We have no evidence to suggest she was otherwise involved."

Rosie gives me another quick glance. I'll bet Eve worked out an immunity agreement in the cabana. Rosie turns to Ward and says, "This changes everything."

"I know."

"In fact, it undermines your case against my client. What do you plan to do about it?"

Ward wrinkles her perfect nose and says, "We have no choice but to drop the charges. We'll be releasing a statement to the press to that effect later today."

*Yes!* Rosie gives me a quick look and then takes the offensive. "You realize jeopardy's attached. Once you drop the charges, you can't refile."

"We can discuss that if necessary when the time comes. The only way we would consider the possibility is if we obtain new evidence."

Rosie can't contain a half smile. She stands and says, "It seems our business here is done. If you'll excuse us, we should call our client with the good news."

# Chapter 48

## "A Matter of Trust"

In a shocking conclusion to a high-profile case, San Francisco District Attorney Nicole Ward announced that murder charges against actress Angelina Chavez have been dropped. Ward explained that new and compelling evidence conclusively showed that Richard MacArthur was killed by his son. Defense attorneys Rosita Fernandez and Michael Daley hailed the decision as a victory for justice.

—KNX Radio
Thursday, June 10. 6:00 p.m.

"How did Angel react to the news?" I ask Rosie. She's sitting in the front seat of the Taurus. Pete's at the wheel and I'm in back. Traffic is heavy on the 110 as we head toward LAX.

She turns to face me and says, "First she was ecstatic. Then she started to cry. Obviously, she's relieved."

There's a tenuousness in her voice. "What is it, Rosie?" I ask.

She turns around and looks out the windshield. I see her shrug. "There was something about her tone," she says. "She regained her composure almost immediately. It was almost as if she expected this."

She knows her niece better than I do. I ask, "Is there something else going on?"

Rosie sighs. "I don't think so. Maybe I was hearing something that wasn't there. Maybe she was tired. Maybe *I'm* tired."

Maybe. I reflect for a moment and ask, "What just happened in Petrillo's office?"

She isn't looking at me as she says, "We got a great result for our client."

It's the correct answer. "I understand. But what really happened?"

I'm still looking at the back of her head when she says, "It isn't our job to ask."

Too glib. "Do you really think Little Richard killed his father?"

Now she turns around and faces me. "It looks as though that's the way it's going to go down," she says. "It was our job to make Nicole Ward prove her case beyond a reasonable doubt. If she thinks the evidence doesn't support a conviction, we shouldn't argue with her. We *can't* argue with her. It wouldn't be in the best interests of our client."

I can see a crooked smile on Pete's face. He turns to Rosie and says, "You really believe that, don't you?"

"It's my job."

"Be that as it may," he says, "if you ask me, the fix was in."

Rosie shrugs. "I didn't ask you. And if it was, it worked to our advantage this time. Next time it won't. Things tend to even out."

Pete's smile gets broader. "Putting aside all the appropriate lawyerly posturing for a moment," he says, "aren't you interested in finding out what really happened? You know—truth and justice—that sort of stuff?"

It's a fundamental question that criminal defense lawyers face all the time. Rosie smiles. "You still sound like a cop."

"I can't help it. So?"

"So what?"

"Don't you want to know?"

Rosie turns serious. "Yes, I do," she says. "As long as it doesn't involve Angel. From a professional standpoint, our work on this case is done."

Pete gives his ex-sister-in-law a playful pat on the shoulder. Then he says, "You guys did a nice job, and you got a good result. Who knows? Maybe Eve was telling the truth." He turns around to look at me for an instant. Then he says, "You've been awfully quiet in this discussion, Mick. What do you think?"

"It doesn't matter anymore."

"Come on, Mick. Not you, too. Just between us—this conversation never leaves this car. What do you say?"

I think about it for a moment. Pete's eyes are back on the road. Rosie's eyes are on mine. I shrug and say, "What was it Dom Petrillo told us? The movie business is all about creating illusions. You should never let the truth get in the way of a perfectly good story."

With that pearl of sage wisdom, I lean back in my seat and close my eyes. We peel off the 110 and head west on the 105 to the airport. We don't say another word the rest of the way.

"HOW'S ANGEL?" Pete asks me.

"She's going home tomorrow," I tell him.

It's eight-thirty the same night. Rosie went to her mother's house to pick up Grace. We're sitting on the restored arsenal at Battery Chamberlin next to the parking lot at the edge of Baker Beach. After two days of planes and cars, we wanted some fresh air. Pete is drinking a beer, and I'm nursing a Diet Dr Pepper. The days are long this time of year, and we're being treated to a spectacular golden sunset over the ocean and the Farrallon Islands.

"That's great," Pete says. "Maybe Jerry Edwards will interview her on *Mornings on Two*."

"You're getting more cynical as you get older."

"It happens." He takes a long draw from his Bud and says, "Well, Mick, Angel got off and they were able to lay it all on Little Richard. All's well that ends well, right?"

There's more than a hint of skepticism in his tone. "You got a problem with that, Pete?"

"No. Do you?"

I don't answer him right away. The sun is reflecting off the towers of the Golden Gate Bridge. The cool sea breeze smells of salt water. After a couple of days running around in the heat of Vegas and L.A., it's nice to be home. I turn to him and say, "What's bugging you, Pete?"

He crushes his beer can and says, "Nothing."

"Come on."

He turns to me and says, "They cut a deal, Mick. You know it. Eve's story was bullshit. Did you see the look in her eyes when you asked her about the bloody clothing? She was making it up as she went along. She says she's an actress, and she didn't even rehearse her lines."

"Why would she have lied?"

"Do I have to spell it out for you? By rolling over on Little Richard, everybody gets exactly what they wanted. Petrillo gets to release his movie on time. He can send his little starlet all over the country on promotional tours and take advantage of the free publicity. He can go into the redevelopment agency tomorrow and put on his song and dance in support of the China Basin project. Even if they say no, he can try again with his pal, Carl Ellis—and without the MacArthurs. It's a win for Petrillo and Ellis."

"It's a loss for Nicole Ward."

"Not necessarily. If Eve is prepared to testify that she picked up Little Richard at the bridge, it creates reasonable doubt in Angel's case. She had to drop the charges. She'll spin it by saying she solved the murder. When the election rolls around in six months, that's the only thing anybody will remember."

"You're forgetting something," I say. "There was nothing in it for Eve. What possible incentive did she have to implicate Little Richard?"

"Money. I'll bet you a trip to the Tuscany that Petrillo gave her some dough to tell her story. She'll get a lot of free publicity. Who knows? Maybe he agreed to let her star in a movie."

Cynic. I grab my soda can and start walking toward the car. "Pete," I say, "we got the result we were hoping for. Angel is going home tomorrow."

"Aren't you interested in finding out what really happened?"

Yes, I am, but I've learned over the years that the truth is very elusive. "Sure, Pete. But not tonight."

"I'm going to find out."

"That's admirable."

"I'm an admirable guy."

"I'll help you out. Do you really think somebody else did it?"

"Maybe."

"Who?"

"Kent. Ellis. Petrillo. Nobody really considered Eve." He reflects and adds, "I still haven't ruled out Angel."

"We've beaten that into the ground. Besides, your guys have spent the last week scouring the area for the bloody nightgown. They didn't find it."

"Maybe she got rid of it someplace else. Maybe she had help."

"You're seeing things."

"Maybe. Maybe not. I'm going to do a little more poking around—just for my own amusement."

I toss my empty soda can into the trash and say, "Let me ask you something. Put yourself in Angel's shoes. If you needed help, whom would you have called?"

He gives me a shrug and unlocks the car. Then he turns to me and says, "I guess it all comes down to a matter of trust."

# Chapter 49

## Family Matters

> The San Francisco Redevelopment Agency has rejected a revised proposal submitted by Millennium Studios and Ellis Construction to build a studio complex in China Basin. Agency head Robert Thompson said there were serious questions about the advisability of placing a high-density development so close to PacBell Park and the UC medical center. Dominic Petrillo expressed disappointment about the decision and indicated that his company may initiate litigation against the city.
>
> —Jerry Edwards. *Mornings on Two*
> Friday, June 11. 7:00 a.m.

The late news is a mix of spin control and bravado. Nicole Ward takes full credit for solving the MacArthur murder. Jack O'Brien is less convincing when he says he considers the case closed. I turn off the lights at eleven-thirty, but my first chance for a good night's sleep in a week is a troubled one. I toss and turn as I replay the highlights of Angel's case. What if Pete's right? What if the fix was in? Then I spend a couple of hours worrying about Rosie's illness. I think about our relationship. Maybe Pete's right about that, too.

I head over to Rosie's at six and find her already up. She tells me she didn't sleep last night, either. We look at Angel's photo on page one of the *Chronicle*. The headline reads, "Charges Dropped Against Movie Star."

"How's Grace holding up?" I ask. She's still asleep.

"All things considered, pretty well," Rosie says. "She had a better day at school yesterday."

"She's very resilient."

"Sometimes I think she has more staying power than we do." She hesitates and adds, "She's looking forward to summer vacation. She told me she needed a break."

So do we.

The TV is tuned to Channel Two. Jerry Edwards looks triumphant. "Angelina Chavez is expected to go home from the hospital today," he says. Next he says the redevelopment agency rejected the China Basin project. "This is a great victory for the residents of the city and a stunning defeat for Millennium Studios and Carl Ellis." His smirk broadens when he says that he will be monitoring the situation with great interest. He adds that *The Return of the Master* will be released today. We are then treated to an interview of Nicole Ward. She expresses her gratitude to the hardworking law-enforcement officers who brought the matter to a speedy conclusion. Jack O'Brien is nowhere to be found.

I flip open the *Chronicle* and turn to the Datebook section. The headline reads, "Mediocre Effort in MacArthur's Swan Song."

Rosie asks, "What's the little man doing?"

Unlike the star system employed by most newspapers, the *Chronicle* rates movies by showing the reaction of a miniature cartoon character known to everyone as the little man, whose opinions range from jumping out of his seat, cheering wildly and throwing his hat (worth seeing) to sleeping in his seat (don't bother). He's expressed his views in this manner for over half a century. I tell Rosie, "Not a ringing endorsement. He's sitting quietly."

"It couldn't have been that bad."

The reviewer can't be accused of pulling punches. "Diehard Richard MacArthur fans may be impressed with his final work," he writes, "but the rest of us will be disappointed. Film buffs who remember MacArthur's early promise will be saddened by his finale, which is a decidedly mixed bag. The writing is solid and, at times, inspired. The directing, as always, is stylish. The acting, however, ranges from adequate to wooden. Of particular note is the strained performance of MacArthur's widow, Angelina Chavez, who was hopelessly miscast. We can only hope that future roles will permit Ms. Chavez to display her limited range in a more productive manner."

"Ouch," Rosie says.

"Let's go see it for ourselves," I say.

"It's a date."

My cell phone rings. It's Pete. "I tried to reach you at home, Mick."

"I'm at Rosie's."

"Kind of early, isn't it?"

"I had trouble sleeping." I glance at Rosie and ask, "What is it?"

"When are you going to pick up Angel?"

"Later this morning."

"Any chance I could talk to you for a few minutes on your way in?"

"Sure. What's up?"

"Maybe nothing."

"IT'S GOOD to be home," Angel says. It's two o'clock Friday afternoon. The color has returned to her face as she is sitting in her grandmother's kitchen. There is still a small bandage on her wrist. Her mother is sitting next to her. They're holding hands.

Sylvia marches in with a tray of broiled chicken. She looks at her granddaughter and says, "I made your favorite."

Angel nods her thanks. Theresa is beaming.

Sylvia says, "You'll stay here for a few days, honey." It isn't a question—it's an order.

Angel agrees.

"You aren't going to move back into that house, are you?" Theresa asks.

"No," Angel says. "Bad memories."

Good choice.

We gather around the small dining-room table and dig into Sylvia's feast. It's the first time in days I've felt hungry. Rosie turns to Angel and asks, "How is your wrist, honey?"

"It feels okay. The doctor said it should be all better in a couple of weeks. I guess I didn't do a very good job of trying to kill myself."

The room goes silent. Theresa looks at her daughter and puts a finger to her lips. Jokes about suicide are not funny.

Angel turns to Rosie and whispers, "Thanks for helping me out, Aunt Rosie. I don't know what I would have done if you hadn't been there."

Rosie nods.

Angel turns to Theresa and says, "You, too, Mama. I would have been a basket case without you."

Theresa's eyes are filled with tears. "It's okay, honey."

Sylvia takes a seat at the head of the table. Then Rosie pulls her chair a little closer to Angel and leans forward. She looks first at Theresa and then at Angel. "Honey," she says, "now that this is all over, there are a couple of things I wanted to talk to you about."

"Sure, Aunt Rosie. What is it?"

Rosie looks at me and then reaches into her briefcase. She pulls out a computer printout.

Angel smiles and asks, "Is that your bill?"

Rosie remains serious. "No, honey."

"What is it?"

"Telephone records."

Angel gives her a perplexed look.

Rosie looks down and swallows hard. I catch another quick glance before she turns back to Angel and says, "Pete's very resourceful."

Angel nods.

"He had a few men helping us search the area on Baker Beach and the Presidio just to be sure that they didn't find anything that might have impacted your case."

Angel's eyes narrow. "Like what?"

Like a bloody nightgown. I remain silent.

"Nothing in particular," Rosie says. "We wanted to avoid any surprises."

"Sure."

"In any event," Rosie says, "Pete's people didn't find anything."

I detect a small sigh of relief from Angel.

"But Pete's very thorough," Rosie continues. "He wanted to be absolutely sure that we weren't overlooking anything. That's what you want from a P.I., right?"

Angel nods.

"In fact, that's probably why you hired him to watch Dick when you suspected him of cheating on you, right?"

An uncomfortable swallow followed by another nod.

"Well," Rosie continues, "his thoroughness may have paid off. In fact, he thinks he might have figured out what really happened."

Angel's eyes start to dance. "Richard killed his father," she says. "Eve admitted it."

Rosie's lips form a tight line across her face. She looks at her niece and says, "We're not so sure."

Angel's face remains impassive. "What are you talking about, Aunt Rosie?"

Theresa gives her sister a stern look and says, "What are you saying, Rosita?"

Rosie places the computer printout on the table in front of Angel and Theresa. "The police gave us printouts of all the phone records from young Richard's house," she explains. "We also got the phone records from Eve's house and the Ritz. We looked at the cell phone records for everybody who was at the screening on Friday night. It took a little while to sift through them."

"What did you find?" Angel asks.

"As it turns out, nothing," Rosie says.

I think I can see relief in Angel's eyes. "Then what's this?"

Rosie leans back in her chair and says, "Pete has a friend who works nights down at Pacific Bell."

"So?"

"Pete asked him to pull the records for every pay phone in the northwest quadrant of the city from early Saturday morning. There are a couple at Baker Beach and several in the Presidio and at the bridge. This listing shows all calls made from the pay phone at the corner of Lincoln Boulevard and Bowley Street from midnight until five A.M. on Saturday morning."

The room is now completely still. All eyes are on Rosie. Angel glances at her mother. Neither of them speaks. Finally, Rosie breaks the silence. "There were only three calls from that phone during that time period," she says. "I guess it's what you would have expected. It was the middle of the night, and it's a secluded area with little traffic."

Sylvia stops cutting her chicken. She takes a sip of water and says,"What's this all about, Rosita?"

Rosie looks at the printout. Then she turns to Theresa and asks, "Do you recognize the last phone number on this list?"

Theresa studies the list for a moment. Then the color leaves her face. She glances at Angel. She turns back to Rosie and says, "It's mine."

Silence. All eyes turn to Angel. Rosie takes her hand and says, "Who do you think called your mother at three-thirty on Saturday morning?"

"I don't know."

Rosie forces herself to keep her tone even when she says, "Why did you call your mother, Angel?"

"I don't remember. I blacked out."

"No, you didn't, Angelina."

"Yes, I did."

"That was the story you made up. I believed you. So did Mike. We *wanted* so much to believe it that we talked ourselves into it." She squeezes Angel's hand. Then she looks at her sister, who is visibly shaken. Rosie says to Angel, "Everything we say here stays in this room. It's time to tell the truth, Angelina." She hesitates and adds, "I want to hear it from you. I don't want to ask your mother."

I can see tears welling up in Angel's eyes. She pulls her hand away from Rosie and takes Theresa's hands. Then she whispers, "I'd had too much to drink, Aunt Rosie. I did some coke with Daniel. I was so angry about the miscarriage. Then Dick embarrassed me in front of everybody. He told everyone my performance was worthless—that I was worthless. He said he was going to ask for a refund for the acting lessons. It made me sick. I was humiliated and went upstairs."

Angel wipes the tears from her eyes with her napkin. She looks at her mother for moral support. Then she turns back to Rosie, and it all comes pouring out. "I did some more coke and came back downstairs after everybody had left. I was so angry. Dick and I had a huge fight."

Rosie asks, "What were you arguing about?"

She lowers her voice and says, "Everything. The movie. The baby. The house. His infidelities." She swallows hard and says, "He was taunting me,

Aunt Rosie. He was shaking the Oscar in my face the entire time. He said he'd given me every possible chance: he'd paid for a new nose, two boob jobs, a tighter butt, a new wardrobe, a new house and a car. He gave me a big allowance."

Rosie and I look at each other in silence.

Angel's voice is now barely a whisper. "He slapped me," she says. "He said he'd spent a million dollars on me for nothing. He shoved the damned statue into my hands and said that was the closest I would ever come to holding an Oscar." She hesitates for an instant and adds, "That's when I lost my head. When he turned around, I hit him. The Oscar was heavy. I had no idea I could have been so strong. I didn't realize what I was doing. Then he fell off the deck and landed on the beach."

Jesus. We sit in stone-cold silence for what seems like an hour, but is probably only a moment. Rosie and I exchange a long glance. Then she asks Angel, "What did you do?"

Angel takes a drink of water and says, "It's all a blur. I panicked. There was blood everywhere. I knew I had to get out of there. I never went back into the house. I ran up the gangway and washed my hands with the hose. His car was blocking mine, so I put the Oscar in the trunk of his car. My gym bag was in the garage. I changed into my sweat suit and put the bloody nightgown into a plastic bag. I loaded everything in the car and started driving. I wasn't sure where I was going. Then I decided to drive up to the winery. I guess I thought the cops might believe me if I told them I left right after everyone else did. It wasn't a great alibi, but it was the best I could come up with."

Rosie says, "But you stopped along the way, didn't you?"

"Yes."

"And you made a phone call."

"Right." She looks at her mother and says, "I needed help. I knew I could trust you." She says she told Theresa what had happened. Theresa's eyes are filled with tears as she confirms Angel's account.

Rosie's hands are folded in front of her. She asks in an even tone, "What did you ask your mother to do?"

"I was desperate, Aunt Rosie. I had just killed my husband. I left the bloody clothes in the garbage can by the pay phone. I asked Mama to pick them up and get rid of them. Then I kept driving."

Rosie asks Angel, "Why didn't you leave the Oscar there, too?"

"I thought it would have been difficult for Mama to get rid of it. I was going to drop it off the bridge on my way to the winery."

"You really thought nobody would see you?"

Angel exhales loudly. "I wasn't thinking clearly."

"So you stopped at the bridge."

"Yes."

Rosie turns to Theresa and asks, "Where did you find the nightgown?"

"Right where she said it was. I took it home and burned it."

"You knew what had happened?"

"Yes." Theresa holds up her hands and says, "My daughter was in trouble, Rosita. What else could I have done?"

What else could she have done? Angel is a murderer. Theresa is at least an accessory after the fact. A look of compelling frustration crosses Rosie's face. She doesn't respond for a moment. Then she turns back to Angel and says, "What happened at the bridge?"

"I couldn't get onto the deck. The gate to the walkway was locked. So I decided to get rid of the Oscar up at the winery. I must have passed out in the car."

"That's when the cops found you?"

"Yes."

"And the coke in the front seat of the car?"

"Daniel gave it to me." Angel emits a painful, sarcastic laugh. "Pretty pathetic, isn't it? I didn't have any plan to get rid of the murder weapon, but I made sure I had some coke with me for the ride."

Rosie holds her chin in her hands and heaves a long sigh. The bottom of my stomach is burning. Rosie glances at her mother, who is staring at her plate with a look of profound pain.

"What made you do it, Angelina?" Rosie asks.

"He hurt me in so many ways, Aunt Rosie. He cheated on me. He humiliated me. He manipulated me. He hit me." She pauses and adds, "He killed my baby."

Sylvia's dining room is completely silent. Angel is still holding hands with her mother. Rosie shoots another look at Sylvia. Rosie's frustration turns to anger. She gives Angel a look that I've seen from her only on rare occasions. "It didn't give you the right to kill him," she says.

Angel looks down at her plate for what feels like hours. "I know that, Aunt Rosie," she says. "And honest to God, I didn't mean to. It just happened." The air of resignation in her voice is palpable.

Rosie emphasizes every syllable when she says, "Murders don't just happen."

"This one did."

"And this had nothing to do with money or movies?" Rosie asks.

"Nothing."

I'm not so sure. "You must have known about the prenup," I say. "You must have known he was planning to file divorce papers and modify the will."

"I swear to you it wasn't about the money," Angel says. "Sure, I knew about the will and the prenup. I knew I was going to be better off if he died. And I knew he would write me out of the will if we got divorced. But it wasn't about money. It was about respecting me—as a person and as an actress."

Rosie is fighting a desperate battle to maintain what's left of her composure. "You can't kill people because you don't think they're showing you enough respect," she says.

Angel is sobbing. "He killed my baby," she says. "He took away my self-respect. Maybe I didn't have the right to kill him. It must have given me the right to do something."

Rosie gives me a helpless look. She hesitates for a moment and asks, "What about Daniel Crown? Was he the father of the baby?"

Angel's eyes turn down. "No, he wasn't. There was nothing between us."

Rosie's eyes are on fire. "And you were prepared to ruin his reputation and his marriage just to save yourself?"

"I was desperate, Aunt Rosie."

"So you lied to us about that, too," she says. "In fact, you lied to us about everything—from day one."

Angel's eyes are full of tears. "I wasn't lying on purpose, Aunt Rosie."

"There's no such thing as an accidental lie."

"What do you want me to say? I didn't mean to hurt anybody. I was—I was—acting."

"Acting?" Rosie's voice gets louder as she says, "There's a big difference between lying and acting, Angelina. This isn't a game. You killed your husband. You *murdered* your husband. You made your mother an accessory to murder. Marty Kent and Dick's son are dead. This isn't acting. This isn't an audition. Three people are dead—in real life."

"I don't expect you to understand, Aunt Rosie."

"I never will."

Angel's mother pulls away from her daughter and says, "Neither will I." She looks her daughter straight in the eye. Her voice is filled with disappointment when she says, "You used everyone, Angelina. You used your husband to get into his movies. Then you murdered him. You used your aunt to help you get off. You lied to her and to Mike. She's delayed her surgery to work on your case. And you have the nerve to talk about respect?"

Theresa starts to cry. Rosie takes her sister's hand. Angel stares at them in stone-cold silence.

Sylvia is looking at her plate. I think I can see her mouthing the words to a prayer.

Finally, Angel looks at Rosie and asks, "Are you going to turn me in?"

Rosie sighs. "There's nothing we can do. The police can't arrest you again without some new evidence. Even if they did, we'd argue that the charges should be dropped because of the prohibitions against double jeopardy." She points a menacing finger at her niece and says, "You have just caught the greatest break of your life. I would suggest that you try to handle it with as much grace as you can."

Angel doesn't respond.

"Bear in mind," Rosie says, "that they may still find these phone records. If they do, you can be sure they'll go running back to a judge to ask if they can file new charges. If I were in your shoes, I wouldn't sleep too soundly tonight." She hesitates and adds, "I want to make one other thing clear to you, Angelina. If they figure this out and they bring new charges, or if you ever get into trouble again, I will not represent you. Do you understand?"

"Yes, Aunt Rosie." Angel bites her lip and says, "Do you think you can help me find a probate attorney? I may need some help with Dick's estate."

The callousness in her tone leaves Rosie visibly shaken. She doesn't respond.

Sylvia has been sitting silently throughout the conversation. A look of cold, hard steel crosses her face. She looks at her granddaughter and says, "You killed your husband, Angelina. Now you want his money? It's blood money."

"Actually, Sylvia," I interject, "she isn't going to see a nickel of it."

This elicits a scornful look from Angel. "I'm going to challenge the amendment of the will," she says. "I'll get something."

You greedy little girl. "No, you won't," I say. "I talked with your husband's probate attorney. He said the amendment of the will complied in all respects with California law. It's perfectly legal. Your husband's son was the sole beneficiary."

"He's dead," Angel says.

"Yes, he is," I say. "But that doesn't mean you're entitled to anything. Your husband's assets will all go to his son's estate." I glance at Rosie and add, "The probate attorney told me that Little Richard had a will, too. But he hadn't gotten around to amending it in anticipation of his pending divorce."

"So?"

"His assets will all go to his soon-to-be ex-wife."

Rosie turns to me and says, "Does that mean—"

"Yes. The stock in MacArthur Films, the house at Sea Cliff, the winery and all the other assets will go to Little Richard's wife."

The irony is not lost on Sylvia, who gives Rosie a knowing nod. I think I see the hint of a smile at the corner of Rosie's mouth. She turns to her niece and says in a tone that remains perfectly even, "If you challenge your husband's will, I will do everything in my power to make sure you never see a dime of it."

## Chapter 50

# Ever After

> The San Francisco Redevelopment Agency announced today that it has received expressions of interest from three Bay Area developers for a low-income housing project and mixed-use development at the China Basin site that was considered for the MacArthur Films studio project.
>
> —Jerry Edwards. *Mornings on Two*
> Friday, June 18. 7:00 a.m.

Rosie's eyes flutter open. A look of recognition crosses her face. "What time is it?" she whispers.

"Nine o'clock."

She gives me a weak smile and asks, "Morning or evening?"

"Evening."

"Is it still Friday?" Her voice is hoarse.

"Yeah."

It's a week later. The private rooms at the UCSF cancer center at the old Mt. Zion Hospital aren't bad. She had her surgery yesterday.

I ask, "How are you feeling?"

"Thirsty."

I give her a sip of water. I look at the IV in her arm and the bandages across her chest. Beautiful Rosie. "Does anything hurt?" I ask.

"Everything hurts. They took out half of my chest yesterday. It's supposed to hurt."

"I can get the nurse."

"Relax, Mike."

"I'll go find a doctor."

Her eyes brighten and she says, "It's okay, Mike. All things considered, I don't feel too bad. The nurse comes in every hour and gives me more painkillers. I haven't felt this good since I was in college."

She had major surgery less than forty-eight hours ago. I'm a basket case and she's making wisecracks. "Dr. Urbach said the surgery went well," I tell her. "She thinks they got all of it."

"I hope so. If they do this again, I won't have any plumbing left."

Two days after her mastectomy and she's ready to fire her doctor. "She told me she was pleased with the result. She said the prognosis looks very good."

"She said that last time."

"I know. She said you'll be able to go home in a few days."

She looks around the hospital room. The TV is tuned to the Giants' game, but the sound is turned down. The dresser is covered with flowers. She looks at them and says, "Did you see the note from Armando Rios?"

"Yes. I thought it was very nice."

"It's retail politics at its finest."

"That it is."

"Leslie sent flowers, too. It was nice of her."

"She's a good person."

"Yes, she is. I'm sorry things didn't work out."

"Me, too."

"Maybe you could ask the nurse to pass some of the flowers around to some of the other patients."

"I will."

She closes her eyes and then reopens them slowly. "Is Grace okay?" she asks.

"Yeah. I talked to her a little while ago. They won their second playoff game tonight. She got two hits and a walk. They're in the finals on Wednesday."

"Maybe Dr. Urbach will let me go watch some of the game."

"Maybe." Grace is staying at Sylvia's tonight. "I'll bring her back over in the morning."

This elicits a smile. "I can't wait," she says. "Has she said anything to you about Angel?"

"Not much." Angel is down in L.A. to do publicity for the movie. "She's keeping busy with baseball." I hesitate for a moment and add, "She mentioned it briefly when we were at home last night."

Rosie perks up. "What did she say?"

"It isn't so much what she said—it's what she did."

"Which was?"

"She took down all the pictures of Angel in her room."

Rosie gives me a troubled look and says, "Did she say why?"

"She just said it was time for a change. Evidently, Angel is no longer the hot item she was a few weeks ago."

Rosie's eyes turn serious. "You don't think she knows the truth, do you?"

I reflect for a moment and say, "I don't think so."

"She's very perceptive."

Just like her mother. "She's only ten, Rosie."

"She watches the news every day."

"There's no way she could have figured it out."

She sighs and says, "I'm not so sure about that."

Neither am I.

Rosie tugs at the IV and asks, "Where did Tony go?"

"He took your mom home while you were sleeping. They didn't want to wake you. He said he'd be back in the morning. He left some oranges for you."

"Everything quiet at the market?"

"Status quo. Rios stopped by on Wednesday. Apparently, he's been asked to help a nonprofit group obtain approvals to build a low-income housing project on the China Basin site."

"Is he going to do it?"

"Yeah. He told Tony he might even do it for free."

"Armando Rios is developing a conscience?"

"Not exactly. Evidently, Dominic Petrillo and Carl Ellis are putting together a competing proposal. I think Armando wants to stick it to them."

"Perhaps he'll do it legally this time."

"Perhaps."

She asks if I've talked to Theresa.

"Briefly. She's holding her own. She persuaded Angel not to contest Big Dick's will."

"That's good news. Where is Angel going to stay when she gets back from L.A.?"

"Theresa's house for the time being. *The Return of the Master* isn't doing very well at the box office. Angel's acting career may be finished."

Rosie takes another drink of water and swallows hard. "My baby niece the sociopathic murderer," she whispers.

I take her hand, but I don't say anything. Then a young nurse comes in and says, "I'm afraid visiting hours are over, Mr. Daley."

Rosie winks at her and says, "Just a few more minutes." The nurse smiles and closes the door behind her. Rosie looks at me and says, "I wanted to ask you about something."

"What's that?"

"I got a phone call from Dean Dwyer over at Boalt on Tuesday."

"Yes?"

"He said he was having trouble getting hold of you, so he asked me if I was going to accept the offer to run the death penalty clinic this fall."

Uh-oh. "You mean he asked you if *I* was going to accept."

"No, Michael. He was very explicit. He wanted to know if *you* had been able to persuade *me* to come help *you* run the death-penalty clinic."

Busted. "He really wants me to do it," I tell her.

"So it seems. Does this mean you're going to break up Fernandez and Daley?"

"No, Rosie. I'm thinking of converting Fernandez and Daley into a slightly different format—one that provides regular paychecks."

She tilts her head and asks, "What do you have in mind?"

"I told the Dean I'd run the clinic only if I could persuade you to do it with me."

"When were you planning to mention this to me?"

"After you got out of the hospital."

I see the corners of her mouth turn up. "And what will happen to our firm?"

"It will remain open on a limited basis. The dean said we can continue to take on selective cases."

"What about Carolyn and Rolanda?"

"They'll continue to run Fernandez and Daley from our lovely offices on First Street. They'll probably have more work than they'll be able to handle."

"How do you figure?"

"The clinic will be high profile. There will be cases that we won't be able to take on. We'll be able to refer them to Carolyn and Rolanda."

She closes her eyes and thinks about it for a few moments. Her expression becomes reflective. "I don't know, Mike."

"It might be nice to have something steady for a while. The benefits are good." Who knows? Maybe we'll be able to put some money away for retirement for the first time. "Besides," I add, "if it doesn't work out, we can always go back to hustling up cases for clients who won't pay us."

She chuckles. "Do we have to move to Berkeley?"

"Only if you want to."

"I don't. I like where we live. Grace likes her school."

"Then we'll stay put."

She tugs at the tape that's holding her IV in place. She turns to me and says, "You've been thinking about this a lot, haven't you?"

"Yes."

"Is it something you'd really like to do?"

"I think so."

"Why?"

"The timing may be good, Rosie. We've been fighting other people's battles for almost twenty years now. I'm going to be fifty next year. You need to take care of yourself. We both want to spend more time with Grace." I take her hand and say, "I think we should take some time for ourselves. Let some eager young law students do the legwork for a few years. You can get healthy. I can coach Little League. We could take the summers off. We might get to go on a real vacation every once in a while." I wink at her and add, "We could go down to the Tuscany for a few days. I stayed in a really nice suite for a couple of hours last week."

This elicits a smile. "I'd like that." Then she turns serious and asks, "Why now?"

"I'm tired, Rosie. I was thinking about my dad when we were in Vegas.

He put off his retirement for a couple of years to make some extra money. By the time he got around to doing it, he was already sick. I don't want that to happen to us. I don't want to wait too long."

She doesn't say anything.

I reflect for a moment and say, "There's something else. We've had a pretty good run in the last couple of weeks. Angel killed her husband, and we got her off scot-free. Tony accepted a bribe and we got him off, too. Carolyn's son may have been selling drugs, and we got him off with a slap on the wrist."

She smiles and says, "Nice hat trick." She adds, "We're good lawyers, Mike."

"I know. But we're not that good. Angel got off because Dominic Petrillo and Carl Ellis cut a deal after they decided it was in their best financial interests to blame Big Dick's death on his son. Tony got off because Dennis Alvarez is a good cop who put the squeeze on Armando Rios, who cut his own deal with Ellis. Ben got off because I was sleeping with a Superior Court judge who did me a huge favor when she felt guilty about breaking up with me."

Her smile gets bigger. "What's your point?"

"In the grand scheme of things, we did very little as lawyers that had any bearing on the outcomes."

"We can still take credit for our successes, can't we?"

I smile. "Of course."

"But you're saying we got lucky."

"Yes."

She gives me a long, hard look. Then she says, "You're right. It's contrary to my nature, but I'm prepared to admit that we caught a couple of big breaks the last few weeks. We may not get so lucky the next time. In my experience, it evens out over time." She shrugs and says, "What does any of this have to do with your decision about whether to take the job at Boalt?"

I try to choose my words carefully. "My dad used to play blackjack. He had a system—or so he said. He tried to explain it to me once or twice, but I was never able to understand it. I couldn't remember the cards."

Rosie is getting tired. "So?"

"I asked him right before he died whether his system really worked."

"And?"

"He told me the smartest guys weren't the ones with the best card-counting systems. The smartest guys were the ones who knew they were lucky when they got on a hot streak. They knew when to quit when they were ahead. For what it's worth, I think we may have just finished our hot streak. It may be time for us to quit while we're ahead."

Rosie takes another sip of water. She checks the final score in the Giants' victory and then turns off the TV. She takes my hand and says, "For what it's worth, Michael, I think you may be right."

There are tears welling up in the back of my eyes. "So you'll do the clinic with me?"

"Yes."

*Yes!*

"Of course," she says, "you can't hold me to anything I say in my current drug-induced stupor."

"I'll understand if you decide to reconsider in the morning."

"And there is one condition."

"Which is?"

"You'll take Grace and me on that trip to the Tuscany as soon as I'm feeling better."

"Deal."

We sit in silence for a moment. Rosie looks out the window at the fog. She tugs at the IV and asks, "Anything else on your mind?"

"Just one thing."

"Which is?"

How do I say this? "I've been thinking about us."

"Us?"

"Yes. You and me. In fact, I've been getting a lot of free advice about it."

She cocks her head and says, "So have I. What are they telling you?"

"They're telling me that we should try to come up with some workable arrangement for our relationship."

"Do you agree with them?"

"I do. Do you?"

She reflects for a moment and says, "I might be persuaded. What do you have in mind?"

I pull the tall vinyl hospital chair next to her bed and sit down. I take her hand and look into her eyes. Here goes. "Rosie," I say, "I don't want to spend the rest of my life looking for somebody else. I love you, Rosita Carmela Fernandez, and I want to be with you."

Her tired eyes turn sad. "We weren't good at being married, Mike"

"I'm not saying we need to get married. Maybe someday, but not now. And I'm not even saying we need to live together. I'm kind of intrigued by the idea, but I think that may be more than we can handle."

"What *are* you saying?"

"I'm saying that I want us to acknowledge that we are a permanent couple. We won't go out with other people. We'll go to weddings, funerals and graduations together."

She smiles. "Are you asking me if I want to go steady?"

"I'm asking you for more than that."

I can see tears in the corners of her eyes. "So, you want me to agree to a committed, dedicated, monogamous and otherwise permanent relationship, where we spend a lot of time together, attend public functions together and hold ourselves out to the world as a couple."

"Right." I give her a big smile and add, "We also get to have sex."

The corners of her tired eyes crinkle as her face breaks out into a wide grin. "Excellent point." She turns serious again and adds, "But we won't move in together."

"Not yet."

"And we won't get married."

"Not right now. Maybe someday." Maybe never.

"And we'll keep our finances separate?"

"Absolutely."

"And we'll continue working togther?"

"Right."

"And you think this is really going to work out this time?"

"Given our history, I don't know." I take her hand and say, "It's worth taking a chance. Last time we moved in together right away and got married in a hurry. That's when everything went to hell. Maybe this time we should try doing things in a more orderly way. Maybe it will work out better."

She gives me a half grin and says, "Are you serious?"

"Absolutely."

"What are we going to tell Grace?"

"Mommy and Daddy are back in business—in a unique way."

Her eyes dance for an instant. Then she turns serious and says, "It isn't exactly the type of relationship I had in mind when I was a kid. I was hoping for a prince—a knight in shining armor. I'm supposed to be a princess."

"Sometimes, fairy tales don't work out exactly the way you think they will."

"That's true. But the good guys are always supposed to live happily ever after."

"In the real world, Rosie, this may be as close as we'll ever get."

She doesn't say anything for a few minutes. We look at each other for the longest time. Finally, she says, "I'm not sure."

"Why not?"

She looks at the IV. Then she looks down at her chest and says, "I'm damaged goods. It isn't fair to you. You may have to spend the next five years taking care of me."

What do I say? "I want to spend the next five years being with you. I want to take care of you if you need me."

She licks her lips and takes a drink of water. Her eyes are now filled with tears. "I can't do it, Mike. It isn't right."

"It *is* right. Love is all about being there when it counts."

She leans back in her bed and wipes the tears from her eyes. Then she looks at me and whispers, "I could die, Mike."

"I'm prepared to deal with that."

"Are you?"

"Yes."

She starts to lift her left hand before she realizes it's hooked up to the IV. She puts it down and raises her right hand to my cheek. She says, "You're a dear, sweet man, Michael Joseph Daley. And if you'll be my permanent, dedicated, monogamous partner, then I'll be yours."

*Yes!* I swallow back my own tears and whisper, "You're on."

She gives me a tired smile and says, "Maybe your luck is changing."

"How do you figure?"

"You finally got the girl."

I did.

Her smile disappears and she adds, "Just your luck, Mike. After all these years, you get the girl—and it turns out the girl is broken."

I close my eyes and feel an enormous lump in the back of my throat. I look into her tear-filled eyes and say, "You're perfect, Rosie. You'll always be perfect."

We cast a longing look at each other. Then the nurse knocks on the door again and pokes her head inside. "You really should get going, Mr. Daley. Ms. Fernandez needs to rest."

"One more minute." The nurse leaves. I turn to Rosie and say, "Anything else I can do for you tonight?"

"I don't suppose you can come up with a cure for breast cancer?"

"I'll see what I can do." I take her hand and say, "You're going to be fine, Rosie."

"How do you know?"

I give her a knowing smile and say, "I made a deal with God."

This gets a grin. "Another one? What deal did you make this time?"

"If God lets you get better, I promised not to screw up our relationship again."

"You had a lot of help from me last time."

"We'll do better this time."

"Did you promise anything else?"

"I promised God that I would love you for the rest of your life."

She's blinking back tears. "What did God say?"

"It's a deal."

"Sounds like a pretty good deal to me."

"It's nice to know all those years in the seminary weren't a total waste."

We sit in silence for a moment. Then she looks at me and says, "Will you do something else for me?"

"Sure. What do you need?"

"Will you hold me for a few minutes?"

"I don't know if there's room in that hospital bed for two people."

She lowers the safety gate and says, "We'll make room."

I climb into bed with her and gently put my arms around her. She rubs my cheek with her hand and deadpans, "No funny business tonight, Michael. You don't get any farther than first base. It's only our first date."

I kiss her softly on the cheek and say, "Okay, Rosie. Besides, the warden will be back in a few minutes to send me home."

Her eyes get a faraway look. "It's been a long time since I've had somebody to hold me. I missed that."

"It's nice to be here," I say.

She kisses me gently on the mouth. Then she yawns and says, "Could you get the light, Michael?"

"Sure, Rosie." I do as she asks. She falls asleep a few minutes later, and I gently ease out of her bed. Then I sit in the chair for a few minutes and listen to her rhythmic breathing. Although her chest is covered with bandages and her arm is attached to a machine, there is a smile on her face. I touch my finger to her lips and whisper, "Pleasant dreams, Rosie." As I'm reaching for the door, I turn around and look at her. I say, "I love you, Rosita."

Her eyes are still closed when I hear her say, "I love you, too, Michael."

# ACKNOWLEDGMENTS

Many readers have noticed that I tend to write long acknowledgments. Writing is a collaborative process for me and I get a lot of help from people who know more about the criminal justice system than I do. I'm going to try once again to thank as many of you as I can.

To my wife, Linda, who has been helping me write stories for more than two decades, and to our twin sons, Alan and Stephen, who are very patient when I'm on deadline and who will be writing books of their own in the near future.

To Neil Nyren, my tireless and patient editor, whose thoughtful comments make my stories far better than the drafts that find their way into his inbox. Thanks also to the hardworking team at Putnam. You make my life a lot easier and I'm very grateful.

To my extraordinary agent, Margret McBride, and to Kris Wallace, Donna DeCutis, Sangeeta Mehta and Renee Vincent at the Margret McBride Literary Agency.

To my mentors, Katherine V. Forrest and Michael Nava, and to the Every Other Thursday Night Writers' Group: Bonnie DeClark, Gerry Klor, Meg Stiefvater, Kris Brandenburger, Anne Maczulak, Liz Hartka, Janet Wallace and Priscilla Royal.

To Inspector Sergeant Thomas Eisenmann and Officer Jeff Roth of the San Francisco Police Department, and to Inspector Phil Dito of the Alameda County District Attorney's Office.

To Sister Karen Marie Franks of St. Dominic's Convent in San Francisco.

To my wonderful friends and colleagues at Sheppard, Mullin, Richter & Hampton (and your spouses and significant others). In particular, thanks to Randy and Mary Short, Cheryl Holmes, Chris and Debbie Neils, Bob Thompson, Joan Story and Robert Kidd, Lori Wider and Tim Mangan,

Becky and Steve Hlebasko, Donna Andrews, Phil and Wendy Atkins-Pattenson, Julie and Jim Ebert, Geri Freeman and David Nickerson, Kristen Jensen and Allen Carr, Bill and Barbara Manierre, Betsy McDaniel, Ted and Vicki Lindquist, John and Joanne Murphy, Tom and Beth Nevins, Joe Petrillo, Maria Pracher, Chris and Karen Jaenike, Ron and Rita Ryland, Kathleen Shugar, John and Judy Sears, Dave Lanferman, Avital Elad, Mathilde Kapuano, Jerry Slaby, Guy Halgren, Dick Brunette, Aline Pearl, Bob and Elizabeth Stumpf, Steve Winick, Chuck MacNab, Sue Lenzi, Larry Braun and Bob Zuber.

To my supportive friends at my alma mater, Boalt Law School: Kathleen Vanden Heuvel, Bob and Leslie Berring, Louise Epstein, Dean John Dwyer and Dean Herma Hill Kay.

To the generous souls who patiently wade through the early drafts of my stories: Rex and Fran Beach, Jerry and Dena Wald, Gary and Marla Goldstein, Ron and Betsy Rooth, Rich and Debby Skobel, Dolly and John Skobel, Alvin and Charlene Saper, Doug and JoAnn Nopar, Dick and Dorothy Nopar, Angele and George Nagy, Polly Dinkel and David Baer, Jean Ryan, Sally Rau, Bill and Chris Mandel, Dave and Evie Duncan, Jill Hutchinson and Chuck Odenthal, Joan Lubamersky and Jeff Greendorfer, Tom Bearrows and Holly Hirst, Melinda and Randy Ebelhar, Chuck and Ann Ehrlich, Chris and Audrey Geannopoulos, Julie Hart, Jim and Kathy Janz, Denise and Tom McCarthy, Raoul and Pat Kennedy, Eric Chen and Kathleen Schwallie, Jan Klohonatz, Marv Leon, Ken Freeman, David and Petrita Lipkin, Pamela Swartz, Cori Stockman, Allan and Nancy Zackler, Ted George, Nevins McBride, Marcia Shainsky, Maurice and Sandy Ash, Elaine and Bill Petrocelli, Penny and Tom Warner, and Sheila, Alan and Leslie Gordon.

To Charlotte, Ben, Michelle, Margaret and Andy Siegel, Ilene Garber, Joe, Jan and Julia Garber, Roger and Sharon Fineberg, Jan Harris Sandler and Matz Sandler, Scott, Michelle, Stephanie and Kim Harris, Cathy, Richard and Matthew Falco and Julie and Matthew Stewart.

Finally, thanks to my readers, who have been so enthusiastic, and especially to those who have taken the time to write or e-mail. Most lawyers don't get fan mail and I'm very grateful.